BLACKMAIL AT BECKWITH PLACE

PIPPA DARLING MYSTERY #4

JENNA BENNETT

The scion of the Sutherlands, Crispin Astley, Viscount St George, has been using Sutherland House in London as his bachelor pad and love nest whenever he's been in Town carousing with his set of Bright Young People. As such, when a young woman with a baby shows up at the door, looking for the Duke's grandson, everyone assumes that Crispin is responsible.

Pippa never expected to have the opportunity to meet the mother and child herself, but that's just what happens one day in July. During a weekend party at Beckwith Place to celebrate Cousin Francis's 30th birthday, there they are: the tired young woman and the baby with the fair Sutherland hair and Astley blue eyes.

Everyone in the family is present for the celebration. Aunt Roz and Uncle Herbert, Francis and his new fiancée, Constance Peckham. Pippa, Cousin Christopher, and Cousin Crispin. Even Crispin's father, the recently widowed Duke of Sutherland, has turned up for his nephew's combination birthday celebration and engagement party.

And when the young woman winds up dead on the grounds of Beckwith Place, bashed over the head with a croquet mallet, the field is wide open. All the men in the family were present. One of them was responsible for getting her with child, and now someone—the same person or someone else—is responsible for ending her life. The only question is who?

If people do not choose to lower their voices, one must assume that they are prepared to be overheard.

MISS JANE MARPLE

CHAPTER ONE

MY COUSIN FRANCIS proposed to Miss Constance Peckham on the 5th of July, 1926, two months to the day after they first met. That might have seemed rash, as if they had something to hide—I'm sure I don't have to spell out what, as we're all familiar with babies being born 'early'—although in justice to them, I don't think that was the case. Constance had been living at Beckwith Place with Aunt Roz and Uncle Herbert, Francis's parents, for most of those two months, so opportunities to misbehave had been few and far between. I didn't think Francis was the type, anyway. Certainly not with Constance. It had been, as the saying goes, love at first sight, and we had all seen this coming for the past month and a half.

For me personally, the 5th was memorable for another reason. It was the day I finally saw the girl with the baby.

The words ought perhaps to be capitalized. The Girl with the Baby, like an impressionist painting or the title of a lurid crime novel. That was more or less how I thought of her, or of them.

I had first heard of the pair at the end of April, during that fatal weekend at Sutherland Hall during which Duke Henry, his valet, and Lady Charlotte, the Duke's daughter-in-law, had all met their ends by various means. At that point, she was just a story that Grimsby the valet told, one of many he had dug up about everyone in the family. The girl had made her appearance at Sutherland House, the Town seat of the Astleys, a month or two earlier, with a baby she claimed belonged to someone in the family. Upon being presented to the then-Honorable Crispin Astley—now the Viscount St George since his grandfather's death, and no more Honorable now, in spite of the title—he had declaimed any knowledge of her.

Naturally, no one believed him. Crispin was a card-carrying member of the Society for Bright Young Persons, with a reputation for fast living and a penchant for seducing anything in a skirt. Sutherland House had been pressed into service as his bachelor pad and love nest during his weekends in Town. There was no reason to think he wasn't as guilty as sin. Ergo, he must be lying, or he had been too drunk to remember, or he had bedded so many women that this one had simply slipped his mind... the excuses were plentiful, and all quite reasonable.

He was adamant, however—to me, to Christopher, to anyone who would listen—that the baby wasn't his, and upon further investigation, I decided that it was just possible that he might be telling the truth. Rogers, Sutherland House's butler, told me that the girl had asked for the Duke's grandson when she knocked on the door that day, and not for Crispin specifically. He's quite well known around London—Crispin, I mean; not Rogers—and he features often in the gossip rags. If he had bedded her, I would have expected her to know his name.

But all that is by the by. In the late afternoon of Monday the 5th of July, while Francis might have been down on one knee in front of Constance somewhere in the wilds of Wiltshire, Evans the doorman called up to let me know that my cousin and flat-mate Christopher Astley had a visitor.

"What kind of visitor?" I wanted to know.

"A young woman, Miss Darling."

"A woman?" I wrinkled my nose.

Unlike his cousin Crispin (or for that matter his brother Francis), Christopher's affections don't incline towards young women. Not in a romantic sense. That doesn't mean that young women don't pursue him, of course. He might only be fourth in line for the title, but he's young and handsome and reasonably wealthy, and he has a strong connection to the Sutherland lands and title. He also has no stomach for chasing off women on his own, which is where I usually come in.

"Yes, Miss Darling," Evans said. "A young woman with a baby."

My heart skipped a beat. The words 'woman' and 'baby' in the same sentence tended to do that to me these days. "Send her..."

No, wait. Did I want her in mine and Christopher's space?

He wasn't at home, or I would be having this conversation with him. I was alone in the flat, and perhaps I didn't want to open it up to someone I didn't know. I'm a friendly sort, but not that friendly.

On the other hand, if I went downstairs to meet her, we'd have to have our confrontation in front of Evans, or alternatively on the street outside, and I wasn't so keen on either of those options, either. The revelations were certain to be sensitive, and I'd rather not have them in front of an audience, even if it was an audience of people I didn't know and who didn't know me.

Evans waited patiently while I weighed my options and made a decision. "I'll be down to fetch her, Evans. Tell her to wait."

This way, I could at least get a look at her before I decided one way or the other.

"Yes, Miss Darling." Evans disconnected.

Christopher and I share a two-bed service flat in the Essex House Mansions in London. It's not overly ostentatious—we're not talking about the Albert Hall Mansions here—but it's quite a nice place for all that. At the moment, it looked as if no one had cleaned it in a while. A pair of Christopher's evening gloves were draped over the back of the sofa—don't ask—and there were stacks of books everywhere, as well as two teacups and saucers with crumbs on the coffee table.

I eyed the mess, and decided it wasn't worth doing anything about. The young woman wasn't likely to stay long. If she was here to confront me with the idea that Christopher had got her with child—he *was* a grandson of the late Duke, after all—I'd soon disabuse her of that notion, and the dust bunnies under the Chesterfield wouldn't stop me.

So I headed for the lift with my head high and my steps steady, only to be met with the glad cry of, "Hullo, Pippa!" as soon as I made it into the hallway.

I managed to bite back the bad word that had come to my mouth, but only just. "Good afternoon, Florence," I said instead, politely, as I made my way towards her and the door to the lift. "Going out for tea? That's a lovely frock."

It was, in fact, quite lovely, at least if you like flounces and ruffles and flourishes.

Like most of Florence Schlomsky's frocks, it was pink, the better to bring out the healthy roses in her cheeks, undiminished by months in the heart of London, and it was girlishly fluttery. Florence likes her chiffon panels. She also likes beads, and tassels, and fringe. You might think the heiress and only daughter of an American business magnate would show better taste, but you'd be wrong. Florence's tastes are delightfully base

—in fact, it was just a month ago that she'd had St George backed into a corner of this very lift, and if that isn't stunningly base, I don't know what would be.

"This old thing?" She brushed the compliment off with a swish of her hand and bared all her teeth in a wide smile. While I know it's physically impossible, I swear she has more than the usual number, all blindingly white and straight. "Say, Pippa..."

I managed to avoid rolling my eyes, but just barely.

"—where's that cousin of yours holed up these days?"

"Christopher's out with a friend," I said.

I knew very well that she didn't mean Christopher, and she doesn't know Francis, but they are my only cousins, at least on the distaff side. I probably have other cousins in Germany, but these days, it's just as well to forget that side of my family. Anti-German sentiment is still high less than a decade after the Great War, and besides, I feel pretty thoroughly English by now.

Flossie giggled and tossed her neck, making the brown curls bounce. "Don't be silly, Pippa. You know I don't mean Mr. Astley. Where has Lord St George been keeping himself?"

"Crispin's in Wiltshire," I said repressively. "If he's been up to London in the past three weeks, he hasn't stopped in."

And small wonder. The last time he dropped by for a visit, he lost two friends to murder and two more to prison, and almost ended up arrested himself. (In addition to being almost devoured by Flossie in a corner of the lift.) By now, he probably thought of me as a jinx and we would never see him again. And while at one time I would have cheered for that prospect, these days I felt rather bad about it.

Not that I *liked* St George. Of course not. But Christopher is fond of him, and he had grown on me lately—like a fungus, in the event that he asked. I was at least able to put up with him for short periods of time without feeling an uncontrollable urge to strangle him.

"Well, if you see him," Florence said, as the lift arrived and the automatic doors slid back. She grasped the grille covering the opening and pulled it aside so I could go in first, "—give him my love."

I crossed into the lift box and made a face as Florence followed. "I'd really rather not."

I had seen Flossie express her love, and there was no part of me that wanted to partake in passing it on.

She giggled, and pulled the grille back the other way. "Of course not, Pippa."

The lift's gears engaged, and we started to descend. Flossie added, quite sincerely, "It's every woman for herself in the matrimonial stakes."

"Oh, God," I said, shaking my head. "No, Florence, you misunderstood. If you can snag him, you're welcome to him. I certainly don't want to marry him. Although you shouldn't want to, either. He's not a good prospect for marriage. He has discarded lovers all over England, you know. In fact—"

In fact, there was a young woman downstairs right now, who might be in possession of the next heir to the Sutherland dukedom.

But the lift arrived at the ground floor before I could throw St George further under the bus, and the door slid away. Flossie got busy pulling back the grille. "Listen, Pippa," she told me over her shoulder, "you don't have to make up stories to keep me away from him."

"I'm not. I assure you—"

But that was as far as I got, because Flossie exited the lift, chiffon panels fluttering, and I followed, and now we found ourselves face to face with two other young women, probably no older than the two of us.

One must be Florence's date for tea, I assumed. She was lavishly dressed—a bit too lavishly, if you ask me. The dotted dress was a bit too smart for her rather plain face, the blue too sharp for her coloring, and the sheer chiffon overcoat was too elaborate for afternoon. She had three strands of good pearls around her neck—they appeared real—and a matching cloche hat from under which she squinted at us.

It took me no more than a second to process all that, and to move on. To the other woman who stood a few feet away from the first, clutching a baby, under Evans's watchful eye.

She had probably been pretty before childbirth and poverty took their toll. She had soft, brown hair and big eyes, and her afternoon dress, a sprigged rayon, was well made and must have been reasonably expensive when it was new. Now it was a couple of seasons out of date, and too large, as if she had lost weight since having the baby. Her hair was lank and could use a shampoo and set, and there were dark circles under her eyes. Unlike Flossie, there was no healthy pink in her cheeks.

The more eye-catching of the two was the baby, however. It was still small enough that I couldn't say with certainty whether it was a boy or a girl, although I leaned towards girl. Either way, it was small and bright-eyed and had all the vigor its mother lacked. Its cheeks were rosy and it was bouncing on its mother's hip, banging a closed fist against her collar bone. A tuft of blond hair stood up on its head, and it had a pink-cheeked, heart-shaped face with a small chin, large blue eyes, and a rosebud mouth.

Now, I will admit that it's difficult to tell with babies. They have a look all their own, and often grow up to appear quite different from the way they did when they were small. But if I were pressed, I would have to say that this particular baby had a Sutherland look to it. In addition to the Astley blue eyes and the Sutherland fair hair, it also had the heart-shaped face and Cupid's bow mouth that Christopher and Crispin share.

I have seen pictures of them both from when they were small, and I have to say that the resemblance was startling.

And of course Francis looks like an older, more muscular version of Christopher. So does his father, Lord Herbert. And Crispin's father, the current Duke, is clearly cut from the same cloth, as well, even if he is taller and more slender than his brother.

Not that I suspected either uncle of being guilty of adultery. I just mention it as a point of fact. Crispin's platinum hair and gray eyes notwithstanding, the Sutherland genes are strong, and all the men in the family look quite a lot alike. Crispin has the blood, so there was no reason to think he couldn't have passed the traditional blue eyes and sunny wheat hair down to a child, even if he didn't sport them himself.

Beside me, Florence's jaw had dropped. She hiked it back up again. "Is that...?"

"It might very well be. That's what I'm here to find out." I brushed past her. "Good evening, Miss...?"

The girl's mouth opened, but nothing came out. After a moment, she cleared her throat and tried again. "Dole. Abigail Dole."

"Miss Dole." I smiled graciously. "Won't you and—"

I eyed the baby.

Abigail clutched him or her a bit closer. "Bess."

How deplorably common. I imagined my late Aunt Charlotte, Crispin's mother, being faced with a grandchild named Bess, and could only be grateful that she—my aunt—was dead and would be spared the indignity.

"Won't you and... um... Bess come upstairs, where we can talk privately?"

Both Evans and Flossie were unabashedly listening, and so

was the young lady in blue. Abigail glanced from one to the other with a flush. "I'm here to see Mr. Astley."

"Christopher isn't in," I explained. "But if you'll come upstairs with me, we can have tea and a biscuit while we wait for him to come home."

She took a step back. "I don't think..."

I took one forward. "It's perfectly all right, I assure you."

"I just wanted to see Mr. Astley—"

"I have photographs," I said, inspired, "although honestly, if you've seen Crispin—and you have, haven't you? Seen Lord St George?"

She took another step back, still clutching the baby. "Yes, I..." Her cheeks flushed. "I have seen Lord St George."

I smiled winningly. "Well, then you've pretty much seen Christopher. They look enough alike—" at least to someone who doesn't know them well, "—that if you've seen one, you've seen the other."

Beside me, Flossie nodded.

"I have to go," Abigail Dole said and turned on her heel.

And that was that. I ended up standing in the middle of the foyer, my mouth open and my hand raised, while she fled through the door into the street, the baby gurgling and bouncing in her arms as she scurried away from me.

The door shut behind her with a *bang*, and I dropped my hand and blinked.

"Well, I never!" Flossie said. Her expression was caught somewhere between appalled and avid. "Was that...?"

I shook my head, more to clear it than in response to the question she hadn't quite got out. "We don't know. She never sticks around for long enough that anyone can find out."

She slanted me a look. "You've seen her before?"

"*I* haven't," I said. "But she's been at Sutherland House, so I knew of her existence."

I turned to Evans while Florence and her friend exchanged a look. "You've never seen her before, have you, Evans?"

Evans shook his head. "No, Miss Darling."

So she hadn't come to the Essex House looking for Christopher before. And—although it probably doesn't need to be said —a year or year and a half ago, whenever little Bess must have been conceived, Christopher and I lived at Beckwith Place in Wiltshire, and she had never, to my knowledge, been seen there, either.

Back then, Crispin lived—as he still did—at Sutherland Hall. His grandfather and his mother had both been alive then, along with Uncle Harold. But even during that time St George had been in the habit of traveling up to Town for occasional weekends of debauchery. The fall of 1924 was a few months after he'd come down from Cambridge, and that was when the infamous treasure hunts had been all over the newspapers.

And Francis, of course, lived at Beckwith Place, but he also traveled up to Town from time to time. He had friends from the war, as well as from school, who lived here, and there had also been a period in Francis's life where he had spent rather more time than he should have in debauchery. Not Crispin's juvenile carousing, either, but rather darker stuff that included a lot less fun and games and a lot more drinking and doping himself into oblivion. It was not impossible that Francis, during one of those periods, had met this girl, and bedded her, and forgotten all about it afterwards.

And she wasn't really Crispin's type, any more than she was Christopher's. Crispin likes girls, yes—likes them a lot—but to my knowledge, he preferred girls from the Bright Young Set, flashy and modern, with privilege and money of their own. Not this pitiful waif in her outmoded dress with her tired eyes.

Part of me noticed, but tried hard not to dwell on, the fact that Abigail Dole looked quite a lot like Constance Peckham, the girl who had turned Francis's head. Dainty and pretty in a soft and old-fashioned way, with the same brown hair and big eyes.

"Let me know if she comes back, will you, Evans?"

I turned to the lift without paying Florence any mind, although I could feel her eyes, and those of her friend, boring into my back as I disappeared inside the box without a word.

CHAPTER TWO

"THAT'S UNFORTUNATE," was Christopher's reaction when he made it home later that evening, and I told him about the girl's sudden appearance and equally sudden disappearance before I could get anything useful out of her.

I nodded. "It's a shame you weren't home. Maybe she would have let something slip with you that she didn't with me."

"I can't imagine what," Christopher said. "It's much more likely that she would have taken one look at me and run, the way she did with you. I'm not who she's looking for either, you know."

"I didn't think you were," I answered. "Although there was that period, the summer after we came down from Oxford, when you did a bit of experimenting, wasn't there?"

"There was, which you very well know. But it never got to the point of getting anyone with child, or doing anything that might achieve that. I didn't like any of them well enough, and Mum would have skinned me alive."

"That was too long ago anyway," I said. "My guess—not

that I know much about it—is that the baby might be five or six months old."

"So she would have been conceived..." He counted on his fingers, "—last spring or early summer. Sometime in the first half of last year."

I nodded. "Six or eight months, at least, after we came down from university. You had finished your phase of experimentation by then."

"Lucky for me."

"I never thought for a moment that she was yours," I said. "Not to mention, I'm sure you got The Talk at some point, didn't you?"

"Of course I did. Mum set Crispin and me down—"

"Aunt Roz? Talked to St George about women?"

His eyebrows rose. "Surely you didn't think Aunt Charlotte would have thought it appropriate to talk to Crispin about sex?"

Well, no. Aunt Charlotte had been rather Victorian on the subject. The last time we visited Sutherland Hall while she'd been alive, she had put me as far into the west wing as Christopher was into the east to keep us away from each other and any suggestion of impropriety. It had been a ten-minute walk to get from my room to his. Never mind the fact that we share a flat in London and can behave as improperly as we want the rest of the time.

Not that we do, of course. None of Christopher's experimentation had been with me. Not only are we the next thing to siblings, but he wouldn't incline my way if I were a total stranger. However—

"I had rather assumed that Uncle Harold would have done the honors," I said, "since he'd care the most about getting a legitimate heir. Or at least care the most about not getting an illegitimate one."

"He might have done," Christopher admitted. "I don't

know what Uncle Harold and Crispin might have discussed. But The Talk—the one about the birds and the bees—came from Mum. Didn't she talk to you?"

Of course she had. But— "That's rather different, don't you think? I'm a girl, or was at the time. I assumed Uncle Herbert and Uncle Harold would have taught you and St George the facts of life."

"Mum understands the facts of life better than either of them," Christopher said. "She was the one who had to deal with the consequences. My mother carried and birthed three boys. My father just stood by and cheered."

After a moment, he added, "Dad did sit me down one Christmas—I must have been fifteen or sixteen, I suppose; home for the holidays from Eton—and he explained about noblesse oblige and that I couldn't go around sticking little Kit into things willy-nilly ..."

"Little Kit?" I made a face.

"What would you have me call it?" Christopher wanted to know. "Or rather, what would you have my father call it?"

"Your father called it little Kit?"

"No, of course not." His cheeks were pink. "He called it something much cruder than that, that I am not about to repeat in front of you. Mum was more clinical about the whole thing—"

I nodded. "With me, too. So Uncle Herbert told you that noblesse oblige and you cannot poke women indiscriminately..."

He nodded. "That was it. I can't go around poking women indiscriminately, because I don't want to have to marry someone I don't care for just because I can't keep my flies closed."

"A pity Uncle Harold didn't have the same conversation with Crispin," I said.

Christopher squinted at me. "How do you know that he didn't?"

"If he had, do you suppose St George would carry on the way he does?"

"I don't think Crispin carries on the way he does because he doesn't know better," Christopher said. "He's well aware of how it all works. Mum made sure of it. Not that we didn't both have a good idea already. But I guess she assumed Aunt Charlotte wasn't going to get around to it, and she didn't trust whatever Uncle Harold might say—not that Uncle Harold ever struck me as someone who was very interested in women, including his wife."

No, he hadn't struck me that way, either. Christopher's aunt and uncle had been married almost as long as Aunt Roz and Uncle Herbert, and it had been years before they'd had Crispin, and then more years after that with no spare. There was either a medical problem, or Uncle Harold just couldn't be bothered.

"You don't suppose...?" I ventured.

"No," Christopher said. "I think I'd be able to tell if my uncle was queer."

"It's not like he'd come on to you. You're his nephew."

"I'd still be able to tell. And thank you for putting that particular image in my head, Pippa."

We both grimaced, since it had now made its way into mine, as well. Bad enough to consider Uncle Harold—who really was a particularly dry old stick—having relations with his wife, which he must have done at some point or Crispin wouldn't exist. Much worse to contemplate him with another man.

"God knows where Crispin gets it," Christopher added thoughtfully.

His proclivity towards being a cad, I assumed, since

Crispin certainly had none of Christopher's preferences for his own gender.

"Must be from Aunt Charlotte. Unless your grandfather was quite the lad in his day."

"I tend to think of Grandfather as having always been a desiccated old mummy," Christopher said, "but I suppose he might have been different when he was young. He was almost ninety when he died. What would that make it?" He counted on his fingers. "Eighteen-sixty or thereabouts when he was our age? Too long ago for me to have any idea what he was like back then."

I wasn't even a Sutherland, so I knew less than he did. "I don't suppose there are family stories?"

"No," Christopher said. "Youthful indiscretions aren't something you want to pass down to your children and children's children after you settle down, I assume. Do you plan to tell your children that their father was a rake before he married you?"

I slanted him a beady eye. "How do you know that my husband will be a rake? Maybe I'll end up with a perfectly lovely gentleman who barely even kissed a woman's hand before he met me."

Christopher smirked, and I sighed. He said, "One of you ought to know what you're doing, don't you think?"

"I know what I'm doing. Or at least I know the theory. I had The Talk with Aunt Roz, too, don't forget."

He nodded. "Dad got around a bit before he met Mum, apparently. That's why Grandfather married him off so young. And Mum was even younger. If you were her, you would be married and have Francis already."

"I'm glad I'm not," I said. "I'm not ready for a husband or babies."

Christopher shook his head. "Nor am I."

"Good thing little Bess doesn't belong to either of us."

Christopher nodded. "Just out of curiosity, did she...?"

"She looked enough like you to be yours."

He made a face. "So she looked enough like Crispin to be his, too."

"Or enough like Francis to be his," I confirmed. "For that matter, she looked enough like all three of you to be Uncle Harold's or Uncle Herbert's. Not that that's likely, I suppose."

"Probably not," Christopher agreed, "although I suppose they *are* both the grandsons of a Duke."

"A very late Duke. When did your great-grandfather die?"

"Before I had a chance to meet him," Christopher said, "but that doesn't make him any less of a Duke. Or them any less his grandsons."

No. But— "Surely you're not thinking that Uncle Harold or your father would have seduced this poor waif and gotten her with child? They were both married last year. Aunt Charlotte was still alive. And I'm sure you're not accusing your father of cheating on your mother?"

"Of course not," Christopher said. "My father wouldn't do that. And while I have no idea what Uncle Harold would or wouldn't do, I don't imagine it's likely. She didn't look like Aunt Charlotte, did she? The girl?"

"Abigail Dole," I said. "And she looked more like Aunt Charlotte than Aunt Roz. Petite and girlish. But dark instead of fair. She looked nothing at all like Lady Laetitia Marsden or Johanna de Vos. Or for that matter like Millicent Tremayne or Lady Violet Cummings or the Honorable Cecily Fletcher or..."

"I get it." He held up a hand. "You can stop. If you're going to run down the entire list of Crispin's conquests, we'll be here all night."

"We'll be here all night anyway," I told him. "We live here. At any rate, you have to admit he has a type."

"And she wasn't it?"

I shook my head. "She was small and dainty, pretty in an understated, old-fashioned sort of way. Not St George's type at all."

"Francis's type, then."

"If Francis's type is Constance Peckham," I said, "then yes. That's who she looked like."

Christopher nodded, looking troubled. He opened his mouth, but was interrupted by the buzzer from the lobby before he could utter whatever was on his mind (as if I couldn't guess perfectly well).

"Telegram for you, Mr. Astley," Evans's voice said.

Christopher turned pale, and so did I. A telegram is rarely a good thing, and we had both dealt with rather a lot of tragedy over the past few months. Neither of us was looking forward to more.

"Open it," I said, "if you please, Evans."

Christopher made an aborted sort of movement, but he didn't end up saying anything. And I understood where he was coming from. Really, I did. It wasn't any of Evans's business why someone might have sent us a telegram. But he'd learn about it, whatever it was, fairly quickly anyway, I figured, and if we'd just put up with him finding out now instead of later, we'd get the news two minutes faster and wouldn't have to worry as long.

There was the sound of paper ripping, and then Evans's voice. "DEAREST KIT AND PIPPA STOP SHE SAID YES STOP ENGAGEMENT PARTY BECKWITH PLACE NEXT WEEKEND STOP BE THERE END." He cleared his throat. "There's no signature."

I blinked. Christopher did the same.

"Thank you, Evans," I said. "I'll be down in a minute to fetch it."

Evans rang off, and I looked at Christopher. He looked at me. "No one died."

I shook my head as I pushed to my feet.

"Francis proposed to Constance."

"So it seems."

"Who did you say this young woman looked like, again?"

"Constance," I told him over my shoulder.

Christopher nodded. "That's what I thought you said."

BECKWITH PLACE, the childhood home of Christopher's mother, my Aunt Roslyn, and also of her younger sister, my own mother, is located in Wiltshire, in an easterly, south-easterly direction from Salisbury. More east, less south-east than Sutherland Hall, but in the same general area. There's less than an hour's drive between the two, and also less than an hour's drive from Salisbury to Beckwith Place. When Christopher and I exited the railway station in Salisbury on Friday afternoon the following week, Uncle Herbert's black Bentley Tourer was waiting outside, with Francis at the wheel.

My eldest cousin is almost thirty: so close, in fact, that he could probably taste it. He'd turn the big three-zero in the middle of next week, and the family gathering this weekend was partly engagement party, partly birthday celebration.

Francis looks like an older version of Christopher: a bit heavier with muscle, but with the same blue eyes and wheat-blond hair. In personality, he falls somewhere between Christopher and Crispin. Louder and more boisterous than the former, not as cutting as the latter. Bantering with Crispin when he's in a mood is an exercise in avoiding injury. Bantering with Francis is mostly good fun, as he doesn't go out of his way to hurt one.

"Hullo, Pipsqueak!" he hollered when I passed through the

doors from the station and into the relative warmth of the July afternoon. "This way, Kit!" He waved energetically.

I rolled my eyes, but headed towards him, raising my voice. "You know what I've told you about that, Francis."

It's an abominable nickname and I wished he wouldn't use it. Not that my wishes on the subject seem to make any difference whatsoever.

"I know, Pippa." He put an arm around my shoulders and gave me a squeeze before he took the bag out of my hand. "Let me take that for you. Hullo, little brother."

He gave Christopher a squeeze, as well.

"Francis." Christopher twitched out of the embrace and stuck out a hand. "Congratulations, old chap."

"Thanks, old bean." They shook and then Francis opened the door to the back of the Bentley. "Pipsqueak?"

I sighed, but crawled in next to the luggage. "Why do I always end up in the backseat?"

"You can have the front, Pippa," Christopher offered, but I shook my head.

"You go ahead. But drive slowly, Francis, so you can tell us all about the proposal."

"There's not much to tell," Francis said, but when he pulled away from the curb, it was at a decorous pace, quite different from the last time we'd been picked up from the railway station in Salisbury, when St George had scattered pedestrians and pigeons in a mad dash out of town in his Hispano-Suiza racing car.

Francis continued, "I timed it for two months from the first time I met her, when we came up the drive at Sutherland Hall and I saw the two of you—" he shot me a glance over his shoulder, "round the corner of the conservatory."

I nodded. I remembered it well. Constance and her family had arrived that afternoon for the funerals of the late Duke and of Crispin's mother, and she and I had been on our way back from a stroll through the garden maze, where we had come upon Lady Peckham's ward, the lovely Johanna de Vos, in the process of swallowing St George (and his title and fortune) whole. It had been quite an uncomfortable interlude, and Constance, who was much nicer-minded than I am, had been battling horrified amusement over Crispin's embarrassment, while I had been loudly and derisively sneering.

"I asked her to take a walk in the garden after tea," Francis continued, "and then I got down on one knee and asked."

"And she said yes."

He nodded. "Surprised the hell out of me, honestly."

I tilted my head. "Why did you ask, if you thought she'd say no?"

He grinned. "I thought there was a chance she'd say yes. And if she hadn't—it's only been two months, after all—I figured I'd simply wait a month and try again."

"There's no reason," Christopher asked delicately, "other than that you want to, that you're proposing so soon, is there?"

Francis arched his brows at him. "Are you old enough to know about such things, Kit?"

"I'm twenty-three," Christopher huffed. "Yes, I'm old enough to know about such things. For God's sake, Francis—"

Francis grinned. "No, Kit. She's not the kind of girl you take liberties with, at least not without a firm understanding of where you're headed. There'll be no small Astleys born early."

Wonderful. And on that note—

I cleared my throat. "Would the name Abigail Dole mean anything to you?"

If I had hoped to see shock—Francis's foot slipping off one of the pedals, the motorcar veering off the road, or even his hands clenching on the steering wheel—I was disappointed.

And that's the wrong word for it, because of course I hadn't been hoping for any of that. I had been hoping for the opposite, which was what I got: nothing. He glanced at me in the mirror. "Should it?"

"I have no idea," I said lightly. "Just curious."

"Of course you are," Francis hummed. "Who is Abigail Dole?"

I avoided Christopher's eyes. "She showed up at the flat a week ago looking for Christopher."

Francis glanced over at his brother, and then back at me. "And what makes you think I would know her?"

"I don't," I said, "specifically. But it seems that someone does. The baby she was carrying had the Sutherland hair and the Astley eyes—or vice versa—and looked enough like all three of you to—"

"Ah." He appeared enlightened. "This is St George's little by-blow, is it?"

"Well..." I thought about it, "yes and no. Abigail Dole is the girl with the baby—"

"Always the girl with the baby, Pippa." He chortled.

"Yes," I said, "but she showed up at the Essex House looking for Christopher. If the baby was St George's..."

"He's made it clear he won't fall for the ruse," Francis said, "hasn't he? So she's trying to put the screws to someone else."

I supposed that might be a possibility. I had assumed, when Abigail and little Bess showed up at the Essex House Mansions, it was to assess Christopher as the potential father. If all she knew was that the man who had seduced her had been the grandson of the Duke of Sutherland, she might just be going down the list of grandsons in order, looking for the right man. And when Crispin hadn't turned out to be him, she had moved on to Christopher.

But of course Francis's explanation made sense, too.

Crispin might have been lying, and Abigail was seeking out someone else in the family to put pressure on him.

And if he had seduced her, then I supposed he'd deserve it.

"She didn't stick around long enough to answer any questions," Christopher told Francis while I was still cogitating. "Pippa went downstairs to talk to her, and as soon as she heard I was out, she ran away."

"And she never came back?"

Christopher shook his head. "Not in the week and a bit more since."

"Perhaps she thought Pippa was your wife, and she was afraid?"

They both glanced at me. I rolled my eyes. That was also a possibility, certainly. I hadn't introduced myself, or explained my relationship to Christopher, so unless Evans had done the honors—and it would have been quite improper for him to give that sort of information about two of the residents to a stranger—it was quite possible that she had assumed we were living together as man and wife instead of, essentially, as brother and sister.

"She didn't give me time to explain anything," I said. "I asked her name, she said it was Abigail Dole, and that she was looking for Mr. Astley. I told her that Mr. Astley was out but that we could go upstairs and wait. She seemed reluctant. I told her I had photographs of Christopher, but that if she had seen Crispin, she had pretty much seen Christopher as well..."

Francis smirked.

"—and then she said, 'I have to go,' and went. I could have run after her, I suppose, although pelting up the pavement yelling for her to come back seemed to be an inappropriate sort of action that Aunt Roz would take amiss."

Not to mention the attention it would have drawn to us both, which I was sure Miss Dole was just as eager to avoid as I was. If she had wanted notoriety, she would have contacted one of the news rags and gotten her story on the front page, hanging St George's indiscretion out for all to see.

I wondered whether that approach just hadn't occurred to her, or whether she hadn't used it because he truly wasn't who she was looking for.

"Mum is hardly going to be happy about this even so."

No, I imagined not. "We don't have to tell her."

Christopher rolled his eyes and Francis snorted.

"No, listen," I said. "There's already quite a lot going on in London that Aunt Roz doesn't know about." Christopher's drag balls, his relationship (or lack thereof) with Tom Gardiner, a detective sergeant at Scotland Yard, that time last month when we were driving around London in St George's Hispano-Suiza with a dead body in the backseat... "There's no need to tell her that Miss Dole showed up at ours. We know it isn't Christopher's baby. Whatever else we may or may not know, or think we do, we do know that."

Francis slanted a look at Christopher. "Little brother?"

"I suppose," Christopher said. "I mean... yes, we know it isn't my baby. I suppose there's no reason to worry Mum when there's nothing to worry about."

Francis nodded. "We won't mention this to anyone, then. It's not our problem anyway, is it? If anyone needs to deal with it, it's St George."

As we left Salisbury proper and headed down the road that ran past the ruins of Clarendon Castle towards Beckwith Place, Francis began to whistle.

CHAPTER THREE

AUNT ROZ'S childhood home is a small (at least in comparison to Sutherland Hall) brick house in the Georgian style. It was originally built with five first floor bedrooms and two attic bedrooms—in addition to, of course, the downstairs sitting room, study, dining room, library, kitchen, scullery, boot room, etcetera. In the early nineteenth century, a wing was added with two additional bedrooms above a drawing room, and in the late nineteenth century, two of the original bedrooms were converted to baths. As a result, when Francis pulled the Bentley to a stop, it was outside a house with seven bedrooms, including the two very small ones on the attic level, and rather a lot of guests.

"Dear me," I said, looking around at the array of motorcars parked along the side of the driveway. "What's all this?"

"Uncle Harold." Francis said, pointing to the Duke's black Crossley Touring Car as Christopher made his way out of the passenger side of the Bentley. "St George." He indicated the blue Hispano-Suiza.

I squinted at it. "They didn't come up together?"

Francis shook his head. "Wilkins chauffeured Uncle Harold and Crispin motored up on his own. I don't know why they didn't both come in Crispin's car, or both in the Crossley, when they were going to and from the same place to begin with, but..."

I snorted. "I'm sure St George would rather die than have someone else drive him anywhere. Although I'm surprised Uncle Harold didn't travel up with him. There's plenty of room in the Hispano-Suiza, and he'd get here faster."

"Maybe Uncle Harold is aware of Crispin's penchant for taking his life in his hands," Christopher suggested as he came to a stop next to me, both hands in the pockets of his flannels, "and he didn't feel like dying today."

It was as likely an explanation as any. I slanted him a look. "He hasn't killed anyone yet. Not as far as we know, anyway."

"But he's come rather close to offing himself," Christopher said.

"Under the influence of rather a lot of alcohol during a treasure hunt or some such foolishness. If he were to convey his father from Sutherland Hall to Beckwith Place in the middle of the afternoon, I hardly think that would be likely to happen. Do you?"

Christopher shrugged. "What's your explanation, then?"

I didn't have one, aside from what had already been mentioned. Uncle Harold knew, as did we all, about Crispin's total destruction of his previous automobile. It might simply be that Uncle Harold preferred not to put his life at risk by traveling with his son and heir. Or it might be that he preferred not to put the future of the dukedom at risk. If he and Crispin both perished in a fiery crash, Uncle Herbert would get the title and fortune. Traveling separately would ensure that if something happened to one of them, at least it wouldn't happen to both.

Or perhaps it was due to the tension between father and son that I had noticed take shape over the past few months.

They'd never been particularly close. Just as Uncle Harold had never really seemed warm towards Aunt Charlotte, he hadn't seemed warm towards Crispin, either. Their relationship had always seemed more like viscount—now duke—and heir than father and son. But since Aunt Charlotte's death, I had noticed things becoming rather more tense than even they used to be.

Perhaps she had been the buffer between them, and without her, all their sharp edges collided.

Or perhaps it wasn't the loss of Aunt Charlotte at all. Perhaps it was the conversation—or shouting match—that Christopher and I had overheard in April, during which Uncle Harold had refused, point blank, to entertain the idea of letting Crispin marry the woman he claimed to be in love with. Not a suitable wife for the scion of the Sutherlands, apparently. Too poor, too common, too foreign.

Uncle Harold had made the suggestion that Crispin should take a different wife, and then make the girl he loved his mistress. Crispin had been appalled, I'm happy to say. I was appalled, too. The whole incident had made me feel rather more kindly towards him, and rather less kindly towards his father.

At any rate, it might be that.

And honestly, it didn't matter in the slightest. They were both here, and that was really all that was significant.

"What about that?" I inquired, indicating a vaguely familiar-looking Crossley Saloon in burgundy.

"Constance's mother's car," Francis said. "Marsden was kind enough to drive it up."

My stomach sank. "Marsden? Not—?"

"Lord Geoffrey, yes." He flicked a look at me. "His parents

are here, too. That's theirs." Francis indicated an elegant dark green Daimler.

"Whose idea was that?"

"Mum's," Francis said with a grimace. "You know how she is. They're the only family Constance has left. I don't think *she* particularly wanted them here, but Mother thought they should be invited. If they chose not to come, that would be up to them. But..."

But of course they'd come. I made a face.

Christopher glanced at me. "What about Lady Laetitia?"

"She's here, as well," Francis confirmed, and added apologetically, "Sorry, Pipsqueak."

"I'm more worried about him than her," I said. "She'll monopolize St George's time to the degree that we're not likely to see much of either of them, which is all to the good. But if Lord Geoffrey tries to touch any part of my anatomy again, I'll hit him, and I'm sure his parents won't like that."

I had refrained from resorting to violence the last time Geoffrey Marsden had squeezed me into a corner of the sofa, because we had been on the Marsden estate and I hadn't wanted to cause a scene, but I'd be damned if I let him feel me up in my own home without doing something about it.

Christopher nodded. So did Francis. "Don't worry, Pippa. We'll make sure nothing happens."

"Someone should warn the servants," I said. "Constance told me that they can't keep staff at Marsden Manor, because Geoffrey moves through them at such a rapid pace."

"I hardly think Cook or Hughes will appeal to him," Francis answered with a snort, and I tilted my head.

"Hughes? Aunt Charlotte's lady's maid, you mean? She's here?"

"Traveled up with Uncle Harold and Wilkins," Francis confirmed. "I assume Uncle Harold doesn't have a need for her anymore, with Aunt Charlotte gone, so he's dumping her on Mum. Or perhaps she decided to leave on her own. However it came about, she's here now."

"To stay? I didn't think Aunt Roz needed—" or wanted, "—a lady's maid, either."

Unlike Aunt Charlotte, who had kept her long hair and Edwardian dress—including corsets—until she died, Aunt Roz has embraced the ease of drop-waist frocks and a shingled bob, and didn't require help dressing herself or her hair.

"Probably feels bad for Hughes," Francis said. "You know how Mum is. Hughes is getting on in age, and she had been with Aunt Charlotte for a long time. It wouldn't be easy for her to find another position. Almost everyone's like Mum these days, dealing with their own clothes and hair. Constance's aunt didn't bring a lady's maid, either, nor did Lady Laetitia. Nor did Constance's mother, for that matter, when they came to Sutherland for the funerals in May."

"Lady P's maid up and left," I informed him. "Got a telephone call one night, a week or so before the funerals, and was gone the next morning. Or so Constance told me."

"How strange."

I nodded. "I'm sure Lady P would have brought her otherwise. She didn't strike me as the type to forego the use of a maid. But I take your point. Most women have less use for them than before. I suppose Hughes would have been left on the street if Aunt Roz hadn't taken her in."

"I think she came from Marsden originally," Francis said. "Constance's mum and Aunt Charlotte swapped maids at some point—they were friends, you know—and Hughes ended up at Sutherland House. Perhaps she's hoping to talk the Countess into taking her back to Dorset."

Perhaps. That would make everything simple, anyway.

"Where will she stay in the meantime? There's not enough room in the house, is there?"

Francis opened his mouth, but before he had the chance to respond, Uncle Herbert's voice cut through the still summer air.

"Pippa!" he called, from the door into the boot room. "Kit! What are you doing, standing around? Come along inside!"

"We're coming, Father," Christopher called back, as he lifted the weekender bags from the back seat of the Crossley. As we approached the house, he added, in less of a shout, "Just discussing what to expect this weekend."

Uncle Herbert nodded. "Well, we'll have to budge up tight."

He stepped back as we all three filed past him into the mess that was the boot room. "The Marsdens are here, all four of them, and so of course is my brother and Crispin. With the five of us and the six of them, it'll be a full house."

"Francis said that Hughes is here, too," I said, "from Sutherland. Where are you going to put everyone?"

"Francis has given up his room to Harold," Uncle Herbert said. "It's the big front bedroom, so it was either the Duke of Sutherland or the Earl and Countess of Marsden."

"And where are the Earl and Countess of Marsden going to bunk down?"

"In the room where Christopher used to sleep," Uncle Herbert said, "above the new addition."

The new addition was roughly a hundred years old, but since it had been built after the rest of the house, it was still called the new addition.

"Constance has agreed to allow her cousin to share her room—"

I made a face. I could only imagine how Constance felt

about that. She didn't like Lady Laetitia any better than I did. "What about her brother?"

"Lord Geoffrey," Uncle Herbert said, "will sleep in your old room."

I gagged, while Christopher winced and Francis smothered a bark of laughter. Uncle Herbert twitched a brow, but didn't inquire. "That leaves the three of you, and Crispin."

"And we're going into the rooms in the attic," Francis said, "I suppose."

Uncle Herbert nodded. "I'm afraid so. Unless you can think of a better division of rooms? We can't have His Grace, or the Earl or Countess Marsden, or even Lord Geoffrey, sleeping in the attic."

"But it's all right to put Crispin there?" He was just as much a viscount as Geoffrey Marsden. Even more of one, actually, since a duke trumps an earl, and so, presumably, the duke's son would trump the earl's son, too.

"He's family," Uncle Herbert said, waving this concern off as if it were a buzzing fly. "The boy won't mind."

He probably wouldn't, actually. In some ways, he's quite easy to deal with. He hadn't minded sharing with Christopher and Francis at the Dower House two months ago, either.

However—

"Those rooms are quite small," Francis pointed out before I could. "I don't know that I and Kit and Crispin can all squeeze into one of them."

Uncle Herbert smirked. "I guess you'll just have to draw lots to figure out which of you gets to share with Pippa."

Oh, Lord. "I'll share with Christopher," I said.

Nobody in the family would think anything of it if I shared a room with Francis, of course. But we couldn't expect the Marsdens to be as *laissez faire*. Consanguineous marriage is legal in England, and it was probably best if the newly engaged man didn't share a bedchamber with his unattached, female cousin.

And as for sharing with Crispin... well, he's neither my cousin nor engaged to someone else, and given his reputation, I certainly wasn't about to ruin what was left of my own by spending the night with him.

Uncle Herbert nodded while Francis grimaced. "Thanks a lot, Pipsqueak."

"Does he snore?" I wanted to know. "Talk in his sleep? Wake up screaming? You know I can't share with him, Francis. It would absolutely ruin the few shreds of my reputation that aren't already in tatters—"

"What's wrong with your reputation?"

"I'm living with Christopher," I said, "aren't I? At least half the people of our acquaintance think we're living in sin."

"You two?" Francis snorted. "That's ridiculous, Pippa. None of us here—"

He stopped when Christopher shook his head. "Geoffrey Marsden certainly thinks so, and he has probably told his parents. He has some suspicion that there's something going on with Pippa and Crispin too, for that matter..."

Uncle Herbert made a choking noise, and we all turned to look at him. He covered his mouth with his hand and made a coughing sound behind it. "Pardon me," he said after clearing his throat. "But I thought you said... Geoffrey Marsden thinks there's something between *Pippa* and *Crispin*?!"

It was difficult to say which of our two names received the most outraged pronunciation.

"It's her own fault," Francis told him and turned to me. "If you would just refrain from flirting with him, Pipsqueak—"

"I do not *flirt* with St George!" I said, offended.

"You did that time. All that 'sometime when we're alone' nonsense..."

Uncle Herbert made another sound. I flicked him a glance —his cheeks were red behind the hand—and then ignored him in favor of Francis.

"That wasn't flirtation, Francis. I was trying to be funny. Everyone who knows us knows that all we ever do is bicker. *He* knows that all we ever do is bicker!"

"Lord Geoffrey doesn't know that all you ever do is bicker," Francis pointed out, "and when you say things like 'when we are alone...'"

I threw my hands up. "I made a mistake, all right? Christopher already explained this to me. I gave Marsden the wrong impression, and as a result we had that whole scene in which he put his hand on my knee and squished me into the corner of the sofa..."

Uncle Herbert made another noise, but this time it was outraged rather than appalled. "He did what?"

I waved it off. "It's ancient history. Happened back in May when we went to the Dower House. St George took care of it."

Uncle Herbert arched a brow before looking from one of his sons to the other. "Crispin had to rescue Philippa from Lord Geoffrey? What were the two of you doing?"

"I was dancing with Constance," Francis said. "I had other things on my mind. Christopher was dancing with... who was it again, Kit? Lady Laetitia or the fair Johanna that time?"

Christopher muttered something, his cheeks hot, and Francis grinned. "That's right. St George was dancing with Johanna, wasn't he? Yet *he* managed to notice that our Pippa needed rescuing, and you didn't. Why was that, Kit?"

"Leave him alone, Francis," I told him, although truthfully I had no idea what he was on about. There was absolutely no chance that Christopher had been so taken with Lady Laetitia's charms that that was why he hadn't noticed my distress. "It's done. Although I'm sure that that unfortunate scene did nothing to persuade Marsden that he was wrong about St George and myself."

"No," Francis agreed, "I don't imagine it did. When a bloke goes out of his way to rescue a girl who isn't his sister from another bloke who's attempting to pet her, it generally tells the other bloke something. At any rate, I won't make you sleep with him. If you're going to—"

He caught his father's eye and trailed off. After clearing his throat, he started again. "I'll share with St George. You share with Kit. And if anyone says anything about it, one of us will be happy to set them straight."

"Marvelous," I said. "Shall we go in, then?"

"The others are gathered in the drawing room," Uncle Herbert said. "It's almost time for tea."

"I'll take the bags upstairs," Francis said. "Do you want the room to the left or the right of the staircase?"

"I don't care," I said.

"Right," Christopher said at the same time.

We glanced at one another. "I'm right," I asked, "or you want the room on the right?"

"Do you care?"

I didn't. "Just pick one. Your right, the house's right, or I'm right. Doesn't matter. We won't be there much, since the rooms are small and uncomfortable and the weather is nice. We can play croquet tomorrow."

Francis nodded and headed for the staircase, bags in both hands.

"This way," Uncle Herbert told us, as if we hadn't grown up here, and gestured towards the drawing room.

CHAPTER FOUR

THE DRAWING ROOM takes up the entire ground floor of
the new, hundred-year-old addition. It's a lovely room, open
and airy, with tall ceilings, walk-out windows on two walls—the
front and side of the house—and a dainty fireplace with a gray
tile surround on the third. A picture rail two feet from the
ceiling holds landscapes and family portraits in gold frames—
one of them of my mother and Aunt Roz as children—while
elegant rugs cover the wood floors.

It's also the biggest room in the house, and with everyone
gathered there—except Francis, until he came back downstairs
—that was useful, since we had quite a crowd.

The first person I saw when I came through the door was
Laetitia Marsden. She was dressed in her usual black, and
looked stunning.

She's an exceptionally pretty woman, I'm not going to deny
that. Tall and slender, with jet black hair cut into a sleek page-
boy, and bright blue eyes outlined with kohl. Her dress was a
black crepe de chine with a ring of rosebuds embroidered
around the neckline, and a scalloped edge circling her hips,

while the skirt below fell to her knees in tiny pleats. She was wearing elegant T-strap shoes and pearls in her ears and around her neck, and her pink lips were curved in a self-satisfied little simper.

The reason for that was sitting next to her, perched on the arm of her chair, looking across at me—at us—with his usual supercilious smirk. "Afternoon, Darling. Kit. My, don't you both look windswept?"

It was probably supposed to be some sort of innuendo. What sort I have no idea, since everyone here, with the possible exception of the Marsdens, knew very well that Christopher and I hadn't stopped off in a hedgerow somewhere between Salisbury and Beckwith Place to do inappropriate things to one another. Crispin certainly knew it. If my hair was disordered, it wasn't because Christopher had had his fingers in it.

I resisted the temptation to smooth it down, which had probably been his aim. Some display of self-consciousness on my part. Instead I smirked back. "St George. How lovely to see you. Florence sends her love."

I crossed the floor towards him as I spoke, and had the pleasure of seeing apprehension flicker across his face.

"She asked me to pass it on personally," I added sweetly, as I stopped in front of him and lifted my hand.

He flinched. Perhaps he thought I was about to give him that slap he's been begging for with every word out of his mouth for the past twelve years, or perhaps he assumed Florence thought he was due one. Either way, it's disconcerting when someone flinches when you lift your hand around them.

I tucked the reaction away in the back of my head and did what I had intended to do all along: cupped my palm against his cheek gently. His eyes widened as I leaned in, and his lips parted. I have no doubt that the whole thing looked terribly intimate, especially since that was the impression I was going for. Out of the corner of my eye I could see Laetitia's eyes narrow into slits.

And that was when I halted two inches from his nose, and smirked at him. "But I've seen what Florence's love looks like, St George, and frankly, I wouldn't lower myself to put my lips anywhere where hers have been. So you're going to have to be satisfied with this, I'm afraid. Flossie says hello."

I distributed a brisk pat to his cheek before I straightened. And smiled at Lady Laetitia over his shoulder. "Pardon my imposition. He's all yours."

Behind me, Uncle Herbert let out a bark of laughter. Crispin didn't move for a second, just sat there, barely breathing. Until someone—I think it may have been his father—cleared his throat, and then his cheeks turned pink. "You're awful, Darling," he told me, with something that was perilously close to a pout.

Behind me, Christopher sniggered. "Serves you right, Crispin. Turnabout is fair play."

He snagged my elbow. "Come along, Pippa. That's enough excitement for both of you for one afternoon."

He towed me towards an empty chair and pushed me down on it, before he draped himself across the arm next to me. I scowled at him, but before I could protest, Aunt Roz had opened her mouth.

"What's this about turnabout, dear?"

She was sitting on one of the Chesterfields next to Constance, and like her husband, she looked rather amused by the whole episode.

"St George decided to practice his wiles on me last month," I told her, with a look at him. "He leaned close and looked deeply into my eyes and breathed my name in this very significant manner..." I shuddered exaggeratedly. "It was horrid."

Uncle Herbert smothered another bark of laughter. "Losing your touch, boy?"

Crispin flicked me a glance before he answered. "Just because Philippa can't appreciate my charms, Uncle, doesn't mean other women can't."

"St George," Uncle Harold rumbled, and Crispin's face closed.

"Sorry, sir."

Uncle Harold looked mollified, and Her Grace, Countess Marsden, tittered. "I can see why you have your hands full with that one, Harold."

Laetitia smirked. Uncle Harold gave his son and heir a look of displeasure. Crispin dropped his eyes to his lap while his lips tightened. I squashed a stab of guilt for putting him into a position where his father was unhappy with him, and surveyed the rest of the room.

This was my first experience with Laetitia's and Geoffrey's parents. They hadn't stopped by during the weekend we had spent at the Dower House, and while Uncle Harold and Aunt Charlotte may have hosted them before, Uncle Herbert and Aunt Roz hadn't.

The Countess looked like an older version of her daughter. Her face was a little more angular and her cheekbones sharper, the skin softer and less dewy. But she retained the same clear, blue eyes and black hair, in the Countess's case leavened with white streaks at each temple. Unlike her daughter—and the rest of us—she'd kept it long and swept back from her face into an elegant chignon at the back of her head. It wasn't *a la mode*, but there was no question that it suited her.

Laetitia and Geoffrey had both gotten their beauty from her, because the Earl was nothing to look at. Shorter than his wife, even while sitting down, he was a portly man with a white walrus mustache and calculating eyes. They flicked between me and Crispin and Lady Laetitia as if weighing us all.

"Miss Darling," Lord Geoffrey drawled. "Mr. Astley."

He was reclining in a chair to the side of the table, and like his sister, looked just as good as he had the last time I laid eyes on him. He may be a cad, but he's a handsome cad. Like his sister, he has sleek, black hair, bright blue eyes, and a perfect nose and teeth. Which were all on display right now, in a lecherous grin.

"Lord Geoffrey," I said politely. "How simply spiffing to see you again."

It wasn't, of course. If I never saw Geoffrey Marsden again for as long as I lived, it wouldn't be too soon.

At this point Francis came back from upstairs, and clapped Crispin on the shoulder as he crossed the floor towards Constance and the Chesterfield. "You're bunking with me, old chap."

Crispin's upper lip curled. "Charmed, I'm sure."

"It was me or Pippa," Francis told him, as he took his seat next to Constance and appropriated her hand. Crispin's gaze flickered to me for a second before settling back on Francis again, as the latter finished, "and we decided that her reputation is in safer hands with Kit than with you. No offense."

"None taken," Crispin said, "although given the way she just schooled me, I don't think there's any danger that I'd compromise her."

Francis chortled. "What did you do now, Pipsqueak?"

"Nothing," I said. "Just a bit of tit for tatting for something St George did to me last month."

After a moment I continued, "I've known you all since I was a girl, you know. I wouldn't worry about sharing a room with any of you."

Crispin's brows arched at this, and I added, "Yes, even you,

St George. But Christopher and I are either misbehaving already, in which case that particular horse has already left the barn and there's no point in keeping us apart, or we're never going to misbehave, and it's safe to put us in a room together. You, on the other hand, have a bit of a reputation—"

He looked somewhere between gratified and appalled.

"—and while you don't worry me, I'd rather not be known as one more of Crispin Astley's conquests. I'll just stick with Christopher if it's all the same to you."

"Delighted," Christopher said, as if this hadn't all been worked out a long time ago.

The Earl and Countess looked from one to the other of us as if we had all sprouted extra heads. I wondered whether they were so oblivious to their own children's lives that they had no idea that Geoffrey's reputation was at least equal to, if not worse than, Crispin's, and that Laetitia had long since lost any semblance of propriety, or whether they were simply pretending.

After a beat, Countess Marsden turned to Aunt Roz. "Roslyn, my dear..."

Aunt Roz blinked and then straightened. "Of course, Euphemia. I forgot you haven't met the rest of our children. This is my youngest son Christopher, and my niece, Philippa. Annabelle's daughter."

Her Grace's glance flickered for a moment to a painting on the opposite wall. I didn't turn to look at it, although Crispin did. "That's right. That's your mother, isn't it, Darling?"

When I nodded, he jumped up from the arm of Laetitia's chair—she pouted prettily—and skirted the Chesterfield with Francis and Constance on it for a closer look. "Which one?"

"Aunt Roz is on the left," I said, "my mother on the right."

Aunt Roslyn was born in 1874 and my mother a couple of years later. The painting was from circa 1890, when they were both young ladies in proper Victorian dress. Aunt Roz's hair was long and piled on top of her head with little curls framing her face—not too dissimilar to the way she looked now, actually, with her bobbed brown locks—while my mother's hair fell around her shoulders in fat ringlets from each side of a center part. They were both dressed in ruffled summer frocks with tiny waists and puffed sleeves, and they both stared out of the canvas with identical blue eyes and solemn expressions.

"We had to stand still for hours," Aunt Roz told Crispin, with her eyes on the portrait, "and Annabelle hated it. She wanted to run and climb trees and wade in the brook and poke wasps' nests..."

Crispin sniggered. "Sounds like you, Darling."

I thought about making a face at him, but he was right: it did sound like me. I'm not terribly fond of sitting still even now, and I had done my best to keep up with him and Christopher, and with Francis and Robbie, when we were younger.

"You look like her," he added after a moment, eyes back on the portrait. "At least what I can remember from this age."

Aunt Roz nodded. "Very much so. Although you have your father's eyes, Pippa. Annabelle's were blue."

And mine are green. Not blue-green, either, but the verdant side of hazel.

The Countess cleared her throat delicately. "So sad, what happened to Annabelle."

I could see an almost imperceptible tightening in my aunt's lips, but her voice was perfectly even when she said, "Thank you, Euphemia. The influenza epidemic stole so many lives, especially just after the war had already taken such a toll on our families."

From the expression on the Countess's face, I deduced that my mother's death during the influenza epidemic of 1919 wasn't what she had been referring to. It was more likely to be the scandal of my mother's mad dash to the Continent some twenty years prior, and her subsequent marriage to a very unsuitable commoner with no title and no fortune—and a German to boot, which became a sin punishable by death a decade and a half later, when the war started.

She—the Countess—had sense enough not to push the issue, though, not after Aunt Roz shut her down, but her eyes landed on me for a second with an expression of dislike.

Crispin cleared his throat. "You were lovely," he told Aunt Roz sincerely. "Both of you."

Aunt Roz beamed at him. "Thank you, Crispin. Such a sweet boy!"

Crispin arched a brow at me as he turned away from the portrait, smirking. *See, Darling?* he told me—silently, but as clearly as if he'd said the words out loud, *some people appreciate me.*

I rolled my eyes. "Think I'm lovely, do you, St George?"

"Of course not, Darling." He made his way back over to Lady Laetitia's chair without looking at me. "I was talking about your mother and your aunt. There's nothing lovely about you."

"You horrible man," I told him, "did you or did you not just say that my mother was lovely, not two minutes after you told me how much I look like her?"

It was his turn to roll his eyes. "Beauty is as beauty does, Darling."

He perched himself on Laetitia's arm again, and she put a possessive hand on his knee. I eyed it for a moment, wondering whether I ought to make a snide remark, but before I could, Christopher leaned down to murmur in my ear. "You're doing it again, Pippa."

I abandoned the spectacle of Laetitia staking her claim to peer up at him. "Doing what?"

"Flirting," Christopher said. "Or your version of it."

I scoffed. "I am not!"

Although to look at the rest of the room—Francis looked amused, Lady Euphemia speculative, Geoffrey fatuous, and Laetitia like a thundercloud—I couldn't prove it by them, clearly.

"We're bickering," I added, for Christopher's ears only, "just as we always do."

"Mmm." Christopher made a noise that absolutely wasn't agreement. "You know, Pippa, one of these days you're are going to wake up and realize what the rest of us have known for years."

I bristled. "And what is that, pray tell?"

"That the two of you—"

The statement was brought up short by a, "Kindly keep your mouth shut, Kit," from Crispin's side of the room.

Christopher flicked him a look, but didn't say anything.

"Don't be ridiculous, Christopher," I sniffed, with a dismissive glance in that direction. "I abhor St George. You know that."

"The feeling's mutual, Darling," Crispin tossed back.

I tilted my nose up. "I'm well aware of it, St George. Which is why it's patently ridiculous for people to accuse us of flirting."

"People accuse us of flirting?"

"These people do," I said, indicating the room.

Crispin eyed them all, one after the other. Francis smirked. Constance did too, but with a blush. Aunt Roz gave him a fond look, and his father contributed a hard stare. Crispin turned his attention back to me. "Absurd."

I nodded. "Glad you agree, St George."

"Of course, Darling. How could I not?"

Christopher snorted. Francis turned a bark of laughter into

a cough. Constance patted him on the back, but her eyes were dancing.

"Hello, Constance," I told her, since I had been too preoccupied thus far to have greeted my old friend when we came in. "We were so happy to receive your telegram last week. Welcome to the family."

"Thank you, Pippa." She smiled demurely. "I'm delighted to be here."

"And we're delighted to have you," Aunt Roz said, and distributed a pat to the back of Constance's hand. "We were starting to despair of Francis ever settling down."

She bent a fond look on her eldest son.

If you asked me, the problem had never been Francis settling down. Crispin settling down, yes, but Francis had never had a habit of flitting from flower to flower, at least not as far as I knew.

Abigail Dole's face—and that of little Bess—rose unasked (and unwanted) in my mind, and I pushed them down and turned back to Constance.

"It'll be lovely to have a sister. I've been surrounded by boys all my life."

The Countess cleared her throat. "You're German, Miss Darling. Is that correct?"

There was a general feeling of stiffening spines around the room. Mine certainly tightened, and both Christopher and his mother sat up straighter. Uncle Herbert's brows lowered.

Lady Laetitia's lips curved, although I'm not sure Crispin noticed, as he, too, was looking at the Countess and at me and then back again.

"I'm English," I told her calmly. "I've spent the past twelve years in England. I'm an English citizen. My mother was English, and so am I."

"But your father was a German."

There was a moment of silence while I thought about what to say. Was I supposed to denounce my parentage? Lie and say no, my father hadn't been German?

Obviously not, since we all knew the truth, and anyway, he'd been my father. I didn't remember him well anymore, but that didn't mean I was willing to pretend he hadn't existed, or that my mother hadn't fallen for him and chosen to settle in Germany to be with him.

I straightened my shoulders, but before I could get the words out, there were footsteps on the floor of the sitting room next door, and then Hughes's form appeared in the doorway between the two rooms.

"Tea is served on the terrasse, my lady."

"THE OLD COW," Christopher muttered as he tucked my hand through his arm to escort me from the sitting room.

The Countess had already been ushered out to the terrasse by Uncle Harold, and her husband had trailed behind them, content to make his own way there, unaided by Aunt Roz. She walked with Uncle Herbert, while Lord Geoffrey ambled after, hands in his pockets. He had slanted a glance in my direction, but must have thought better of approaching when Christopher and I both responded with looks of loathing.

Crispin, meanwhile, was taken in hand by Laetitia and swept through the door with no more than a glance over his shoulder at us. He looked concerned, but there was very little he could do about it without bucking Laetitia's grasp on his arm, and he seemed unwilling or perhaps unable to do that.

So it was me and Christopher, and his opinion of the Countess of Marsden.

"Like mother, like daughter," I said philosophically as I let him escort me out of the drawing room and through the sitting room to the hall. Laetitia was still close enough to us that she could probably hear me, but if she did, she didn't react. "It's no problem, Christopher. Yes, I'm half German. We all know it. I'm certainly not going to pretend I'm not, just because some old crone has decided to put me on the spot."

"Trying to make her daughter look better by making you look bad," Christopher grumbled.

I shook my head. "That's ridiculous. Is this about your peculiar notion concerning me and St George again?"

"Is it peculiar if the Countess Marsden got the same impression and moved to make you look bad because of it?"

The look he slanted me was victorious. I rolled my eyes. "I can't help it if people get the wrong impression, Christopher. There's nothing going on with me and St George, and you know it. We simply like to bicker. He's clever, and I enjoy matching wits with him. I can't help it if other people read something into that. But Laetitia Marsden is welcome to him. Or Flossie Schlomsky. Or Abigail Dole, if she can snag him. Or Millicent Tremayne or Violet Cummings or... Thank you, St George."

"Don't mention it," Crispin said with a smirk as he held the hall door open for me to pass through. "Do go on, Darling. Millicent Tremayne or Violet Cummings or...?"

"Cecily Fletcher. Or that woman with the artistic grandfather you dallied with last year sometime. Or the waitress you mentioned last month, the one who prevented you from getting back to Sutherland Hall in a timely manner the day after Freddie Montrose died. They're all welcome to you, singly or together. And I, for one, hope that when the competition is over, they've torn you into tiny pieces and scattered them across the landscape so that none of us have to deal with you anymore."

I swept past him with my head held high. He sniggered and

fell into step with Christopher as we headed down the hallway through the back of the house towards the terrasse doors.

IT WAS some ten or fifteen minutes later, just as the sun was dropping below the tops of the aspens to the west, that Laetitia stopped with a cucumber sandwich halfway to her mouth and asked, "Who's *that*?"

We weren't sitting at the same small wrought-iron table on the terrasse. Of course not. For a moment, when Crispin attached himself to Christopher and me at the door, I had been afraid that I was destined for tea with him and Laetitia. But the Countess Marsden swooped down and whisked them off to a table for four with herself and Uncle Harold on the north end of the terrasse. Her husband ended up with Aunt Roz, Uncle Herbert, and Geoffrey—I breathed a sigh of relief at that, at any rate—and Christopher and I sat with Francis and Constance, which made for a very comfortable and happy meal for us. The only thing worth notice was when Hughes, who was helping Cook with tea, approached Lady Marsden to inquire whether the Marsdens had heard anything from Lydia Morrison.

"Lydia Morrison?" I repeated, with a glance at Constance. "Who's she?"

The name sounded vaguely familiar, but I couldn't place it. And what would make Hughes think that Lady Marsden would know, anyway?

Constance answered in the same soft tone so we wouldn't overpower the conversation at the other table. "My mother's lady's maid."

"The one who left without giving notice a couple of months ago?"

Constance nodded. "Hughes asked me about her, too, when she arrived this afternoon. But of course I've been here at

Beckwith since shortly after Morrison left. I told Hughes to ask Lady Marsden or Laetitia instead."

Over at the other table, Lady Marsden had finished looking down the length of her nose at Hughes, and deigned to inform her that no, no one at Marsden-on-Crane had heard from Lydia Morrison since she'd left Lady Peckham's employ in late April. The Countess's tone indicated deep offense that Hughes had dared to address her.

"Thank you, Hughes," Aunt Roz said pleasantly. "Go on inside and get your own tea, if you would. We'll be fine here."

Hughes murmured her thanks and withdrew, looking chastised, although I'm fairly certain that the tightness in Aunt Roz's voice was in response to the Countess's behavior and not Hughes's. Aunt Roz is invariably polite to the staff.

"How does Aunt Charlotte's maid from Sutherland know your late mother's maid at the Dower House?" I wanted to know, as Lady Marsden returned her attention to Uncle Harold and to Crispin.

"It's like I told you, Pipsqueak," Francis said. "They switched places at one point."

"Truly?"

Constance nodded. "Hughes worked for my mother at Marsden, and Morrison worked for your aunt at Sutherland Hall. And when one of them wanted a change, the other agreed to a swap."

"Interesting."

Constance shrugged. "It was a very long time ago. Morrison worked for Mother my whole life. I never saw Hughes until today. She told me Mother had promised to bring her back to the Dower House after the funerals, but..." She trailed off.

"But your mother died," I nodded, and then winced, appalled at my own insensitivity. "Sorry."

Constance didn't respond, and I added, "And you haven't heard from Morrison since she left?"

She shook her head. "But I didn't expect to. Mother gave her her wages, and there'd be no other reason why she'd contact me."

"Not even to offer her condolences after your mother's and Johanna's deaths?"

And there I went, stuffing my foot in my mouth again.

"Never mind," I said, and it was at this point that Lady Laetitia lifted a cucumber sandwich to her mouth and stopped halfway.

"Who's *that*?"

We all turned in the direction she was staring, in time to see a slender figure in a sprigged rayon frock, with a fair-haired baby on her hip, stagger out of the bushes onto the croquet lawn and promptly crumple into a heap on the grass.

CHAPTER FIVE

THERE WAS a moment when nothing happened, when no one moved or even breathed. Then Laetitia squealed, and slapped a hand to her mouth. Not the one with the cucumber sandwich, sadly; the other one.

Constance gasped. Francis swore, and the legs of his chair scraped on the flagstones as he pushed it back. Aunt Roz's chair fell over with a clatter as she shot to her feet and started running with Francis right behind.

I met Christopher's shocked stare across the table.

"Is that—?" He couldn't seem to find the words to continue, so he just stared at me.

I nodded. And pushed to my feet, too, a little less violently than either Aunt Roz or Francis. "Excuse me, please. I'm going to see if there's anything I can do."

Christopher nodded.

"Who...?"

I glanced at Constance—she had turned pale and looked faint—and back at Christopher. "Stay with her. Explain."

He nodded. "Be careful."

"Of course." Not that there was anything to worry about. Abigail Dole wasn't likely to be contagious, or a danger to me in any other way.

By the time I reached the cluster of people on the lawn, it had swelled to include Uncle Herbert and Crispin as well as Francis and Aunt Roz. The latter two were on their knees on the grass, one on either side of Abigail. She was, for all intents and purposes, pale as death. Her eyes were closed, with dark circles like bruises against her translucent skin, but her chest was moving, so at least she was alive. Her pale arms looked like sticks poking out of the sleeves of the dress.

Uncle Herbert had taken it upon himself to pick up little Bess. When Abigail had crumpled, the baby had tumbled out of her arms onto the grass, and had started wailing.

It hadn't been a far drop and the landing had been soft, so it was probably shock more than pain, and the shrill cries died into wet hiccoughs as Uncle Herbert cradled the baby in the crook of one arm and rocked back and forth with her, crooning.

"Well, hello there. Aren't you a pretty girl? Who do you belong to, then?"

Crispin was standing a few feet away staring at them both, eyes wide in his pale face.

"You've seen her before," I asked him briskly as I brushed past with a—quick deliberate—knock of my shoulder to his arm, "haven't you?"

He slanted his eyes my way before turning back to Uncle Herbert and Bess. "It was a few months ago. She—it—didn't look like this then."

No, I could well imagine. A two-month-old looks quite different from a five-or-six-month old. She'd been a bit less distinctly a Sutherland the last time he'd seen her, I imagined.

"Are you sure you don't know her mother?" I asked, looking over at Abigail. Aunt Roz was patting her hand now, while

Francis was peeling back her eyelids to look at her pupils. Crispin examined her, too, for a moment, and then shook his head.

"No, Darling. I realize you have no reason to believe me, given my—" he grimaced, "reputation, but I swear I don't. I saw her at Sutherland House in March, of course, you know that, but that was the first time I saw her."

After a moment he added, "I do try to be careful, you know. The last thing I want is to have to marry someone just because I had a bit too much fun one night."

"Of course." It would be about his own convenience and no one else's. Of course it would. "If you're worried about that happening, you could just keep your flies closed, you know."

"In this case," Crispin said coldly, "I did."

Uncle Herbert was still rocking the baby, shifting from one foot to the other. Her cries had died to sniffles and she had found her thumb and was sucking on it, eyes on his face. One pair of Astley blue eyes contemplated another.

"Are you all right," I asked, "or would you like me to take over?"

He shot me a quick look. "I imagine I have more experience with this than you do, Pippa, having had three of my own. She's fine for now, and so am I."

I nodded. "Her name is Bess. Elizabeth, I guess. Last name Dole. Her mother is Abigail. She came to the flat last week, looking for Christopher."

At those words, the color drained out of Uncle Herbert's cheeks, too. "Kit?" he croaked.

"Obviously not," I said. "I mean, yes. She was looking for Christopher. But he's not who she's really looking for. We all know that."

I looked back down at Abigail. By now, Francis was

scooping her up off the ground and into his arms, and Aunt Roz was getting to her feet, too.

"—don't know what we'll do," she was saying. "We don't have a single available bedroom. Wilkins and Hughes have to put up above the pub in the village as it is. Perhaps one of you boys wouldn't mind...?"

The three of them started for the terrasse and the door to the house. Aunt Roz was still talking.

"—should have a doctor look at her, I suppose, although it's probably just exhaustion and the heat. She may not have eaten anything recently. Some rest and food might be all she needs. But—"

As they moved past us, Aunt Roz took Uncle Herbert by the elbow and tugged. "Come along, dear. She'll want to see her baby when she wakes up, I expect. If we keep him or her—"

"Her," I said quickly as I fell in behind. "Bess."

Aunt Roz gave me a look, but didn't inquire, "—her away, I'm sure it won't be a good idea..."

The procession moved across the flagstones. From out of the corner of my eye I could see Lady Laetitia and her mother, their heads together in a whispered conversation, and Uncle Harold, with his face like stone. Crispin had followed the rest of us up on the terrasse, and was making his slow way back to their table, seemingly deep in thought.

"Crispin, dear?"

When Aunt Roz said his name, he jumped, and his eyes shot to her, startled. "Yes, Aunt?"

"Drive down to the village, would you? Fetch Doctor White and bring him back here."

Crispin nodded and turned on his heel. By the time his feet hit the grass, he was running.

"Come along, Pippa," Aunt Roz said, and I held the door as we all passed through and into the house.

. . .

A MINUTE LATER, Abigail had been deposited on one of the Chesterfields in the library, and Francis was dusting off his hands, almost literally. He was brushing them down his sleeves repeatedly, as if trying to get rid of the imprint of Abigail's body.

"Here." Aunt Roz took little Bess out of Uncle Herbert's arms and dropped her into mine. I held on as best I could as Aunt Roz continued. "Better go back outside. We can't leave Harold and Euphemia in charge for too long. One of us should be there."

Uncle Harold nodded, eyes lingering on Abigail. "What do I tell them?"

"The truth," Aunt Roz said. "The doctor's coming, and until he's looked at her, we have no idea what's going on."

"Did you hear what Pippa said?"

Aunt Roz glanced at me.

"The girl's name is Abigail Dole," I said. "This is Bess. They came to the Essex House Mansions last week looking for Christopher."

Aunt Roz looked unfazed by this statement. "Well, we know she isn't Christopher's. Francis, do you have something you'd like to confess?"

Francis shook his head. "No, Mother."

"Herbert?"

Uncle Herbert looked offended. "Of course not, Roslyn. How can you even suggest—?"

"It's just as well to be sure, dear." She patted his arm and then nodded towards the door. "Go on out there and mitigate whatever damage you can. I'll stay with her until the doctor gets here. You push off too, Francis."

Francis hesitated, glancing from Abigail to Bess to his mother and back. "What if—?"

"The doctor will be here soon," I told him. "The village isn't far." And Crispin wouldn't be holding back, I assumed. I added, significantly, "Constance must be worried."

Francis blinked, and then panic streaked across his eyes for a moment as that thought penetrated, before he spun on his heel and headed for the door.

"Well done, Pippa." Aunt Roz waited for them both to get out of sight before she sank down next to Abigail with a sigh. "Tell me everything."

"There's not much to tell," I said, eyeing her. "She showed up a few months ago at Sutherland House. According to Rogers, she was looking for the Duke's grandson. This was—"

"Before Henry died." Aunt Roz nodded. "Naturally they thought she was looking for Crispin."

"Of course. And it makes sense that they would, given how free he is with his favors." Not to mention his habit of using Sutherland House as his own private love nest whenever he was in Town. If Abigail had been there before, it made sense that she would come back.

After a moment, when Aunt Roz hadn't said anything, I added, "Who else is there? We know the baby isn't Christopher's, and Francis said she wasn't his..."

"What Francis said," Aunt Roz told me, and there was an edge to her voice, "was that there wasn't anything he wanted to confess. It's not exactly the same thing, is it?"

Well, no. Now that she mentioned it, I supposed it wasn't.

"Surely you don't think...?"

"I don't think anything," Aunt Roz said, which was clearly a lie. She was thinking all sorts of things; she just wasn't sharing them with me. "Go on. She went to Sutherland House, and Crispin refused her. Then she came to your flat?"

"Last week. It must have taken her all this time to track down where we live, I assume."

Aunt Roz nodded.

"Christopher wasn't home. I asked her to come upstairs and wait for him, but instead she ran away. All I got out of her that time, was her name and the baby's name."

"And now she's here."

Indubitably.

"It seems, then," Aunt Roz said, "that one of two things is happening. She got herself in the family way by someone in the Astley family—"

"There's really no denying that, is there?"

Aunt Roz looked at little Bess, now contentedly chewing her thumb while perched on my hip. "That the baby is a Sutherland? No, there's no denying that, I'm afraid. So either Miss Dole went to Sutherland House looking for her baby's father, and when she determined that Crispin wasn't he, she found out where Christopher and you live, and went to look at Christopher. And then—"

"I told her that if she'd seen Crispin she'd seen Christopher," I said, "and Flossie Schlomsky agreed with me..."

"—and now she's learned where Francis lives, and has come to take a look at him."

So she was essentially going down the line of Astleys looking for the right one. "Or?"

"Or," Aunt Roz said, eyeing the unconscious figure critically, "she knows exactly who little Bess's father is, and she's here to force him to acknowledge her."

"Blackmail?"

She shrugged, and I added, "When you say that she knows exactly who he is...?"

"She went to Sutherland House first," Aunt Roz said, "didn't she?"

"So you think it's Crispin."

She slanted me a look. "Don't you?"

Did I? "Every time we've talked about it," I said, "he has told me it isn't. He said it again just a few minutes ago. He's said it every time I've asked." And I had asked more than once.

"He has every reason to lie," Aunt Roz pointed out. "If this truly is his baby, Harold will go spare. And the last person he'd want to admit it in front of—"

"Is Laetitia Marsden. Of course."

"No," Aunt Roz said, blinking. "That wasn't..."

I brushed her off. "It doesn't matter. He could be lying. Or he could have forgotten. Or he could be telling the truth. I don't know how we'd ever know for certain. People lie. Even if Abigail wakes up and says he's Bess's father, it won't be proof."

"It'll be proof enough for me," Aunt Roz said. She turned to look at the unconscious girl. "I'm surprised it has taken as long as it has, honestly. I don't suppose you carry smelling salts, Pippa?"

"Of course not. I'm hardly in the habit of fainting."

She nodded. "Nor am I. And I don't suppose Euphemia or her daughter are the swooning sort, either. Perhaps Constance...?"

"I could go inquire," I said. "Unless something's wrong with her that smelling salts won't fix. Did you check her for injuries? Maybe someone shot her, or conked her over the head..."

"To many murder mysteries, Pippa." She smiled at me fondly, but shook her head. "If she'd been shot, we'd have heard it, and besides, there'd be blood. If she were conked on the head, we'd be able to see that too, I imagine. Besides, who would do it? We were all on the terrasse when she walked up. Unless you imagine Cook was running around in the bushes with a rolling pin?"

Hardly. "I guess we just wait for St George to come back with the doctor, then."

"Not much more we can do, I imagine. I'm sure Gerald will have a way of waking her when he comes."

She sat in silence for a few seconds before glancing at the door. "I wonder what's going on out on the terrasse. Whether Herbert managed to calm the waters."

The waters hadn't struck me as being particularly choppy, but what did I know? There was bound to be some curiosity, certainly, although Uncle Herbert hadn't the information to quell any of that. None of us did.

"I could stick my head through the door and see," I suggested. "I'm not doing you any good standing here. Or *her* any good, either."

"You're holding her baby," Aunt Roz said, and pushed herself to her feet. "I'll go."

She looked older than usual, and tired. "I'll be back in a minute. Come fetch me if anything changes."

I nodded, and Aunt Roz left the library and left me alone with Abigail and Bess. For a few seconds, I could hear the heels of her shoes clicking against the wood floors, and then that was gone, too.

A minute passed. Bess babbled and bounced on my hip. Abigail didn't stir. Then there was the sound of a motorcar outside, and a blue blur shot past the windows. Crispin was back, and hopefully he had brought the doctor.

I heard the car doors slam outside, and then the boot room door opened, and rapid steps crossed the floor of the hallway. "Aunt Roslyn?"

"In here," I called. "Library."

The steps headed my way: Crispin's, and a heavier and slightly slower pair that must belong to the doctor.

I turned towards the door in time to face them, and had the

pleasure of seeing Crispin come to a stop in the doorway and rock back on his heels. For several seconds he just stared at me, eyes wide. By then, the doctor had caught up, and shoved him to the side so he could waddle in. "Out of my way, boy. Where is my patient?"

"Hello, Doctor White," I said politely. "That's her, on the sofa. She walked onto the lawn earlier, and collapsed. Francis carried her in here. She hasn't woken up yet."

Doctor White has been the local doctor for as long as I've lived at Beckwith Place. He saw me through the influenza that ravaged the world in the wake of the war—saw us all through it, and well enough that we all survived, too—and has seen me for every other ailment I've had in the past dozen years, so he's practically family. Anyone who has listened to my lungs and examined my chest for rashes is close enough to be considered a relative, I think.

Even so, I didn't expect the look that traveled from me to Bess and then to Crispin, before Doctor White said, "You two?"

Crispin opened his mouth and closed it again. He looked horrified.

"Hers," I told the doctor, "actually. Nothing to do with me at all."

Crispin opened his mouth and shut it again without saying anything. Doctor White grunted. He was peeling back Abigail's eyelids the same way Francis had been doing earlier, peering intently at her pupils.

"Go fetch Aunt Roz," I told Crispin. "She went back onto the terrasse, but she told me to fetch her if anything happened before she came back."

He nodded and turned on his heel, after a last look at the baby. Over on the Chesterfield, Doctor White picked up Abigail's wrist and checked her pulse before pulling down her lip and opening her mouth. Finally, he listened to her heart before sitting back. At no point did she show any sign of life other than that she kept breathing.

By then, Aunt Roz had come back inside. Without Crispin, so he must have got caught by Laetitia, or perhaps his father. Instead, it was Christopher who tagged along behind his mother. Like Crispin, he stopped in the doorway and looked at me, but instead of behaving as if he'd seen a ghost, a corner of his mouth turned up.

"What?" I wanted to know.

He smirked, and looked astonishingly like his cousin for a second. "I can see why Crispin looked the way he did when he reached the terrasse."

"Doctor White asked whether there was something going on between us," I told him. "I'm sure he was appalled and nauseated by the suggestion."

Aunt Roz gave me a jaundiced look before turning to the doctor "What can we do for her, Gerald?"

"Nothing, Roz," Doctor White said. "It looks like a mixture of perfectly normal things. Exhaustion, malnutrition, overexertion in the heat..."

Perfectly normal things, were they?

"She'll be all right once she wakes up and we get some food and water into her. Although there's no telling when that'll happen. She could be asleep for a while. I can take her to the infirmary in the village if you'd prefer?"

"That might be best," Aunt Roz allowed. "We have a full house here, Gerald. Constance is here, as you know, and so is Francis. Pippa and Christopher are visiting. So are Harold and Crispin. And so is the entire Marsden family. I have to put Pippa and Christopher in the same room as it is..."

Doctor White lifted a hand. "Say no more. We can keep her overnight in the infirmary."

Aunt Roz's face melted into appreciation. "Thank you, Gerald."

"It's what it's there for, my dear." He reached out and patted her shoulder. "Now, the child..."

They both looked at me, and at little Bess. And at Christopher, who was standing next to me. We probably looked like a little family, which was a strange thing to contemplate.

"Oh, we can handle *that*." Aunt Roz waved it off as if taking care of someone else's baby was nothing. Perhaps it was, to someone who had brought up three of her own, plus a niece.

Or perhaps she realized, as I did, that if Bess was here, Abigail would have to come back too, even if Doctor White took her to the village now. Without that, she might vanish again, and then we'd never get the answers we wanted.

Yes, much better to keep little Bess with us, as assurance of her mother's return. Besides, the baby would probably be more comfortable here than in the infirmary, anyway.

"Christopher," Aunt Roz said, "run out and fetch... No, on second thought we'll just leave them all where they are. Can you carry her?"

Christopher gave Abigail a dubious look, but he nodded.

"Lift her, then, and let's take her outside. Can either of you drive Crispin's car?"

"He'd kill us," Christopher said, as he headed for the sofa. I nodded.

Aunt Roz huffed exasperatedly. "He would not. He loves you both."

He didn't. And even if he did, at least in Christopher's case, he loved the Hispano-Suiza more. But before I could say anything about it, she had gone on. "We'll take the Bentley. Or perhaps we can find Wilkins. Harold won't mind if we take the Crossley down to the village and back. Go on, Christopher."

She nodded towards the door, and Christopher headed for

it with Abigail in his arms. I was impressed, I have to say. I know Francis had lifted and carried her earlier, with no problem, but that's Francis, isn't it? He's a fully grown man almost seven years older than Christopher. Of course *he* would be able to lift and carry eight or nine stone of dead weight. Christopher is both younger and slighter, and I was rather impressed that he managed it, without apparent effort, too.

Aunt Roz hurried ahead of him through the library and toward the hallway.

"Go on, Philippa," Doctor White said, and nudged me into motion ahead of him. "You're on baby duty, it seems?"

"I'm sure Aunt Roz will take her away from me shortly," I said, "but for now, it seems I am. Anything we should know about taking care of a baby?"

"I'm sure Roslyn has it covered. She's had several of her own, after all. It's about time for grandchildren, isn't it?"

He beamed at little Bess.

I smiled politely. It was all I could do when I didn't know whether he was fishing for information or a confirmation or what. Anything I said would likely give an impression I didn't want to give, so it was much safer just to keep my mouth shut. And by then we had reached the boot room, where Aunt Roz was holding the door open and giving Christopher instructions for how to navigate through the mess.

"Turn sideways... yes, that's right. Be careful with the Wellies, there on your left. Don't stumble. Now watch her head... I said watch it, Christopher—"

"I'm watching," Christopher grumbled. "I'm not going to bash her head against the door jamb, Mum. I'm not stupid."

"Of course you're not, dear. Just turn a little bit more... yes, that's right—"

Christopher rolled his eyes, but maneuvered the body—the unconscious body—through the doorway.

"After you, Philippa," Doctor White said with a touch to my back. I made it through the door in time to see Christopher head down along the driveway towards the parked cars with Aunt Roz scurrying beside him.

Five minutes later, Uncle Harold's Crossley made its sedate way towards the village with Wilkins at the wheel and Doctor White enthroned in the passenger seat next to him, while Christopher was in the back holding onto Abigail. I had offered to come along instead, in case a woman's touch was needed, but the doctor had assured me that the nurse would manage and that he'd rather have two strong, young men capable of wrangling the body than my feminine touch.

"You stay here and mind the baby, Philippa," he told me, with a pat on the shoulder.

So that was that. Off they went. The excitement was over, at least for now.

"Better give her to me," Aunt Roz said, reaching for the baby, "or Harold will have a conniption."

She tucked Bess onto her own hip with practiced ease, and turned toward the back of the house and the croquet lawn. "Let's just go this way, shall we?"

Certainly. "Why would Uncle Harold care...?" I began, but she was already several feet away, and there was nothing I could do but follow.

CHAPTER SIX

THE TERRASSE WAS MOSTLY BACK to normal by the time I got there. Uncle Herbert was entertaining the Earl of Marsden and his son, and from the way they were chuckling, the subject must have been either hunting or women. Crispin had been gathered back in by Lady Laetitia, and between her, her mother, and his father, he was being kept on the straight and narrow with no opportunity for escape. He didn't even glance my way when I stepped onto the terrasse, although that could have been for other reasons. Something was obviously going on with him, considering the way he had looked at me like he'd seen a ghost in the library earlier.

"Stupid idiot," I grumbled as I dropped into the chair between Aunt Roz and Francis.

Aunt Roz glanced at me. "What's that?"

"St George. I don't know why he puts up with Lady Laetitia draping herself all over him like that."

She was leaning in, swaying towards him, as if she wouldn't be close enough until she were in his lap.

Which she certainly wasn't going to be on the terrasse in the middle of the afternoon.

"It doesn't appear as if he minds, Pippa," Constance said softly.

Well, no. It didn't. But—

"Two months ago, he told her flat out that he didn't want to marry her. I heard him. She was trying to cajole him into it, telling him how much they have in common and how much fun they'd have, and he made it clear that he didn't want to."

Nicely, I'll admit—he'd told Laetitia that she deserved a husband who was in love with her, not a husband who was in love with someone else—but it had been direct and unmistakable.

"I thought she'd given up," I said, "but it doesn't look that way, does it?"

We all contemplated the table, and the way Laetitia had her hand on Crispin's arm and was leaning close, eyes sparkling.

"No," Aunt Roz said, while Francis chuckled. "That looks like a woman with matrimony on her mind."

"Someone should have a word with him."

"He's not stupid, Pipsqueak," Francis said. "If he didn't want to be there, he wouldn't be."

"I'm not so sure. He has a bad habit of listening to Uncle Harold, and Uncle Harold has a bad habit of *not* listening to St George."

"That's their business," Aunt Roz said, "although I share your concern, Pippa. But if he won't stand up for himself, the rest of us can't stand up with him."

I suppose not. And it was none of my affair who St George ended up with, anyway. If he was idiotic enough to let himself be drawn in by Lady Laetitia again, and she was idiotic enough to pursue him after being told why he didn't want to marry her, then I supposed they deserved each other.

"What happened out here while I was inside?" I asked instead.

Constance and Francis looked at one another, and Francis nodded for Constance to go first.

"Not much. At first, there was a lot of whispering. Laetitia and her mother had their heads together, and His Grace, Duke Harold, looked like he was about to have an apoplexy..."

"Probably thinks she's Crispin's," Francis sniggered.

We all glanced at little Bess, who peered back at us with those big, blue Astley eyes. Yes, I'm sure we all thought she might be Crispin's. "And then?"

"Eventually, everyone but you and Lord St George came back," Constance said. "Laetitia made a fuss about it until Roslyn reminded her that she had sent Lord St George for the doctor and that while you were with the body, the two of you were not together."

"She isn't dead, Constance," Aunt Roz reminded her, bouncing the baby on her knee. Bess looked perfectly comfortable and perfectly at home, gurgling and cooing. "Not quite a body yet."

Constance flushed. "Of course not. My apologies."

"No apologies needed," I told her. "She looked dead. Christopher had to carry her out to the car when the doctor took her away. Wilkins turned as pale as a ghost when he saw us coming. For a second, I think he thought he'd be asked to get rid of a dead body."

Which sounded uncomfortably like the situation we had found ourselves in last month, in London, and it took me a moment to shove the memory down. "Anyway," I managed brightly, "St George and I were certainly not making eyes at one another over the not-dead body of his maybe-mistress while Lady Laetitia was sitting out here."

Francis smothered a chuckle.

"But the doctor said she'd be all right. He agreed with Aunt Roz that it was just exhaustion and heat and malnutrition and something else, and rest and food would set her right."

"Poor thing," Aunt Roz murmured, cradling the baby a little closer, protectively.

"Don't get attached, Mum," Francis advised her. "You can't keep her, you know. She isn't Dad's."

Aunt Roz gave him a crushing look. "I know that, Francis. She isn't Christopher's, either, and I hope she isn't yours..."

"Of course not," Francis said.

Aunt Roz nodded. "I'll give her back to her mum tomorrow. I just feel bad for the poor thing. Alone with a baby, and at her age. She's no older than Pippa, perhaps not even. And no money to speak of. That dress was several years out of date, and she clearly hasn't had enough to eat lately; God only knows how she got here from London..."

"How do you know she came from London?" Constance wanted to know.

"She came to the flat to see Christopher last week," I said. "And I'm sure she's the same woman who came to Sutherland House a couple of months ago to look at St George, too."

Although I didn't know that for a fact, admittedly. He hadn't actually said so. But how many young women with Sutherland babies were likely to be roaming England at any given time, really?

Then again, considering St George's proclivity for getting under women's skirts, there might actually be more than just this one.

This time, when I scowled at him, he was actually looking my way, and arched a questioning brow. I opened my mouth, but before I could say anything, Laetitia noticed that his attention had strayed and brought him to heel with a tap on the nose.

I closed my mouth again and huffed.

"The girl, Pipsqueak," Francis said, and I turned my attention back to present company.

"She was in London a week ago. She was in London this spring. She's likely to live in London."

She didn't look like a country girl, certainly. Not enough tweed.

"Do you know anything else about her?" Constance wanted to know. "Other than—" she hesitated, "the obvious?"

"I know her name," I said, "if she told me the truth. Abigail Dole. I know the baby's name. Abigail called her Bess. I assume her given name is Elizabeth."

"There are no Elizabeths among the Astleys," Aunt Roz said. "Not for several generations."

"Abigail might just have liked the name." If she didn't even know the name of Bess's father, she wasn't likely to know about any Astley family names, after all. "The Duke and Duchess of York did just have a baby they named Elizabeth."

Aunt Roz nodded. "In any case, there's no helpful information there. If her name had been Charlotte, it would have been a different story."

It would. Although even that wouldn't have been proof of anything.

"And that's all I know," I told Constance. "Her name and the baby's name. And the fact that Bess's father almost certainly has to be a Sutherland. When Abigail first knocked on the door at Sutherland House, she told Rogers that she was looking for the Duke's grandson."

We all chewed on that bit of information for a moment.

"This was when Henry was alive," Aunt Roz said.

I nodded. "Sometime in the spring. Before the end of

April." Before Duke Henry and Crispin's father died. Before Grimsby the valet shared all his blackmail information with us.

"Herbert's father had four grandsons. Robbie's gone—"

"Too long ago to have had anything to do with this," Francis said gruffly. Even after almost a decade, he doesn't like to be reminded of his dead brother.

Aunt Roz nodded. "Then there's you, and Christopher, and Crispin."

And there was us, going around the same mulberry bush, beating the same dead horse.

"I'm as certain as I can be that Christopher didn't bed this girl," I said. "It's impossible to be one hundred percent certain, but he said he didn't, and besides—"

Besides, Christopher isn't attracted to women.

Aunt Roz nodded. "You say you didn't, Francis..."

"I don't think I did," Francis said coolly, while beside him, Constance flushed pink. "I don't remember her. And I can't imagine when it would have happened. I don't spend much time in Town, and unlike my cousin, I'm not in the habit of bedding women indiscriminately..."

Although Francis does occasionally go up to London, and in the past, he had also done enough dope that certain things might have slipped his mind. It was just possible that a single encounter with Abigail Dole could have been one of those things. So like with Christopher, we could be almost certain it hadn't happened, but not one hundred percent.

"Crispin has told me categorically, over and over, that it wasn't him," I said. "He's been absolutely adamant about it."

Aunt Roz threw the hand up that wasn't supporting little Bess. "Then I don't know what we're supposed to do."

"Wait for her to wake up and accuse somebody, I suppose," I said. "I'm sure she'll recognize him when she sees him, don't you think?"

And if she hadn't recognized Crispin, and by default Christopher, then there was only Francis left.

His jaw was tight as he sat next to me. "The doctor said she'd wake up by tomorrow?"

"He didn't say specifically. But that was the impression I got. We'll just have to wait."

He nodded. "Excuse me. I feel the need for a stiff drink."

He didn't look at either of us—not even Constance—when he pushed to his feet and strode into the house. Uncle Herbert watched him go with a concerned wrinkle between his brows, and Constance flushed, sinking her teeth into her bottom lip. She stared down at her hands, blinking hard. Aunt Roz and I exchanged a glance across the table, but I don't think either of us knew what to say.

"I'm going to go wait for Christopher and the Crossley," I said, pushing my chair back. "Would you like to come with me, Constance?"

Constance hesitated, with a tortured glance at the house.

"He'll have to deal with this on his own," Aunt Roz told her. "He'll be back when he gets his head on straight."

Constance nodded, but she didn't look as if she believed it. "What if—?"

"He won't break the engagement," I said. "Not unless you ask him to."

"That's not what concerns me." She lowered her voice. "He hasn't used Veronal for more than two months now. Not since the funerals. Not even while Christopher was unconscious for those few days, and you were all worried that he wouldn't wake up. But now..."

Now, with this hanging over his head, Francis might seek oblivion in alcohol and dope again.

"That's a valid concern," Aunt Roz told her, kindly, while Bess gurgled happily on her lap, "but there's nothing you can do about it, Constance. Francis has to decide on his own not to drown his emotions. You can't do it for him."

"But if we are to be married…"

Aunt Roz shook her head. "You will still be two different people, Constance. You cannot take on Francis's problems as if they are your own. You can help him with what troubles him—"

Constance opened her mouth and Aunt Roz lifted a finger to pause her, "—but only if he asks. Don't manage him."

"Please don't," I muttered, slanting a glance over at Lady Laetitia, who was managing Crispin for all she was worth.

"The secret to a happy marriage," Aunt Roz intoned, "is to be together as equals. You have a life of your own, and let him have a life of his own. Then you can meld your two lives together, and neither of you will get swallowed up by the other. If you let yourself be subsumed by your husband's life, or you let him be subsumed by yours, you'll come to trouble down the line. Mark my words."

Constance gulped, nodding. I nodded, too. Not from personal experience, but because I had watched Aunt Charlotte be Uncle Harold's wife and Crispin's mother with absolutely no life of her own for years, and it wasn't something I wanted for myself.

"Go with Pippa," Aunt Roz told Constance. "Francis will do what Francis will do. If he needs a stiff drink, let him have one. And when he comes out of it, be there for him. That's all you can do besides staying healthy yourself."

"Come on," I told her, taking her elbow and giving her a boost out of the chair. "We'll figure this out. We're smart girls. We can do it."

Constance nodded. "Thank you, Roslyn."

"Don't mention it, dear." Aunt Roz smiled sweetly and got to her own feet. "If you girls are leaving, I think I'll join

Herbert's table. They're enjoying themselves far too much over there."

She drifted off in that direction, baby on her hip, while Constance and I headed down the steps onto the grass. Crispin watched us go, until Laetitia tapped him on the cheek and he turned back to her with a practiced smile.

"Stupid man," I grumbled under my breath.

Constance slanted a look my way. "Francis?"

I shook my head. "St George. Also known as the most annoying man in England."

Her dimple made an appearance. "Only in England? Are you sure you wouldn't like to add in the Continent too?"

"I suppose I might as well," I said. "Although if I add in the Continent, there might actually be someone else equally annoying. A Frenchman, perhaps. The French are notoriously rude and awful."

"Has Lord St George been rude and awful today?"

I thought about it. "No more than usual, I suppose. There was that comment about looking windswept when we first arrived..."

"You got revenge for that," Constance said, sticking her hand through my arm as we arrived on the gravel of the driveway. "Poor boy, he looked positively overcome. Whatever was that about, Pippa?"

"The greeting? Flossie Schlomsky is a neighbor of ours at the Essex House Mansions. She made St George's acquaintance a few months ago, and was quite taken with him. When she found out that I would be seeing him this weekend, she told me to give him her love."

"And that was how you chose to do it? In full view of everyone?"

"I certainly wasn't about to do it privately," I said. "Besides, he did it to me first."

"Did what, exactly?"

"Leaned close," I said, demonstrating; Constance's brown eyes widened, "and called me darling in this very low, very seductive voice. Totally different from the way he normally says it. Even his eyes changed." I shuddered. "It was awful."

Constance tittered. "It can't have been that awful, surely. He's ever so handsome."

"He's a menace," I said, "and you know it. But I got him back." I smiled in satisfaction.

"You certainly did," Constance agreed. "For a moment there, it looked like he had forgotten how to breathe."

"Serves him right."

"I don't know, Pippa." We turned the corner of the house. "You know how Laetitia is. The more interested someone else is, the more adamant she becomes about keeping what's hers."

"He's not hers," I said.

"Tell that to Laetitia," Constance answered, looking around. "I don't see them."

I didn't, either. There was only the Daimler, and Aunt and Uncle's Bentley, and the Peckham's—now Constance's—burgundy Crossley parked outside the carriage house. There was no sign of Christopher, or Wilkins, or Uncle Harold's motorcar, or for that matter Francis.

"Let's go this way," I said, and headed for the boot room door. "We may as well move St George's car back while we wait. I don't see him escaping to take care of it any time soon."

Constance trailed behind me as I headed for the H6. "Do you know how to drive a motorcar, Pippa?"

I glanced at her over my shoulder. "Of course I do. Uncle Herbert let me practice on the Bentley."

"Have you driven a motorcar recently?"

I hadn't, but— "Surely it's like riding a bicycle, don't you think? Once you know how, the knowledge doesn't leave you?"

"I don't know," Constance said. "Mother would never let me learn. Gilbert—" She trailed off for a moment before she squared her shoulders and tried again. "Gilbert knew how, but Mother liked letting the chauffeur do the motoring. I don't think she trusted Gilbert."

"Was he a bad driver?" I opened the door to the Hispano-Suiza and fitted myself behind the wheel. The leather seat was cold against my back, even in the heat of the summer, and the pedals were farther away than expected. I felt around for a way to adjust the seat, but none was readily available. It probably didn't matter, anyway, when I was only going to travel a few yards.

"Does it need a key?" Constance asked, leaning into the window and watching me look around. "Are you certain you should be doing this, Pippa? He's rather protective of his motor-car, isn't he?"

He was, rather. We'd had a small set-to over it back in May, on our way home from the Dower House. I had threatened to take over the motoring, and he had behaved as if I had suggested that I wear his trousers rather than merely that I drive his automobile.

"He's on the terrasse with Laetitia," I said. "She's keeping him busy, never fear."

There was a starter pedal on the floor of the car. I raised my foot, and was just about to stomp on it, when there was a wordless bellow of fury and consternation from the boot room door. I jumped, and so did poor Constance. She banged the top of her head against the top of the window and staggered back, rubbing her crown.

The bellow had sounded like Francis, but surprisingly it was Crispin himself who came rushing towards me, or more accurately, towards his precious vehicle. I guess Laetitia wasn't keeping him busy after all. How very strange.

"Out," he told me, flapping his hands, for all the world as if he were shooing recalcitrant chickens. "Get out. Out."

I didn't get out, of course. Instead, I leaned back in the seat and sniggered as he came closer. "Goodness gracious, St George. Whatever is the matter?"

Constance stepped out of the way as Crispin yanked the door open and grabbed me by the arm. "Out, I said. You do not get to drive my motorcar, Darling. Absolutely not."

"We were just doing a good turn," I told him as he pulled me through the door with enough force that I staggered and had to brace myself on his shoulder so I wouldn't fall. "Ouch. Stop it, St George, you're hurting me. We were merely going to move your precious to the parking area for you."

"No." He shook his head. "Not you. Not *my* motorcar."

I dusted my hands off and took a step back so his hands fell from my upper arms. "Strong feelings from a man who destroyed his own motorcar not even a year ago."

"That was different," Crispin said. "I told you before, I don't trust you behind the wheel of my car."

"It's a matter of a few feet! How much damage do you suppose I could do in the time it would take me to motor across the driveway?"

He squinted at me. "You weren't planning to go into the village to look for Kit?"

"No! I told you. We were going to take it back to the carriage house with the others. Your precious tires would not have touched the road."

"Very well, then." He took a step back.

Very well? "You mean, you'll let me drive?"

"Of course not, Darling." He looked at me down the length of his nose. "*I* will move *my* motorcar to the carriage house, since its presence here offends you."

"Oh, fine. Be that way. Although you owe Constance an apology first. Your carrying on made her hit her head."

"Did it really?" He swung on his heel. "My dear Miss Peckham..."

"She's soon to be your cousin," I reminded him. "I think you can probably call her by her first name."

Crispin arched a brow. Not at me, at Constance. "Truly?"

"If you would like," Constance said primly.

"In that case, my dear Constance—" He poured on the charm, which included kissing her knuckles and dropping his voice into that seductive register he had attempted to use on me last month, "—please let me apologize most abjectly..."

Constance blinked, her cheeks flushing.

"Any more abject, and Francis will have your hide," I told him. "Let go of her hand, St George, and stop being a nuisance."

"I'm merely being myself, Darling, as you know very well." But he did let go, and took a step back. "What are you two girls doing out here? The party's on the terrasse."

"We're waiting for Wilkins and Christopher," I said. "The terrasse was becoming rather uncomfortable. I'm almost certain Lord Geoffrey and his father were telling bawdy jokes..."

Constance nodded.

"—although I suppose Aunt Roz probably put a stop to that when she went over there. But the Countess kept glaring at me, and the way Lady Laetitia was carrying on is frankly disgraceful."

He smirked. "Jealous, Darling?"

"Frightfully," I said dryly. "If you're not careful, you'll be betrothed by the end of the weekend, St George."

He scoffed. "Don't be ridiculous, Darling. I made it clear back in May how I feel about the idea of marriage. You heard me."

"I did," I said. "And so did she. But instead of accepting your rejection, she seems to have merely withdrawn to devise a different—better—battle plan. And now she has regrouped, and has recruited her mother to help. And it looks as if they've roped in your father, too."

Constance nodded, although she added, "It's more likely that Laetitia told Aunt Euphemia what happened, and this was Aunt Effie's idea. Although I don't suppose it matters."

"Not in the slightest," I agreed, since Laetitia was clearly going along with it either way. "I think the best thing you could do for yourself is get in your motorcar and hightail it back to Sutherland Hall, St. George."

He sneered. "You'd like that, wouldn't you, Darling?"

"I would positively adore it, St George."

The sneer deepened, and I huffed. "I'm not trying to get rid of you, you moron. I'm simply concerned about what will happen if you stay. You said it yourself two months ago: Your father would be delighted to hand you over to Lady Laetitia. And as you have somewhat grown on me over the past couple of months..."

Crispin's eyes widened, but whatever he might have planned to say was interrupted by the clearing of a throat from in the vicinity of the door.

Crispin flinched, and so did I. I think we all probably expected it to be Laetitia Marsden.

It wasn't. Nor was it her mother, the Countess. Instead, it was Uncle Harold standing there, looking from me to his son to Constance and back.

"A word, St George?"

Crispin grimaced but gave in to the inevitable. "Yes, Father."

Uncle Harold stepped aside so Crispin could precede him

into the boot room. The door shut behind them with a sort of final *bang*, leaving Constance and me alone outside.

CHAPTER SEVEN

IT TOOK LESS than a second for me to decide what to do. And I suppose I'm not proud of it... no, actually, that's not true. I'm perfectly fine with eavesdropping. As Crispin had told me once, you learn such interesting things.

"I'll be right back," I told Constance.

She opened her mouth, perhaps because she was thinking of saying something to stop me, although if she was, she thought better of it. Instead, she simply nodded, a resigned look on her face, and watched, silently, as I trod over to the door and depressed the latch, as softly as I could.

There was a chance, of course, that Uncle Harold and Crispin had stopped just inside the door, and if such was the case, it wouldn't matter how quiet I tried to be. They'd see the door open and would know that I was there. But if Uncle Harold had taken Crispin somewhere else for better privacy, then I stood a chance of getting inside undetected, and of perhaps hearing something interesting.

So I opened the door as quietly as I could, and held my breath as I eased it open and peered around it.

The boot room was empty. So far, so good.

Beckwith Place is a rather small place as far as country houses go. The foyer at Sutherland Hall, for instance, could swallow several of the rooms at Beckwith Place whole. The boot room, obviously, is one of them. It's fairly minuscule, and full of Wellington boots and rain slickers and umbrellas and Uncle Herbert's golf clubs and things like that.

I eased the door shut and made my way across the room as quietly as I could. And stopped in the doorway and contemplated my surroundings.

On my right was the hallway to the terrasse, along with the kitchen and scullery, and the library. On my left was the door to the front of the house, and the stairway down to the cellars. Directly in front of me was the door to Uncle Herbert's study.

Where would Uncle Harold have taken Crispin for a private chat?

Not to the kitchen, obviously. Cook and Hughes were still there. I could hear the faint sound of voices, and of running water and dishes clacking together.

Nor to the library, I thought. They'd have to pass the kitchen door, and Cook and Hughes, to get there, and it was also closest to the terrasse, where the others were. I assumed Uncle Harold would want to avoid an audience for this confrontation, or he would have had it out with his son in front of me and Constance, most likely.

The study, perhaps? It's a small room, tucked away between the scullery and the cellar staircase. Quite private, if you're looking for that type of thing, and I assumed Uncle Harold was.

I crept across the hallway. The study door was open a crack, and there was no noise and no voices from inside. I inched the door open until I could get my head around the jamb, and peered around. The study was dark and empty.

They must have gone into the front of the house, then.

Unless Uncle Harold had yanked Crispin straight down the hallway and back onto the terrasse, of course. That was possible. But if he had wanted to have an actual conversation with his son, they must have gone in the opposite direction.

So I did the same: went to the door that separated the front of the house from the back, and pushed the latch down on the door. I could be a little less careful here, as there was another door between me and the foyer. The little area beyond the first door was essentially the landing for the cellar steps, and the cool draught that filtered up from below was enough to explain the reason for the doors. What was a cool draught now, in the middle of July, was a chill breeze in winter, and Aunt Roz had insulated both doors with felt to keep the cold air from escaping into the rest of the house.

I couldn't hear anything from beyond it.

So I swallowed my anxiety and depressed yet another latch. And eased the door between the cellar stairs and the front of the house open a finger's breadth, holding my breath in case it creaked.

"—idiot boy!" Uncle Harold's voice snarled, so close that he might as well have been standing on the opposite side of the door, and if I pushed it open any farther, I'd hit him in the back. "When are you going to get it through your head that—"

"Don't you dare call me an idiot!" Crispin retorted angrily, and unlike his father, he took no particular care to keep his voice down. "I am *not* stupid, I—"

He stopped talking as something hit a wall nearby with a *thump* that made the door vibrate. I jumped, and almost let go of it, and caught myself at the last moment, eyes wide. Had Uncle Harold shoved Crispin into the wall? Surely Crispin hadn't pushed his father? Or perhaps he had simply taken his frustrations out with a swing of his fist into it?

"Then stop behaving like it," Uncle Harold hissed. If anyone had been slammed into the wall, it didn't sound like it had been him. "You're damned lucky the Marsdens are still willing to consider you as a suitor for their daughter's hand—"

"I don't want Laetitia's hand!" Crispin said shrilly.

"You should have thought of that before you ruined her," Uncle Harold snarled. "And furthermore—"

"I didn't ruin her," Crispin retorted, "you imbecile. I didn't even seduce her. *She* seduced *me*! And—"

"That's hardly something to brag about," Uncle Harold told him, viciously, and there was another *thump* as something else—or, at a guess, Crispin's back—hit the wall. Again. "And don't you call me an imbecile, you insolent brat—!"

"Get your hands off me," Crispin said breathlessly. I could hear scuffling beyond the door. "Let go, damn you. Bloody hell, that hurt!"

I winced. Into the silence that followed, I could hear small sounds, like the rustling of fabric—Crispin straightening his clothes, where his father had grabbed him?—and the shuffling of feet. One of them getting away from the other, presumably.

Then—

"I'll hear no more about it," Uncle Harold said. "Stay away from Miss Darling and leave your cousin's fiancée alone. Spend your time with Lady Laetitia instead. And for God's sake, try to convince her that the bastard isn't yours. We can deal with—"

"The bastard," Crispin said, his voice just as vicious as Uncle Harold's had been earlier, and ice cold, "is, in fact, not mine. I'm many things, Father, but I'm not a liar. When I have a child, it will be born in wedlock, to a woman who's my lawfully wedded wife, and who I won't have to worry is sneaking around behind my back to sleep with my—"

But before I could find out whether he was going to say groom, or chauffeur, or perhaps cousin, there was yet another *thump* of something hitting the wall, this one accompanied by a sharp exclamation of pain.

I jumped, and accidentally let go of the door. And because I had, I moved as quickly as I could in the other direction. Hopefully they had both been too preoccupied to notice that I'd been there—had Uncle Harold really knocked Crispin's head into the wall three times? Hard enough for him to cry out? —but just in case they hadn't, I wanted to make tracks before they could find me.

So I scurried through the door into the hallway and from there around the corner into the boot room, and out the door to the driveway.

Nothing had changed in the time I had been gone. Constance was still standing beside the Hispano-Suiza, looking from one side to the other. Christopher and the Crossley were nowhere to be seen. And while it felt like I had been inside a long time, I didn't think it had been more than a minute or two, perhaps three. The row had been vicious and surprisingly violent, but short-lived.

Hopefully Crispin was all right, and Uncle Harold hadn't done permanent damage to him.

I scurried across to Constance and grabbed her by the arm. "Come on."

"What happened?" She stumbled over a tuft of grass as she struggled to keep up with my longer legs. I was still wearing brogues from traveling, while Constance was in delicate strap shoes with higher heels. "Are you all right?"

"I'm fine," I said, and let go of her arm once I determined we were far enough away from the house not to be overheard. "I'm not so sure about St George."

Constance lowered her voice. "What did your uncle do to him?"

Uncle Harold wasn't actually my uncle any more than

Crispin was my cousin, but now was not the time to quibble. "Knocked him into the wall. More than once."

Constance winced.

"The first time he seemed to be fine. It knocked the wind out of him and made him shut up, which I assume was the point. The second time he complained that it hurt. The third time he cried out."

Constance sank her teeth into her bottom lip. "That's not right."

I shook my head. No, it wasn't.

"Why did he do it?"

"I don't know," I said. "The first time, Crispin got angry and told his father not to call him an idiot. The second time, *he* called Uncle Harold an imbecile—"

"Understandable," Constance said.

I nodded. Understandable that Crispin would be upset with his father after being knocked into the wall, but also understandable that Uncle Harold would object to the appellation. "That's no excuse for manhandling someone, though. And the third time..." I shook my head. "I'm not even sure. They were talking about children. Or about Bess, specifically. Uncle Harold told Crispin that he had to convince Laetitia that Bess isn't his, and Crispin said that she *isn't* his, and that when he has a child, it'll be in wedlock, with a woman who's his wife and who isn't running around on him with someone else..."

I shook my head. "I can't imagine what there might be about that, that would be objectionable to anyone, especially to Crispin's father. Of everyone, he should be most invested in Crispin having a legitimate heir."

Constance nodded.

"It was probably just his tone. I frequently feel inspired to violence when St George opens his mouth, too." Especially when it's accompanied by a sneer, which it so often is.

"But you don't do anything about it," Constance said.

No, I don't. I might feel like it would be a nice thing to smack the pratty expression off Crispin's face, but I don't actually hit him. We're civilized people, after all, and besides, I'm not entirely certain he wouldn't hit back. He's done it before, after all. And yes, he has been told that it's wrong to hit girls, but when the girl hits first, he can hardly be blamed for retaliating in kind.

"I'm sure he's fine," I said, although between you, me, and Constance, I wasn't as certain as I would have liked to have been. Although I couldn't very well ask him about it, not without owning up to having eavesdropped on the conversation, so there was very little I could do about the whole thing.

"I hear a motor," Constance said.

I dragged my thoughts out of the quagmire they were circling and paid attention. And heard it, too. "This must be them."

We both turned our attention to the road, in time to see the front of Uncle Harold's Crossley come around the hedge and proceed majestically up the driveway towards us. We stepped out of the way and watched as Wilkins... no, as *Christopher* pulled the motorcar to a stop between the Bentley and the Marsdens' Daimler. Wilkins was in the passenger seat, chauffeur cap pulled low over his face as if he were trying to avoid being recognized.

I turned a chuckle into clearing my throat. "Wilkins, if you don't mind..."

He slanted a look my way.

"Do you suppose you could go and move Lord St George's H6 away from the door? I offered to do it earlier, and he told me, in no uncertain terms, that I was to go nowhere near his precious. But I assume he can't object to *you* doing it."

Wilkins nodded. "Right away, Miss Darling."

He walked away. The early evening sun reflected in the polished, knee-high boots that went with his spiffy uniform, and burnished the sandy hair peeking out from below the peaked chauffeur's cap.

I waited until he had vanished from sight before I grinned at Christopher. "Talked him into letting you drive the motorcar home, did you? Or did you have to resort to bribery or blackmail to be allowed?"

"Do you know something blackmail-worthy about Wilkins?" Christopher wanted to know, but continued before I could answer. "It took bribery. Although that's an ugly interpretation of an exchange of coins for favors. Naturally he was concerned about what Uncle Harold might say."

"Of course he was." I rolled my eyes. "Uncle Harold is in a foul mood, actually, so it's just as well that he didn't see you. But I might know something blackmailable about Wilkins."

Christopher perked up. "What's that? And why do you say you might, and not that you do?"

"It was over that horrible weekend back in April. Tom told me that Wilkins has—or had back then—a habit of taking the Crossley to Southampton to visit family."

"Not sure that's much of a blackmailable offense," Christopher said, disappointed. "Grandfather might have known all about it, and so might Uncle Harold."

"That's why I said that I might know something, and not that I do for certain. Wilkins might have had your grandfather's permission. He seemed to treat the staff better than he did his own family, at least judging by Grimsby. Although I doubt Uncle Harold would put up with the chauffeur taking off on personal errands whenever he felt like it."

I had never had a high opinion of the old Duke's personality—stingy, hard-necked old man that he was—but over the past few months, I had developed an even lower one of his successor.

And Christopher could tell by the sound of my voice that something had happened, I assume, because he asked, "What's he done now?" in a resigned sort of tone.

"How do you know that he's done something?"

"I know you," Christopher said, which was certainly true. "You only get this way when someone does something you deem unfair or unjust."

"Well, your uncle abused your cousin again."

Christopher's brows lowered. "How do you know that?"

"Followed them inside and eavesdropped," I said. "Uncle Harold kept grabbing St George and knocking him into the wall. Or at least that's what it sounded like from where I was standing."

"What did Crispin do to deserve it?"

I gave him a look. "Do you think anyone deserves being knocked about by their father?"

"Of course not, Pippa. But you have to admit he can be quite trying."

I grimaced. "He shot his mouth off. You know how he is. But that's no excuse, Christopher."

"Of course it isn't," Christopher said. "What do you want me to do about it?"

It was an actual question, not the rhetorical kind that implied that I shouldn't expect him to do anything at all, and I could have kissed him for it.

However— "I don't think there's anything you can do," I admitted. "Crispin's supposed to devote himself to Laetitia, and to making sure she knows that the bastard—direct quote from your uncle—isn't his."

Christopher rolled his eyes.

"See if you can get a look at his eyes, at least."

"His eyes," Christopher said blankly. "I'll admit they're pretty, Pippa, but you want me to stare deeply into Crispin's eyes? Why?"

Constance let out a titter, and then flushed when we both glanced at her.

"I'd do it myself if I could," I said. "And don't look at me that way, you know what I mean. But Uncle Harold warned him away from having anything to do with me, or with Constance. Laetitia only."

"Yes," Christopher repeated, "but why?"

"Because if Uncle Harold kept knocking his head into the wall, he could be concussed. He said it hurt."

Christopher pressed his lips together, but nodded. "I'll see what I can do."

"Thank you."

We all three looked up as the front of the Hispano-Suiza, with the stork emblem and the name in ornate script across the grille, rolled slowly up the driveway towards us.

"We'd better move out of the way," Christopher said. He grabbed me by the wrist and Constance, a bit more politely, by the elbow, and moved us aside as Wilkins slotted the H6 into place next to the Daimler.

"Thank you, Wilkins," I told him as he exited the car and shut the door behind him.

"No problem, Miss Darling." He tugged on the brim of his cap before disappearing into the carriage house with long strides.

I tucked my hand through Christopher's arm. "Enough about St George. Did anything interesting happen in the village?"

Christopher offered Constance his other arm, and she put her hand on it, too.

"Not aside from what you might expect. She didn't wake

up on the drive. I held onto her as best I could. Wilkins carried her into the infirmary. He's a strapping lad, isn't he?"

He was, and no lad, either. Older than Francis by at least a year or two, and with the same broad shoulders and muscular arms, most likely honed on the Continent during the war. A decade older than Christopher, I'd say.

He was certainly attractive, if one happened to like the type. And Christopher might. Although Wilkins wasn't the sort to appreciate Christopher's charms, I thought.

The latter shook his head when I said so. "Certainly not. Nor was that why I brought it up. I had to haul her out to the car, you know, and for all that she's small and skinny, it's no easy task. But Wilkins scooped her up like she weighed nothing. He even got a little grunt out of her, and I think her eyes opened, but if she woke up, it was only for a second. Once he'd put her on the cot in the infirmary, she was out cold again."

"Did Doctor White say anything interesting?"

Christopher shook his head. "Just that he'd take care of her, and let us know when there's a change. He said we'll probably hear from him tomorrow morning."

I nodded. "Nothing to do but wait, then."

"I suppose not." He looked around, at the bushes and trees and the croquet lawn where Abigail had swooned earlier. "I wonder how she made it here from London."

"I imagine she must have taken the train to Salisbury," I said, "like we did, and either walked or hired a car from there. Perhaps begged a ride with someone part of the way. A young woman on foot carrying a baby might appeal to someone's better instincts. And I don't imagine she was flush, really." Not judging by the out-of-date frock and the fact that she couldn't have been eating well lately.

"Seems a long way to come without some sort of luggage. Or a bag with extra nappies for the baby, if nothing else."

It did, now that he mentioned it.

"Might she have dropped it?" I asked, looking around. "Before she lurched onto the lawn and fainted?"

"I suppose she might have done."

"Should we look, then?" There was no part of me that wanted to go back onto the terrasse only to watch St George try to please his father by buttering up Lady Laetitia and her parents. I understood why he'd do it—Uncle Harold held the purse strings, as well as the title and all the power—but I still didn't think I wanted to watch.

"No reason why not," Christopher agreed, looking around. "She would have come up the driveway, I assume, the same way we are. And she came through the bushes... over there, was it?"

He indicated a break in the foliage up ahead. We could just hear the buzz of discourse on the terrasse from where we were standing. Not clearly enough to make out individual voices, but the general rise and fall of conversation.

I nodded. "Looks like."

"Let's look about, then. She would have traveled light, I assume, so probably not a trunk or weekender bag..."

No, Abigail had had the baby to carry. She would have been traveling quite light, I thought. No weight that she didn't need, since she had a fifteen pound baby on her hip and wouldn't want to carry anything else unless absolutely essential.

"Over there?" Constance ventured hesitantly. "Under the bush?"

She indicated a healthy specimen of lilac, seven feet tall, leafy green, but with no flowers left in the middle of July.

"Good eye," Christopher commented. He started forward, and we both withdrew our hands from his arms to let him proceed. A moment later, he had pulled a cheap cloth tote from under the branches and extended it towards her. "Your discovery, my lady."

Constance took it, but looked reluctant. "Do you think we should go through someone else's personal belongings?"

"Aunt Roz will need nappies for the baby," I pointed out. "It's long enough since Christopher was small that I'm sure she doesn't have any sitting around. And if there's anything in there that'll give us an idea of what's going on, I think we owe it to ourselves to find out. Don't you?"

She hesitated.

"It could exonerate Francis. She might have something in there that proves, without a doubt, that he isn't responsible."

Of course, there could be something that proved, without a doubt, that he was responsible, as well. But Constance didn't seem to think about that. Her lips firmed. "Here? Or should we take it somewhere?"

I glanced around. The door to the boot room was nearby, but so was the carriage house, and aside from Wilkins's presence, it might be more private. "In there."

Christopher shot me a look. "Why are we hiding, Pippa? We're not doing anything wrong."

"Just humor me," I told him, as I headed for the row of cars again. "I don't want everyone to see. Not until we know what we're looking at. Although you're right, there's no reason to hide. Let's just stop beside one of the cars and use the seat to lay out what we find."

Christopher shrugged, but acquiesced. When we got there, he was the one who opened the door to Crispin's blue H6 and gestured Constance forward. She placed the tote on the seat and bit her lip.

"Would you like me to do it?" I asked.

She slanted me a look. "Would you? It's really more your place than mine."

I wasn't sure it was anyone's place, but I also wasn't about to let the opportunity go by to see what Abigail was carrying. Call it healthy curiosity, although I have been told, more than once, that I have a tendency to stick my nose into things where it has no business being.

Nonetheless, I turned the tote upside down and shook it. A shower of small items dropped and fluttered out and hit the seat, and a few bounced off.

"Coin purse," Christopher said, as he fetched it from the floor of the Hispano-Suiza. "Ticket stub. Third class fare from London to Salisbury."

I nodded, as I sorted through the things on the seat. "Nappies. A change of clothes for the baby. A blanket."

It had 'Elizabeth Anne 1-14-1926' embroidered in one corner, surrounded by small, blue flowers. I squinted. "Violets?"

"Looks more like forget-me-nots," Christopher said, not that he knows much more about flowers than I do. "Pretty, whatever they are."

It was. A christening-gift, perhaps, or something for when the baby had been born. It was clearly not off the rack, but something a friend or relative—or Abigail herself—had made, perhaps while she'd been waiting for little Bess to be born.

"There's something written on this, too," Constance said, holding up a small piece of paper that had been folded a few times, and now unfolded again. Christopher and I crowded in.

At the top of the page was the logo of the Great Western Railway, the shields of the cities of London and Bristol. Below, in round, somewhat unformed script, was a list of words or phrases.

HAMMERSMITH PALAIS

Fair hair
Blue eyes
Black motorcar
Grandson
Duke of Sutherland
Astley

CHAPTER EIGHT

"SHE MUST HAVE BEEN MAKING a list of everything she knew about the baby's father," I said. Unnecessarily, since none of us were stupid and the other two had surely figured that out for themselves already. "I guess we can assume that they met at the Hammersmith Palais de Danse."

"In April of last year," Christopher nodded, "judging from little Bess's birthdate."

"And he had fair hair and blue eyes and drove a black motorcar," Constance added.

"They must have left together, for her to have seen the vehicle."

"He probably took her back to wherever she lives," Christopher said. "Or where she lived at the time. It's a shame she doesn't know a bit more about motors. She might have noticed a make instead of just a color."

I nodded, looking from Uncle Herbert's black Bentley to Uncle Harold's black Crossley. Every man in the family had access to a black motorcar in April of last year, so knowing that the vehicle had been black was remarkably unhelpful.

"At least Crispin's car is blue," Christopher said.

I shook my head. "He still had the Ballot last spring. He didn't destroy it until autumn. And anyway, he had access to his grandfather's car, I'm sure."

Christopher snorted. "Have you lost your mind, Pippa? Do you really suppose Grandfather—or for that matter Wilkins—would have allowed Crispin to drive Grandfather's precious Crossley? Besides, why would he have needed it, if he had a motorcar of his own?"

He wouldn't have, of course. Unless it had been during that period when the Ballot was out of commission, before he had replaced it with the Hispano-Suiza. But that had been nine or ten months ago, not last spring. "At least the blue eyes take him out."

"Not necessarily," Christopher said. "In that kind of setting, and in the dark, gray can look very much like blue. I'm not sure we can eliminate anyone based on the eyes or the car."

"Well, you all have fair hair," I said, "so that's hardly helpful. You're all grandsons of the Duke of Sutherland. Or were, back then. Now, nobody is the grandson of the Duke of Sutherland."

There was a moment's silence.

"I hate this," I said. Constance nodded fervently.

"At least Mum will have nappies for the baby." Christopher began shoving everything back into the tote again, only to stop, guiltily, when there was a scuff of a foot nearby.

We all looked up, and I daresay we looked very much like we had something to hide. But it was only Wilkins, back outside the carriage house again. He had a cigarette in one hand and a lighter in the other, and he had probably expected us to be long gone, because he looked from us to the tote and the stack of folded nappies Christopher was busily shoving back inside with consternation.

"We found the girl's bag," I said brightly. "We thought we'd... um... take a look inside before we brought it to Aunt Roz and Uncle Herbert."

Wilkins didn't say anything, and I'm sure I sounded very much like a fool, trying to explain myself to the chauffeur. And not even my own chauffeur, but Uncle Harold's.

"Never mind," I added. "Carry on, Wilkins."

"Yes, Miss Darling." He gave the bag one last look before he walked in the other direction. Away from the house and the cars, towards the hedgerow screening the property from the road, where he could suck on his gasper in peace.

"Done," Christopher said. "Come on, Pippa. Let's get this to Mum before the baby needs a change."

He handed the bag to Constance, who looked dubious but took it.

"Coming," I said, with a last look at Wilkins. "How much did he take you for, anyway?"

"Who?" Christopher glanced at him, too. "Oh, just a few shillings. Not much."

He shook his head. "It must be terribly boring, just waiting around for my uncle to require the car again. Especially when we all know that he won't need it until it's time to go back to Sutherland on Sunday. What is Wilkins supposed to do with all this time?"

"I imagine he'll retire to his room in the village once dinner starts. Uncle Harold isn't likely to need him after that."

"Uncle Harold isn't likely to need him at all," Christopher said, and moved aside the branches between me and the croquet lawn. "Go ahead, Pippa. Constance."

"Thank you, Christopher."

"Anyway," Christopher added, "I imagine Wilkins will retire to the pub but not to his room, if I'm any connoisseur."

"Connoisseur of what, exactly?"

"Men," Christopher said, with a final look over his shoulder at Wilkins before he ducked through the branches after us. "It's a pity."

"What's a pity?"

He grinned. "That he doesn't incline my way. Good-looking bloke."

"It's just as well that he doesn't," I told him. "Running after the staff is just about the lowest of low tastes."

Constance nodded fervently.

"It's one of the few things I've always appreciated about St George," I added. "At least he stays away from the servants."

"Faint praise, Darling," a voice drawled, close enough that I jumped.

It was St George himself, of course, tucked away in the shade of the stairs, below the terrasse, doing what Wilkins was doing: smoking a cigarette. I don't know how he so often manages to be in a spot to overhear me when I wish he wouldn't.

Unlike Wilkins, he had company. Lady Laetitia was enjoying her own fag through the length of a lovely ivory cigarette holder. She eyed me down the length of it, like I were some lowly caterpillar that had crawled out from the trees and onto the lawn, and had the temerity to speak in her presence.

I ignored her. "St George," I said instead, pleasantly. "I didn't see you there."

"Clearly." He turned his head to blow the smoke the other way instead of straight into my face. "Who would you be running after, Darling, if he were inclined that way?"

"Oh," I began, since he'd clearly misunderstood that part of the conversation. But before I could continue, Christopher got in before me.

"We were talking about Wilkins." He gave Crispin a smirk that could equal one of his cousin's own.

"Is that so?" Crispin's eyebrow rose. "I didn't realize you had such low tastes, Darling."

Laetitia tittered. Constance opened her mouth, perhaps to explain the misunderstanding—it would have been nice after Christopher essentially threw me to the wolves—but before she could say anything, the latter had put out a hand and stayed her.

Crispin watched the byplay, but didn't comment. "What's that you've got?" he asked instead, eyes on the tote over Constance's arm. "You didn't have that earlier."

She lifted it, but this time I got in first. "Abigail Dole's things. We thought Aunt Roz might need fresh napkins for the baby."

He flicked me a glance. "And where did you find Abigail Dole's things?"

"Under the lilac bush," I said. "She must have dropped the bag before she staggered onto the lawn earlier."

Crispin nodded. "So to return to Wilkins..."

"Let us not return to Wilkins, St George. Wilkins is none of our affair. Although, since we're on the subject of Wilkins and of returning, I had him move the H6 back in front of the carriage house for you. You're welcome."

He squinted at me. "Did you talk him into letting you drive?"

Christopher sniggered. I said, "No, St George. I said I wouldn't, and I didn't. Your precious is safe from my clutches. How's your head?"

"My head?" He sounded sincerely confused, which was nice—if something had been wrong with it, surely he would have said so.

On the other hand, it was surprising that he didn't catch on to the reason I was asking. He's usually quicker than that, so maybe something was wrong after all. "What are you implying, Darling?"

"Nothing whatsoever," I said. "Carry on. We'll take the bag to Aunt Roz."

He nodded, looking past me out to the lawn. "Croquet in the morning, I assume?"

"First thing after breakfast." Beckwith Place has an actual, honest-to-goodness, dedicated croquet lawn, which should tell you how much we all enjoy playing. Or enjoy beating one another, at any rate. As far as I could recall, Crispin had beaten me the last time we'd played each other, and I was eager for my revenge. "Make sure you're rested, St George."

"Of course, Darling." He glanced at Christopher. "You'll be at supper, won't you?"

Christopher nodded. "Pippa's just getting ahead of herself. Looking forward to rubbing your nose in your defeat, no doubt."

"Unquestionably," Crispin agreed. "As I recall, I beat you last time, Darling."

"I know you did," I said. "I'm looking forward to returning the favor." I turned to his companion. "Do you play, Lady Laetitia?"

She looked at me as if I had uttered an obscenity. "Lawn croquet at dawn?"

I smirked. Not, then. "We'll see you at supper, St George. In the meantime, don't do anything Christopher wouldn't do."

"You're awful, Darling," Crispin said. "You realize that that leaves me at loose ends?"

"You could help Aunt Roz with the baby. Get some practice in for the future."

He paled. "I'm not certain I like what you're implying, Darling."

I was quite certain he didn't. Whether that implication was

that he'd be responsible for little Bess soon, or that he'd be expected to provide Laetitia with a son and heir shortly.

She didn't like it, either. She gave me a narrow look, and then gave him one. "Crispin? Didn't you tell me...?"

"I did, Laetitia." He flicked her a glance. "Darling's just having some fun."

I smirked. "Whatever you say, St George. See you at supper."

I flounced away, up the stairs to the terrasse with Christopher and Constance trailing in my wake. Constance was wide-eyed and silent, Christopher sputtered like a tea kettle in his effort not to laugh out loud.

"You're evil, Pippa," he told me when we were far enough away that Crispin and Laetitia wouldn't hear him. "You know as well as I do that he's supposed to convince Laetitia the baby isn't his."

Of course I knew. However— "That's his problem. Mine is to keep her from becoming part of the family."

Constance nodded fervently.

"If Uncle Harold is determined to make it happen," I added, "and Crispin won't stand up for himself, someone has to ensure it doesn't come off."

By now, we were inside the house, making our way down the hallway past the kitchen, with no one to hear my outburst except Hughes, who was clattering about with the remains of tea.

I slowed to a stop. "Good evening, Hughes. What's going on with Miss Morrison, if you don't mind my asking?"

She straightened, face blank. "Miss Morrison, Miss Darling?"

"I heard you ask Lady Marsden about her earlier," I said. "Lydia Morrison, Lady Peckham's maid."

A shadow crossed her face and she turned back to the table. "Nothing you need concern yourself with, Miss Darling."

"Constance told me she left Lady Peckham's employ suddenly," I said, with a glance at Constance, who nodded. "She didn't give notice or anything. Was something wrong, and that's why she left? And now you're concerned about her?"

Hughes shook her head. "This is none of your affair, Miss Darling."

"She worked for my mother for as long as I can remember," Constance said from beside me. "If something's wrong, I would like to know."

Hughes eyed her. And eyed me, and eyed Christopher. We both attempted to look as if we weren't asking out of sheer, idle nosiness. Hughes sighed and turned her attention back to Constance. "We corresponded occasionally over the years. I was your mother's lady's maid at Marsden a long time ago. Lydia Morrison was Lady Charlotte's maid at Sutherland before the young lord was born."

The young lord being Crispin. So we were talking about things that had happened almost a quarter-century ago.

"Were you the one who wanted a change of position," I wanted to know, "or did Morrison?"

Hughes eyed me for another moment, but eventually she deigned to answer. "After Master Crispin was born, things at Sutherland weren't the same."

Obviously not. Although she probably wasn't referring to the obvious. People can be so annoying, with the way they don't just come out and say things.

I did my best to look politely expectant, and eventually she gave in and went on. "I wasn't there at the time, but apparently His Grace became... peculiar."

I arched my brows. So did Christopher. "His Grace

meaning my grandfather?" he asked. Hughes nodded. "Peculiar, how?"

Normally, when a peer is referred to as peculiar, it's because he has found religion or a chorus girl or some such nonsense. Or has lost his faculties in some other fashion. I had never noticed any such peculiarities in Duke Henry. He'd been a sour old man for as long as I had known him, but I wouldn't have called him peculiar by any of the usual standards.

"Wasn't this right around the time when his own father died?" I asked, looking at Christopher. "The old Duke, the one we talked about, who was a lad around eighteen-sixty? Perhaps your grandfather just had a difficult adjustment into the role?"

Christopher shook his head. "I have no idea, Pippa. I was just a few months old myself at the time."

"So Morrison wanted to leave," I said. "Is that it?"

"Yes, Miss Darling," Hughes nodded.

"And she went to Marsden instead of you, and you came to Sutherland Hall instead of her. Did Duke Henry behave peculiarly towards you too?"

"I never noticed anything amiss in my lord's manner, Miss Darling."

"That's all quite interesting," Constance said politely, in a tone that indicated that she didn't find it interesting at all, "but I would like to know whether there's a reason to worry about Morrison's current whereabouts. This is all ancient history. But she left the Dower House more than two months ago and didn't leave a forwarding address. Do you have reason to think something's wrong?"

Hughes hesitated. "I phoned Dorset the evening after His late Grace's valet was found dead. My lady was uneasy in her mind, and wished to speak to Morrison."

"Aunt Charlotte? Did you hear what they talked about?"

She eyed me again, much as one does an insect on a pin. "No, Miss Darling."

The corollary—*"and I wouldn't tell you if I did,"*—was implied but not stated out loud.

"Hughes..." Christopher tried.

She shook her head. "I don't know, Master Christopher. She took the call in the study, away from everyone. I stood in the hallway so she wouldn't be disturbed. I couldn't hear the conversation."

"But you think it had something to do with Grimsby's death?"

She gave me another look. "I don't know, Miss Darling."

Fine. "You haven't heard from Morrison since she left the Dower House. And you're concerned."

She nodded.

"Perhaps you can prevail upon your aunt or uncle to make some inquiries," I told Constance, "when they get back to Dorset. Or perhaps Laetitia or Geoffrey would be willing to oblige. It's possible one of the other servants has heard from her. Or perhaps she had friends in the village that she's kept in touch with."

Constance nodded. "I'll let you know if I hear anything, Hughes."

"Thank you, Miss Constance," Hughes said politely. She went back to the tea things, and we headed for the cellar steps and the door into the front of the house.

"You don't suppose anything is really wrong with her," I said, "do you?"

"I can't imagine what," Constance answered, and Christopher nodded.

"It was Aunt Charlotte who did away with Grandfather and Grimsby. By the time Morrison left the Dower House,

Aunt Charlotte was already dead. She couldn't have done anything to Morrison."

No, I suppose not. "And Morrison was in Dorset, so she couldn't have had anything to do with what happened at Sutherland."

"I don't see how," Christopher said.

"So why do you suppose Morrison hasn't got in touch with Hughes?"

"Is there any reason she would want to get in touch with Hughes?" Christopher didn't wait for me to answer, just went on. "She'd been working in Dorset for more than twenty-two years. She had no ties to Sutherland anymore. She might not actually like Hughes. She might not have liked Aunt Charlotte either, and that's why she wanted to leave her employ back in 1903. She didn't bother to come to the funeral, did she?"

No, she hadn't.

"It had been twenty-three years," Constance said in her soft voice. "Half her life, probably, since she worked for your aunt. She would have formed new friendships and connections during that time. Sutherland was a lifetime ago."

"She's probably on the beach in Blackpool," Christopher added, "under an umbrella. Or in London working at a dress-maker's shop. Or sitting in a cottage in the Cotswolds with a husband and two stepchildren."

"I suppose." Someone would have to work fast to acquire a husband and two stepchildren in two months' time, but the others were at least theoretically possible. "I don't suppose your mother is likely to know what was going on at Sutherland Hall back then, is she?"

"If she is, she wouldn't tell us," Christopher said. "It's none of our concern, and that's what she'd say. And Uncle Harold would tell us it's none of our concern, and he'd be right."

"And that's if anything was going on at all," Constance

reminded me. "We only have Hughes's word for it that something was. Morrison might have wanted a change of scenery for her own sake. Perhaps she had a love affair in the village that went wrong, or something like that."

I made a face, and she continued, "Don't do that, Pippa. Twenty-two years ago, she wasn't much older than we are now. Just because she's a servant, doesn't mean she doesn't have normal thoughts and feelings."

Of course she did. "Fine," I grumbled. "Never mind Morrison, then. What do we do now?"

"I intend to go upstairs to see if I can find Francis," Constance said. "I haven't seen him since tea."

Since he'd stalked off into the house looking for a stiff drink, more specifically. I hadn't seen him since, either.

"I'll take the bag to Aunt Roz," I said, reaching for it. "I'll see you in the dining room for supper, if I don't see you before."

Constance nodded, and headed up the stairs to the first floor. Christopher and I followed the sound of Aunt Roz's voice, and the gurgling of the baby, into the drawing room.

She had spread a blanket on top of the rug, and little Bess was lying on it, kicking her legs, while Aunt Roz sat on the floor next to her. Uncles Harold and Herbert were arranged on the Chesterfield. They each cradled a glass of something amber, possibly bourbon.

"There you are," Aunt Roz said brightly when we came through the door. "Did everything go well, Christopher?"

"As well as can be expected," Christopher said. "Wilkins carried her into the infirmary. Doctor White said she might not wake up until tomorrow, but he'll let us know."

Aunt Roz nodded. "And what's that you've got there?"

"We found it in the garden." I handed her the bag. "It's full of nappies and baby clothes."

"Perfect." She peered into it. "This will come in handy."

I perched on the chair Laetitia had sat on earlier, and Christopher folded himself onto the arm next to me. "There was a note inside, as well." I dug it out of my pocket and passed it to Aunt Roz. "She must have sat on the train and compiled it. The paper has the GWR logo on it."

"What does it say?" Uncle Herbert wanted to know, peering over his wife's shoulder.

Aunt Roz cleared her throat. "Hammersmith Palais. Fair hair. Blue eyes. Black motorcar—"

Uncle Harold harrumphed, but let her read through to the end before he said, "St George's eyes are gray. And his motorcar is blue."

Aunt Roz nodded. "My boys both have blue eyes. But I imagine gray might look a lot like blue in the dark. And—forgive me, Harold—Crispin would have had access to his grandfather's motorcar."

"The Ballot was black," I added. Uncle Harold gave me a look of concentrated dislike, but he didn't say anything.

Uncle Herbert cleared his throat. "Do we have any idea when...?"

"There's an embroidered blanket in there," I said, indicating the bag; Aunt Roz dove in, "with a name and a date on it. If it's accurate—and I don't see any reason why it wouldn't be—Elizabeth Anne was born in January of this year."

"That would put their meeting sometime in April of last year," Aunt Roz said, peering at the blanket, "if the baby was born at term. This is lovely."

She stroked the soft blanket and embroidery.

"I've been to the Hammersmith Palais de Danse," Christopher said, "although I didn't go anywhere near this girl. But I don't suppose my word is good enough for anyone."

"It's good enough for us, Christopher," Aunt Roz said, with a glance at Uncle Herbert. "We know you'd never..."

Uncle Harold harrumphed. "But I suppose you'll say that Crispin—"

"Your son does have a habit of tom-catting around, Harold," Aunt Roz said apologetically. Uncle Herbert winced. "You heard what Euphemia said..."

I hadn't heard what Laetitia's mother had said, but I could guess. "He isn't the aggressor in that relationship," I said. "She seduced him, not the other way around."

All three of them looked at me. Four, including Christopher. Uncle Harold's gaze was particularly piercing, and I fought back a wince. It occurred to me, a moment too late, that I had just paraphrased what Crispin himself had told his father earlier.

Now Uncle Harold probably suspected that I had listened in on their argument.

"Sorry," I added. For form, not because I actually felt sorry. "But I watched them together for a full weekend at the Dower House in May, you know, and she's relentless. Ruthless, too. At one point she smacked him across the face with her fan because he wasn't quick enough to cross the room to her."

There was a moment's silence. "Might be just what he needs," Uncle Harold muttered. "A wife who will keep him in his place."

My eyes narrowed, and so did Aunt Roz's. Uncle Herbert's jaw tightened. "With all due respect, Harold—"

"The boy is out of control," Uncle Harold said. "Someone has to rein him in. If Laetitia Marsden can do it, more power to her."

He put his glass on the table with a sharp click, got to his feet, and stalked towards the door.

"He's not a boy," I told his back. "He's a grown man. You can't make his decisions for him."

He swung around in the doorway to glare at me. "If he

knows what's good for him, he'll do as he's told. And so will you, Miss Darling."

He vanished from sight, and we could hear his footsteps slap against the wood on his way across the sitting room and foyer and up the stairs.

Christopher didn't breathe out until there was silence in the room, punctuated by the slamming of a door from upstairs. Bess made an inquiring sort of sound from the floor. "That went well," Christopher said sarcastically.

"Did you expect it to?" Aunt Roz turned to me. "What on earth was that about, Pippa?"

"I overheard him talking to Crispin earlier," I said. "I'm fairly certain he knocked him into the wall a couple of times. Crispin sounded like it hurt."

Uncle Herbert winced again. He's never been the kind of father who disciplined his children with corporeal punishment. "Is he all right?"

"I asked him about his head outside, and he made it sound as if nothing was wrong, so I assume so. I'm still not happy about it."

"And about Lady Laetitia..."

"Harold and Pippa are both right," Aunt Roz said. "Crispin is grown and should be allowed to make his own decisions. But he *is* running wild, and it's understandable that Harold would support anything that would force Crispin to calm down."

"Not anything," I answered, a bit ungrammatically. "St George would settle down if his father allowed him to marry who he wants to marry. Until Uncle Harold does, I think he's fighting a losing battle."

Aunt Roz had nothing to say to that. Nor did Uncle Herbert. They exchanged a glance.

"Do you need us for anything?" Christopher asked as he got to his feet.

His mother shook her head. "No, Christopher, dear. You two go on upstairs and rest. Supper at eight in the dining room. Black tie."

Christopher nodded and held out his hand to me. "Come along, Pippa."

"Coming," I said, and let him pull me to my feet.

CHAPTER NINE

WE WERE an uneven number at dinner, which is what happens when you have a family with a lot of sons and no daughters. Although Francis not turning up ended up for the best, since Aunt Roz was able to put Geoffrey Marsden to her left, with Constance beside him. Then came Uncle Harold, and then Euphemia, Lady Marsden. Uncle Herbert sat on the other end of the table with Crispin on his left. That was unorthodox, but it allowed us to maintain a man-woman-man formation for the rest of the table. Laetitia sat next to Crispin, Christopher next to Laetitia, and then there was me between Christopher and Laetitia's father, who was on Aunt Roz's right.

Speaking for myself, I was delighted with the arrangement. I was a bit too close to Lord Geoffrey for comfort, but I thought I could trust that he wouldn't try to play footsie with me practically under the eye of Aunt Roz and his father. The first time he accidentally kicked Aunt Roz or the Earl trying to get to me would hopefully put a stop to that. And I was also at a safe distance from both Uncle Harold, whom I still wanted to scream at, and from Lady Laetitia, who never failed to get on my nerves. I had Constance across from me, and Christopher on my right, and the Earl of Marsden turned out to be pleasant enough for the few minutes I was forced to converse with him.

"So you're Annabelle's daughter," he said. "And you went to the Godolphin School with little Connie."

I nodded. "I did, Lord Marsden."

"Call me Maurice, my dear. And how did you like Godolphin?"

We conversed on Godolphin—the school I had attended while Christopher and Crispin had been away at Eton—and then the next course was served and the Earl of Marsden—pardon me, Maurice—returned his attention to Aunt Roz and I returned mine to Christopher.

The only fly in the ointment, so to speak, was the fact that Francis was gone. "Any idea where he is?" I asked Christopher under cover of wiping my mouth with a serviette.

He slanted me a look. "I expect the village pub, since all of the motorcars are still here and he'd hardly attempt to bicycle all the way to London."

"Surely he wouldn't go to Town, anyway? Not with a house party and an engagement to celebrate tomorrow?"

"Not sure he was thinking straight when he left," Christopher said. "But at least if he's on foot we won't have to worry about him killing himself when he comes home, dead drunk, in the middle of the night."

No, we wouldn't. "I'm sure he's all right," I said, more for Constance's benefit than for Christopher's. She was sitting across the table and was hanging on our every word. "He'll be back later tonight, no doubt, and then tomorrow Abigail will wake up and give us a definitive answer about the baby's father, and then we'll move on from there."

Constance's mouth opened, and then closed again.

"What?" I asked.

She lowered her voice so far that it was hard to hear it across the table. "What if it turns out to be Francis's baby?"

"Then you'll either marry him, knowing that he had sexual relations with another woman before he knew you, or you won't, and he'll deal with it on his own. At least he didn't cheat."

Constance's jaw dropped at this rather brutal, but dare I say it, accurate, description of the situation. "But won't he want to...?"

"Oh, no." I shook my head. "She can't force him to marry her, you know."

I raised my voice a little on the last sentence, just to make sure that Crispin could hear me. "Francis loves you. If the baby is his, he'll have to provide for her, I suppose. But nobody can force him to marry someone he doesn't want to marry."

Lady Euphemia eyed me from down the table, where she was seated between Uncle Herbert and Uncle Harold. "Would you marry a man who had sired a child with someone else, Miss Darling? Someone who then left that woman to raise the child on her own?"

I think it was intended to be a trap. I'm fairly certain I was expected to return a negative answer. However, expectations often make me go out of my way to do the opposite, whether I actually agree with what I'm saying or not.

I eyed her back. "If I loved him, I suppose I would. Although if I loved him, he wouldn't be the sort of man who would abandon a woman he had gotten with child, would he?"

She hummed. "I don't know, Miss Darling. Would he?"

"I don't know, Lady Marsden. I guess we'll have to wait and see."

I hadn't meant anything by it, other than that I wasn't in love with anyone at the moment, and this was all a hypothetical situation, as far as I was concerned. But her nostrils flared as if I had said something significant. She exchanged a glance with her daughter, and then went back to her discussion with Uncle Harold. He gave me a cold sort of look, too. I guess he was still upset with me from earlier. Aunt Roz arched her brows questioningly.

I placed my napkin next to my plate. "May I be excused, Aunt Roslyn?"

"Go ahead, dear."

"Me as well?" Christopher asked.

His mother sighed. "Yes, Kit. Go on."

Constance didn't say a word, just watched with large, pleading eyes until Aunt Roz nodded. "You, too, Constance."

"Thank you, Roslyn." I waited for Christopher to pull out my chair. Geoffrey was gentleman enough to do the same for Constance.

"I expect you'll want to use the gramophone in the drawing room," Aunt Roz said. "I would be grateful if you'd close the door so the rest of us won't have to listen to the caterwauling you call music."

I had no plans of playing the gramophone and dancing, actually. Giving Lord Geoffrey that kind of proximity to me was the last thing I wanted. I had just desired to get away from the table and from the Marsden family, not to mention Uncle Harold. If the evening was warm, we might go out on the terrasse for a cigarette. But there was no need to say any of that, so I just nodded pleasantly. "Of course, Aunt Roz."

"Off you go, then." She waved a hand at us. Christopher offered Constance his arm. To my consternation, Lord Geoffrey hadn't sat back down at table, and now he offered me his.

"Miss Darling."

I forced a smile. "Thank you, Lord Geoffrey."

He leered down. "The pleasure is mine."

It certainly wasn't mine. If it had been up to me, I would

have told him that I didn't need his help to walk out of the dining room and across the foyer. But he and his family were honored guests, and Aunt Roz would never forgive me if I caused a scene. The way I had addressed Her Grace the Duchess had been bad enough.

So I rested my fingertips—the very smallest part of me I could manage—on Geoffrey's arm, and let him escort me from the room. Behind me, I could hear the Countess tell her daughter, "Why don't you and Lord St George join the other young people, darling. It can't be any fun for you to sit here with us old relics."

Aunt Roz and Uncle Herbert are certainly not relics. They're vibrant, engaging, smart people that it's fun to spend time with. I snorted.

"*Gesundtheit*," Geoffrey said.

I blinked. German? Really?

"Move along, Darling," St George's voice told me, before he gave me a nudge in the back to get me going again. "You're holding up the queue."

"Sorry, St George." I kicked back into motion. "There was no need for you to join us, you know. I didn't intend our departure to take you away from your supper."

"Believe me, Darling, I wouldn't have done it if I hadn't been told to run along and play."

Yes, that had been the long and short of Lady Marsden's remark, hadn't it? Move along, children, and let the grownups talk business.

I wondered what the topic of conversation was going to be after we left the dining room. How to prevail upon Crispin to propose to Lady Laetitia, or how to determine who was responsible for the baby currently asleep in my aunt and uncle's room upstairs?

Or perhaps the whereabouts of the eldest son of the house,

or the rudeness of the poor relation, who clearly didn't know her place?

I snorted again. And right on cue—

"*Gesundtheit*," Geoffrey said.

Christopher turned to look at me over his shoulder. "Are you developing a cold, Pippa?"

"No, Christopher," I said. "I'm incredulous."

"Ah." His lips twitched, and for a second, I saw him glance over my shoulder to, presumably, share an amused glance with his cousin. Then he added, "Where to?"

"Where would you like to go?"

"This was your idea, wasn't it? If you hadn't asked Mum to excuse you, we'd all still be sitting in the dining room."

"I just wanted to get away from the table," I said. "As long as we're not there, I don't care where we are."

He nodded. "It's a nice evening. Terrasse?"

The terrasse seemed like as good a place as any, so we headed that way and ranged ourselves along the balustrade. Crispin lighted Laetitia's cigarette and then his own. And then turned to me. "Darling?"

"Please," I said.

It was a lovely night. One of those clear, starry ones you sometimes get in summer when the temperature is perfect, there's no moisture in the air, and the smell of the flowers in the garden pervade everything. It would have been romantic had it not been for Geoffrey Marsden, who insisted on standing too close to me, and his sister, who carried on a heavy-handed flirtation with St George to the point that all I wanted to do was tell her to get a room. We all understood that she considered him her personal property. She had made that part very clear. Neither Constance nor I was a threat to her ownership. There was no need to stake her claim quite so vociferously. Frankly, it was making her look a bit desperate.

I crushed out my cigarette on the balustrade and prepared to get up and go inside, since I'd had all I could take of both Marsden siblings. But before I could get the words out, Constance's head rose. "Someone's coming."

We all quieted, Lady Laetitia a few seconds after the rest. "—so happy…"

I sharpened my ears, and after a moment I could hear what Constance's sharper ears had picked up on. Shuffling footsteps, or at least the passage of something or someone up the driveway and into the bushes at the corner of the house.

A muffled curse.

"Francis!" Constance jumped up from the parapet and ran for the stairs.

Down at the edge of the croquet lawn, in the shade of the house and the bushes, a many-legged creature appeared. It took a second for it to resolve itself into two figures, closely entwined, matched in height and breadth of shoulder. It wasn't until they came a bit closer that we could make out Francis on the left and Wilkins on the right. The twin rows of shiny buttons on the latter's uniform was a dead giveaway once the light hit them.

Constance hurried over and tucked herself under Francis's other arm. He beamed down on her with the easy affection of the extremely drunk. "Hullo, Connie!"

"Hello, Francis." She wrapped an arm around his waist and let out a soft grunt when he transferred his weight from Wilkins to her. Christopher headed down the stairs to help them.

"What happened?" he asked as he traded places with the chauffeur on Francis's other side.

Wilkins retired a few steps to the side and rotated his shoulder and then his neck. Francis was no lightweight. Then again, nor was Wilkins. "His Lordship having indicated that he wouldn't need my services for the rest of the evening," he said, "I retired to the village pub, where I've taken a room. When Mr. Astley expressed a desire to leave, I offered to drive him up the hill."

Translation: Francis had been drunk enough that Wilkins was worried he might end up face down in a ditch on his way home, and had thought to spare him that.

"Thank you, Wilkins," I said. "We'll take it from here."

"Yes, Miss Darling." He turned and headed towards the driveway.

"Wilkins?" I called after him.

He turned around. "Yes, Miss Darling?"

"Any news on the girl?"

"No, Miss Darling."

"No talk in the pub? Doctor White didn't come in for a nightcap and let anything slip?"

He shook his head. "No, Miss Darling."

"All right," I said. "Thank you, Wilkins. Sleep well."

"Yes, Miss Darling."

He disappeared into the bushes. After a moment, we could hear his footsteps on the driveway and then, eventually, there was the sound of the Crossley starting. By then, I had turned my attention to the threesome making their slow way up the stairs and across the terrasse. "There's simply no way we'll be able to get him up three flights of stairs to the attic."

Christopher shook his head. He was out of breath, but not as severely as Constance. Francis must be leaning quite a lot of his weight on them both. "I say we put him in the library," he told me. "It's the closest, and no one's likely to enter at this time of night."

"Fine by me." I moved to get the door, but Crispin got there ahead of me.

"He's all right, isn't he?"

"Drunk out of his mind," Christopher panted, stepping through the doorway first and dragging his brother in behind him, "but not hurt otherwise. He must have refrained from picking a fight at the pub, at any rate."

"Does he often pick fights in pubs?" Constance managed, staggering through the doorway behind them.

Christopher shot her a glance over Francis's bowed head. "It's been known to happen. Not much lately."

"More when the war had just ended and he was trying to adjust to civilian life," I added, as I slipped past Crispin and into the house behind them. "Thank you, St George."

"Don't mention it, Darling."

He shut the door behind the rest of us and followed me down the hallway as Christopher and Constance navigated Francis through the door into the library. "Someone should fetch a bucket," he added dispassionately from behind me.

I eyed him over my shoulder. "Do you think he'll need it?"

He gave me a look. "Better safe than sorry, I'd say."

True. "I'll check the kitchen." I moved down the hallway while the others passed through the door into the library.

By the time I came back with one of Cook's enameled buckets, Francis had been lowered onto one of the library sofas, and was resting with his head on an embroidered pillow. His eyes were closed and his breathing slow and even.

"I'll stay with him," Constance said, and sat down in one of the overstuffed chairs with her hands folded in her lap, quite as if she planned to spend the rest of the night there.

"At least go get yourself a blanket," I told her. "And change into something comfortable. If you're going to spend the night in a chair, you don't have to do it in a beaded gown."

"Someone ought to tell Mum and Dad, too," Christopher added. He was standing next to the sofa with his hands in his pockets and his eyes on Francis. "I'm sure Mum's worried.

She's got other things on her mind, but she'll want to know that Francis is all right."

"You go ahead," I told him. "Constance, you go on upstairs and get ready. Bring a blanket for Francis, too. I'll stay with him until you get back. And then we'll all leave the two of you alone."

Constance nodded, and headed out, followed by Christopher. I perched on the chair and told Crispin, "Take a look at him, St George, if you don't mind."

He arched a brow, but squatted next to the sofa, the better to peer at Francis's face. "What am I looking for?"

"Anything to indicate that he isn't all right."

He shot me a quick look over his shoulder. "No, Darling. He's perfectly fine. Marinated to the gills, but otherwise in tip-top shape."

"No sign of anything else?" Anything other than alcohol, I meant. Veronal, opium, cocaine... all the other things that Francis had been known to indulge in to keep the darkness at bay.

Crispin shook his head. "Not that I can see."

"His brat, is it?" Geoffrey asked genially, while Crispin rose to his feet.

I fixed him with a stare. Lord Geoffrey, I mean. Crispin had actually been helpful, so there was no point in glaring at him. "If you had been paying attention, you'd know that we don't know whose baby it is. At this point, it could be anybody's."

"Anybody in the family," Geoffrey clarified.

"Obviously. Unless you'd like to confess. She has blue eyes. So do you."

He sniggered. "Not it."

No, that would be too easy. I'd positively adore it if Handsy Geoffrey were to blame for Abigail's predicament, but blue eyes aside, that fair Sutherland hair was hard to dismiss.

"Crispin..." Laetitia whined and reached out. I rolled my eyes, but he moved obediently in her direction and allowed himself to be gathered in. When she had a tight grip on his arm, she turned to me. By now, her voice was crisp and cool. "What do you think, Miss Darling?"

I thought she was a horrible cow who ought to be taken outside and... well, no. Not shot. But I thought she was a horrible cow. That was not, however, likely to be what she meant.

"I think we don't know enough to make a determination. After all, anyone can say they're the grandson of the Duke of Sutherland, can't they?"

"Is that what happened?" Geoffrey asked. He looked like he was thinking deeply. I hoped I wasn't giving him ideas.

"That's what we surmise happened. She hasn't actually been awake to tell anyone anything. But she started with St George, then she came to see Christopher, and now here she is, where Francis lives."

"So it's not Crispin," Laetitia said, and in her favor, she actually sounded relieved.

I flicked him a glance. "He says it isn't."

"But if she moved on..."

"That's if she decided he isn't the baby's father. She could equally well have moved on because he denied her, and now she's trying to drum up sympathy in other quarters, so she can have support for when she nails him to the wall."

Crispin winced. "Thanks a lot, Darling."

I smirked. "Just telling the truth the way I see it, St George."

"But you said she came to see Christopher Astley after seeing St George," Geoffrey said.

I nodded. "And she took one look at me and ran, without telling me anything at all."

"So you don't know that Mr. Astley isn't the baby's father." Laetitia grasped hold of this idea in the manner of someone who's looking for something—anything—solid in a storm.

Her brother chuckled, but before he could voice whatever inanity had come to his mind, I told her, "*I* know that Christopher isn't, if he's the Mr. Astley you're referring to. But there's no proof of that, any more than there's proof for or against anyone else. And clearly some Mr. Astley or other is responsible."

Laetitia opened her mouth, but before she could say anything else, there was the sound of rapid footsteps in the hallway outside. A moment later, Aunt Roz swept through the door to the library, followed by Uncle Herbert. Christopher trailed behind them. I looked beyond him, in case Uncle Harold or the elder Marsdens had chosen to come along, too, but they must have decided to stay in the dining room, or wherever else they were gathered at this point.

"Francis!" Aunt Roz made for the sofa.

Francis opened his eyes to slits. "Mum?"

"What have you done to yourself, silly boy?"

She perched on the sofa next to him and pushed the hair out of his face.

"Got drunk," Francis muttered.

Aunt Roz's nose wrinkled. "So I smell."

Uncle Herbert smothered a laugh.

"Constance wants to stay here with him," I said. "She's gone upstairs to change into her night clothes and to bring down a pair of blankets. I don't see any reason why she can't, personally. He's in no condition to take advantage of anyone, and if he were going to, chances are he would have done it already."

"I'm not sure the Marsdens will agree with that reasoning, Pippa," Aunt Roz said, with a sideways look at Laetitia and

Geoffrey, "although I suppose Constance is of age and can make her own decisions."

I nodded. "That's what I assumed." And let's be honest, it wasn't as if Lady Laetitia or Lord Geoffrey had any claim to chastity. To demand that Constance behave like a lady while they carried on however they wanted seemed like the height of hypocrisy.

"Let's just not mention anything about it to them," I said. "What they don't know can't hurt them and all of that. And as you said, Constance is of age."

Aunt Roz nodded. "We'll just let you deal with it and go back to our guests. Sleep well, son." She patted Francis on the shoulder before sweeping out of the library with Uncle Herbert right behind. He winked at me on his way past.

"We'll go to Mummy and Daddy, as well," Laetitia said and made to follow. The personal pronoun seemed to include Crispin, because she took him with her. "Come along, Geoffrey."

She made her exit with both young men in attendance.

"Good God, Christopher," I said, when I thought she must be far enough down the hallway that she wouldn't be able to hear me, "please say it isn't just me. I know I roll my eyes a little extra hard because it's St George, but please tell me she really is as insufferable as I think she is. It can't be just me, surely?"

"She's a trial," Christopher said. "So is he, of course, in his own way."

"She's already taken possession of him, you know. She acts as if it's a done deal."

Christopher nodded. "Perhaps it is."

"If he has proposed, I haven't heard anything about it. Surely we would. She wouldn't be able to keep her mouth shut, would she? Nor would her mother, I bet."

"I would expect us to hear if my cousin got engaged,"

Christopher agreed, "although with everything else that's going on here this weekend, who knows?"

That was a fair point. "He'd tell you, though. Wouldn't he?"

"Again," Christopher said, "I would expect him to. But—"

He stopped talking at the sound of soft footsteps in the hallway. It was only Constance, though, arrayed in a dressing gown, with quilted slippers on her feet and a pillow and two blankets in her arms.

"We'll let you get to it," I told her. "Lock the door behind us if you don't want to be disturbed."

She nodded. "Are you going back to the drawing room?"

Christopher nodded. I shook my head. "I've had enough for tonight. If I have to deal with one more imbecilic comment from Lord Geoffrey—no offense, Constance..."

"None taken," Constance said, dropping the pillow and blankets on the chair before draping one lovingly over Francis's still form. A corner of his mouth turned up, even in sleep, and he snuggled in underneath it. Constance straightened and glanced at me. "I didn't choose him."

"Well, I have listened to enough of Geoffrey's inanities, and have watched Laetitia do her worst vis-à-vis St George, for long enough today. I'm going to bed. I'll see you upstairs, Christopher."

"Since Francis is down here," Christopher said, with a glance at him, "I'll share with Crispin."

"Since Constance is down here, St George might not come upstairs. Laetitia may drag him into Constance's room with her."

"If she has relations with him in my bed," Constance said, "I will absolutely tell Aunt Effie about it."

Good. If Laetitia had relations with St George in Constance's bed, she'd deserve a dressing down by her mother.

"I'll see you both in the morning." I made my own way towards the door. "If St George proposes to Lady Laetitia—or vice versa—in what's left of tonight, you have my permission to wake me, Christopher, so I can give the happy couple my felicitations."

"I'll make sure to do that, Pippa," Christopher said. "Sleep well."

CHAPTER TEN

I DID, indeed, sleep well. Nothing disturbed my slumber that night. Christopher didn't burst in at any point to tell me that Crispin had lost his mind and proposed to Laetitia, nor did Francis sleep off his bout of drunkenness and come upstairs to bed. I spent a peaceful nine hours in oblivion, all by myself, without even a bad dream for company.

Saturday dawned sunny and bright, with rays of light peeping around the draperies. I lounged luxuriously for a few minutes before I remembered that today was the day we would (surely) get answers from Abigail Dole about the paternity of little Bess, and it was also the day in which I would get another chance to beat St George—and everyone else in the family, but particularly St George—at croquet.

The tiny windows on the top floor of Beckwith Place, the ones that go along with the tiny rooms in the attic, look out over gray roofing slates and, below, the croquet lawn. When I bounded out of bed and over to the window, I only wanted to look at the smooth and even greenness of the grass, so as to gloat over my possible defeat of St George later.

Instead, as I pulled the curtains back and peered down, past slate gray tiles and the edge of the roof onto the bright green of the lawn, I experienced a distinct sense of déjà vu when I spotted the patch of sprigged rayon on the grass, and the pale limbs extending from it.

For a second or two, it felt like I had gone back in time twelve or fifteen hours, and Abigail Dole had just walked out of the trees and collapsed. But of course I knew that such was not the case. We had lived half a day since then. We had picked her up and carried her inside, and Doctor White had come and taken her to the village, and Aunt Roz had minded little Bess all evening and night. Christopher, Constance, and I had found Abigail's tote under the lilac bush and read the list of things she knew—or thought she knew—about her baby's father.

It was Saturday morning, not Friday at tea time, but Abigail Dole was sprawled on the lawn.

I pushed back from the window and ran across the room to the door. And yanked it open and ran across the landing to the next door. "Christopher!"

Two almost-identical faces peered at me from over the top of the blankets. One pair of Astley blue eyes, one pair of cool gray.

"Darling?"

I ignored him—ignored them both—in favor of rushing across the room and yanking the curtains back. Crispin winced as the sunlight hit him full in the face.

"What's wrong, Pippa?" Christopher asked as he sat up and rubbed his eyes. "A bit early, isn't it?"

"Abigail," I said, waving at the window. "On the lawn."

They both glanced at the window, and then back at me. "That was yesterday," Crispin said.

I shook my head, and continued to shake it. "She's there again. Now."

They exchanged a look, and then Crispin threw the blankets off to stride to the window. I kept my eyes on Christopher. "We have to go down. We have to see if..."

I couldn't finish, and Christopher looked at me with concern for a second before he turned to his cousin. "Crispin?"

The latter turned from the window, his face pale. "She's there."

Christopher breathed a bad word and pushed the blankets off himself. "We'd better go, then. But let's do try to be quiet, so we don't wake the whole household. At least until we get past the first floor."

He stuffed his feet into slippers and waited as Crispin, who had taken off his pyjama top to sleep, pulled it back over his head. "Something for your feet, Pippa?"

"I suppose I'd better. Just a moment." I scurried back across the landing, picked up my brogues, and carried them in my hand as we slipped down the two sets of stairs and through the back of the house onto the terrasse. There, I took a second to shove my bare feet into the shoes before I followed the boys across the flagstones and down the lawn.

By the time I caught up, they were kneeling, one on each side of her, with their knees in the dewy grass. Christopher was pale. Crispin was paler. He had his hand on Abigail's throat, and must be unable to feel a pulse, because the hand trembled.

"Looks like someone whacked her on the back of the head," Christopher said. His voice shook, too.

"With that?" I eyed the croquet mallet lying a few feet away.

Christopher glanced at it. So did Crispin. "I would assume so. Don't touch it."

I hadn't planned to. I'm not stupid. I did take a few steps towards it and bent down for a closer look, though. "There's blood and maybe hair on it."

My stomach rolled, and I backed away and closed my eyes and focused on pushing air into and out of my lungs.

"All right, Darling?" Crispin asked. His voice came from quite far away, down a long, echoing tunnel.

I nodded and continued to breathe. "Fine. Or I will be fine. Someone should phone the constables."

"I'm phoning Tom," Christopher said. I opened my eyes in time to see him push to his feet. "They'll have to call in Scotland Yard anyway. It's us. And she was from London. It makes sense."

"Whatever you say," Crispin told him. "I'll stay with her, shall I, until we know what to do?"

"If you don't mind." He turned to me. "Pippa—"

"I'll stay with Crispin," I said.

Both of them eyed me as if I had said something extraordinary.

"What?" I wanted to know. "Someone has to stay with you to make sure you don't tidy away any of the evidence."

He rolled his eyes. "Of course, Darling. You know, if I had evidence to tidy away, I would have done it last night."

"It was dark," I said. "You may not have seen clearly."

It was Christopher's turn to roll his eyes. "Be nice, Pippa. Don't kill each other while I'm gone."

"No promises," Crispin told him. "Hurry, won't you?"

Christopher did just that, headed for the terrasse at a jog. Crispin turned to me, "You know, Darling, your suspicions of me are getting ridiculous. First you thought I shot Grimsby, then you thought I strangled Johanna. You probably played with the idea that I may have killed Gladys, too—"

"Actually, I didn't." I sank to the ground on the other side of the body, far enough away that I didn't have to look at her, and folded my legs. "I made a good case for why you may have wanted your grandfather and Grimsby out of the way. It made sense. But I never believed that you'd strangled Johanna, and not just because you hadn't had the time to do it. If you haven't strangled me in all the years we've known each other, you're not going to strangle anyone else. And the idea that you might have done something to Gladys never even crossed my mind. When we tracked you down at Sutherland Hall that evening, it wasn't because we thought you'd hurt her. It was because we were worried about you."

He blinked.

"And I don't suspect you of this—" My eyes flicked down to the body and away again, quickly, "either. Not more than I suspect anyone else. You've always seemed sincere when I've asked you about it. And if Bess isn't yours, then you'd have no reason to murder Abigail."

He looked caught somewhere between gratified and appalled. "Then why are you making remarks about tidying away evidence?"

"Isn't that what we do?" I said. "Say awful things to one another to annoy?"

"You, perhaps," Crispin answered. "I, on the other hand..."

"Oh, spare me."

He grinned, a quick flash of white teeth, and I added, "Every time you say anything to me, you intend for it to grate. Why else do you insist on calling me Darling every time you open your mouth?"

He opened his mouth, and I continued before he could say anything. "Yes, yes. I know it's my name. Or approximately my name." An anglicization of my German surname of Schatz, if you want to be precise. "But that isn't the reason you use it."

He smirked. "No, Darling. It isn't."

"You do it because you know it irritates me. And in return, I do what I know irritates you."

"It's hardly on the same level," Crispin said. "You seem to

actively despise me. I don't despise you. I don't even particularly dislike you, except when you do something that reminds me that you loathe me."

I opened my mouth. And closed it again. "I don't loathe you," finally fell out.

He arched a brow.

"I don't! I'll admit that I have, at times, disliked you. You were a horrid little boy. You used to take me into the garden maze at Sutherland Hall and leave me there."

He sniggered. "Only until you figured out how to get yourself out. And it didn't take very long, as I recall."

Well, no. It hadn't. But— "It happened more than once. And you also took me into the cellars and implied you'd shut me in the dungeon, and you threw mud at me, and snowballs in the winter, and you put spiders and caterpillars down the back of my dress..."

"I'm sure I did, Darling. I'm sure I did worse than that, too. But I haven't been a horrible little boy in quite a long time, and I haven't done anything like that to you in years. You should have gotten over it by now."

Perhaps that was true. However— "You're still exceedingly annoying, you know."

"It's hardly my fault that everything about me bothers you, Darling. Unlike you, I don't go out of my way to annoy you."

"Oh, that's rich," I said. "So in May, when you told me I looked like a Bramley—"

He held up a finger. "I did not tell you that you looked like a Bramley, Darling. I said that you looked edible."

"But what you meant was that I looked like a Bramley. Because my dress was green."

He smirked, and I added, "Fine. Last month, when you decided to treat me to a sampling of your charms..."

"I was proving a point," Crispin said. "Unlike you, when you went out of your way to embarrass me in front of my entire family yesterday. Not to mention in front of the woman my father wants me to marry, plus *her* entire family. Thanks a lot, Darling."

I shook my head. "You can't, St George."

"Can't what?"

"Marry her. What else?"

He tilted his head inquiringly. "And why is that?"

"You don't love her. We both know it. *She* knows it. You've told her. I heard you."

He nodded. "And she wants me anyway. Unless you think she's after the title and fortune?"

He quirked a brow. I pressed my lips together in a concerted effort not to take the bait. For years I had been telling him, at every opportunity, that that was all he had to recommend him, that the Sutherland title and Sutherland money are the only reason that women buzz around him like bees around a flower. It's a lie, of course. I'm neither stupid nor blind. He's clever, he's handsome, he can be charming when he wants to be (and vicious when he doesn't)... but the fact that he's Crispin Astley, Viscount St George, and first in line for the Sutherland dukedom, isn't the only reason why a woman might find him attractive.

Naturally I didn't say so. Not in so many words.

"She has a title and money of her own," I said instead, crossly. "She doesn't need yours. We both know she thinks you'd have *fun* together."

My nose wrinkled on the word, and Crispin chuckled. "You could have fun of your own, you know, Darling. Plenty of girls these days aren't opposed to a bit of slap and tickle."

Well, he'd know, wouldn't he?

"Thank you, St George," I said repressively, "but I prefer to wait until I find someone I want to have more than just fun with."

He smirked. "Well, she does want more than just fun, doesn't she? So tell me why I can't marry her, Darling. If she wants me, and it isn't for the title, and we both know my father won't let me marry who I really want to marry... why shouldn't I marry Laetitia?"

"You'll be unhappy," I said.

"I'm unhappy now, Darling."

I blinked at him. Opened my mouth and then closed it again before saying, "This is a strange conversation to have over the dead body of a woman you may have gotten with child a year ago."

"I thought you said that I seemed sincere when I told you I hadn't."

"You lie like a rug," I told him. "I wouldn't trust you any farther than I could throw you."

He rolled his eyes. "There's the Darling we all know and love."

Yes, there she was. The conversation had gotten heavy, and I had become uncomfortable, and I had done what I usually did, and lashed out at him.

He turned to glance over his shoulder. "Here's Kit. Good conversation, Darling. I'm going to go upstairs, if you don't mind."

He uncoiled in one smooth motion, and was on his feet. And then he walked away. He met Christopher on the stairs between the grass and the terrasse—I heard a quick exchange of, "Something wrong?" and, "Nothing out of the ordinary. I'm going up to change,"—and then he was gone and Christopher bore down on me.

"What did you say to him?"

"Nothing," I said.

"Then why did he look like that?"

"Like what?" He had looked perfectly normal when he'd stepped away from me. "He asked me why he shouldn't marry Laetitia if she wants him. I said it would make him unhappy. He said he's unhappy now."

Christopher nodded. "I got through to Tom. He said to call in the local constabulary."

"He's not coming?"

"He's coming," Christopher confirmed. "He said he'd contact Inspector Pendennis and get him to get in touch with the chief constable for the area, but we have to follow procedure. So I called the village and asked for a bobby. When he gets here, I'll explain the situation. Tom said he'd be on his way as soon as he updated Pendennis."

Chief Inspector Arthur Pendennis is Tom's boss, or his team leader or some such thing. When Pendennis investigates a case, Detective Sergeant Tom Gardiner goes along as photographer and general dogsbody. There's also a Detective Sergeant Ian Finchley who serves the same purpose, but his specialty is fingerprints. Sometimes, Scotland Yard Police Surgeon Curtis tags along with them, too.

"Tom's coming before it's officially Scotland Yard's case?" I asked.

"Tom's coming because someone in the family committed murder," Christopher answered bluntly. "He was coming anyway, for Francis's engagement party this evening. Now he's just driving down a few hours early. Is that a problem?"

"Of course not. Not at all." I'd rather have Tom investigate than some flatfooted bobby from the village. "It's just... Aren't you afraid it might look like... well... favoritism? Or bribery or something?"

He arched his brows. "Do you intend to pay him?"

"Of course not," I said.

"Then it isn't bribery." He shook his head. "He said he was on his way, Pippa. I wasn't going to tell him that I didn't want to see him, was I?"

No, I imagined he wasn't. "When will he get here?"

"Not for a few hours yet." He reached out and flapped his hand at a fat fly that took aim at the body, probably attracted by the sticky area of blood on the back of Abigail's head.

I averted my eyes. "Should we cover her with something?"

"Hard to say," Christopher said. "Some coppers would appreciate us preserving the evidence and keeping the body mostly untouched. Others would be upset because we didn't leave it alone."

I eyed him. "Is there a reason you're suddenly overly concerned with this?"

Christopher made a face. "Would you happen to remember a local boy by the name of Samuel Entwistle?"

"Of course." He was a few years older than Christopher and I, and had lived in the village for as long as I could remember.

And then I made the connection. "Oh. He's Constable Entwistle now, isn't he? Did he answer the telephone at the constabulary?"

Christopher nodded.

"So he's the one coming? Is that going to be a problem?"

"He and Robbie never got along," Christopher said.

"That's a shame. But—forgive me—Robbie's gone." Christopher's elder brother, younger than Francis by a couple of years, had died in the Great War.

"I know that, Pippa." Christopher sounded impatient. "However, Francis is not. And whenever Sammy picked on Robbie, it was Francis who hit back. Twice as hard."

"So Sammy doesn't like Francis." I knew that, actually. I had lived here for a long time, after all. It was just that a lot of this history had happened before I arrived, before the beginning of the war, so I hadn't been here for it.

Christopher shook his head. "And Francis is very much alive. Not to mention a prime suspect in this murder."

Yes, of course he was. "We'll just have to make sure Sammy thinks someone else is guilty, then."

He huffed. "And who do you think we should throw under the bus, Pippa?"

"Well," I said, thinking about it, "not me or you, obviously."

He shook his head. "No, let's not. Nor Crispin, if we can avoid it."

I supposed not. There was no part of me, not anymore, that wanted to see St George go down for murder, especially one he hadn't committed.

"I'd rather it not be Aunt Roz or Uncle Herbert, either. Who does that leave?"

"Laetitia or Constance?" Christopher proposed. "Or Uncle Harold, because he thought she was after Crispin?"

"I'd rather not take Constance away from Francis," I said thoughtfully, "although I'd be all right with framing Uncle Harold."

I'd be more than all right with it, in fact. Truthfully, the idea was not unpleasant, and came with benefits other than just fixing on a suspect for the murder. If Uncle Harold was sent away to prison, it would rid us all of the prospect of Laetitia Marsden as part of the family, and it would also get Crispin out from under his father's thumb. He might be able to marry who he wanted to marry, which might give him a shot at being happy, or as happy as he could be with a father who was incarcerated.

Yes, framing Uncle Harold was an idea with merit.

"I like my cousin better than my uncle," Christopher agreed, "so if I'm going to throw one of them to the wolves, it'll be Uncle Harold. Although it's probably not either of them, you know."

"Guilty, do you mean?

He nodded.

"Well, if it isn't Uncle Harold or Crispin, and it isn't Constance or Laetitia, and it isn't you or Francis or your parents, then who is it?"

He smirked. "I don't suppose it's you, Pippa?"

I stared at him, appalled, and he continued, "You had a room to yourself. You could have seen her from the window, and come down to talk to her, and lost your temper. You have one, you know. And you swing a mean croquet mallet."

"Surely you're not serious, Christopher?"

He sniggered, and sounded like his cousin for a moment. "No, Pippa. Although I don't doubt that you would viciously attack anyone who threatened me or Francis, or even Crispin."

"But I wouldn't whack her over the head with a croquet mallet," I said. "I'm not a murderer, Christopher!"

"Of course you aren't. I just can't think of anyone else who would do such a thing, either."

No more could I. However— "I don't think Sammy Entwistle is going to care who we think is capable of it, Christopher. He'll be more concerned with alibis, I'm sure. I don't have one. You and St George were together in the other attic room. Did either of you leave at any point?"

He shook his head. "Not after Crispin came upstairs. But that was after I did. So there was a period of time—long enough to hit someone with a mallet—that we weren't together. He might have been with someone else—"

I made a face. Laetitia, most likely. Lip-locked in a dark corner somewhere.

"—but I wasn't."

"Francis and Constance were together in the library," I

said. "But Francis was sleeping off a drunken binge, and I don't suppose he would have noticed if Constance slipped out."

"And Constance might not have noticed if Francis slipped out, either. I don't know how soundly she sleeps."

"Not that soundly. I shared a room with her at the Dower House for a couple of nights. Besides, she was curled up in a chair, and probably uncomfortable. I doubt she would have stayed asleep had Francis started stumbling around in the dark. But again, I don't think Sammy would take my word for it."

Christopher hummed agreement.

"Laetitia had Constance's room to herself," I said. "She might have been afraid that Abigail was going to point the finger at St George this morning. And her room has a window onto the croquet lawn, so she could have seen Abigail arrive. If she were awake."

Christopher glanced up at the house, and the window to Constance's—currently Laetitia's—room. The curtains, pale blue, were still shut against the morning sun.

"Uncle Harold also has a private room," I added. "Right next to the stairs, too. It would be easy for him to come and go."

"But no window on the lawn."

No. But that didn't matter. He might have been looking out the front window just at the time when Abigail turned the corner from the lane into the driveway, which wasn't any more unlikely than that Laetitia had looked out onto the lawn and spied her.

And we didn't know that it had happened by chance, anyway. Uncle Harold might have had a pre-arranged assignation with Abigail. She might have contacted him at Sutherland Hall and arranged to meet him here. She might even have traveled up from Sutherland in the Crossley with him and Wilkins. We didn't know that she hadn't. Crispin had motored up on his own, so he wouldn't have known. They could have set her down in the village and instructed her to walk the rest of the way here. If she had been Crispin's paramour, and Uncle Harold wanted Crispin to marry Laetitia, he had reason to want Abigail gone. Bringing her here to Beckwith Place, where the suspects were more plentiful, before he did away with her, made sense in that context.

"Geoffrey slept alone, too," Christopher said, derailing my train of thought, "but I don't suppose there's any reason to think he's involved."

Sadly not, although he was someone else I wouldn't be disinclined to frame for murder.

"I would love it to be him," I said. "He pokes little Geoffrey into anything that moves, so it wouldn't be at all surprising if he had gotten some poor girl with child at some point or another. Although he wouldn't need to say he is the grandson of the Duke of Sutherland to make himself sound important, would he? He could claim to be the next Earl of Marsden, and it would come to the same thing."

Christopher nodded. "Unless he was specifically trying to put the blame on one of us. But in April last year I didn't even know who he was, and Crispin hadn't taken up with Laetitia yet then, either."

"Nor does he have fair hair," I said regretfully. "Besides, it's really a bit too much of a coincidence that he'd be here the weekend she shows up, isn't it?"

"Probably so," Christopher agreed, his voice equally regretful. "I wish it were this easy."

I nodded. And then we both turned towards the edge of the lawn as a strapping young constable wheeling his bicycle through the trees looked around and said, "What's all this, then?"

CHAPTER ELEVEN

UP CLOSE, Constable Samuel Entwistle was eminently recognizable as the young lout who had made Cousin Robert's life a misery during his formative years. He had the same carrot-red hair, the same snub nose, and the same sneer on his round face as he had had back then.

Of course, I hadn't been around for much of that—it had mostly happened before Robbie went off to Eton at thirteen, at which point I was still just eight years old and living with my own parents in Germany.

But I did remember him from a few holidays after I arrived in England, when Robbie and Francis were home for the summer, before they had to go off to France and fight in the war. Robbie, with his fine clothes and fine manners, had turned the head of one of the village girls that Sammy had his eye on. At this point I couldn't even remember her name, but I did remember the incident. Sammy had convinced his foul friends to pile on Robbie after the latter had dropped the girl off at her home in the village one evening, and Robbie had staggered into Beckwith Place two hours later with a black eye and a bloody lip and torn clothes and two flat tires on his bicycle. Uncle Herbert had wanted to involve the constabulary and come down on them all like the wrath of God, but Francis had prevailed upon his father to let him take care of it. Two days later, it was Sammy walking around with a fat lip and a black eye. Needless to say, there was not much love lost between any of the Astleys and Sammy Entwistle.

I did my best to calm what I assumed would turn out to be turbulent waters. "Constable. I'm Philippa Darling. I don't know if you remember me from when we were children..."

He sneered. "My lady's German niece, aren't you?"

That was distilling it into its basest form, and without any provocation at all. I gave up any hope of civil discourse and narrowed my eyes. "Listen, you—"

"That's Constable Entwistle to you," Sammy said, and rose to his full height of almost six feet, chest out and shoulders back.

I put my hands on my hips and glared up at him. "I don't care who you are, you prat—"

He smirked. "That's abusive language, that is. I can arrest you for that."

"I'd like to see you try," I began, but Christopher seemed to think that this had gone on for long enough, because he interrupted.

"Constable Entwistle. I'm Christopher Astley. And that's the victim."

He pointed to Abigail. Sammy looked at her as if this was the first he'd noticed her lying there.

"Whacked her over the head with a croquet mallet, did you?"

"*We* didn't," I said, "for God's sake..."

Christopher stepped on my foot. Thanks to the fact that I was wearing brogues and he was wearing slippers, it didn't hurt, but I could feel the pressure. "Listen," he said, "Constable Entwistle. I have already rung up a friend at Scotland Yard…"

Sammy's face twisted into another sneer. "Friends with Scotland Yard, are you? Well, until *my* chief constable decides that *we* need help with this investigation…"

"He'll be here by midday," Christopher cut in. "I suggest you prepare yourself. Until then, we realize that you have a job to do. But—"

Sammy scowled. "Who do you think you are, ordering me about? Just because you're one of the Astleys from Beckwith Place, thinking you can get away with murder by involving your *friends* from Scotland Yard…"

"You're being ridiculous," I told him. "We followed procedure. Christopher called the local constabulary. They sent you. Now I suggest you get on with your job."

He gave me a look. "And what do you think my job is?"

I wanted to roll my eyes so hard that I could see the inside of my skull, but I refrained. "If it were me, I would start with the body. You'll find Crispin's fingerprints on her throat, where he checked for a pulse. Neither Christopher nor I touched her. And no one touched the murder weapon."

Sammy eyed the croquet mallet. "How do you know that that's the murder weapon?"

I didn't. But— "Educated guess? There's blood and hair on the head of it, and it's lying next to the body. I made an assumption. Anyway, you should take a look at it."

Sammy made an irritating, humming little noise. "Refresh my memory," he said. "Who's Crispin?"

Seriously? "Viscount St George," I told him. "Future Duke of Sutherland. Christopher's cousin. Him."

I nodded towards the house and the door to the terrasse, which had opened far enough to let Crispin slip through. He was dressed for the day in tweed and plus-fours, with his hair slicked back and his best supercilious look firmly attached to his face.

Sammy looked him up and down for a moment before turning back to me. "And why did he have his hands around the girl's neck?"

His voice was pitched high enough that Crispin could, undoubtedly, hear every word.

"He didn't have his hands around her neck," I said, "you imbecile. Don't you listen? He had his fingertips against her throat to check for a pulse. Besides, does she look strangled to you?"

Sammy glanced at her, blankly. Maybe he truly didn't know what a victim of strangulation looked like. My mind served up an image of Johanna de Vos sprawled across the Dowager Lady Peckham's bed, and I gagged.

"Listen, Constable—" Christopher began, eyes narrowing.

"Easy, Kit." Crispin must have seen the look, because he put a hand on Christopher's shoulder for a moment before he came to a stop next to him. "Constable." He directed a look down the length of his nose at Sammy. "I'm Lord St George."

And he sounded every bit of it, I must say, with his posh vowels and condescending tone.

Sammy sneered. "Of course you are."

Crispin arched a brow. And waited.

"So you touched the victim," Sammy said, when nothing more was forthcoming.

Crispin nodded blandly. "I put my hand on her neck, yes. To check if her heart was beating."

"Couldn't tell from the back of her head that she was dead?"

Crispin flicked a glance that way. I did, too, and wished I hadn't. "Not really," Crispin said faux-apologetically. "I'm afraid I lack your vast experience with murder victims, Constable."

That wasn't true, actually. From his grandfather and Grimsby to Johanna and Frederick Montrose, Crispin had probably seen more murder victims in the past few months than Sammy Entwistle had in most of his career. Rural Wiltshire isn't exactly a hotbed of criminal activity.

Of course, Sammy might have been in France or Belgium during the war, and that would put rather a different complexion on things. Not as far as murder victims go—unless you consider victims of war to be murdered, and I suppose you could—but at least as far as violent death was concerned.

"Who was she to you?" Sammy wanted to know.

Crispin flicked another glance at Abigail. "Nothing."

"Nothing?"

"I didn't know her."

Sammy scoffed. "A likely story."

"It's true, nonetheless," I told him. "None of us knew her. I met her once before yesterday. Last week, in London, for less than five minutes. Crispin met her once, several months ago. Also in London, and also for just a few minutes. Christopher hadn't met her at all."

"She wasn't a guest, then? Here for the engagement party?"

"No," I said. "The engagement party so far consists of our family and Constance's family. We were expecting a few friends later today, although I suppose we'll have to try to head them off after this. The only women here, apart from myself and Constance—and of course Aunt Roz—is the Countess of Marsden and her daughter, Lady Laetitia. This is neither of them."

Sammy looked at the body. "Who is she, then?"

"As far as I know," I said, "her name was Abigail Dole. That's what she told me."

"And what was she doing here?"

"We don't know," I said.

Both Christopher and Crispin reacted to that, with a little flinch each, and Sammy raised his brows. "Don't know?"

"We never got a chance to talk to her. She staggered onto the lawn in the middle of tea yesterday, and collapsed. Francis carried her inside."

Sammy's jaw twitched, but he didn't interrupt.

"We sent for Doctor White," I added, "and he took her to the village infirmary in the Duke's Crossley. Wilkins drove and Christopher went along for ballast."

Sammy had looked from Crispin to Christopher during this recitation. Now he returned his attention to me. "Wilkins?"

"Father's chauffeur," Crispin said.

Sammy sneered, but didn't comment with a remark on people who had chauffeurs. "And when did the victim return?"

"Sometime between ten o'clock last evening and about an hour ago, That was when I looked out the window and saw her."

"Midnight," Crispin said.

I shot him a look. "Really?"

"No, Darling. I have no idea when she returned. But that's when the rest of us went to bed."

"You and Laetitia, you mean?"

He shook his head. "The rest of us. Kit had gone up early. It was me and Laetitia, her parents, my father, and Aunt Roz and Uncle Herbert."

"What about Geoffrey?"

"Somewhere," Crispin said. "Maybe he went to bed early, too, or maybe he roamed the house hoping to find a stray female."

"He was out of luck, then. I locked my door, and Constance

was with Francis in the library. Not that Geoffrey would try to seduce Constance, I imagine."

"He'd seduce anything in a skirt," Crispin said, which was rich considering the source.

Before I could say so, Sammy cleared his throat. "Who's this, then?"

"Lord Geoffrey Marsden," I said. "Only son of the Earl of Marsden and his countess. Cousin to the bride-to-be."

"And what was his relationship to the deceased?" By now, he had pulled the standard issue notebook and pencil stub out of his pocket and was actually taking notes. Perhaps he could be taught after all.

"None that we know of," I said. Although if Geoffrey had been roaming the house last night, hoping to come across an unattached female, and Abigail had showed up... well, who knew what might have happened?

Although how would Geoffrey know where to find a croquet mallet? We hadn't played last night, so they weren't easily accessible. As far as I knew—as far as everyone in the family knows—the croquet set is stored in the carriage house.

Then again, Geoffrey had been here a good part of the day yesterday. There was no reason to think he might not have explored the grounds closely enough to figure out where the sports equipment was kept.

Sammy made no inquiries about the croquet mallet, so I didn't say anything about it. He asked a few more very basic questions and then he dismissed us to the house to change. And while he managed to give the impression that my pyjamas were entirely beneath his notice, he also managed to make it seem like I must be the loosest of loose women to be wandering around outside in them accompanied by two young men.

I flushed with irritation but kept my mouth shut. Hopefully, we'd only have to deal with Sammy for an hour or two more, before Tom got here and took over, and then I wouldn't have to see Constable Entwistle again.

So I kept my head high as I stalked up the stairs to the terrasse and across the flagstones to the back door. Once we were inside and out of Sammy's hearing, however, I said, "I suppose we should knock up the others. Cook will be arriving soon, too, I imagine."

"I'll get started on that," Crispin offered, "while you two get changed. While your pyjamas are lovely, Darling, you clearly shocked poor Constable Entwistle down to his toes. I can only imagine how he'd react to Constance's virginal frills or Laetitia's lace and satin."

"I'm sure Lady Laetitia would take it in her stride," I said, since she wasn't the shy and retiring type. "Constance, on the other hand..."

He sighed. "Yes, Darling, I'm aware." He stopped outside the library door. "I'll wake them up, shall I, and then work my way upstairs? Knock up Aunt Roz and Uncle Herbert, then my father? Aunt Roz will want to deal with the Marsdens herself, don't you think?"

"We'll knock on Aunt Roz and Uncle Herbert's door on our way upstairs," I said. "You concentrate on your father and Lady Laetitia. She would undoubtedly rather have you walk into her bedchamber than me or Aunt Roz. Although with everyone else around, I suppose it's just as well if you don't, actually. Best not to give anyone the opportunity to say you've compromised her."

"I'm afraid that ship sailed months ago, Darling."

"Yes, thank you," I said. "There's no need to rub it in, St George."

He opened his mouth and then closed it again. "Go on upstairs. I'll get started on this."

He twisted the knob, and when the door didn't open, he

applied his knuckles to the wood. "Constance? Francis? Open up."

"Come on, Pippa," Christopher said and took my elbow. "Let him deal with it. We'll go get changed."

I let him pull me away from the door and along the passage to the door beside the study and into the front of the house. From there, we climbed the stairs to the first floor, where Christopher lingered to knock up his parents and I headed up the second flight of stairs to the attic level where I got busy changing into proper attire for the day.

By the time I was dressed in a sprigged summer frock of my own—yellow and violet with a dropped waist, cap sleeves, and three ruffles on the skirt—Francis had made his way up to join Christopher, and was asking questions about what had happened. When Christopher mentioned Sammy Entwistle's name, Francis's face contorted in a snarl. "Sodding bastard."

"I take it you've met again since you were children?" I inquired delicately.

He scowled. "You take that right. The tosser threw me in the village jail overnight to sober up a couple of months ago. Gave me a beat-down while he did it, too. Said I had 'resisted arrest' when I woke up the next morning with a black eye and bruises."

"That's not right," Christopher said.

Francis shook his head. "Nought I could do about it, though. It was just the two of us, and I was drunk off my arse. And while I don't remember putting up a fight, I suppose I might have done."

"I can't imagine that you wouldn't," I told him, leaning against the door jamb with my arms crossed over my chest, "if Sammy Entwistle tried to arrest you."

Francis made a face. "You're probably right about that.

Now, do you mind, Pipsqueak? A bit of privacy, if you can? I'd like to change out of these clothes."

"Of course," I said and pushed off from the wall. "I'll go downstairs and see how far Crispin has gotten with his notifications. He might need help."

"You just want to stop him from walking into Lady Laetitia's room," Christopher said.

I sniffed. "And what if I do? His father and her mother are just looking for an excuse to tie him into an engagement. He'd play right into their hands by being caught in there with her in her negligee. And you know he's not going to be able to resist if she reaches for him and coos his name in that voice she uses when she wants to wheedle something."

Francis sniggered. "Go ahead and try to prevent him from ruining himself if you want, Pipsqueak. But I fear you'll be fighting a losing battle."

I feared he was right. But all the same, I intended to try. "I'll see you downstairs," I said, and headed for the stairs. Christopher stayed behind to talk to Francis—or perhaps it just took him longer to get ready than me; men have to wear so many layers.

Downstairs on the landing, I tripped right into Crispin coming out of his father's—aka Francis's regular—room at the front of the house. He shut the door behind him and stopped for a second to let out a breath and pinch the bridge of his nose as if he had a headache.

"Everything all right?" I ventured.

He jumped, as if he truly hadn't noticed me coming. "Oh! Darling. Yes, fine. Talking to my father is always a bit of a strain."

He kept his voice low, presumably so that Uncle Harold wouldn't hear him. Beckwith Place is built quite solidly, if not as solidly as Sutherland Hall, so I didn't think there was much danger of that. I lowered my own in deference anyway. "Surely he didn't take the opportunity to push his marriage agenda while you were telling him about Abigail Dole's death?"

"Oh, didn't he?" He shook his head. "Never mind. He knows what happened; that's the important part."

"Come along downstairs, then." I tucked my hand through his arm. "Let's see what Constable Entwistle's up to."

For a moment he stiffened, and threw a glance at the door to Uncle Harold's room, but then he let me pull him towards the stairs. Above my head, I could hear Christopher's—or perhaps Francis's—footsteps enter the staircase and start down. Elsewhere on the first floor, there was the murmur of voices. Perhaps Aunt Roz talking to the baby or Uncle Herbert updating the Marsdens or Constance and Laetitia conversing behind the closed door of their room.

We landed in the foyer, and I pulled Crispin towards the door to the back of the house.

He resisted. "Where are you taking me?"

"Don't you want to see what Sammy's up to?"

"I expect he's up to his job," Crispin said, twitching his sleeve out of my grasp. "And no, Darling, since you asked, I feel no need to present myself for his consideration any sooner than I have to. You know he'll suspect all of us of having killed her."

"You spent the night with Christopher," I said. "The two of you can provide one another with an alibi. Besides, if you had started to walk around on the landing in the early hours, I'm sure I would have heard you."

He quirked a brow. "Did you hear me come up?"

Well, no. I hadn't, now that he mentioned it. "Were you alone at any point last night?"

He sniggered. "Only the time it took me to climb the stairs from the first story to the attic. After you went upstairs, Kit and I spent some time in the drawing room with the others. He excused himself to go up to bed. I stayed. At the end of it, I walked Laetitia to her door, managed to avoid being pulled inside her room, and came upstairs. By then, Kit was asleep, although I woke him stumbling in."

Stumbling, was it? "Were you drunk, St George?"

"With my father and Laetitia's parents watching my every swallow? Please, Darling. I tried to be considerate by not turning on the hall light, but it made it difficult to see."

Of course it did. "What did you fall over?"

He grimaced. "Kit's shoes. He'd left them in the thorough-fare. I just barely avoided clipping the side of my head on the bedpost."

I sniggered. "How very debonair of you, St George."

He shrugged. "I do better when it's someone I care to impress in the bed."

"Of course you do. Must you keep bragging about it?"

He smirked. "I had no idea my escapades bothered you so much."

"They don't," I said. "I just wish you wouldn't constantly feel the need to remind us all that you go through women the way other men go through socks. It's not an attractive quality, you know."

"Sorry, Darling." There was nothing in his tone or his demeanor to indicate that the apology was sincere.

I was saved from responding by Christopher, who entered the staircase above us at that point, followed by his mother. She had little Bess on her hip and was chattering. "—slept through most of the night, thankfully. Although what we'll do now..." She trailed off and then picked up the conversation with another thought. "We know nothing about this girl save for the fact that she lives somewhere in London, and that's if we can even surmise that. She might have come up from somewhere else the few times you've seen her."

As she stepped off the staircase she looked up and saw us standing there. "There you are. Crispin, dear, help your aunt for a moment."

"Of course, Aunt Roslyn," Crispin said obediently. He's perfectly lovely to practically everyone but me.

Or at least he was until Aunt Roz stepped forward and dropped Bess into his arms. "Hold the baby for a moment. I have to arrange for a bottle."

She disappeared through the door into the back of the house without a backwards look at him. She did, however, tip me a very small wink on her way past.

CHAPTER TWELVE

IN THE FIRST MOMENT, I was afraid Crispin would drop little Bess. I had visions of her hitting the floor and bouncing—and then hitting the floor and not bouncing, which was much worse. The situation—and the astonished expression on his face—would have been rather funny if not for my fear that she'd get hurt. But then he fumbled her into a more secure hold and dragged his eyes from the door where Aunt Roz had vanished to peer down at the baby.

She peered back: wide blue eyes against wide gray, and matching cupid's bow mouths slightly parted in shock at this turn of events.

You might have expected her to be upset at being unceremoniously dumped into the arms of a stranger, but no. She looked fascinated. So, rather remarkably, did Crispin.

Fascinated, but wary. He looked at her rather as if she were a shell that might go off at any moment.

And of course seeing them stare at one another, faces a foot apart, just emphasized the resemblance. I had known it was there, but seeing them together drove it home, and made something churn uncomfortably in my stomach. They looked like father and child. Knowing that that was a possibility was one thing, seeing it with my own eyes was another.

Christopher sniggered. "They make quite the pretty picture, don't they, Pippa?"

Crispin's brows lowered, and he flicked a glance at me before turning a scowl on Christopher. "You've no room to remark, Kit. If you were the one holding her, it'd look very much the same, you know."

"Mum didn't give her to me," Christopher pointed out, smugly. "She gave her to you."

"And I'm holding her, aren't I? I can't help it that she looks like me."

He turned his attention back to the baby, who was bouncing on his arm, trying to get his attention back on herself now that it had wandered. "Yes, I see you. You're lovely, aren't you? Such a pretty girl."

He made cooing noises, and Bess responded by cooing right back. When she reached out and wrapped a chubby fist around his tie, he winced, but didn't do anything to stop her.

I rolled my eyes but took pity on him. "Not the tie, Elizabeth. He'll wrinkle, and then Lady Laetitia will feel compelled to fix it for him, and if she does, I might gag."

I pried the baby's fingers from around it and smoothed it back down myself.

"It's a bit uncanny," Christopher said, in all seriousness now, looking from his cousin to the baby and back. "She really does look enough like you to be yours, Crispin. There's no denying that face."

"Or those eyes or that hair," I added.

"But not *my* eyes nor *my* hair," Crispin pointed out. "Abigail Dole is not my type, and I'm not as unrestrained in my affections as you seem to think I am. If I had bedded her, I would remember. And if this—" he glanced at the baby, "—was mine, I'd own up to it."

Christopher nodded. "Well, she isn't mine, either. I can count on the fingers of one hand the women I've had any kind of relations with, and none of it would have resulted in this."

Crispin nodded back, or would have, had Bess not hooked a finger in his mouth and pulled his bottom lip down. "Owch," he sputtered.

I rolled my eyes but grabbed her chubby little hand again, and pulled her wet fingers away. They let go of Crispin's lip with a pop, and I grimaced. "Handkerchief?"

Christopher held his in front of me.

"Thank you." I wiped my fingers, and Elizabeth's, and then I dabbed at Crispin's lip for good measure. And that, naturally, was when the door opened and Aunt Roz came back into the foyer.

"Dear me," she said, when she saw us, "what happened?"

Crispin flushed but glowered. "I know what you're doing, Aunt Roslyn. And I'll have you know I don't appreciate it."

"Of course not, dear boy." She grinned and reached out. "I'll take her now. There's milk heating on the stove."

She headed for the back of the house, baby in her arms. I tucked Christopher's handkerchief into my pocket—he wasn't likely to want it back after what had happened to it—and followed.

"Aunt Roz? What's going to happen to Bess now?"

Aunt Roz passed into the kitchen and sighed. "I don't know, Pippa. Tell me again what you know about her mother?"

"Me?" I began to busy myself with pouring the now gently steaming milk into a clear glass bottle with the name S. Maw & Sons stamped on it. One of Christopher's baby bottles that had languished at the back of a cabinet for twenty-two years, I assumed. "I know very little. Just her name and the baby's name, plus the items on the list we found. That's all."

Aunt Roz took the bottle and squirted a drop of milk on the inside of her wrist. The temperature must have been acceptable, because she handed it to Bess with a distracted, "Yes, yes. There you are."

The baby grabbed the bottle in both hands and latched on, greedily.

"Christopher wasn't at home when she showed up at the Essex House," I said, watching as little Bess swallowed rhythmically, "so I went downstairs to greet her. It was Wednesday of last week, tea time. I tried to get her to come up to the flat with me but she wouldn't. If she had, I might have been able to find out more."

Aunt Roz nodded, watching the baby suck on the bottle. "And before that?"

"Rogers said that when she came to Sutherland House this spring, she asked for the old Duke's grandson. They showed her Crispin, and he denounced her—"

"There's no need to put it that way, Darling," the scion of the Sutherlands drawled from where he was lounging in the doorway with a shoulder against the jamb. "We're not Victorians, you know."

Aunt Roz fixed him with a stare. "Anything to add, Crispin? Since you're the only other one of us who has actually met her?"

He shook his head. "No, Aunt Roslyn. The occasion wasn't auspicious. It had been a long night, and I wasn't myself."

"Hung over?" I inquired tartly. "Asleep? Still foxed?"

He eyed me. "All three, Darling. And also not alone."

Oh, ouch. "That must have gone over well. Dragged away from one woman only to be confronted with another and a baby that looks just like you."

"She looked less like me back then," Crispin said, with a glance at little Bess. "Just any old baby with blond hair, really. She looks more like a Sutherland now. Although—" he smirked, "I don't have to worry about Violet Cummings trying to drag me to the altar anymore."

"Oh dear," Aunt Roz said, although her eyes were dancing. "You got nothing out of her, I assume?"

He shook his head. "It's like Darling said. She took one look at me and ran. I was in no condition to follow. And it wasn't as if I could ask Rogers to tackle her in the street."

Aunt Roz nodded. "So we know nothing about her other than her name."

"We might have Bess's birth date," Christopher offered, "if the date on the blanket is correct. We—or someone—could check the London parish register. Not today, of course..."

"And," I added, "it seems she might have met this man at the Hammersmith Palais de Danse, probably sometime in April of last year. I assume it must have been a one-time thing, or she would have known more about him."

I glanced at Crispin for his thoughts, since I figured he was the one among all of us with the most experience in such matters.

He made a face, but nodded. "Likely, yes. Some bounder swept her off her feet and then left her to face the consequences on her own afterwards."

"A good thing you'd never do that," I said sarcastically, since I had certainly gotten the impression that he was quite experienced at the hit-and-run.

He fixed me with a look. "I wouldn't, Darling. Not that I haven't swept my share of young women off their feet, but I've made sure there are no consequences. If there had been, I would have dealt with them."

My eyes narrowed. "Dealt with them, how?"

He rolled his own. "Not by killing the messenger, for God's sake. I'm not a murderer. And these circumstances..."

He shook his head, eyes on little Bess who was still sucking lustily on the bottle. "Anyone who kills the mother of a baby just because he can't be bothered to take responsibility for his own actions deserves to hang."

There was a moment's silence, and then—

"It's likely she's a Londoner, then," Aunt Roz said briskly, yanking the conversation back on track with ruthless efficiency. "You didn't notice an accent, I suppose?"

I shook my head. "She spoke perfectly properly, the little bit that she said. She was English. She wasn't posh, but she wasn't a Cockney, either. Just a perfectly average girl with a perfectly average voice."

Crispin nodded. "She was pleasant. Polite. Soft-spoken."

"We'll have to have the police try to track her down, I suppose. Christopher..."

"I called Tom," Christopher said. "He was going to talk to his superiors at Scotland Yard, but I don't think they can simply choose to come and take over the investigation just because we want them to. They have to be invited in, I believe."

"Like vampires," Aunt Roz said brightly.

I arched my brows. "Have you been reading Stoker again, Auntie?"

"Never mind, Pippa, dear." But she grinned. "The engagement party is off, of course. We can't celebrate such a happy occasion while the police is crawling all over the house and the crime scene on the lawn. It wouldn't set the right tone at all. Constance and Francis will have to uninvite all their friends, I suppose. It's a good thing most people are on the telephone these days..."

"I guess we're stuck with the Marsdens for the duration," I

said, "even if it's unlikely that any of them had anything to do with this."

"I'm afraid so, Pippa." Aunt Roz sighed. "I wish we could cite a murder on the grounds and send them on their way, but I'm afraid the police would look askance at that."

Yes, I was afraid so, too. "We'll just have to do the best we can. And speaking of..."

There was the sound of footsteps in the front of the house. We could also hear, or at least I could, the sound of a motorcar outside. "Sounds like someone else is coming, as well."

"Probably the other police," Christopher said with a glance over his shoulder. "It's too soon for Tom, I think."

"Might be Wilkins," Crispin added. "Coming to spend the day in the carriage house just in case my father needs the motorcar for something."

That sounded like a horribly boring way to spend a day. "Perhaps you should go and head him off. Once he sees him, Sammy isn't likely to let him leave again. But there's also no chance that Uncle Harold will be allowed to leave Beckwith Place at any point today, so there's no reason for Wilkins to have to sit here."

"I can't imagine that Constable Entwistle will appreciate my telling anyone what to do," Crispin said, removing himself from the door jamb, "although I suppose someone should give him the news. I doubt Father will think of updating the chauffeur."

No, I didn't think he would, either. To Uncle Harold, Wilkins was the equivalent of furniture. He made the motorcar go, but other than that, he wasn't really a person to the Duke of Sutherland. Which was how Uncle Harold could rationalize having Wilkins sit around all day with nothing to do except wait for a summons that might never come.

But that begged the question of whether Abigail Dole had

been a person to Uncle Harold, or if he had simply seen her as an obstacle to what he wanted for Crispin. And if he had, how easy or hard would it have been to swing that croquet mallet at her head?

Not that there was any reason to think he had, of course, any more than anyone else currently in the house. Just because he could have—just because he'd had a motive and the opportunity, and probably the means, too—didn't mean… well, anything, really. Those things were true for quite a few of us.

"Excuse me," I told Aunt Roz, and headed for the now-empty doorway. "I'll be right back."

She nodded, and turned her attention to her youngest son. "Would you like to hold the baby, Christopher?"

"No," Christopher said as I left the room, a noticeable shudder in his voice. "Not at all, if you don't mind, Mother."

And then I was through the door and into the hallway. Crispin had made his way to the boot room, and as I approached the door, I heard his half-raised voice from inside. "Wilkins! Over here!"

I stepped through the doorway and saw him with his head outside through the crack in the door, and the rest of his body inside the house.

There was the sound of Wilkins's footsteps on the gravel, and then his voice. "My lord?"

"Wilkins," Crispin hissed. "There's been a murder!"

There was a beat of silence. "A murder, my lord?"

"The girl from yesterday," Crispin said, "the one you drove to the infirmary. She's dead."

"Is that so, my lord? How did that happen?"

"We don't know," Crispin said, "do we? Miss Darling saw her through the window this morning." He huffed. "That's not important."

"Indeed, my lord?"

"Of course it's important, Wilkins. Someone's dead! But it's none of our concern, is it? My father isn't going to need the motorcar today—the police won't allow him to go anywhere—so there's no need for you to remain here. Get yourself back to the village before the constable sees you, and decides you have to stay, too."

"Yes, my lord," Wilkins said, and—I assumed—turned on his heel.

And had only walked a couple of steps by the time Sammy Entwistle's voice cut through the silence. "What's all this, then?"

Crispin sighed, and I imagined he rolled his eyes towards the heavens before he straightened and pulled the door open all the way and said, stuffily, "Wilkins is my father's chauffeur. I told him his services won't be needed today and that he could leave."

"Now that's for me to decide," Sammy said, "and not you. I'm in charge here. Isn't that right, my lord?"

His tone twisted the last two words from an honorific into an insult. I ducked under Crispin's arm and opened the door wider so I could look out.

He bit back an oath, even as he gave Sammy a look that ought to have curdled his blood. I could almost feel the hairs on the top of my head sizzle. "Of course," he said, "Constable."

"But Wilkins wasn't even here when it happened," I protested. "He stayed in the village last night."

Sammy looked at me, and his brows rose. "Is that so, miss? But he had the motorcar, didn't he? And even if he hadn't, the village is in walking distance. Someone could easily walk from there to here."

Of course someone could have. That must have been how Abigail had made it here, after all.

She must have woken up in the middle of the night and

realized that she was alone. Perhaps the doctor or infirmary nurse had told her that the baby had remained behind at Beckwith Place.

Then again, perhaps not. If that had been the case, surely they would have talked her into staying in the infirmary until morning. Or if she had refused, at least they would have found someone to drive her up to Beckwith Place. Surely they wouldn't have simply let her walk off in the middle of the night on her own, in a strange place full of strangers.

No, it was far more likely that my initial thought had been correct: Abigail had woken up on her own and remembered that Beckwith Place was the last place she'd seen Bess. And then she had sneaked out of the infirmary and set out on foot to find her child.

While all this had been going through my mind, Sammy Entwistle had been addressing Wilkins. "—have to have a parley about what you know."

Wilkins shied like a spooked horse. "Know? I don't know anything. Why would you think I know something?"

Crispin rolled his eyes and slammed the door shut. "That was a waste of time."

"You couldn't know that Sammy would hear you and interrupt," I said, taking a step back. "You were trying to help."

His eyebrow rose. "Assigning me noble motives, Darling? Perhaps I just wanted to know what he knew."

"Why would he know anything? He's the chauffeur!"

And I was clearly no better than Uncle Harold. Furniture, indeed.

Crispin's lip twitched. "My, my, Darling. How very unenlightened of you."

"Oh, sod off, St George." I plunged out of the boot room and into the hallway, only to fetch up in front of Uncle Harold, who gave me and then his son a narrow look. "St George?"

"Good morning, Father," Crispin said politely. "I was trying to head off Wilkins, but the constable overheard, and now I'm afraid he's stuck here with the rest of us."

Uncle Harold gave him a look down the length of his nose. "Is there a reason he shouldn't be—" his tone made quotes around the words, "stuck here with the rest of us?"

"As Darling just reminded me," Crispin flicked me a look, "he's the chauffeur."

I wrinkled my nose, and he sniggered before telling his father, "We thought we'd spare him the ordeal of sitting here all day when there's no chance that the police will let you leave."

Uncle Harold's brows rose while his voice lowered. "And what do you mean by that, boy?"

"Nothing." Crispin sighed. "Absolutely nothing."

"What St George meant," I said, with a flicker of a look at him, "is that they aren't likely to let any of us leave. Not while they're investigating the murder. We simply thought there was no need to have Wilkins spend his day in the carriage house when he wouldn't be needed."

"Where else would he spend his time?" Uncle Harold wanted to know. He sounded sincerely baffled, as if he couldn't conceive of Wilkins possibly wanting to spend the day anywhere but Aunt Roz's and Uncle Herbert's carriage house.

"The village?" I suggested, in exactly the same baffled tone, as if I couldn't understand why he didn't understand something so obvious. Before I dropped the tone—I was being rude, after all, and fully aware of it—and added, "It's moot at this point, anyway. Sammy caught him, and now he's stuck."

Uncle Harold eyed me for a moment in silence before he moved past me towards the kitchen. "Come along, Crispin."

He didn't quite snap his fingers, but I got the impression he would have liked to.

"Yes, Father." Crispin slipped through the doorway and past me with a murmured, "Pardon me, Darling."

I turned to watch him go. "Head all right, St George?"

He glanced at me over his shoulder. "Yes, Darling. Should I be worried that you keep asking?"

"I don't see why," I said and flapped a hand at him. "As you were, St George."

He nodded and ducked into the kitchen after his father, who had started talking to Aunt Roz. "—cannot conceive of why, Roslyn—"

I rolled my eyes and went in the other direction, back to the boot room door. After putting my ear to the crack, I could hear the continuation of the conversation outside.

"—nothing!" Wilkins's voice said belligerently. "I spent the night in the village, didn't I? Had a pint or two in the pub and went up to my room."

Sammy's voice said something, too softly for me to catch, and I eased the door open a centimeter, the better to hear.

"Full house up here," was Wilkins's answer. "Between His Grace and his young lordship coming from Sutherland Hall, and all the Marsdens visiting from down in Dorset, and Master Christopher and his bird down from London, Lord and Lady Herbert's got a houseful, don't they?"

I rolled my eyes. Not that it wasn't all true, of course, but did Wilkins really imagine that I was involved with Christopher? His 'bird'? How deplorably low class.

"—girl?" Sammy asked. "Had you seen her before?"

"I haven't seen her now," Wilkins pointed out.

"She was here yesterday, the others said. Swooned on the lawn and was taken to the infirmary in the village."

"I don't know nothing about that," Wilkins said.

"So you hadn't seen her before?"

"Before...?"

"Before she ended up dead on the lawn," Sammy said, with rather strained patience.

Wilkins sounded reluctant, and it was hard to blame him. Nobody likes to admit to having seen dead people before they were dead. "I saw her yesterday. Drove her and the doctor back to the village after his lordship ran down in the H6 and fetched the doctor in the first place."

"Why didn't his lordship drive them back?"

"Got pulled into orbit by the other bird," Wilkins said, and I smirked at the description of the very elegant, highly-born Lady Laetitia Marsden.

Until Sammy asked, "The one that was here with him a minute ago?"

"That's Miss Darling," Wilkins said dismissively. "His Grace would never allow that."

"She's Lady Roslyn's ward, ain't she? Her niece or something? What's wrong with that?"

"German," Wilkins said grimly.

"Oho."

Neither of them said anything else for a few moments. Remembering the war, no doubt. They must have both taken part, given their ages.

I grimaced. It's never pleasant to come face to face—or ear to crack in door—with the prejudice. I know it's there, but most of the time I'm able to forget about it. Until something like this happens, or until someone like Euphemia Marsden expresses what a pity it is that my mother chose to leave England for Germany and my father, and then it all comes back.

Sammy cleared his throat. "What can you tell me about the dead woman?"

"Nothing," Wilkins said. "I don't know her, do I?"

"Don't you?"

"'Course I don't. She's here looking for one of the Astleys, ain't she?"

"Was she?"

I wondered whether Wilkins flinched at the change of tense. I did, a little.

"That's what I heard," Wilkins said.

"Which Astley was she looking for?"

"We don't know," Wilkins said, "do we? With the way that baby looks, it could be any of 'em."

"Baby?" I could practically hear Sammy's ears prick up.

"Had a babe with her yesterday afternoon," Wilkins said, while I tried to figure out whether we'd truly forgotten to mention little Bess, or whether Sammy was just playing stupid to get Wilkins to talk. "Blond hair. Looks like the Sutherlands."

"Is that so?" Things went silent. When Sammy spoke again, there was a faint note of jubilation in his voice. "One of them got her up the duff, then?"

"Must have."

"But you don't know which?"

I assumed Wilkins must have shaken his head, because the next thing he said was, "Could have been any of them."

"Francis Astley?"

"Like as not," Wilkins said. "No way to know."

There was a moment's silence. Then—

"Thank you, Mr. Wilkins," Sammy told the chauffeur. He tried to be professional about it, but I could tell that for him, Christmas had come early. He probably thought all his wishes were about to come true. "Don't go anywhere."

Wilkins muttered something. I eased the door shut before they could see me eavesdropping and vanished back into the hallway.

CHAPTER THIRTEEN

IN THE KITCHEN, it was business as usual. Aunt Roz was still feeding the baby, while Uncle Harold was looking on, scowling. Every so often, he'd glance from Bess to his son, as if he were comparing them, and his scowl would deepen. Occasionally, he'd look from Bess to Christopher or Francis instead, and then his face would relax a little.

Francis had made it to the kitchen while I'd been tucked away in the boot room, and was leaning on the wall next to Christopher. Constance had not, and I guessed she was upstairs in her room with Laetitia, still getting ready for the day. None of the other Marsdens were anywhere to be seen. Too good to sit in the kitchen with the rest of us, I assumed. Uncle Herbert might be keeping them company, because he wasn't in attendance, either. Crispin was propping up the wall on the other side of Francis, and seeing the three of them in a row, all with their fair hair and light eyes and Sutherland features, brought home, yet again, just how much alike they all look. Christopher and Crispin, especially, could be brothers—twins—instead of cousins.

I averted my eyes and headed across the room. "Shall I turn on the kettle? I could use a cup of tea. Or coffee."

"Or something stronger," Francis muttered.

I busied myself with water and the hob. "I know we've indulged rather early in the day before, but surely drinking before eight is pushing it a bit far."

"I was considering it more as an extension of last night, Pipsqueak."

"Hair of the dog?" Crispin inquired, and Francis shot him a look.

"Not like you've never done it, is it?"

Crispin shook his head. "No, indeed."

"If you want a splash of something in your tea or coffee," Aunt Roz told him, "go ahead and fetch it, Francis. I wouldn't mind a drop of something myself. It isn't every day we wake up to a dead body on the lawn."

Francis pushed off from the wall and departed in search of alcohol.

"What's going to happen now?" Uncle Harold wanted to know.

"I imagine Constable Flatfoot will blunder about the croquet lawn until he has destroyed any evidence that might have been there," his son answered acerbically, "and eventually the chaps from Scotland Yard will show up and take over."

Uncle Harold eyed him severely for a moment. "St George..." he began, clearly with the intention of going on.

Crispin shook his head. "I've already told you, Father. Not my circus, not my monkey."

Aunt Roz looked pained. "Crispin, dear..."

Crispin turned to her. "It's a proverb, Aunt Roslyn. Some sort of Eastern European thing. I learned it from a Russian girl." He smirked—I rolled my eyes, which made him smirk harder—before he added, "There's no offense intended against the baby."

Aunt Roz sighed. "Of course not. That would be silly, wouldn't it, seeing as she looks exactly like your baby pictures?"

Uncle Harold bristled. "Now listen here, Roslyn—"

Aunt Roz waved him off. "Never mind, Harold. She looks exactly like Christopher's baby pictures, too, and quite a lot like Francis's. I don't suspect Crispin of being responsible for this any more than I suspect my own children."

"When you say 'this'..." I got busy pulling cups and saucers from one of the cupboards and lining them up on the counter next to the stove, "you're referring to Bess, I assume, and not the murder?"

"Of course, Pippa." Aunt Roz gave me a look that might almost have been a glare. "No one here would bash that poor girl over the head and leave her on the lawn."

She glanced around the kitchen once before repeating it. Firmly. "No one."

The impression I got—that we all got, I'm sure—was that no one had better confess to such a thing, because my aunt would simply not have it.

"Then who did?" I wanted to know as I lifted the kettle off the hob. "Who wants tea?"

Everyone did, it seemed. By the time I had finished fiddling with the leaves and water and had poured the result into cups, Francis was back with the liquor, and we seated ourselves around the table with cups and saucers, tea, milk, sugar, and brandy.

"I don't know who did, Pippa," Aunt Roz went back to the question I had asked. "I can't imagine anyone in the family doing something like that. I know I didn't raise my boys to kill."

Of course not. Although at least in Francis's case, the war had intervened. Francis had surely killed before.

And I think he must have been thinking it, too, because he put his cup into the saucer with a noticeable *click*. "I spent the night in the library with Constance. She would have heard it if I left."

"Of course, Francis, dear," his mother said.

"Judging from the condition you were in last night," I added, "you wouldn't have been able to make your way back to the lawn, let alone see straight enough to hit anyone's head."

Francis squinted at me. "Not sure I appreciate that assessment, Pipsqueak."

"Don't worry about it," I told him, with a pat of his hand. "It couldn't have been you. You were out cold, too drunk to aim, and spent the night with someone. If anyone's alibied, it's you."

He looked only partly mollified by that. "I'd really rather be thought innocent because you know I would never do something like this."

"Of course we all know that, Francis," Christopher said. "But a solid alibi will be a lot more helpful in the long run. Be glad for it."

Crispin nodded. "Kit and I are covered. I was with the party in the drawing room until we all went to bed, and after that, we slept in the same room."

"I went up before you," Christopher reminded him. "There was an hour or so when Pippa was asleep and Constance and Francis were in the library and the rest of you were in the drawing room. I could have killed her then."

There was a moment's pause. Then—

"Don't be ridiculous, Christopher," I said, at the same time as Crispin exclaimed, "For God's sake, Kit, are you trying to get arrested?"

"Of course not. I didn't do it. I'm just saying I could have. *You* have an alibi for the whole night. I don't."

"You had no reason to want her dead, though," I pointed out. "Of everyone here, it's least likely that the baby is yours."

Uncle Harold huffed and looked like he wanted to say something, but Christopher merely shrugged. "That's easy for you to say, Pippa. You know me. The police doesn't."

"Tom does."

"Tom's not in charge," Christopher said. "Sammy Entwistle is."

"Of anyone, Sammy Entwistle is going to try to pin this on Francis." I shot the latter a look. "Sorry, Francis, but you know as well as I do—"

Francis nodded. "No love lost between me and Sammy Entwistle."

"Which is why it's very good that you have a solid alibi. Less good that Christopher doesn't have one."

"I'll lie," Crispin said. "I can say we went upstairs together."

I shook my head. "If it were just us, that might work. But there are too many other people here who can dispute it."

And I wouldn't trust the Marsdens not to spill the beans. Laetitia would certainly prefer to see Christopher hang for murder rather than Crispin, and so, I'm sure, would her mother.

I added, "It'll be easier if we just say that he and I went upstairs together at the beginning of the evening, and spent the night in the same room. That's what we were supposed to do, anyway, before Francis ended up in the library."

Crispin looked like he didn't think much of this idea, but it was Christopher who shook his head. "That leaves Crispin without an alibi, and he's at least as likely to be guilty as Francis..."

"Thanks a lot, Kit."

Christopher shot him a look. "You know what I mean. You

say you didn't do it, and I trust you. But that's somebody's child—" he glanced at little Bess, "—and somebody picked up that croquet mallet and killed her mother. I know it wasn't me. I don't think it was Pippa. I don't see how it can have been you or Francis. But I'm not going to lie to cover my own back, especially if it leaves someone else without an alibi. They can't prove I had anything to do with it, because I didn't."

"Fine." I rolled my eyes. "We'll all tell the truth. Francis was in the library with Constance, you two were together, I was by myself. Happy now?"

"Ecstatic," Crispin said dryly. "How do you plan to prove that you didn't kill her, Darling? You have no alibi at all, do you?"

I didn't. But I also didn't need one. "Don't be ridiculous, St George. What reason would I have to kill her?"

"None," Christopher said.

Crispin shot him a look. "You know that, and I know that. But does Sammy Entwistle know that?"

"Sammy Entwistle knows sod all," Francis grumbled.

Aunt Roz shook her head, but fondly, and Crispin continued. "Sammy Entwistle is going to look at this baby, and come to the same conclusion we've all come to. One of us is responsible for getting this girl with child. He's going to say that one of us killed her. If we've all got alibis, he's going to look further afield, to the other people who may have had a reason to want her out of the way. That means Constance—"

"Constance would never," I interrupted.

"Constance was with Francis," Christopher added.

Crispin glanced at him. "In that scenario, Francis is the one with the alibi, not Constance. She would have noticed him sneaking out. He was too drunk to notice anything at all."

"Listen..." Francis growled, and Crispin rolled his eyes.

"I'm not saying *I* believe it, Francis. I'm saying it's what Entwistle will say."

When none of us objected, he went on, holding up another finger. "It means Philippa, because I'm sure he knows that she'd commit murder for Kit."

He probably did. Sammy Entwistle, I mean. He'd seen enough of both of us growing up to assume that.

"It means Laetitia," I shot back, "for the same reason it means Constance."

"Not quite the same reason, Darling. I'm not engaged to Laetitia, am I?"

"You might as well be," I told him, "considering how possessive she is of you. And she has no alibi, either. She slept in a room by herself. One with a view of the lawn. She might have seen Abigail arrive, and decided to go downstairs and deal with her. I saw her expression yesterday, when she saw the baby. Do you really suppose she wouldn't kill to keep you?"

"Now, listen here, Miss Darling..." Uncle Harold began, and Crispin shot him a look. So did Aunt Roz, who must have assumed that I was likely to start accusing both Uncle Harold and the other Marsdens next.

"Well," she said brightly, "this has all been quite illuminating, hasn't it? But I think perhaps it's time you and I join the others now, Harold, and let the children be."

I huffed, but quietly, so she wouldn't notice. "Shall I clean up the kitchen, Aunt Roz?"

"Yes, thank you, Pippa." She balanced little Bess against her shoulder and began patting her back. "Rinse the bottle so it's clean for next time, too, if you please. Hopefully Cook will get here soon, so we can get some food on the table."

"I can begin on breakfast," I offered, "if you'd like."

"No, no, Pippa." She looked faintly alarmed. "Leave it for Cook, dear."

She swept Uncle Harold out the door ahead of herself, and herded him down the hallway towards the front of the house.

Crispin sniggered as I began to gather the teacups. "Was that a reaction to your cooking, Darling? Afraid you'll poison us all if you attempt to make breakfast?"

"At least I'm able to feed myself," I shot back. "Christopher and I don't have live-in help, you know."

Unlike him, who had the entire staff at the Hall, or at Sutherland House, available to him when he was in residence.

"You live in a service flat, don't you?"

"We have a kitchen," I said. "For God's sake, St George, we're not incompetent."

He smirked. "Truly, Darling? You know how to cook?"

"I can cook enough that Christopher and I won't starve. I could manage breakfast right now, although I'm sure Lady Euphemia wouldn't be likely to appreciate my efforts. Nor would your father, I'm sure." Or Lady Laetitia, for that matter. "Mostly, we end up boiling eggs and eating sandwiches and the like. But whoever I marry, assuming he'll be someone without a staff, won't starve. I'm sure that's more than you can say, St George."

"Luckily, I'll never have to worry about it," Crispin said languidly. "Are we done here, then?"

He glanced at the door.

"If you can't wait to see Laetitia," I told him, turning toward the sink with the cups and saucers, "I certainly won't keep you. Goodbye, St George."

I waved him off. He scowled, but went. Francis, who had been watching the two of us like a spectator at a tennis match, chuckled. "You know, Pippa—"

"Yes, Francis. But all the same, we do have to figure this out, you know. Sammy—Constable Entwistle—is going to want to pin this murder on somebody. If we can't figure out who actually did it, I'm afraid he'll choose you."

"Of course he'll choose me," Francis said, and got to his feet. "I'm the most likely suspect, and not just because he has a bone to pick with me. She'd already visited Sutherland House and your flat in London, hadn't she? So she looked at both Crispin and Kit and decided they weren't who she was looking for. That leaves me. With a history of drinking too much, and doping myself to the gills, and doing stupid things I can't remember the next day—all of which Sammy Entwistle is well aware of. And with a brand new fiancée I'm presumably willing to do anything to keep. Even murder."

When he put it like that, it sounded unpleasantly possible. "We know you'd never—"

"Of course *you* know that, Pippa. And you saw me last night, and you know I wouldn't have woken up for anything but a crack of lightning that hit the roof. But Sammy's going to say that I was pretending, and that I fooled you, and Constance, and that I was able to sneak out when she didn't notice and kill that poor girl, and there's going to be no way of proving that I didn't!"

His voice had risen until he came to the last word, and after he had finished speaking, the silence rang. I swallowed a nervous hiccough.

"We won't let that happen," Christopher said. "I promise, Francis. Tom's on his way. He knows you wouldn't. And I don't care what we have to do. I'll kill Entwistle myself if I have to, before I let him arrest you for this murder."

Francis choked back a laugh, although it was a wet one. "Don't even say that, Kit." He put his hand on Christopher's shoulder for a moment. "You have no idea what that's like, and I don't want you to ever know. But I didn't do it, and hopefully Tom will be able to prove it. If it's up to him, that is."

"If it isn't," I said, as I put my own arm around Francis's waist, "I'll prove it myself. We will not allow anyone to arrest you for a crime you didn't commit."

"Thank you, Pippa." He leaned into me for a second before he straightened again. And cleared his throat before telling us, "We should go find the others. Cook will be here soon, and won't want us in her domain, and I should find Constance."

"I'll just peek out the back," I said as we entered the hallway and the others turned towards the front of the house. "Just to see if anything more has happened."

Christopher hesitated, and I added, "It's only going to take a minute. I just want to see whether Sammy's back on the lawn and if he has rung for reinforcements. He can't investigate everything by himself, I imagine. I mean, we're in here, and she's out there, and there are rather a lot of us..."

"If he's rung anyone, he hasn't done it from in here," Christopher said, but he followed Francis down the hallway. "Don't dilly-dally, Pippa," he told me over his shoulder.

"Of course not." I didn't wait for him to disappear through the door above the cellar steps, just turned in the other direction and headed for the terrasse. A few seconds later, I had closed the back door behind me and was on my way across the flagstones, as quietly as I could manage.

There turned out to be no need to sneak around, however. The lawn was perfectly empty except for the dead body still sprawled there, with the croquet mallet nearby. Sammy was nowhere to be seen. He was either still speaking to Wilkins by the boot room door, or he had gotten back on his bicycle and gone down to the village to request help from the rest of the constabulary.

If he had done anything at all to protect the crime scene, it wasn't immediately evident to me. I could have walked up to the body and touched it, had I wanted to.

Of course I didn't. Want to, or do it. I had already seen poor Abigail up close; I had no need to examine her again. I certainly didn't want to touch her. Watching Crispin do so had been more than enough for me.

I did think Sammy ought to have covered her with something, though, now that he had seen her. It seemed polite, as well as a prudent way to protect the crime scene as much as possible.

Although I didn't know what there was to protect, to be honest. The croquet lawn was... well, it was a lawn. It wasn't likely that the killer would have left footprints. It hadn't rained recently, and the grass was thick.

I put my back to the balustrade—and the body—and surveyed the terrasse. This was where we'd sat yesterday, when Abigail had staggered out from the bushes and collapsed on the lawn. Crispin on the far right now, with Uncle Harold, Laetitia, and her mother. Christopher and I, Constance and Francis, at the table in the middle, and Aunt Roz and Uncle Herbert with the Earl and Lord Geoffrey on my left.

But what good did it do to think about any of that? Nothing had happened then. She had collapsed, and some of us had run for her while others had stayed in their seats. I supposed those reactions, or lack thereof, might have said something about our individual attitudes towards those less fortunate than us, but I couldn't see what it might have to do with the murder, since at that point, more than half the assembly hadn't even known who Abigail Dole was.

Something moved, just at the upper edge of my vision, and I glanced up, at the soft, faded brick of the old Georgian house. It was glowing a lovely pinkish peach, a result of the sun just creeping above the trees to the east.

Up on the third floor, in the room where I had spent the night, a shadow stepped back from the six-over-six paned windows. I squinted against the reflection of the sun to see if I could make out who it was, but by now, the window was empty.

Aunt Roz, maybe, tidying up. Or Christopher, whose room it was supposed to have been originally. His weekender bag with his spare clothes had still been on his unused bed when I ran out of there this morning.

Or someone else, wanting a private look at the crime scene, from a vantage point where they weren't likely to be seen?

I contemplated the empty window, blank now but for the mullions crisscrossing it, for another moment before I headed back across the flagstones to the terrasse door.

CHAPTER FOURTEEN

EVERYONE WAS in the sitting room by the time I made my way there. Laetitia looked quite comfortable cozied up to Crispin, not quite on his lap, but as close as she could get without being there. Constance was perched next to Francis on one of the Chesterfields, hand between both of his. Christopher was next to them. Aunt Roz stood by the window, swaying back and forth, still holding the baby, while Uncle Herbert watched from one of the armchairs. His expression was half concerned, half indulgent. If little Bess turned out to be their grandchild—or even if she didn't—it looked as if they were quite ready to shower her with attention. Uncle Herbert was probably concerned that Aunt Roz was getting attached, actually.

Uncle Harold kept a keen eye on Laetitia and Crispin, and so did Lady Euphemia. Although when I walked in, she gave me a cold up-and-down look before turning her attention back onto her daughter. It wasn't quite blatant enough for me to justify being rude, so I ignored it and headed for Christopher. "Budge up, please."

He scooted closer to Constance, and I fitted myself on the edge of the sofa next to him. "Quiet crowd."

Quiet enough that I couldn't ask him who might have just arrived in the sitting room from upstairs, not without having everyone present hear me.

He nodded. "Anything going on outside?"

"Not that I could see. The body hasn't been covered, and Sammy was nowhere to be seen. When I checked outside the boot room, both he and Wilkins were gone from the driveway. I think perhaps he headed back to the village for reinforcements."

Or perhaps Sammy had been the one upstairs in my room. Looking for... evidence?

"He left," Christopher reiterated, "and left the body on the lawn?"

I shrugged. "Hard to say what else he could have done with it, to be fair. He can't move it until it's been photographed and examined *in situ*, and for that, I assume he needs the medical examiner. Would that be Doctor White, do you suppose?"

"I think so, Pippa," Aunt Roz said from over by the window. "Did Wilkins drive Constable Entwistle to the village?"

He might have done, now that she asked. I had assumed Wilkins had merely vanished into the carriage house to await His Grace's pleasure, but it was possible that Sammy had commandeered the Crossley and Wilkins's services instead of setting off on his bicycle. It would make sense, if he planned to bring people back with him.

I wouldn't mind at all if they came back with the doctor, actually. I had a few questions for Gerald White. Including why no one had noticed Abigail walk off in the middle of the night, and also whether she had woken up at any point yesterday, and had perhaps said something to someone about what she was—or had been—doing here at Beckwith Place. Something more specific than what we already knew, or thought we did.

"This is intolerable," Lady Euphemia said, with another look at me, as if it were my fault. "Isn't there something that can be done?"

"Done about what?" was the obvious answer, and I thought about giving it. Aunt Roz got in first.

"I'm afraid not, Euphemia, dear. When poor Grimsby was shot in the Sutherland Hall garden maze in April, all we could do was wait for the police to finish their job and let us go home. I'm afraid it'll be the same now."

"We'll have to figure out what to do with the baby," Francis said, and sounded as if the words were dragged out of him by force. "If the girl... if her mother isn't here to take care of her, what do we do? We can't simply keep her."

He glanced at little Bess, snuggled up on his mother's shoulder with her thumb in her mouth, and quickly away.

"Of course not," Aunt Roz said, rubbing the baby's back. "Not unless someone in the family wants to claim her. I assume none of you has changed his mind since yesterday?"

She waited. No one had, of course, and it was hard to blame them for that. If it had been difficult to claim responsibility for little Bess before the murder, it was doubly hard now.

"We can put Tom on figuring out who she belongs to," I said, "once he gets here. I'm sure there are records somewhere in London. Abigail may have had other relatives. Parents, or a sibling. A flat-mate, even. Someone who can be notified about her death. And there's the baby's father, unless he's the one who killed her. If he did, giving him the baby wouldn't be a very healthy thing to do, I suppose..."

There was a beat of silence. Crispin, of course, was the first one to break it. "Which one of us are you accusing, Darling? Kit, Francis, or me?"

I met his eyes. The gray was darker today, and troubled, like storm clouds. "None of you, St George. You've all told me it wasn't you, and I trust you. All of you."

"Who else is there, though?" Constance wanted to know, with a shrill hint of hysteria in her voice. She was clutching Francis's hand with both of hers now, instead of him keeping her hand enfolded in both of his. "I mean... just look at that baby. That can't be a coincidence!"

We all stared at the baby. She blinked back at us with those big blue Astley eyes, under that fuzzy mop of fair Sutherland hair.

"A lot of babies have fair hair and blue eyes," Maurice said. "Why, even Geoffrey when he was little—"

His wife and son both sent him matching looks of fury, and he snapped his mouth shut.

"All I know is that she isn't mine," Francis said into the silence that followed. "And I certainly didn't kill her mother. We were together all night, Connie. You know that."

Constance nodded. "I know, Francis. But someone did. And I imagine it must have been one of us."

There was a beat of silence. Then—

"Well, I never!" Laetitia said, at the same time as her mother exclaimed, "Really, Constance!"

"Sorry, Aunt Effie. But what are the chances that someone random came onto the grounds and murdered her? She wasn't a local. Nobody here knew her."

She glanced around the room. No one spoke up.

"If she had been from here," Constance continued, "Pippa would have recognized her when she saw her in London last week, and so would Doctor White, surely. And Lady Roslyn and Lord Herbert, not to mention Francis..."

"She wasn't local," Christopher interrupted. "You can forget that idea. None of us have ever seen her before."

Francis nodded. So did Aunt Roz and Uncle Herbert.

"Well," Constance said, "then what are the chances...?"

"She might have gotten a lift from the village," I suggested, "late in the night or early this morning, and something happened."

"The croquet mallet, though, Darling," Crispin said. "Who outside the family would have known where to find that?"

Not many people, for certain. He did, obviously. He wasn't a resident of Beckwith Place, but he had spent enough time here to know where the croquet sets were kept. Uncle Harold might have known, too. Everyone in the family probably did. Constance would have figured it out by now for certain.

But it also wasn't impossible that one of the others had wandered into the carriage house sometime between their arrival yesterday afternoon, and Abigail's arrival in the middle of the night.

Lady Laetitia had been glued to Crispin's side every time I had seen either of them yesterday, but before Christopher and I arrived, she might have done a recce of the grounds, including the carriage house. I couldn't picture either the Earl of Marsden or his wife clambering around our carriage house— why would they?—but again, they could have, had they chosen to. And the same was true of Geoffrey. I had no idea why any of them, save for Laetitia, would have wanted Abigail dead, but any and all of them might have known where the croquet mallets were kept.

Crispin had even mentioned that Geoffrey had not been with the others in the drawing room last night, hadn't he? Geoffrey might have decided to motor into the village last evening. He'd had access to several of the motorcars, his parents' Daimler or Constance's Crossley, at least. He slept alone, so no one would have noticed him being gone. And Geoffrey was definitely the type to pick up a lone female begging a lift up to Beckwith Place.

Abigail had been out of her element here in the countryside. The walk from the village to Beckwith Place was a distance in the dark, especially for someone not familiar with the shortcut through the fields. The dark and silence of the country can be quite disturbing when you're used to the hustle and bustle of Town, too. So yes, if a nice-looking gentleman in a nice car—and Geoffrey Marsden was decidedly nice-looking, for all that I can't stand him—if he had offered Abigail a lift, she might have taken it.

And if he had done, he was also the type who would have expected something in return. And when Abigail refused—which surely she must have done, considering what the consequences had been the last time she had let some smooth-talking, good-looking bloke wheedle his way into her unmentionables...

"Excuse me." I got to my feet, abruptly. Crispin blinked. He had been watching me, perhaps waiting for me to answer the question he hadn't quite managed to get out earlier, the one that had started me down this path of conjecture. I avoided his eyes and turned to my right instead. "Christopher?"

"Of course." He rose politely.

"Don't do anything stupid," Aunt Roz said.

"Of course not. When do we ever?" He grinned as Aunt Roz rolled her eyes, and put his hand on my back to guide me out of the room. "Come on, Pippa. Let's go."

We ducked out of the sitting room and towards the front door. Behind us, I could hear Lady Euphemia clear her throat. "Roslyn, my dear..."

"What are we doing?" Christopher wanted to know, heading for the front door.

I glanced up at him. "Checking the motorcars. It occurred to me—"

He changed direction. "We'll need gloves, then. Don't want to leave any evidence of our own."

No, indeed. I let him pull the door open to the back of the house, and then followed him into the boot room, where he rummaged around until he found a pair of driving gloves for himself and a pair of Aunt Roz's gardening gloves for me. They looked ridiculous with my outfit, all ratty and stained with dirt, but at least they would keep me from getting my fingerprints all over everything.

"We'd better hurry," Christopher added, pulling the door to the driveway open. "We don't know how long we have until Sammy comes back with reinforcements. Would you tell me why you decided this was necessary?"

"It was what St George said about the croquet mallet, and from there a detour into how Abigail might have arrived at Beckwith Place last night."

"She walked, don't you think?"

He nodded me towards the row of cars parked along the driveway.

"It occurred to me," I said as we took off in that direction, "that she might not have. That perhaps Geoffrey went to the village—St George said he wasn't in the drawing room last night—and that he might have come upon her walking back here, and offered her a lift. And then one thing led to another."

"Say no more." Christopher headed for the sleek green Daimler and the burgundy Crossley. "He would have taken one of these two, don't you think?"

Rather than the Duke's Crossley—which wasn't here, I noted—or Crispin's Hispano-Suiza? Almost certainly.

"What are we looking for?" Christopher pulled open the Daimler's door and bent over the leather upholstery.

"I have no idea," I said. "Hair? Makeup smears? She left her tote in the garden before she fainted, so I don't suppose it's likely we'll find a reticule or anything of that nature. And I don't think she was wearing jewelry, was she? A dropped earring would come in uncommonly handy..."

Christopher sniggered. "Chance would be a fine thing. But I don't think we'll be that lucky, Pippa. And she was wearing both her shoes, too."

I nodded. "I doubt we'll find anything at all, to be honest. But I couldn't sit there any longer. The desperation was choking me. Constance is scared out of her mind about what might happen to Francis, and the way Laetitia was petting St George..."

"Was she petting him?"

"Playing with his hair," I said. "Stroking the back of his neck. Dipping her fingertips under his collar. It was indecent."

He looked at me. "You know, Pippa..."

"Fine," I said. "It wasn't indecent. We've both seen her do worse. But it was inappropriate for eight o'clock in the morning in your mother's and father's sitting room. Not to mention the other circumstances that make it in poor taste."

The dead body on the lawn, the police investigation, and the now-motherless baby that might be Crispin's.

Christopher shot me a look. "Are you quite certain you aren't just jealous, Pippa?"

I gave him one back, a longer and more narrow one. "Why on earth would I be jealous, Christopher? I can barely stand St George. I have no desire to touch him. And I certainly wouldn't want to run my fingers through his hair. It's full of brilliantine, isn't it?"

Really, it would take real indulgence for any woman to run her fingers through any man's hair these days, sticky as it's likely to be.

Christopher laughed. "You have to admit that for someone who swears up and down that she dislikes the man, you're rather opinionated when it comes to other women liking him."

"I don't mind women liking him," I said. Or sniffed, rather. "But her parents were sitting right there, Christopher. So was his father. So were the rest of us. Why on earth can't she keep her hands to herself when we're all forced to watch?"

"I imagine her staking her claim works better when we're all there to see it," Christopher said and closed the door to the Daimler's driver's side. "I don't see anything inside."

I nodded and followed suit. "I don't, either. It's more likely that Geoffrey would have used Constance's Crossley anyway. He drove it up here, didn't he? And his father might have had something to say about it if he took the Daimler to the village pub."

We headed for the burgundy saloon car.

"Anyway," I continued, picking up the thread of the conversation where we had dropped it, "I just don't see why her mother and father put up with it. Aunt Roz wouldn't put up with me brazenly petting a young man in polite company. I don't think she would let Constance behave that way towards Francis, either, and they're engaged. It's simply not proper."

"There's a reason for that," Christopher answered as he pulled open the door to the Crossley. "The Countess has her eye on the Sutherland title. I'm sure she'll put up with her daughter's behavior for as long as she has to, in the hopes that it will turn into an engagement."

I ran my eyes over the leather seat of the Crossley, burgundy to match the exterior paint. "Do you think it will?"

"I think," Christopher said precisely, "that the longer he lets it go on without saying anything about it, and the longer the rest of us do the same, the more likely it is that he'll have to come up to snuff at some point."

"Should we say something, then?"

"He's capable of saying no himself if he wants it to stop, Pippa. If he doesn't, he mustn't mind."

"Hard to believe," I said. "It would be different if he cared for her. Then he'd presumably enjoy the public petting. But he isn't in love with her. So what does he get out of it?"

"I imagine it must feel pleasant," Christopher said without looking at me, "and of course there's the fact that he can flaunt it in everyone's face."

"So he simply enjoys making us all squirm? I don't know why we should have to put up with that."

"Feel free to say something to him about it," Christopher said. He was running his fingers between the seat cushion and the back of the driver's chair, not looking at me. "I imagine he'd get rather a kick out of it if you did, actually."

I scowled at him. "You know very well that I can't do that. He'd certainly take it the wrong way, and then he'd never let me live it down."

"Best leave it alone, then," Christopher said, "and simply stop looking." He straightened up. "There's nothing here that I can see."

I shook my head. "It was a bit of a long shot, anyway. Mostly I just wanted to get out of the sitting room. It was uncomfortably close in there."

Christopher nodded and leaned his posterior against the front of the motorcar. "This situation is going to get ugly, you know, Pippa. Sammy Entwistle is almost certainly going to try to pin this on Francis. He's the one with the new fiancée, and I imagine Sammy will think twice before he tries to accuse the future Duke of Sutherland of murder."

"There's you," I said.

He nodded. "But between the two of us living together, and

the fact that I've never been one to run after the local girls, I'm sure people have drawn their own conclusions."

He shot a glance my way. "Sammy is welcome to try to pin it on me—in fact, I wish he would; much better me than Francis—but I don't think he's going to."

Likely not. "So it's Francis we have to worry about."

He nodded, and glanced down the driveway towards the road. "I wish Tom would get here."

"It's a bit of a trek from London," I said. "And he might have got caught up with Pendennis before he was allowed to leave. If he was allowed to leave at all."

"He'll come," Christopher said. "He may not be able to take over the case. Sammy might think he can handle it without help, and if they don't ask, Scotland Yard can't cut in. But Tom will want to be here. He won't let us deal with this on our own."

"I hope you're right," I told him, as I turned to look at the doors to the carriage house. "Before we go back inside, let's look in there, too." It was where the croquet mallet had come from, after all. "Maybe there's a clue in there."

"Better put the gloves back on, then." He pushed off from the Crossley and headed for the doors to the carriage house. "And hope we don't leave any clues of our own to what we've been doing. Sammy won't like us interfering with his investigation."

No, he wouldn't. Given how he felt about the Astleys in general and Francis in particular, he'd undoubtedly take it very amiss, and would also do his best to make something of it. Something like, we were trying to do away with evidence that would implicate someone in the family.

That didn't stop me from moving forward behind Christopher. Sammy might be determined enough to blame Francis for the murder, or certain enough that Francis was guilty, that he would overlook something pertinent. We owed it to ourselves, and to Francis, to discover everything we could.

And yes, I quite realize that I was basing that opinion on nothing but worry and old history. Sammy had done nothing so far to indicate that he was interested in railroading Francis, or for that matter anyone else, into a murder charge. But better safe than sorry, and all that. When Christopher ducked inside the dusk of the carriage house, I followed. For a couple of steps, before I stopped.

"Where are you going? The croquet set is over here, by the door."

"I know, Pippa." Christopher glanced at me over his shoulder. "I lived here too, remember?"

Of course he did. I looked around at the piles of things—rakes and spades, croquet mallets, old wooden sleds and bicycle tires, and the dust motes dancing in the streaks of sunlight coming through the cracks in the walls—and fought back a wave of revulsion. "Now I remember why I never go in here. It's creepy."

"It's just an old carriage house," Christopher said, "full of old things we no longer use. It's only creepy because of the spiders."

"Precisely. Crispin used to drop them down the back of my dress. Spiders and caterpillars and anything else small and wiggly that he could catch."

Christopher smirked. "I remember. And handfuls of snow and fallen leaves and whatever else was available. He kept doing it for far longer than he should have, too."

"Lord, yes." I shuddered. "I think I must have been fifteen before he stopped."

"He was probably hoping you'd tear off your frock and he'd get a look at your unmentionables," Christopher said with a snigger. "That would have been before he started getting access to women's unmentionables of his own."

"He wouldn't have been interested in mine, Christopher. I'm sure he just enjoyed hearing me squeal." I took another look around the room now that my eyes had adjusted to the gloom. "Do you see anything interesting?"

"Can't say I do," Christopher said. "You?"

"Not really. It seems as if whoever used the croquet mallet must have known where to find it, though. They're not terribly visible over there, are they? Not something you'd stumble over accidentally, it seems."

Christopher nodded. "Takes out the itinerant wanderer, then."

"Was there an itinerant wanderer in the village last night?"

"Not aside from Abigail," Christopher said. "But they make for such handy scapegoats, don't they?"

They did. "I'm fairly certain it has to be someone in the family, you know. Or in the household, I should say. Not only is it too much of a coincidence that she'd come here all the way from London only to get herself murdered by a stranger, but nobody else would know where the croquet mallets are."

Christopher nodded.

"Before we go in, let me ask you something."

"Of course." He put his back against a rickety shelf cobbled together from rough pieces of wood and proceeded to listen attentively.

"When you and Francis went into the front of the house and I went onto the terrasse earlier, who was in the sitting room when you arrived? Was everyone there, or was someone missing?"

Christopher threw his mind back. I could see his eyes grow unfocused. "The Marsdens were there. Except Lord Geoffrey.

He came down a few minutes later. But Laetitia was there, as you say, already petting Crispin. Her mother was talking to Uncle Harold and her father was talking to Mum. Constance came down before Geoffrey but after Francis and myself."

"And your father?"

"There from the beginning," Christopher said, "riding herd on the Marsdens. Why do you ask?

"There was someone in my room, looking down at me. Or at the body. I couldn't see who, they stepped back out of sight as soon as they noticed I had seen them."

"Must have been Constance or Geoffrey," Christopher said. "Everyone else was downstairs."

"Why would Constance or Geoffrey be in my room?"

"For a look at the body?" Christopher suggested. "Constance's room has its own window on the croquet lawn, I guess. But Geoffrey's room faces the front of the house."

"Why *my* room, though? Why not his sister's room?" It would be much more convenient, on the same floor as his own as it was.

"No idea," Christopher said and stripped off his gloves. "Maybe he has some sort of illicit passion for you and wanted to sniff your bedding and imagine himself sharing it with you."

My face twisted, and he added, "Just joking. I'm sure he wouldn't do that. He probably just wanted a look at the body from somewhere he wasn't likely to be seen."

Perhaps. Although I did wish he hadn't chosen to do it from *my* window.

"Are you ready to go back inside," Christopher added, "or is there something else you want to look at?"

"I can't think of anything." I peeled off my own gloves, or Aunt Roz's, while we turned towards the entrance. "This is all very upsetting. I can't imagine how we're going to figure out what's going on. The only people with a reason for wanting

Abigail dead are people I don't think are guilty. Where am I supposed to go from here?"

Christopher opened his mouth, but before he could speak, another voice said, rather gloatingly, "I suggest you go inside and stay there until I call for you."

CHAPTER FIFTEEN

IT WASN'T ST GEORGE. Of course not.

No, it was Sammy Entwistle, God only knew how.

"Where did you come from?" I wanted to know. The Duke's Crossley was not back from the village, yet Sammy was here.

"I've been here all along." He smirked.

I shook my head. "You can't have been. We looked for you."

Or at least I thought that I had. He hadn't been on the lawn with the body, and he hadn't been in the driveway with Wilkins, and the Crossley had been gone, and I guess I had put those three things together and assumed that Sammy had gone with it, when there had been absolutely no proof of that anywhere but in my own mind.

"I heard you come out of the house," he said now, with a triumphant look at both Christopher and me, as if he believed he'd caught us doing something we shouldn't be, "and I was curious, so I kept an eye on you. What were you looking for in the motorcars?"

"Nothing." I refused to share a guilty look with Christopher, even though I could feel him trying to catch my eye.

"Planting evidence?"

"Of course not!"

Sammy hummed doubtfully. "I suppose we'll see."

I stuck my hands on my hips. "We absolutely will. Besides, what sort of evidence do you suppose we might want to plant? Everything is out in plain view. The body's on the lawn with the murder weapon right next to it. What could we possibly have that we'd want to plant?"

"An alibi for your brother?" Sammy suggested with a glance at Christopher, which was proof positive, if we had needed it, that he was eyeing Francis.

I snorted. "How do you plant an alibi, pray tell?"

His brows lowered, and I added, "If you're talking about Francis, he already has one. Wilkins drove him back here, three sheets to the wind, from the village pub last night. He fell asleep in the library and didn't stir again until this morning. Constance spent the night with him."

"But she'd lie," Sammy said, as if there was no question about that.

I blinked and opened my mouth, but Christopher got in before me.

"That's a bit cavalier, isn't it? To assume that she'd lie before you've even spoken to her?"

Sammy snorted. "I've seen her around the village. Well-bred, mealy-mouthed little thing."

"She's not—" I began, irately, and then I stopped, because, yes, she was.

Sammy smirked. "I suppose it's high time I have a talk with everyone anyway."

It absolutely was. We'd been sitting in there, chatting about anything and everything, for the past two hours. He really should have corralled us all and written down anything anyone said right from the start.

"They're all in the sitting room," Christopher said, gesturing to the house, while I asked, incredulously, "Are you just going to leave the body there, on the lawn?"

Sammy looked at me. "What do you want me to do with it? Doctor White is on his way. He has to look at it next."

"Can't you at least cover her with something? There are insects and—I don't know—birds?" Not to mention that there was us, having to look at Abigail every time we turned our eyes to the croquet lawn. "I'm sure Aunt Roz will give you a sheet, if you didn't come prepared."

"Doctor will be here soon," Sammy said indifferently.

I stomped my foot. It did absolutely nothing, because we were standing on the grassy verge of the driveway. My voice, however, was both loud and demanding. "I insist that you cover her with something! Her daughter is inside the house, and while we have no idea how much babies understand..."

"Yes," Sammy said, diverted, "I heard she had a baby. Where's the brat?"

"In the house," Christopher said tightly. "My mother's minding her."

Sammy smirked, but before he had the opportunity to say whatever foul thing had come to his mind, I cut him off. "Someone had to mind her, you brainless clod. Her mother collapsed in a heap on the grass yesterday and was removed to the infirmary. Someone had to take care of the baby, and it's my aunt's house, so who else was going to do it?"

"Doctor's wife?" Sammy suggested, which I suppose was a reasonably good suggestion, everything considered.

"Aunt Roz thought the baby was better off here," I said stiffly.

Sammy made a humming noise. "Are you sure your aunt didn't just—"

"Why don't you simply ask her?" Christopher cut in, exasperated. "If you're not going to cover the body, or do anything else useful out here, let's just go inside and you can ask my mother exactly what she was thinking."

Sammy nodded. "Why don't we just do that?"

He grabbed my upper arm, and then he grabbed Christopher's, and then he proceeded to frog-march us both to the boot room door. At that point he had to let go, since we couldn't all fit through the opening at the same time. The same thing was true for the boot room itself, and the hallway, but once we arrived in the foyer, he made a point of taking us both by the arm again as he pushed us ahead of him into the sitting room.

"Kit!" Uncle Herbert jumped to his feet.

This caused Aunt Roz to turn from the window, where she'd been standing watching the road. "Pippa? What on earth is going on?" Her eyes dropped. "Are those my gardening gloves?"

"Yes. I'm sorry." I held them out. "We wanted a look inside the motorcars in the driveway, and we thought it better not to add any fingerprints."

Aunt Roz nodded, as if this made perfect sense. She put the gloves down on the nearest table and turned her attention to Sammy. "Constable Entwistle."

Sammy pulled his gaze from little Bess, who was staring at him with those big, blue Astley eyes. "My lady."

"Are you arresting my son and niece?"

Sammy let go of Christopher and me. "Not at this time, my lady. I caught them snooping around in the carriage house."

"We didn't snoop," I said irritably, twitching my sleeve back into place. "We stood inside the carriage house doors looking around. We didn't even touch anything."

"Be that as it may…"

"It is not against the law to stand inside one's own carriage house! And it's not like you're doing anything to figure out who murdered Abigail anyway—"

"Darling," Crispin said, cutting me off mid-rant just as I was getting to the expletives. I turned to him, and he put a finger to his lips. "Shhh."

My mouth dropped open as Sammy looked from me to him and back. "What's this, then?"

"She doesn't always know when to shut up," Crispin explained, and I scowled at him.

"Very funny, St George. If anyone doesn't know when to shut up, it's you. You actually shushed me?"

"I'm sitting here quietly letting the constable do his job," Crispin sniffed haughtily, "while you're carrying on like a fishwoman. You need to pipe down so Constable Entwistle can get on with it."

I opened my mouth to blister him with my next retort, but Aunt Roz got in first. "Crispin is right, Pippa. Do take a seat and be quiet so we can figure this out."

She eyed me, steadily, while I dug my fingernails into my palms until I managed an, "Yes, Aunt Roz." And then I leveled Crispin a look that ought by rights to have killed him on the spot. He smirked.

"You too, Christopher," Aunt Roz added.

"Yes, Mother." Christopher dropped onto the Chesterfield next to Francis and Constance, where he had sat earlier. He left enough room for me, but I pretended I didn't notice. Instead, I wandered over and perched myself on the other arm of Crispin's chair, so he had Laetitia on one side and me on the other. His eyes widened at my approach, while hers narrowed.

Sammy watched until I was situated, and then he opened his mouth. "Is there some reason you don't want the lady to speak, Lord St George? Something you don't want her to say, perhaps?"

Crispin blinked. I guess he hadn't thought about the fact that him shushing me made it look like he had something to hide. It was my turn to smirk.

He cleared his throat. "No, Constable. Just trying to prevent her from getting herself arrested for verbal assault, you know. She can be quite mouthy when she's riled up."

"You're vile, St George," I informed him, but without any heat whatsoever.

He flicked me a cool look. "Likewise, Darling."

Sammy, meanwhile, fastened his eyes on little Bess. "So this is the babe."

Aunt Roz clutched her a bit tighter. "This is she."

"Belonged to the dead lady, did she?"

"So we believe," Aunt Roz said.

Sammy nodded. He looked from Crispin to Christopher, who was draped on the Chesterfield with one leg folded over the other, elegantly. Neither of them turned a hair at the examination.

Then it was Francis's turn. When the latter narrowed his eyes under the constable's examination, Sammy looked pleased that he had gotten a reaction. His voice was practically a purr. "Astley."

"Entwistle," Francis growled.

Sammy's smirk widened and his attention dropped to where Constance was clutching Francis's hand. Her engagement ring, an heirloom ruby surrounded by small brilliants, sparkled in the sunlight. "I understand congratulations are in order."

Francis's jaw tightened, but he didn't speak, just gave a short nod. He might be afraid of what would come out of his mouth if he opened it.

"Thank you," Constance breathed. I swallowed a sigh. I love her, really I do—or at least I'm beginning to, now that it looks like she's going to be my cousin's wife—but does she have to be so meek all the time?

"Brand new, isn't it?"

"Last week," Francis grunted.

"Happy, I assume?"

"Of course," Constance said. The firmness of her tone was somewhat compromised by the fact that her voice shook.

Sammy looked at her for a moment and then turned his attention back to Francis. "Anything you'd like to tell me about the dead lady?"

"No," Francis said.

"Didn't know her?"

Francis shook his head.

"Yet she came here, where you live? And brought her child?"

There was nothing any of us could say to that, of course, so nobody tried.

"Had you met her before yesterday?" Sammy wanted to know.

"I didn't meet her yesterday," Francis answered, with the air of someone who was forcing the words past his teeth. "She staggered onto the lawn and collapsed. I picked her up and carried her inside. She never woke up."

"But you hadn't met her before?"

"No," Francis said. "I've never met her."

Sammy eyed him in silence for a few seconds. "You know the penalties for perjury, don't you, Astley?"

"It's hardly perjury," I said, offended. "Perjury is when—"

It was all I got out before Crispin shifted on the chair and accidentally—or perhaps not so accidentally—swept me off the arm and onto the floor. I landed with a squeal, and he gave me a bland, "My apologies, Darling," as I scrambled to my feet. Sammy took a moment to admire my legs—they're quite good, according to Christopher—while Laetitia and her mother exchanged a cautiously pleased glance that I pretended not to see.

"Really, St George," I told him as I crossed the floor and dropped down next to Christopher on the Chesterfield, cheeks hot, "if you wanted to be rid of me, you could have just said."

"I said I was sorry, Darling. It was an accident, I assure you."

And I was a monkey's uncle. It had one hundred percent been deliberate. He wasn't even pretending to match his expression to the words he was saying.

Although, since I assumed he had done it to prevent me from saying something stupid, and not simply because he didn't want me sitting next to him, I couldn't really indulge in the hissy fit that was threatening. I took a deep breath instead, and told him, "You could have done the gentlemanly thing and helped me to my feet, you know."

"You must have me confused with someone else," Crispin answered. After a moment he added, blandly, "That color is quite becoming to you."

I hoped he was talking about my cheeks, which were bright pink, and that I hadn't flashed him (and everyone else in the sitting room) a glimpse of my unmentionables while I was kicking around on the floor, but I wasn't about to ask.

Sammy cleared his throat. "Has anyone present met the victim before yesterday?"

I thought about lying, but what good would it do? "She came to our flat in London last week."

Sammy's brows arched. "Came to see you, did she?"

"She came to see Christopher," I said.

"And what did she want?"

"We don't know. Christopher was out. When I told her so, she left."

"And she didn't come back?"

I shook my head. Sammy looked around the room. "Anyone else?"

Crispin raised a languid hand. "She came to Sutherland House a few months ago."

"What's a few months, Lord St George? February? March? April?"

"Not February," Crispin said. "The babe was at least a couple of months old. Maybe March or April."

"And what did she want?"

"To speak to the Duke's grandson," Crispin said with a smirk. "Rogers dragged me out of bed to meet her. I told him I'd never seen her before. She ran away. I went back to my guest."

"Who was your guest?"

He eyed me, and he eyed Laetitia, and then he had the nerve to eye Constance. She flushed. Francis growled.

"Lady Violet Cummings," Crispin said.

Sammy wrote it down. "And that's the only time you saw the girl?"

"Until she walked onto the lawn yesterday, yes."

"And you can prove that, I suppose?"

"Of course I can't," Crispin said, irritated, and both Lady Euphemia and Uncle Harold drew in a breath. "You won't be able to find anyone who's seen us together, because I didn't know her, but that doesn't mean that I can prove I didn't know her."

"St George..." his father rumbled, and Crispin shot him a look.

"Sorry, Father. But there's just no way to prove something like that."

"So you have no alibi for the murder?"

"Of course I do." Crispin glanced at Christopher. "Kit and I shared a room. We were together from midnight until Darling knocked us up this morning to tell us about the body."

"Darling. You two are..." Sammy looked from him to me and back, dubiously, "together?"

I wasn't the only person who snorted derisively at that. Crispin did, and so did Francis. So, for that matter, did Uncle Harold.

"Certainly not," Crispin said. "I don't pass muster with Darling. Do I?"

"Not at all," I agreed. "You're a cad and a vile seducer, and I wouldn't have you if you were giftwrapped with a ribbon around your neck."

He gave me a mock bow, just as if I had paid him a genuine compliment. "Just so."

I rolled my eyes. "I suppose you could be worse, St George. I'm not certain off-hand precisely how, but if you put your mind to it, I'm sure you could manage, being so uniquely gifted in that way."

His smirk widened. "Thank you, Darling."

Sammy snorted and turned back to the conversation. "Who of you slept alone last night?"

There was a beat, then— "What cheek," Crispin drawled. "Do you really suppose all of us are comfortable with that line of questioning, Constable?"

"This is an official inquiry—" Sammy began stiffly, but before he could say anything further, Uncle Harold had butted in.

"That's enough, St George. Don't make this any more difficult than you already have."

"Yes, Father." Crispin didn't quite roll his eyes, but I'm fairly certain I saw the intent and watched him squash it. I don't know whether Uncle Harold noticed.

"I spent the night alone," I told Sammy. "On the third floor, across from Christopher and Crispin, in a room of my own. I had a view of the lawn and if I had looked out the window at the right moment, I might have seen her." Or seen the murder.

"But you didn't?"

I shook my head. "Not until I woke up this morning. I was the first one to notice."

Or at least the first one to say anything about it.

"And no one can vouch for your whereabouts between midnight and six this morning?"

"It was more like ten last night. But no."

"Why did you retire early?" Sammy wanted to know.

The truth was that I had had enough of Geoffrey's idiocy as well as Laetitia's shenanigans, but I couldn't really say that. So — "I'd had enough of St George for the evening," I said.

The latter's brow arched. "Is that so? I don't recall being there with you when you made that decision."

"You weren't. You can annoy from a distance, too."

"Of course."

"So no," I told Sammy. "From ten last night until this morning, I have no alibi. Not unless the boys heard me snore when they came upstairs."

Crispin and Christopher both shook their heads. "Pippa—" Aunt Roz began.

"It's the truth, Aunt Roz. I slept alone. He can't prove that I went downstairs and killed Abigail, because I didn't, but I slept alone."

She nodded. Sammy looked around the assembly. "Who else has no alibi for the night?"

Geoffrey and Laetitia both raised their hands. Uncle Harold didn't, I noticed, although he had certainly spent the night alone, too.

"Names?"

Geoffrey eyed Sammy down his nose. "I'm Lord Geoffrey Marsden, and this is my sister, Lady Laetitia."

"And you are?"

Geoffrey opened his mouth, probably to reiterate their names. He's extremely literal and not very bright. Laetitia got in first. (There's nothing wrong with her head, much as it pains me to admit it.) "Cousins of the bride-to-be."

Sammy flicked a glance at Constance before turning his attention back on Laetitia. "And you spent the night alone."

Laetitia nodded. "I was supposed to share Constance's room, but she ended up in the library with Mr. Astley. Lord St George had made other plans."

She lowered her lashes demurely. She's an extremely lovely woman, in case I've neglected to mention that. A couple of years older than Crispin (and the rest of us), with big, crystal-clear, blue eyes, perfect porcelain skin, and shiny black hair. Her thick, dark lashes barely needed the coating of mascara she had given them, and the look she slanted Crispin from underneath would have made Sarah Bernhardt proud.

The Countess sucked in a breath, but Crispin just gave Laetitia an apologetic look. "Sorry, Laetitia. But I'm not using my cousin's engagement party and my aunt's house to misbehave."

"And quite right, too," I said. "We should all misbehave on our own time and in our own houses. Good for you, St George."

He shot me a look. "Thank you, Darling."

Uncle Harold cleared his throat. "I also slept alone. Although I'm sure you're not insinuating that I would murder this unfortunate waif, Constable?"

Sammy hesitated. There was clearly a correct answer here —"Of course not, Your Grace,"—but I suppose he didn't think that being a duke absolved Uncle Harold of suspicion. (Nor should it.) And in justice to him—Sammy—I guess he didn't want to say that it did when it didn't.

"I assume we're all suspects until we can prove otherwise, Harold," Aunt Roz said, and took Sammy off the hook. He looked relieved. "Herbert and I spent the night together, Constable, as we always do. He didn't stir, and I didn't either. Although we did have a window onto the croquet lawn, so it's possible we might have seen her arrive, had we looked out that window. At that point, however, I'm afraid we were probably asleep."

Sammy nodded. "You didn't hear anything through the window at any point? An argument? Any..." He hesitated delicately, "...noises?"

My mind supplied the sound a croquet mallet might make when it made contact with the back of a skull—the closest my imagination could come was the *thwack* of a spoon against a soft-boiled egg, magnified several times—and I winced.

"I'm afraid not, Constable," Aunt Roz said composedly, and Uncle Herbert shook his head. "We slept through the night with no interruptions. Except for the baby, of course."

Of course.

"We, as well," Laetitia's mother hurried to say. "I'm Euphemia, Countess Marsden, and this is my husband, Lord Maurice. We had no window onto the lawn, and didn't know this unfortunate girl existed until she collapsed in front of us yesterday afternoon."

She divided a displeased look between myself and Aunt Roz, as if she blamed us for it. I have no idea why, since I'd not had anything to do with that, nor had Aunt Roz. It was her house, I suppose, and her son who had proposed to Lady Euphemia's niece, thus forcing the Marsden family to be here— although between you and me, I think we would have all been better pleased if they had just stayed home.

At any rate, it wasn't as if Aunt Roz could have foreseen this happening, nor as if she would have wanted it to, if she had.

"Lord Geoffrey?" Sammy turned to him.

"Slept alone," Geoffrey grunted. "Saw no one."

"Didn't know the girl?"

"Never saw her before in my life," Geoffrey said.

And that was that. Sammy looked around the room. His eyes lingered for a second on Constance and Francis, and on Crispin and Laetitia, and then on me. I arched my brows at him —surely he didn't seriously suspect me?—and he pursed his lips, but didn't do me the courtesy of looking abashed.

I suppose he thought the five of us were the most likely suspects. Francis and Crispin because they might be little Bess's father, Laetitia and Constance because they were afraid of losing Crispin and Francis, respectively, and me... God only knew what Sammy thought my motive was. While there were people here I would kill for, at least in the heat of the moment, there was nobody for whom I would commit coldblooded murder. Certainly not the coldblooded murder of a poor waif whose only crime was to have gotten herself in the family way by some smooth-talking bloke who told her he was a Sutherland.

If she had threatened Christopher with bodily harm, I would have squashed her like a bug. I wouldn't have snuck downstairs in the middle of the night and hit her over the head with a croquet mallet, however. And more to the point, she hadn't threatened Christopher. As far as I knew, she hadn't had the chance to threaten Francis, either. Crispin... well. Him, she might have threatened. And while I knew I wouldn't have murdered her for it, even if the baby had been Crispin's, I suppose I couldn't expect Sammy to know that. Crispin's insistence on calling me Darling, which made sense to the two of us, may not make sense to Sammy. He might think it meant something it didn't.

But Crispin had an alibi for last night and couldn't have committed the crime. Nor could Francis and Christopher.

Unless someone was lying, of course. Christopher had suggested telling a fib to give me an alibi, so he might have been willing to fib for Crispin, as well. And Constance would certainly have lied for Francis, although he truly hadn't been in any condition to commit murder last night, so I was fairly certain it hadn't been him.

That left Laetitia, last of the group Sammy had been eyeing. In my opinion, Sammy ought also to consider Uncle Harold and Geoffrey, both of whom had also spent the night alone.

The case for Geoffrey was simple. He might have seen her, might have made a play for her, and might have lost his temper when she wouldn't play along. If it was Geoffrey, it had been a crime of passion, heat of the moment, and nothing more.

Uncle Harold was a grandson of a Duke of Sutherland, albeit a long-dead one, and could have passed down the Sutherland hair and eyes to Bess. On the other hand, it was difficult to imagine him being interested in someone like Abigail Dole—difficult to imagine him interested in sex at all, really—and just as difficult to imagine Abigail letting herself be swept off her feet by Uncle Harold. Surely her beau must have been someone younger and better-looking?

On the other hand, he might simply have believed that Crispin was responsible for Bess, and so he got rid of Abigail to keep her from entrapping Crispin. I could see someone like Uncle Harold justifying murder in a case like that, especially if the victim was no one of consequence.

And then there was Laetitia. I had believed her capable of strangling Johanna de Vos at the Dower House back in May, and I believed her completely capable of killing Abigail Dole now. She wanted Crispin, and from where I was sitting, she seemed willing to do almost anything to get him.

I glanced over at her, perched on the arm of his chair, angled towards him as if she were a flower and he was the sun. I shivered.

"All right, Pippa?" Christopher whispered. He reached over and took my hand.

I nodded and leaned closer, putting my head on his shoulder. "Ready for this to be over."

Sammy Entwistle, as if he had heard me, cleared his throat. "Let's start over from the beginning."

CHAPTER SIXTEEN

RESCUE CAME in the form of Wilkins and the Crossley, and the reinforcements from the village. Sammy dismissed us so he could go and give his minions orders, and I turned to Christopher. "Walk with me."

He nodded. "Excuse us."

"Of course, dear." Aunt Roz waved us off. We ducked out into the foyer and then through the front door and into the fresh air.

"Where do you want to walk to?" Christopher wanted to know when we were outside in the sunshine and warm July breezes. The sun was up now, and it was turning into a nice day. Excepting the dead body on the lawn, of course, and the constables crawling all over everything, and the suspicion that was attached to the family in general.

I shook my head, feeling a combination of hysteria and helplessness creep into my head and my voice. "Nowhere. There's nowhere to go. We're stuck here, with nowhere to go and nothing to do. Somebody murdered someone on the lawn, and I don't know who or why!"

"It's not your job to figure out who or why," Christopher pointed out as we approached the intersection between front door path and driveway. The Duke's black Crossley was yet again parked beside the other cars outside the carriage house. "This way."

He turned me in the other direction, down the driveway towards the lane, away from where there were likely to be other people.

"I know it's not my job to figure it out," I told him. "But do you really trust Sammy Entwistle to do it? He'll arrest Francis just for old times' sake! He made it clear in there that he suspects him. We always thought he would, but that made it clear."

"He can't do that," Christopher said, although there wasn't any kind of conviction in his voice. Not much of anything else, either. He must feel as overwhelmed and helpless as I did. "Francis has an alibi. Besides, Tom's coming."

"You hope Tom's coming. But even if he does, as long as Sammy's in charge, there's nothing Tom can do."

"He's from Scotland Yard!" Christopher said. "Sammy would listen to him, don't you think?"

"Knowing Sammy—" Not that I did, "I doubt he'd listen to anyone or anything he didn't personally want to believe. And the thing is, what he believes makes sense, Christopher! Abigail went to Sutherland House and met Crispin. Then she came to the Essex House, and I told her you look just like him. If she knew Crispin wasn't who she was looking for, at that point she would have known that you weren't, either."

Christopher nodded. "I'm not who she was looking for. We both know that."

Of course. "Then she came here. If the old Duke of Sutherland had three grandsons, and it wasn't you or Crispin who got her with child, Francis is the only one left."

"But even if he did," Christopher protested, "and I'm not saying he did, but if he did... he still couldn't have killed her. Constance aside, we both saw him when he came home last night, and he wasn't in any kind of condition to get up and walk out and fetch a croquet mallet and bash anyone over the head."

No, he hadn't been. "You don't suppose he could have been feigning, do you?"

He gave me a look. "Affecting being drunk? To what purpose? He couldn't have known she'd show up, could he? She was still unconscious when we took her to the village. They didn't have a chance to set up an assignation for later."

"Francis was in the village last night, too," I pointed out, kicking at pebbles in my path. "He might have stopped by the infirmary. And if she was awake, they could have arranged to meet at Beckwith Place later. She'd want her baby back, so it wouldn't be difficult to convince her to come here."

Christopher looked reluctant, but he admitted, "I suppose it's possible. Although even if he did set up a meeting, it makes no sense that he'd go to the carriage house for the mallet. There are weapons closer to hand."

I supposed that was true. There were fireplace pokers in the library and rolling pins in the kitchen and golf clubs in the boot room. No need for anyone to go to the carriage house for a croquet mallet.

"Besides," Christopher added, "if it was premeditated, why would he—why would anyone—kill her on our own lawn with our own croquet mallet? None of that makes sense."

No, it didn't. Anyone who was thinking straight and had planned the crime would have killed her in the village without bringing her back to where we—where *he*—lived.

The only problem with that, of course, was that Francis hadn't been thinking straight last night. I doubted he had been able to think at all, as soused as he'd been.

But it was still unlikely that he could have made it out of the library and onto the lawn to kill her. Not without alerting Constance, and surely Constance would have stopped him had she realized what he was doing.

"So we're back to where we started," Christopher said, kicking out viciously at a particularly offending pebble. "Even if Francis got her with child—and that's a big if, because he says he didn't—he couldn't have killed her."

"That's how it looks to me," I agreed. "The way I see it, we have two issues here. Someone got her with child, someone who said he was the grandson of the Duke of Sutherland, and someone killed her. That could be the same person, or two different ones."

"You mean, if Francis got Abigail with child, Constance might have killed her, because she was afraid Francis would have to marry Abigail instead of herself."

It didn't sound like a question, but I nodded anyway. "Or Crispin got Abigail with child, and Laetitia murdered her. Or Uncle Harold did, because he didn't want Crispin to have to acknowledge Bess. They both had their own rooms—Uncle Harold and Laetitia, I mean—so they could have come downstairs without anyone noticing. And Constance could easily have gone outside. She was close to the back door, and Francis isn't likely to have noticed."

"No," Christopher agreed. "By that measure—opportunity —it would have to be one of those three, or Geoffrey."

"Or me," I said.

"You had no reason to want her dead."

"I had a better reason than Geoffrey. I don't think he loves his sister quite enough to commit murder for her, do you? Or is invested in her marriage to St George enough for that?"

He didn't answer, and I added, "I'm a different story. I would commit murder for you, and I'm sure Sammy knows it.

We live together, and some people think we're living in sin. You could have gotten her with child, and if you had, I might have wanted her gone."

Christopher scoffed, and I added, "Or you and I do not live in sin, but I'm in love with St George—eeurgh! Just saying that makes my mouth pucker—so I killed her out of jealousy. Sammy perks up every time Crispin calls me Darling, as if he thinks it means something. Although honestly, if I were in love with St George—eeurgh!—I'd be more likely to go after Laetitia, honestly."

"No, you wouldn't," Christopher said. "You said it yourself, he's not in love with Laetitia. There's no need to worry about her."

"He seems willing to marry her, even so. If I'm in love with him—eeurgh!—I wouldn't want that to happen."

He slanted me a look. "You said he wasn't."

"Two months ago, he made it clear he wasn't. But he's not doing much to avoid it right now, so he must have changed his mind."

"Maybe he doesn't realize what she's planning?"

"He'd have to be stupid not to," I said crossly, since I don't like to admit it, "and he's not."

We walked in silence for a moment, until Christopher said, "Perhaps he thinks he made himself clear and she won't try again."

I shrugged. "Perhaps. I guess we'll have to wait and see. I just hope he won't end up doing something he regrets later. Once she gets that ring on her finger, she'll never let him go."

We had reached the end of the driveway now, and peered left and right up and down the lane. It was empty, of motorcars, horse-drawn carriages, and pedestrians.

"I suppose we'd better turn around," Christopher said. "We don't want Sammy to think that we're trying to escape."

"Definitely not." I turned my back on the lane and looked at the house. "Do you miss living here?"

"I miss Mum and Dad," Christopher said as we started back up the driveway. "But I'm happy that we get to live our own lives in our own space."

"If you ever find someone you'd like to live in sin with…"

He wouldn't be able to marry whoever he found, after all. Not unless his tastes changed, and I didn't think that was likely. Or unless the laws changed, but that was perhaps even more unlikely.

He squeezed my arm. "We'll figure it out. You're more likely than I am to find someone to be with, anyway."

"Not at the rate I'm going," I said, disgruntled. "Every man I've met lately has had something wrong with him. Geoffrey Marsden's a womanizer. Freddie Montrose is dead. Ronnie Blanton's a dope addict. Dominic Rivers is a dope merchant. Graham Ogilvie is queer. Nigel Hutchison—"

"You know, Pippa," Christopher cut in, "there's always—"

"If you say St George, I shall pummel you."

"I was going to say Sammy, actually."

My face twisted. "That's even worse. Could you imagine the family dinners? Francis and Constance, Crispin and Laetitia, and me and Sammy? Good Lord, we wouldn't make it through the soup course before there was bloodshed!"

"I'd pay money to see that," Christopher said with a wistful sigh, before he added, "don't worry though, Pippa. I'd never let you marry Sammy. Nor would Francis or Crispin."

"Nor would I," I said. "I already told you, Christopher. If we're not married by thirty, we're marrying each other."

"I'm not worried," Christopher said, as we turned the bend in the lane and the carriage house came back into view. "What do you say we go back to the lawn and see what's happening? The worst Sammy can do is send us back inside."

I nodded, and we meandered in that direction.

There was a motorcar parked beside the bushes, that must belong to the mortuary, and there was the sound of rattling and clanging from inside the carriage house. Some flatfooted constable trampling all over the evidence, no doubt. I rolled my eyes, but didn't say anything. What was the point of grousing to Christopher, after all? There was nothing he could do about it, either.

"Here they come," he said softly, and I pulled my attention away from the carriage house and towards the motorcar in time to see two men emerge from the bushes, at each end of a stretcher. The body was covered by a sheet, I was happy to see. It was about time that someone afforded Abigail Dole that final dignity.

Doctor White came out from the bushes behind them, and he was the one who opened the back doors of the motorcar so they could slide the stretcher and its burden inside. That done, they closed the doors again, and exchanged a few words we couldn't hear, before the driver and his helper, both dressed in black with bowler hats, got into the car and backed down the driveway past us.

Christopher and I moved aside to let them pass, and then waited for Doctor White to approach.

"Doctor," I said politely.

He shook his head, and pulled a gigantic handkerchief out of his pocket, and used it to mop his forehead. "Dreadful state of affairs. Dreadful."

"What happened?" I asked.

He peered at me. "We don't chain people to their beds, you know. If there are children, one of us stays in the infirmary overnight, in case there's a need. But she was an adult, and there was nothing wrong with her, nothing that a good night's sleep couldn't cure. So we went to bed and let her sleep."

"Of course." No point in losing sleep over someone who for all intents and purposes was perfectly healthy, after all.

"I thought she'd still be there in the morning," Doctor White said. "But by the time my wife got down to the infirmary, the young lady was gone." He clicked his tongue. "Nothing wrong with that. She wasn't a prisoner. She could leave when she wanted. But this..." He dragged the handkerchief across his brow again, shaking his head, "this is dreadful."

"It certainly wasn't your fault," I assured him. "As you said, she wasn't a prisoner. She could leave when she wanted to."

He nodded, but vacantly, as if the reassurance didn't matter in the least.

I paused for a polite moment before I asked, "She didn't wake up at any point, did she? Or say anything to anyone?"

The doctor shook his head. "I'm afraid not. She slipped from unconsciousness into sleep without waking up. There was a moment, when we jostled her into the car yesterday afternoon, that I thought she might be coming to—"

Christopher nodded.

"—but nothing happened. We put her to bed and she stayed there, never saying a word."

"That's too bad," I said. "We thought she must have woken up in the night and realized that the baby wasn't there. And so she came here to find her."

Doctor White nodded. "As like as not, young lady. As like as not."

"And then someone found her instead. And whacked her with a croquet mallet."

Doctor White shook his head. "Not a croquet mallet."

Not a...?

"What do you mean, not a croquet mallet? It was next to her on the grass! It had..." I gulped, "it had blood and... and hair on it."

"That's as may be," Doctor White said primly, "but the mallet wasn't what killed her."

Christopher blinked. "You mean, someone hit her with something else first, and then hit her with the mallet?"

But Doctor White was shaking his head again. "Nobody hit her with the croquet mallet."

"But the..." He glanced at me, "the blood, and the other matter...?"

Urk. There was that word I hadn't wanted to think, let alone say. I could feel the blood drain out of my head, leaving me dizzy.

"Catch her, young man," Doctor White's voice said, from farther away than it should have been, "before she falls down. You really ought to know better than that."

"Sorry." I felt Christopher's hand under my elbow. "Come along, Pippa. Over in the shade. This way." I heard one of the motorcar doors open, and then he nudged me onto a seat. "There we are. Deep breaths."

"Sorry," I said, keeping my head down and my eyes closed. "I'm not usually so feeble. It was just that word..."

Plus the fact that a month ago, I had driven around London with the head of a dead man in my lap, wrapped in a towel. There had been blood and brain matter then too. This brought back bad memories.

"Hmph." Doctor White cleared his throat with irritation. "You wouldn't have lasted a week on the ward during the war, young lady. Amputated limbs and infected wounds and maggots..."

No, I wouldn't have, and I didn't want to hear about it now. My stomach flopped over in an unpleasant manner.

"Carry on," I told him—told them both—with a flip of my hand. Perhaps moving on with the conversation would help. "You were saying that the mallet wasn't the murder weapon?"

The doctor harrumphed again, but said, "No. She was hit with something else first."

Something else? "What?"

I admit it, I had visions of fireplace pokers and rolling pins and golf clubs flitting through my head. All the things we had talked about just a few minutes ago, that had been readily available to anyone who wanted to commit murder.

"Something with a smaller circumference, likely metal," Doctor White said. "There were specks of rust in her hair."

So not just metal, but rusty metal.

That would explain why someone was rustling around in the carriage house, anyway. There were sure to be plenty of metals in there, rusty and otherwise. The entire building is a lock-jaw accident waiting to happen.

"But that doesn't make any sense," Christopher objected. "Why would someone hit her with something else, and then go get the mallet and hit her with that, only to leave the first thing lying around in the carriage house?"

"Who said anything about the carriage house?" Doctor White wanted to know. "And she wasn't hit with the mallet. I thought I made that clear. She was hit with something else, and then someone fetched the mallet."

"But didn't hit her with it? How did the blood and... um..." Christopher glanced at me.

"You can say it," I told him grumpily. "By now, that's hardly the most disturbing thing about this situation. Someone hit her with something else, then went and fetched the mallet, and rubbed the head of the mallet in the wound, so it would look as if she was hit with the mallet?"

"In a word," Doctor White answered. He seemed pleased, either because I'd figured it out or because I wasn't fainting after articulating it all.

"But that's barbaric," Christopher said, and the doctor turned to him.

"Less barbaric than hitting the dead corpse with the mallet a second time, I would say. Although I'll readily admit that none of it is pleasant."

No, it absolutely was not. And furthermore, it was well-nigh unbelievable. I couldn't imagine any of us doing something like that. The idea of Constance or Laetitia first wielding the classic blunt instrument—and in rusty metal; where would either of them have got their hands on rusty metal? It's not like we keep our fireplace pokers or kitchen utensils rusty.

But all right, so we had Constance or Laetitia bashing poor Abigail over the head with a rusty, blunt instrument, and then, not being satisfied with that action, running into the carriage house, fetching one of the croquet mallets, dipping it into the blood and brain matter on the back of her head—I gagged—and throwing it on the grass to make it look like the murder weapon, before gathering up the original blunt instrument and restoring it to whence it had come, presumably to divert suspicion from herself.

If that was the case, the real murder weapon must be something that could implicate whoever had used it. Otherwise, why not just leave it on the lawn?

Of course, it might have been as simple as fear that the rusty poker contained the murderer's fingerprints, but if it truly was as rusty as all that, it didn't seem likely that it would. And besides, why not just take it away without substituting the mallet? And if he, or she, could keep his or her fingerprints off the mallet, why not keep them off the original weapon, as well?

"Better now?" Christopher asked me. He must have noticed that I had slipped from nauseated silence into the quiet of contemplation.

I nodded. "Much, thank you. I suppose all we have to do

now is find the rusty poker—or whatever it is—and it'll lead us straight to the guilty party."

"I'm sure Sammy is trying to do exactly that," Christopher said, and turned to the doctor. "What can we do for you, Doctor White? Do you want to go back to the village? You'll have to do the post mortem on the body, I assume, even if it's already obvious what caused her death."

Doctor White nodded. "Yes, my boy. For the inquest, you know. Best to have all the details figured out and sound like I know what I'm testifying about."

"Would you like us to take you to the village?" I asked. It would be an opportunity to look around. An opportunity to get away from Beckwith Place for a few minutes, too, with an excuse that Sammy couldn't use to haul us off to jail. "Or do you want to go inside and see Aunt Roz and the baby, and maybe get a cuppa before you head back?"

Doctor White looked like he might have been tempted, but he shook his head. "My wife's waiting. And so is the body. I'd better get to work."

"I'll find Wilkins." Christopher glanced around. The Duke's Crossley was definitely still parked in front of the carriage house, so Wilkins must be somewhere on the premises.

"If Christopher can't find Wilkins, we'll take you to the village ourselves," I assured Doctor White. "We both know how to drive a motorcar, even if we don't get much practice these days. There are four thousand double decker buses in London, and the underground train we can use, not to mention all the taxis."

Doctor White nodded. "It's been a few months now, hasn't it? Do you like living in Town?"

I did like living in Town, and told him so, as I watched Christopher peer into the Crossley, which must have been empty, before he ducked into the carriage house. "Wilkins?" I heard his voice faintly. "Are you in here? Wilkins?"

"We were happy to see Francis bring Miss Constance home," Doctor White commented. "He's had a rough few years since the war. It's nice to see him finally move on."

Yes, it was. "The events of this weekend surely haven't helped. He was a wreck at Sutherland Hall, after Duke Henry and Lady Charlotte died."

"He's better now," Doctor White said. "I haven't had to prescribe any morphia for him in a few months. This may have been a small setback, but overall, he's doing much better."

"That's good. I think he became scared after Aunt Charlotte killed herself with the Veronal, you know? But then he met Constance, and I'm sure that made a big difference."

He'd been so busy making sure that she was all right after losing her mother, and making sure that Christopher was all right after being poisoned, that there hadn't been much time, or need, for any pain-numbing of his own.

"He'll be all right," Doctor White said, as Christopher came back out of the carriage house again, by himself. "In a week or two, this weekend will be a memory, too, and he'll marry Miss Constance and they'll live happily ever after."

Hopefully he was right about that. The alternative was that Sammy would find some way to arrest Francis in spite of his alibi, and that he'd find the evidence to convict him in spite of his not having had the opportunity to kill Abigail, and then there would be no marriage and no happily ever after. But it didn't seem worthwhile for me to say all that, not out loud, and besides, by then Christopher had reached us.

So what I said instead was, "No Wilkins?"

Christopher shook his head. "He must be inside with Uncle Harold. Or perhaps on the lawn with Sammy. Or somewhere else. But he isn't here."

"I guess it's up to us, then." I eyed the row of cars. "I don't suppose the Marsdens would be very happy if we took their Daimler, although it would be great fun to drive it..."

"There's no 'we,'" Christopher told me, sternly. "I have an alibi for last night. You do not. If you leave Beckwith Place, Sammy would have an excuse for arresting you. You're staying here."

"But it's just a trip to the village—"

"In a borrowed car," Christopher said. "Which will not be the Daimler, by the way. And I'll spare my cousin's feelings, too, since I know how much he loves his Hispano-Suiza."

I sniggered. "He'd marry it before he'd marry Laetitia."

Christopher nodded. "Mum and Dad won't mind if I borrow the Bentley. We'll take that."

He waved the doctor to follow him down the gravel path towards the Astleys' motorcar.

"Be careful," I told him as I trailed behind. "It's been a while since you had the chance to motor anywhere..."

"I motored home from the village yesterday," Christopher said, "remember? And it was just fine. It's like riding a bicycle. You don't forget."

"I could run inside and fetch St George..."

"No," Christopher said, as he started the Bentley with a growl of the engine. "You're just looking for an excuse to get Crispin away from Laetitia. Just be honest about it. You don't need an excuse."

The doctor perched his bag on his lap and eyed me over the top of his glasses. "Like that, is it?"

"Absolutely not," I said. "I abhor St George. I just like Laetitia Marsden even less. I don't want him to marry her. But it's absolutely not like that."

"I'm perfectly capable of handling this," Christopher told me. "If anyone asks, I'll be back in half an hour."

I nodded. "Be careful, please."

He snorted. "It's a quiet country lane at nine in the morning. I'm not likely to meet another vehicle. But I'll go slow. I'm not my cousin."

"Then I'll see you when you get back," I said. "Goodbye, Doctor White. And good luck with the post mortem."

"All in a day's work," the doctor grunted. "Onwards, young man. Onwards."

He pointed, like Columbus at the Americas. Christopher let out the clutch, and the Bentley rolled off down the driveway. I waved, and waited until they had turned into the lane and were out of sight before I turned away and contemplated my next move.

CHAPTER SEVENTEEN

THERE WERE STILL SOUNDS COMING from within the carriage house. One of Sammy's constables, I assumed, or perhaps Sammy himself. I supposed I could simply go over and have a peek, but Christopher hadn't made mention of anything particularly exciting going on inside, so it was probably just the equivalent of a constabulary bloodhound sniffing at everything and nothing.

The boot room door turned out to be locked, something that hadn't happened, in my recollection, more than half a dozen times before during the day. I turned my feet towards the croquet lawn and back door instead.

The body was gone, obviously, and so, I assumed, was the croquet mallet. I hadn't looked in the mortuary van before it rolled off down the driveway, but I assumed the mallet had been there, carefully wrapped. It ought to be. Unless Sammy had it stashed somewhere, but I couldn't imagine where, since the constabulary seemed to be getting around on bicycles, and surely he didn't plan to carry it down to the village strapped to his back at the end of the investigation?

The lawn was empty but for a bobby squatting on the grass next to where Abigail's body had lain. He had his hat off and the sun shone on brown hair, instead of the flaming carrot red of Sammy's head. I thought about engaging him in conversation, just to see if he might let some inside information slip, but he looked like he might be praying, or at least doing something else important, and besides, Sammy had surely warned the constables away from telling anyone anything. I would have done, had I been in charge.

So I merely walked past him with a muttered "Pardon me," giving both him and the crime scene a wide berth, and made my way up onto the flagstone of the terrasse and across to the door.

Inside, the house was quiet. Neither the library nor the study are rooms that particularly invite anyone to kick their heels up in them, and someone must have warned off Cook, because the kitchen and scullery were empty. Hughes hadn't arrived, either, or so I assumed, until I heard her voice float out of Uncle Herbert's study as I approached.

"—knows."

"I have no idea what you mean," Uncle Herbert answered, but there was a brittle note in his voice that stated, as plainly as words, that he was lying. He had understood exactly what she meant, and furthermore, he wasn't pleased about it.

I stopped, of course, out of sight of the door, while I waited to see whether they had heard my approach.

And it seemed as if they hadn't, because Hughes made a sound that might have been a giggle in someone younger and less dignified. In either case, there was nothing particularly servile about it, nothing like what a domestic servant should do to the master of the house. I arched my brows and eased a bit closer, holding my breath.

"I can't make it much clearer than that, Lord Herbert."

"But he can't possibly," Uncle Herbert protested. "We said we'd never speak of it. I don't know how *you'd* know. You weren't even at Sutherland then."

"Lydia Morrison and I compared notes," Hughes said composedly. "I know His late Grace's idea was to get rid of anyone who knew anything—"

The late Duke Henry, obviously. She must be talking about whatever had happened when Lydia Morrison had been sent to Dorset to work for Constance's mother, and Hughes had come back in her place.

"—but you know, Lord Herbert, how servants gossip."

There was a hint of something like satisfaction in her voice, or maybe more like triumph; something almost threatening, or at least suggestive that a threat might be in the offing, or could be if she so chose.

"That wasn't even the first time it happened," she added maliciously, "was it?"

I could almost feel the question shiver in the air.

There was a moment of silence, and when Uncle Herbert's voice came back, it was tight with what I judged to be a mixture of anger and fear. "What do you mean by that?"

"Surely you remember Maisie Moran?"

I blinked. My thoughts whirled, scrabbling. Was this someone I should know?

Then I realized that no, I didn't remember Maisie Moran. I had no idea who Maisie Moran was, or had been.

Uncle Herbert clearly did. "That was a long time ago," he said roughly. "Before I met Roslyn. Before we got married. It had nothing to do with us."

"Of course not." Hughes's voice oozed poisoned sympathy. "But one child with a woman not your wife is one thing. Two is quite another."

Child?

I gasped out loud, and then slapped a hand over my mouth, my heart beating faster.

But they must be too involved in their own conversation to have heard me, because Uncle Herbert was already speaking again. "Maisie never—" he began, voice hot, and then he choked on the rest of the sentence. There was a moment, one during which I was every bit as shocked as he was, I might add, before he spoke again. "No one ever told me!"

"Of course not," Hughes said, her tone dripping with false kindness. "His Grace sent her away, didn't he?"

"Did he?" Uncle Herbert sounded almost confused. "He did? My father?"

"Of course he did, my lord. You were engaged to Miss Roslyn by then, weren't you? It wouldn't do to have Miss Moran show up with a claim."

"But..."

Hughes waited, but Uncle Herbert didn't end up saying anything more. If his thoughts were anything like mine, scurrying like crabs in a bucket, I couldn't blame him for that. Unless I had misunderstood something, he had just been told that an affair he'd had—with one of the maids? Really, Uncle Herbert?—before he married Aunt Roz, had resulted in a child he hadn't known existed.

"Why bring this up now?" Uncle Herbert finally managed, which was a salient point, I thought. It wasn't as if we didn't have plenty of other things to worry about this weekend.

"If not now," Hughes wanted to know, smoothly, "then when?"

After a second she added, "Now is when it matters, isn't it?"

"You mean—?"

Uncle Herbert must have thought better of what he was

going to ask, because he stopped. And thought for a moment before he asked, instead, "What do you want?"

"Money," Hughes said bluntly. When he didn't immediately respond, she added, "You, my lord, have every incentive to help me with that. I'm sure you, like your father, wouldn't want someone with too much knowledge hanging around your wife and children."

There wasn't much Uncle Herbert could say to that, of course. Nor did he try. "How much?" he asked instead, voice rough, and I was vividly reminded of Christopher, sitting on the bed in his room at Sutherland Hall after his audience with the Duke his grandfather, asking Grimsby the same question.

"Enough to go somewhere else for a fresh start," Hughes said. "Somewhere far away from Beckwith Place and Sutherland Hall. I think perhaps it would be better not to tempt fate."

Indeed. I focused on holding my breath and not shifting my feet as Uncle Herbert mentioned a sum. Hughes countered with one quite a bit higher, and they dickered back and forth before settling on the same amount which Grimsby had tried to extort from Christopher two and a half months ago. While Christopher and I hadn't had it, I didn't think coming up with a thousand pounds was going to be a problem for Uncle Herbert. He might have to do some fast talking to Aunt Roz to explain where it had gone, however. It was enough that she'd notice it missing.

Enough for Hughes to buy a small cottage somewhere out of the way, and live quietly on what was left for a good, long time.

"It'll have to wait until after this mess is sorted," Uncle Herbert warned, and Hughes tittered.

"Of course, Lord Herbert. We wouldn't want to draw any extra attention to the current situation."

I rolled my eyes even as I toed my shoes off as quietly as I could. It sounded as if they were winding up the conversation, and the last thing I wanted was to be caught outside the door with my ear to the metaphorical crack. Whatever this had been about, it had clearly been important enough to Uncle Herbert to pay a thousand pounds for Hughes's silence, and it was probably best if he didn't know that any of the rest of us knew about it.

So I slipped my feet out of the shoes and bent and picked them up, and then I scurried, as quietly as I could in my stockings, across the hall and through the door of the boot room. And placed my shoes on the floor there, as if I had just come in from outside. In the event anyone happened to notice me—say, if Hughes made for the side door, the quickest way out of the house—it might look as if I had just arrived from outside.

For good measure, I slipped my feet back into the brogues as my thoughts churned. Uncle Herbert had had an affair with a woman named Maisie Moran before he and Aunt Roz got engaged, and she'd had a child?

Francis was turning thirty next week, and Uncle Herbert and Aunt Roz had been married at least a year or two by the time he came along. He hadn't been one of those 'early' babies, as far as I knew. Maisie Moran's son or daughter would be thirty-two or -three by now, then.

That was if he or she existed at all, of course, and Hughes wasn't just making the whole thing up. She hadn't given Uncle Herbert any proof of anything she'd said. He had tacitly admitted to the affair with Miss Moran, and hadn't claimed that a child couldn't have come from it, so I supposed I'd have to take that part of it as fact. But just because there could have been a child, didn't mean that there had been one.

I knew nobody whose last name was Moran. But then Maisie might not be a Moran any longer. Uncle Herbert had married. She might have married, too, and taken her husband's name. And so might her child.

And whatever name it bore, Maisie's child would be a decade too old to have been Abigail Dole. But Hughes had said that it happened again. And it sounded as if it had happened around the same time that Hughes had come up from Dorset in exchange for Lydia Morrison, which had been when Crispin (and Christopher, and for that matter myself) had been infants. Around the same time, I would guess, that Abigail had been one, too.

For Uncle Herbert to have had another child the same age as Christopher, he would have had to—I winced—commit adultery while Aunt Roz was expecting. I don't know why that should make it worse, but somehow it did. I didn't think I would ever be able to forgive my (hypothetical, future) husband if he cheated on me, but if he did so while I was carrying his unborn child, not only would I not forgive him, but I'd probably go after him with a mallet of my own.

But perhaps Christopher had come about as a result of the affair. After, not before. If Uncle Herbert and Aunt Roz were trying to repair their marriage after Uncle Herbert's indiscretion, and they thought another child would do it, they might have had Christopher.

I made a face. The idea of my best friend being the result of an attempted reconciliation between his parents was a bit unpleasant, honestly. I wanted him to be a product of a happy mother and father deciding, after a few years, to try for another child, not a last ditch attempt to fix a failing marriage after one party cheated on the other.

Although none of this was my affair—pun totally intended. What mattered, was that it was possible that Abigail Dole was Uncle Herbert's child by someone other than Aunt Roz. And that would explain why little Bess looked like a Sutherland.

Abigail didn't, or hadn't, but if the genes were there, she could have given birth to a child with Sutherland hair and eyes.

What it didn't explain, was that list of items we had found in her tote. Fair hair, blue eyes, black motorcar, grandson of the Duke of Sutherland.

Unless that wasn't Abigail's list, of course, but her mother's. Uncle Herbert had been the grandson of the (previous) Duke of Sutherland at the time when Abigail would have been conceived, before the old man died and Henry succeeded to the title.

I had never been able to reconcile the idea that either Christopher, Crispin, or Francis had lied to me about Abigail. They'd all three sounded very sincere in their denial of her and her child, and this explained why.

What it didn't explain, was who had killed her. But that really seemed like something of a side-issue at this point. I could reason that away as having been done by Laetitia, or in a pinch by Constance or Uncle Harold. Someone who wasn't actually family and whom I would feel better about throwing to the wolves than my own flesh and blood.

No, this was all very much to the good, actually. Yes, my uncle was being blackmailed, and he had, apparently, been unfaithful to my aunt at some point before I'd been born. But while that was bad, nobody in the family appeared to be guilty of murder. I could relax.

And so I did, so much so that I actually staggered, and accidentally knocked into a walking stick that was leaning in the corner of the boot room. It fell over, clattering against the door, and that caused my uncle, who was still lingering in the hallway after seeing Hughes on her way, to appear in the doorway, as pale as a ghost and with terror in his eyes.

It was only slightly mollified by the sight of me. "Oh." He

sounded out of breath, although he had certainly not exerted himself on his way across the hallway, so it must be nerves. "It's you, Pippa. What are you doing here?"

He glanced around the tiny boot room, probably to ascertain that I was alone.

"Just came in from outside," I said brightly. "The vehicle from the morgue left with the body, and Christopher offered to take Doctor White to the village in the Bentley. I hope you don't mind."

I'm a reasonably good liar, if I do say so myself. I don't think my voice gave anything away. It sounded perfectly normal and cheerful in my ears.

"No, no." Uncle Harold waved it off as if it were nothing. Under normal circumstances, I would have expected at least a wince at the idea of letting his youngest son go off in the beloved automobile, but right now there was no reaction to that bit of news at all.

"Did you..." He eyed me, "Just now, did you say?"

I nodded.

"Through this door?"

"Of course. Where else would I—?" *Oh.*

"I locked it earlier," Uncle Herbert said gently. "After I let Hughes in. I didn't want people coming and going through all areas of the house, so I locked this door."

Oops. I glanced at the key in the lock, and then back at Uncle Herbert. I'm sure guilt was writ all over my face in large letters.

"How much did you hear?" he wanted to know.

I winced. "Not all of it. Enough to know that you had an affair with one of the servants before you married Aunt Roz, and another with someone else before Christopher was born. And that there may have been children."

"May have been?"

"I didn't hear any proof," I said.

Uncle Herbert nodded. "What do you plan to do with this knowledge, Pippa?"

I blinked. I hadn't thought that far ahead, actually. "Is there something I should do with it?"

His lips curved hopefully. "I suppose it would be too much to ask you to keep it to yourself?"

"I'm not in the habit of keeping things from Christopher," I said.

It wasn't a threat. I wasn't trying to be clever or calculated or whatever it might have sounded like. The words simply fell out of my mouth because they were true. I don't keep things from Christopher. That's not to say that I tell him everything. I don't. But I've never held something like this back. Something that affects him as much as, if not more than, me.

"And we love you for it," Uncle Herbert said sincerely. "You've been the best friend we could have asked for, for Christopher. All these years you've been like a sister to him, and to Francis."

I nodded. We'd shared everything for twelve years, Christopher and I. The idea of keeping this secret from him made my stomach hurt.

However, so did telling him what his father had done.

"He doesn't need to hear this, Pippa," Uncle Herbert said, with something that hit in the neighborhood between anguish and persuasion in his voice. "It would only upset him, when there's nothing he can do about it. It would upset them all."

'Them all' being Francis and Aunt Roz, I assumed. Perhaps Uncle Harold, who might hold his brother in higher regard than to suspect him of having indulged in multiple affairs—not that there was any part of me that wanted to run to Uncle

Harold to tell tales. This was none of Uncle Harold's concern, and aside from that, he might know already.

But there was one person who really ought to know.

"Aunt Roz..." I began, and Uncle Herbert flapped a hand.

"Roz knows."

My jaw dropped. "Aunt Roz... knows?"

He nodded. "Of course. Did you think I would keep secrets from my wife? I told her about Maisie before we were married."

Before I could say anything, a shadow crossed his face. "I didn't know that there was a child, of course. If I had known, I might have been forced to act differently. My father was right about that..."

Duke Henry had been right in sending Maisie Moran away, I assumed, or Uncle Herbert might have felt compelled to marry her, once he knew about the child, instead of Aunt Roslyn.

"But the other—"

He shook his head. "There were extenuating circumstances, Pippa. And I'm not discussing them with you. But you will not—*will not*, do I make myself clear?—you *will not* ask your aunt to explain them. Roz knows, but that doesn't mean I want it dredged up again. Bad enough that I'll have to tell her about Maisie's child."

"You'll tell her about that?"

"I don't keep secrets from my wife, Pippa," Uncle Herbert said sternly. "And when you marry—"

He stopped, rather abruptly, and breathed in and out through his nose a couple of times. When he continued speaking, he sounded less peremptory, so maybe he had realized that he wasn't really in a good position to be giving marital advice. "When you marry, I hope you won't keep secrets from your husband, either. A happy marriage is built on trust."

Easy for him to say. It couldn't be simple to trust a man who had cheated on you before, so more power to Aunt Roz. But I did love her, she was my blood, and Uncle Herbert was right: I didn't want to cause her any more pain than he must have already caused with this behavior.

"I won't say anything," I said grudgingly. "Not to Aunt Roz nor to anyone else. Not Christopher or Francis or even Constance."

"Or Crispin," Uncle Herbert said.

"No, of course not. It's none of his concern, is it?" Uncle Herbert didn't respond, and I added, "It's not like we're close, you know. Everyone's acting as if something's going on with us, but the truth is that I can barely stand to be in the same room with him, and he doesn't like me any better. I'm certainly not going to confide family secrets in him."

Uncle Herbert nodded. He stuck out a hand. "Shake on it?"

"I suppose," I said grudgingly.

"Good girl." He gave my hand a squeeze. "I promise you there are extenuating circumstances, Pippa. I can't tell you what they are, and I beg you not to interrogate your Aunt Roz or Hughes, but I swear I'm not such a cad as I seem. There were reasons, good reasons, for doing what I did."

"I believe you," I said, even if I wasn't sure I did. I loved my uncle, though. He had taken me in and had become my surrogate father when my parents sent me to England before the war. I didn't want this to come between us.

"Thank you, my dear." He put a hand on my shoulder for a moment. "Now... will you come into the sitting room with the others?"

"I think I need a few minutes to myself," I said. "I think perhaps I'll go back outside and wait for Christopher to come back."

If I tried to go upstairs, there was a chance that someone would see me, and I didn't think I could face Aunt Roz, or Francis or Constance, right now. "Not to talk to," I added. "Not about this. I promised, and I won't. But I think I could use some fresh air. Is it all right if I go out this way?"

"Of course, Pippa." Uncle Herbert turned the key in the lock and pulled the door open. "I'll just lock this behind you again. Better not to have people wandering in and out everywhere."

Definitely. Especially considering the things they might overhear.

"Has Sammy... has Constable Entwistle got around to doing individual interviews yet?"

"He spoke to the Earl and Countess Marsden," Uncle Herbert said, "and to Lord Geoffrey. I can only assume he thinks they are the least likely to be involved, since they have no connection to the Astleys except through their niece."

"No interview with Laetitia?"

Uncle Herbert shook his head. "I hope you have a plan, Pippa, or she'll have Crispin hogtied and bound for the altar before the weekend is over."

"I didn't realize it was up to me to prevent that," I said.

"Someone has to," Uncle Herbert answered, which wasn't an answer, although it was at least nice to know that someone else shared my reservations.

"I've tried to speak to him about it. Two months ago, he was adamant that he didn't want to marry her. I don't know why he isn't putting up more of a fight now."

"Try again?" Uncle Herbert suggested.

"I suppose I'll have to, if nothing changes. Although he might be more inclined to listen to you. Crispin's never liked me much, you know."

"I doubt that," Uncle Herbert said, surely in response to my first statement and not my second. He shook his head. "I can't go behind my brother's back, Pippa. Crispin's his heir, and Harold seems to want him settled down. And I can't say that I blame him. The boy's running wild."

No question about that. "But surely sticking him in an arranged marriage he doesn't want isn't going to make him any less likely to play the field? He'll just be more unhappy and more likely to act out, won't he?"

"I imagine so," Uncle Herbert admitted, "but it's up to my brother what he arranges, and up to Crispin what he'll accept. Perhaps just encourage him not to do anything rash?"

I had no idea why he thought it was my responsibility to affect this, and furthermore, I had no expectation that Crispin would listen any better than he had the last few times I'd brought it up, but I didn't want Laetitia as part of the family either. "It can't hurt to try again, I suppose. I'll try to get him alone at some point today."

"Perhaps we can just hope that Lady Laetitia was responsible for what happened to the poor young lady," Uncle Herbert said, "and Constable Entwistle will take her off to prison for us."

That would be nice. However— "That's what I hoped would happen when Johanna de Vos died. But alas."

Uncle Herbert chuckled. "You'll figure it out, Pippa."

I had absolutely no expectation that I would, but I told him, "Thank you, Uncle Herbert. I'll see you later, then. I'm going to get some air before Christopher gets back."

"He took Doctor White into the village in the Bentley, you said?" Uncle Herbert looked pained. He must have finally realized what I had told him earlier.

I nodded. "I'm sure he'll be fine, Uncle. Wilkins let him drive Uncle Harold's Crossley back from the village yesterday, and that was no problem."

"Let's hope so," Uncle Herbert said. "I'll go join the others. Don't go far, Pippa."

I told him I wouldn't, and then I let him shut and lock the boot room door behind me as I set off down the driveway in the direction of the lane.

CHAPTER EIGHTEEN

THIS WAS a pretty pickle I found myself in, I admitted to myself as I kicked small pieces of gravel out of my way as I walked. Having to keep things from my best friend—my flatmate, my cousin, my other half. And worse than that, I now *knew* things about his family that I had no business knowing. Personal things that Christopher didn't even know, and that I couldn't share with him, both because I had promised, and because Uncle Herbert was right: knowing would only hurt Christopher.

But even as my conscience fought with itself, my logical brain was telling me that this opened the field of suspects by two. If Abigail Dole had been Uncle Herbert's daughter from his second affair, the Sutherland hair and Astley eyes that little Bess inherited would be adequately explained.

And if Abigail was not Uncle Herbert's daughter, then there was Maisie Moran's child, who would be older than Francis by now. If that child had been a boy—and the Astleys did run to a lot of boys—he could be little Bess's father. He could have met Abigail Dole at the Hammersmith Palais, and told her that he was the grandson of the Duke of Sutherland, and it wouldn't even have been a lie.

Of course, Uncle Herbert's second illegitimate child might have been a boy, as well. The one Aunt Roz knew about, because there were extenuating circumstances, whatever that meant.

And he would be younger than Francis. As young as Christopher, even, Or anywhere between thirty and twenty-three.

A head of red hair intruded on my inner vision, followed by the rest of Sammy Entwistle's freckled face. Moran was an Irish name. Maisie might have had red hair that she passed on to her child. He did have blue eyes. And it would explain Sammy's ongoing resentment towards all the Astleys, but especially Robbie. The legitimate son who was the same age as himself.

God—I winced—that would explain rather a lot, wouldn't it?

"No." I shook my head. "Surely not. That can't be. Not Sammy."

Only to be interrupted by a disembodied voice from my left. "Dear me, Darling, what are you muttering about? Surely not Sammy, what?"

"Oh." I managed to swallow my heart back down to where it belonged, although it was still beating hard enough to hurt my chest. And the palm I pressed against it didn't help at all. "St George. I didn't see you there."

"That's rather the point, Darling, don't you think?"

He was crouched on the running board of the Hispano-Suiza, out of sight of the house and with a lit cigarette dangling from his fingers.

I eyed it. "What's the matter, St George? Won't Laetitia let you smoke in public anymore, so you have to hide to get your fix?"

"Of course not, Darling." He dropped what was left of the fag to the dirt and ground it under his shoe. After blowing out the last mouthful of smoke, he added, "Laetitia smokes quite as much as I do. She doesn't mind."

"Why are you over here skulking, then?"

"Needed some fresh air," Crispin said, which was ridiculous, considering that he'd been sucking in lungfuls of smoke.

I sniggered. "Fed up with the adoration, are you?"

He gave me a look. "I'm sure I don't know what you mean, Darling."

"No, I'm sure you don't." I leaned against the opposite car, which happened to be Constance's burgundy Crossley, and folded my arms across my chest. "You don't have to put up with it, you know."

"Unbridled devotion is hardly a burden, Darling."

"No? The constant cooing isn't a bit much?" He didn't react, and I added, "I could understand if you were in love with her, but we both know you're not."

I waited another moment, but when he didn't say anything, I continued, "What happened to the girl you said you were in love with? Have you given up on that?"

"She doesn't want me," Crispin said sulkily, without meeting my eyes.

"How do you know?" I nudged the toe of his shoe with mine to get him to look at me. He did, but only for a second. "Have you told her? And not just in your usual nonchalant fashion? You know, sincerely, with some actual feelings behind it?"

"No." He moved his foot out of the way of mine, and addressed the ground between his feet rather than me. "I told you. I have nothing to offer. Father would never approve, so we would have to run away and live in squalor on the Continent, because I'd have to renounce the title and estates and become a pauper."

I giggled. "At least you're able to properly articulate 'renounce' this time. Last time you mangled it."

Last time had been a month ago, when he'd showed up at my and Christopher's flat and tried to talk me into going out to celebrate his birthday with him. He had used almost exactly the same words then.

He scowled. "It's not funny, Darling."

"Of course it is. If that's how you propose to all your women—" Three sheets to the wind and with the delivery (and sincerity) of a musical comedy actor—

"It's not."

"—it's no wonder they don't take you seriously."

He glared at me. "I didn't intend for you to take me seriously. Although I suppose you'd insist that I get down on one knee, wouldn't you? The heir to the Sutherlands, tractable and obedient and kneeling at your feet, offering up the Sutherland parure in the hopes that you'd have me? Is that the kind of husband you're looking for, Darling?"

"Not at all," I said with a shudder. "The Sutherland parure is hideous, and certainly no incentive to marriage. Besides, I gave you my answer last month, St George. Don't you dare."

I could just imagine the scene that would ensue if Laetitia, or Sammy Entwistle, or—God forbid—Uncle Harold came outside and found him down on one knee in front of me, mock-proposing.

He nodded blandly. "I remember, Darling. 'Keep the title and fortune,' wasn't it? Followed by, 'I don't want them—or you?'"

It was. Or had been. That was pretty much word for word what I'd told him, as a matter of fact. Although I was surprised that he remembered it so clearly, because he had been thoroughly potted at the time. "If she loves you," I said carefully, "she'll live in squalor on the Continent with you."

"I don't want her to!" Crispin retorted angrily. "Besides, I told you. You just—"

—*don't listen*, I assumed. He stopped before he could finish the sentence, and said instead, more calmly, "She doesn't want me."

"Crispin..."

He looked up, and for a second his eyes were the clear gray of water, open and completely transparent, and so sad that my chest clutched.

Until the shutters slammed down and the corner of his mouth curved up. It took only a moment. "Don't feel sorry for me, Darling. I don't want your pity, and I certainly have no reason to whinge. I can marry Laetitia next week if I want to, and if it isn't love, it's close enough."

No, it wasn't. "Just because your father thinks it's time you settle down and stop running wild—"

He chuckled. "Did he tell you that?"

I snorted. "Of course not. Your father and I aren't on speaking terms. Especially not now, when I would gladly throttle him for pushing you at Laetitia the way he's doing. If you're not careful, you'll be engaged by the end of the weekend."

"There are worse things," Crispin said with a shrug. "Better than being arrested, at any rate."

"Is there a chance of that?"

He squinted at me. "I figure it's an equal chance that he'll haul in any one of us, Darling. He'd prefer for it to be Francis, no doubt, but he'll take any one of us he can get. We've all got alibis, but they're all from people who'd lie for us anyway. I'd lie for Kit, and I'm sure Kit would do the same for me. Constance would lie for Francis. You'd lie for either of them, or for Constance—"

"Or for you," I said.

"Would you, Darling? Charmed, I'm sure."

I shrugged. "Don't be too flattered. I just don't think you did it. I'm sure Christopher didn't, and I don't think Francis did, either. But none of you should need me to lie. Your alibis are good and neither of you had the opportunity to kill her."

Crispin nodded. "Well, someone did. If not one of us, then someone else. What was that you were muttering about when you first turned up? Not Sammy what?"

"Oh." I flushed. "None of your concern, St George."

"Hmm." He looked me up and down, with special attention to my flaming face. "Dear me, Darling, have you formed an illicit passion for Constable Entwistle? Is he your idea of the perfect husband?"

"Don't be ridiculous," I said. "He beat up Robbie. How could I form an illicit passion for someone who beat up my cousin?"

"I'm sure I don't know, Darling. Not Sammy what, then?"

"I told you. None of your concern."

He arched that infernal brow. "If you don't tell me, you'll have to put up with me drawing my own conclusions, you know."

"I guess I'll have to," I said crossly, "because I promised, and..."

"Oho!" He grinned. "And who did you promise, pray tell?"

"No one," I said, since I had already admitted more than I should have.

He gave me a shrewd look. "Uncle Herbert, was it? Oh, relax—"

Because my eyes widened and my jaw dropped.

"I'm not a diviner or anything. I saw him let you out through the boot room door."

"Oh." I started breathing again. "Well, I'm sorry, St George, but I can't—"

"No, no." He waved a hand. "I bet I know what it is anyway."

I certainly wasn't going to fall for that twice. So I put my hands on my hips and scowled at him. "You do not!"

"I may not. But I heard a few things when I was hiding in that secret passage outside Grandfather's room before he died. Things I didn't tell you at the time."

"I'm sure you did," I said, "you infernal cockroach—"

"Now, now, Darling. Name-calling will get you nowhere."

"I'm not trying to get anywhere! Unless it's away from you, you awful excuse for a human being!"

"Uncle Herbert fathered a son with someone other than Aunt Roslyn," Crispin said flatly, and I slapped my hand across his mouth.

"Be quiet!" For good measure, I leaned in until we were practically nose to nose and I could see his pupils dilate. "He told me not to tell anyone, and that means that I'm not to speak of it. Not even to someone who already knows. Certainly not where anyone else can hear! I want you to promise me that you won't mention it again. Promise me, St George!"

He said something, lips moving against my palm, and I snatched my hand away. "What?"

"I said, how am I supposed to promise anything when you've got your sweaty palm over my mouth?"

I narrowed my eyes. "That's not what you said. It was something much shorter than that!"

"I said, unhand me." He fished his handkerchief out of his pocket and dragged it across his mouth. "God, you're awful, Darling. It was all I could do not to bite you."

"Fine," I said. "I won't do it again. Just promise me, St George. Promise you won't talk to anyone about this."

"I did," Crispin said. "That's what I said. I promise. Besides, I'm not the one you need worry about, you know. I've known for months, and I haven't said a word to anyone. You found out ten minutes ago, and you've already told me."

He moved to stuff the handkerchief back into the pocket of his trousers.

"Give me that." I snatched it out of his hand to wipe my palm with it. *Cooties, ugh.* "Although you're right about the rest of it. I'm a horrible person. I broke my uncle's confidence, and it didn't even take a quarter of an hour."

He sighed, and accepted the handkerchief back. "You're not a horrible person, Darling. I tricked you, all right? You wouldn't have said anything otherwise."

"You did not. You already knew. You said it first."

He shrugged, and I added, "But we can't talk of it again. Any of it. Maisie Moran's child or the... the other thing. He doesn't want Christopher and Francis to know."

Crispin nodded. "Believe me, Darling, I feel the same. It would only make them feel awful. Better we keep it between the two of us. Or three."

"Four," I said. "Apparently Aunt Roz knows."

He rolled his eyes. "Of course she does. Four, then."

"But he doesn't want me to talk to her about it, either."

"No," Crispin said, "I can quite imagine why. Very well, then. If you feel the need to jabber, I suppose you'll just have to come to me."

I rolled my eyes. "I'm sure Laetitia will appreciate that."

"She'll cope," Crispin said. "It's not as if she has to worry about you giving her competition for my attention, is it?"

"Of course not. She's welcome to you. You know that."

He nodded. "Precisely."

"I just don't think you should marry her. For your own sake, you know. And a little bit for ours, too, I guess—she's bloody awful, St George—but mostly for yours. I don't care what you do, but I also don't see any reason why you should set yourself up for unhappiness with the wrong woman when you know that the right one is out there, and all you have to do is suck up your pride and tell her how you feel."

"She doesn't want me," Crispin said. "And even if she'd take me, which she wouldn't, I have nothing to offer her. But I thank you for your concern, Darling. I'll take it under advisement."

It sounded like a dismissal, so I nodded. "I'm going to walk down to the lane and see if Christopher is coming. You may join me if you wish."

"I think I'd better go back inside," Crispin answered. "If I delay much longer, Laetitia is likely to come look for me."

"At least she's not carrying her ostrich feather fan today. You don't have to worry about being slapped with it. And that's another thing—"

"Just a love tap, Darling. Nothing to worry about."

It hadn't been, actually. I'd been watching, and it had been rather more than a love tap. But if he was the one she'd hit, and he didn't complain, who was I to do so? So I merely told him, "I'll see you inside, then, St George. Don't do anything I wouldn't do."

He quirked a brow. "Propose?"

I shuddered. "God, no. Not at ten in the morning with a murder and an illegitimate child hanging over you." And not to Laetitia Marsden.

"See you later, then, Darling. Enjoy your walk."

He set off for the front door. I watched for a moment before I headed down the driveway to look for Christopher.

· · ·

WHEN A VEHICLE APPEARED, however it was not the Astleys Bentley. It was yet another Crossley, one of the less luxurious and more utilitarian Tenders that the London Metropolitan Police had invested in after the war. From behind the wheel beamed the handsome face of Detective Sergeant Thomas Gardiner with Scotland Yard. "Hullo there, Pippa. Waiting for me?"

"Waiting for Christopher, actually," I said, "although I'm happy to see you."

"Hop in, I'll give you a lift back up to the house."

It was a three-minute walk, no more, but it seemed silly to let him drive it alone while I ran after the motorcar, so I swung myself up into the passenger seat and watched him let out the clutch. Once we were moving again, he slanted me a look. "Is Kit not here?"

"He drove the doctor down to the village in Uncle Herbert's car," I said. "You must have passed it on the way."

"I wasn't paying much attention. I was concerned with getting here as quickly as I could."

"And we appreciate it," I said. "You can park just over there, with the others." I waved to what was essentially a car park in front of the carriage house. "We have more motorcars than we know what to do with right now. Uncle Harold and St George motored up separately, God knows why, although it looks like Wilkins took the Crossley back to the village, actually..."

It wasn't with the others, anyway, so unless he'd made a run for it, the black Crossley was likely parked in front of the pub. He must have gotten away while I'd been eavesdropping on Uncle Herbert and Hughes.

"The Marsdens brought their Daimler up from Dorset,

along with the Peckhams' Crossley, since I guess that belongs to Constance now..."

Tom didn't say anything, just slotted the Tender into the spot where the Duke's Crossley had been, turned it off, and let me ramble.

"The only ones with no vehicles are the constables. They're getting around on bicycles. But the vehicle from the mortuary was here earlier and picked up the body and the croquet mallet..."

Tom nodded. "Would you like to tell me what's going on before we go inside? Kit didn't have time to go into much detail when he rang up this morning."

"Of course." I took a breath and let it trickle out again. "Where would you like me to start?"

"At the beginning," Tom said. "That's usually best."

Right. The beginning.

I thought back, over what he might reasonably know and what it was likely that he didn't. Tom had been there during the weekend at Sutherland Hall when Duke Henry and Grimsby were killed, when I'd first heard about the girl with the baby. Crispin had known about her earlier, of course, but that was my introduction to the subject, and I assumed it had been Tom's as well, so I decided to start there, with a recap of that story and then everything that had happened since.

"And this morning she was dead on the lawn?" Tom asked when I had gone through it all. "You saw her through the window?"

I nodded. "I knocked up Christopher and Crispin, and we all went down together."

"Was there a reason you thought you might need rein-forcements?"

"I suppose..." I hesitated. "They were there, just across the hall. We were all three of us on the top floor. It seemed silly not to wake them while I was up there, that way I wouldn't have to run back in and up three flights of stairs if I needed them later."

Tom nodded.

"But also, it was a bit eerie to see her again, so similar to yesterday afternoon. Sprawled on the grass in almost the same spot. I suppose I was, subconsciously at least, thinking that someone might have to carry her inside."

"You didn't see the blood until you came outside?"

I shook my head. "It's a long way down. And her hair was brown. It blended. And the sun wasn't fully up yet, either. And I don't think there was much blood on the grass, just on her head."

Tom nodded, and I added, "By the way, Doctor White came and looked at her, and he said that the croquet mallet wasn't the murder weapon. Someone hit her with something else first, something metal, and then fetched the mallet and—" I winced, "rubbed it in the wound so it would look like the murder weapon."

"Cold," Tom commented.

I nodded. Yes, indeed. Not only to take the time to replace the actual murder weapon with something else—and in full view of half the bedrooms in the house, too, even if it probably had been the middle of the night and we were all asleep—but to do *that* to it!

"I suppose I should go introduce myself to the chap in charge," Tom said.

"Are you taking over the investigation?"

I asked it hopefully, but I wasn't surprised when he shook his head. "We have to be called in by the Chief Constable, and your Constable Entwistle doesn't seem to think that's necessary."

"He's not *my* Constable Entwistle," I said; that was all I needed, for someone other than St George to latch onto that fallacy, "and besides, he probably thinks it's going to be easy. I'm sure he's just looking for a reason to arrest Francis."

"Why Francis?"

That necessitated an explanation which included Robbie, who had been Tom's best friend during their years at Eton, before they were both sent to France and Robbie didn't come back.

At the end of it, Tom nodded understanding, but said, "I thought you told me Francis has an alibi."

"He does! He was thoroughly spiflicated, for one thing. Absolutely blotto. I'm sure, if he'd tried to hit someone over the head in that condition, he wouldn't have known which head to aim for."

Tom chuckled, and I added, "Constance spent the night with him. They both ended up in the library. She hadn't had anything to drink—she never drinks much—and she spent the night in a chair. She would have heard him get up if he tried to leave."

"Not Francis, then. Who else does he suspect?"

I had no idea who Sammy suspected, or whether he suspected anyone at all, or perhaps he was just busy building a case against the person he most wanted to arrest. "I don't see who it could be," I told Tom honestly. "Christopher and Crispin spent the night together. In the same room, I mean. And while they might lie for one another, I don't think either of them is capable of committing murder."

Or at least not this murder.

"I slept alone," I added. "So did Laetitia Marsden. Constance was supposed to be in with her, or she was supposed to be in Constance's room, but Constance stayed in the library with Francis, as I said, so Laetitia got the room to herself."

"Shades of the Dower House situation," Tom commented.

I nodded. "Geoffrey Marsden also slept alone, and so did

Uncle Harold. Aunt Roz and Uncle Herbert shared, of course, and so did the Countess and Earl of Marsden. I slept alone."

"No one else on the premises?"

I shook my head. "Not overnight. Aunt Roz runs the house with very little help. Cook lives in the village, and Hughes ended up above the pub with Wilkins, I think."

"Your late aunt's maid from Sutherland Hall, you mean? She's here?"

I nodded. "She came here with the party from Sutherland Hall yesterday. And I suppose I ought to tell you..."

I hesitated, wondering whether I truly ought, or whether I just felt like I should. Tom wasn't in charge of the case, although I personally thought he stood a much better chance of solving it than Sammy Entwistle did. He wasn't biased, for one thing. Or at least if he was biased, it was in our favor.

On the other hand, I had told Uncle Herbert I wouldn't talk about it. But surely I could mention Hughes's blackmail without going into the reasons for it? If Tom had to solve the case, surely he needed to know about that. And it was a criminal offense, wasn't it?

"I overheard her blackmailing my uncle," I said.

"The Duke?"

I shook my head, and then tilted it curiously. "Does Uncle Harold have something he can be blackmailed over?"

Tom didn't answer beyond an arched eyebrow, and I made a face. "It was Uncle Herbert. They were in the study talking earlier, and they didn't hear me come down the hallway. And it was over something that happened ages ago. Before Christopher was born. And before Hughes arrived from Dorset to work for Aunt Charlotte. Apparently Lydia Morrison told her."

"Who's Lydia Morrison?"

I explained who Lydia Morrison was, and Tom nodded. "I already know what Hughes was holding over your uncle's head.

You don't have to tell me."

"I wasn't going to," I said grumpily. "I just wondered... You know about the child, I assume? Or children? Who they are? Or ended up being?"

Tom didn't answer, just gave me another inscrutable look, and I sighed. "Just answer this. Abigail Dole. She wasn't Uncle Herbert's daughter, was she?"

Tom looked at me. After a moment, a corner of his mouth turned up. "No. She wasn't."

I nodded. "So whoever the baby's father was... by the way, you should go inside and see little Bess. Aunt Roz has been taking care of her since yesterday afternoon. There's really no denying that she's a Sutherland. And if Abigail wasn't one, then one of the men in the family must be responsible."

"I thought you'd always assumed that."

I had always assumed that. But— "When I learned that Uncle Herbert had had a child with someone other than Aunt Roz, I thought maybe..."

"No," Tom said. "Abigail Dole was not your cousin. I actually spent some time this week looking into her, as it happens, so I can assure you of that."

I must have looked surprised, because he added, "Kit told me last week that she had turned up and might be thinking of causing trouble. I decided to do some digging."

Good for him. "And?"

"Abigail Dole is from Bristol originally. Her parents still live there. She has lived in London for the past four years or so, working as a shop clerk. That ended when the baby was born."

"In January?"

He nodded. "The baby was born at the East End Maternity Hospital in Stepney. The father's name on the birth certificate was noted as unknown. Abigail listed the Blackwall Buildings in Thomas Street in Whitechapel as her home address. Finch is there now, trying to learn what he can."

He glanced at his watch before he added, "He's probably back at the Yard by now, actually. It took me a while to get here. I should ring up and see what he's discovered."

"Let me take you inside," I said, and fumbled for the handle on the door. "You've been here before, haven't you?"

He nodded. "With Robbie, when we were lads. It's been ten years or more, though."

"Uncle Herbert locked the boot room door," I explained, taking Tom's arm, "so we'd better go through the front. Unless you'd like to see the croquet lawn and the scene of the crime. If so, we can go through the terrasse door instead."

"I wouldn't mind getting the lay of the land, and a look at the crime scene. As I said, it's been a while."

"This way, then."

We pushed through the trees and bushes—"That's where we found Abigail's tote last night," I pointed out, "with the list she made on the train," —and emerged at the back of the house. The constable who had been squatting on the crime scene earlier was nowhere to be seen now, and I indicated the general direction of where the body had been. "That was where she was this morning. Yesterday, she collapsed more in this vicinity. Just a few steps out from the bushes."

Tom had stopped, and was looking around. "And the doctor said what, exactly?"

"About the collapse? Exhaustion, heat, dehydration. Nothing criminal or sinister. Probably just from making her way here from Salisbury, and from not taking care of herself generally."

Tom nodded, eyeing the grass. "They haven't secured the crime scene in any way."

No, they hadn't.

"I guess Sammy thinks he's gleaned everything there is to

glean," I said.

Tom scuffed the grass with the tip of his shoe. "He might be right. Not much hope for footprints on this."

"No. Come on, let's get you inside so you can make your presence known, and then you can ring up London and Detective Sergeant Finchley."

We abandoned the grassy lawn and headed up the steps to the terrasse and the back door.

CHAPTER NINETEEN

INSIDE, I pointed out the library to Tom, and then the entrance to the kitchen. Hughes was inside, helping Aunt Roz prepare some sort of food. She's not a cook nor scullery maid, of course, and I could see from her expression—sour—that she did the kitchen work only reluctantly. But then Aunt Roz was right there next to her, with her title and her money, and I guess Hughes felt like she couldn't in good conscience refuse when Lady Herbert was doing the work right alongside her.

"Thomas!" Aunt Roz seemed delighted to see Tom. So much so that she dropped what she was doing and came to embrace him. "You darling boy! How lovely to see you!"

"Lady Roslyn." Tom embraced her back, a bit gingerly.

"Is Christopher not with you?" She peered past him to me, and past me to where there was no one.

"He went to the village in the Bentley," I said. "I told Uncle Herbert and he said it was all right."

"Of course, Pippa, dear. Why would he do that?"

Christopher and not Uncle Herbert, I assumed. "He took

Doctor White home. Or to wherever the post mortem is taking place."

"Ah." She looked partly enlightened and partly nauseated. "That poor girl."

I nodded. "Speaking of poor girls, Tom would like a look at the baby."

"Constance has her," Aunt Roz said. "She's quite good with her, as a matter of fact. Much better than I would have expected for someone with no experience with babies."

"I don't think we'll get to keep her," I said, since it was obvious that my aunt was already getting attached to little Bess.

She brushed me off. "Of course not, Pippa. I'm just ready for grandchildren, and none of you have seen fit to give me any. But hopefully Francis and Constance will get on that shortly."

Better them than me. "I'll take Tom in," I said. "Do you need me to come back and help you with anything?"

"No, no, dear." She shook her head. "Hughes and I are managing. She's been invaluable, really."

She beamed at Hughes, who responded with a colorless, "Thank you, my lady."

"We'll be off, then," I said. "Let me know if you change your mind."

Aunt Roz nodded. "I will, dear. But with Christopher gone, you had better stick with Thomas. Don't let Sammy bully him."

"Of course not." It was far more likely—and would be much more satisfying—to watch Tom bully Sammy.

"You can let Euphemia know that it won't be long now. She was quite put out by the lack of a tray in her room this morning."

"Spoiled," I said. "Like her daughter."

Aunt Roz rolled her eyes. "I do hope poor Crispin comes to his senses before she manages to tie him down. Harold should be ashamed of himself for encouraging it."

Yes. He should. "We'll just have to hope that His Grace sees the light and lets Crispin have what he wants without disinheriting him," I said. "He's quite as spoiled as Lady Euphemia, you know. He wouldn't last a week without his creature comforts. Truly, he probably does have the right idea about not subjecting his lady-love to himself in penury. No matter how much she might love him—if she does—I wouldn't wish that fate on anyone."

I turned to Tom. "Ready to go?"

He nodded.

"Let me know if you change your mind about the help, Aunt Roz."

She flapped a hand in my direction. "We're almost done, dear. You two go on. And if you find a way to disrupt your uncle's plans along the way, do go ahead and take it."

I promised her I would, and then Tom and I left the kitchen and headed for the front of the house. The study was empty this time, and so was the boot room. The stairwell to the cellars was lit up, however, with scrabbling sounds coming from below, and once we were in the foyer we could hear voices from the sitting room, as well.

"—can't believe your cheek!" Euphemia Marsden's voice said.

I expected her to be talking to Crispin, or perhaps to Francis, who had been known to be cheeky on occasion, too. I didn't expect for it to be Constance who answered back.

"I'm sorry, Aunt Effie—" She didn't sound sorry at all, "—but the constable is just doing his job. If you didn't have the opportunity to hurt Miss Dole, you can simply say so."

"Well, I'm saying so," Euphemia said with a sniff. "I was in bed with my husband all night, and I do not appreciate the impertinence of being asked to verify that! I had no reason to want that unfortunate girl dead—"

She went on in this vein for another half minute, while Tom smirked.

"Hazard of the job," he told me, when I quirked an inquiring brow his way. "We often have to ask impertinent questions of people who think they're too good to answer. I suppose Constable Entwistle hasn't had much opportunity to deal with the upper classes."

Probably not. Murders in high society aren't plentiful here in Beckwith. Aside from the war and the occasional partridge party, we're a peaceful group overall.

"Just go introduce yourself," I told him. "You'll have her eating out of your hand in no time. Sammy might even be grateful for the rescue."

Tom gave me a jaundiced sort of look—yes, I didn't really believe what I was saying, either—but he stepped forward into the doorway.

The sitting room went quiet as people noticed him standing there. Even Lady Euphemia wound down. Then—

"Tommy," Francis said, and the relief was evident in his voice.

"Thomas," Uncle Herbert added, genially. "You made it."

"Detective Sergeant." This was Laetitia, and she was fluttering her eyelashes. She did it when presented with any good-looking young man, which Tom definitely was, and it had, no doubt, the added benefit of possibly making Crispin jealous.

I rolled my eyes and stepped into the doorway behind him, as he made his way into the room.

"Gardiner," Crispin said, while Constance simply smiled demurely. If Crispin was jealous of Laetitia's fluttering, it was not evident in his voice.

Tom greeted them all before turning to Sammy, who was seated awkwardly on one of Aunt Roz's spindliest chairs with his notebook open against his thigh. I wondered whose idea it had been, whether someone had done it deliberately—Crispin, perhaps; it was the sort of petty maliciousness he delighted in— or whether Sammy had simply chosen poorly when he found a seat. "Constable. I'm Detective Sergeant Thomas Gardiner with Scotland Yard."

"Didn't call in Scotland Yard," Sammy grunted.

Tom nodded pleasantly. "I'm here off duty, as a friend of the family."

Sammy eyed him. "You look familiar."

"I'm not surprised." Tom's voice was nicely even, even as he added, pleasantly, "I remember you, too. I gave you a black eye once, when you tried to jump Robbie and me in the village one Christmas when we were visiting from Eton."

"Swotty nancyboys," Sammy muttered, and Tom's eyes— usually a warm hazel—frosted over.

"Be that as it may—" And it hadn't been, at least as far as I knew; Robbie hadn't been inclined that way, and he and Tom had been friends, nothing more, "—I wanted to offer my assistance, should you need it. Murder investigations can be tricky when you're not used to them."

"Don't need help," Sammy said, offense clear in his tone, and Tom inclined his head courteously.

"In that case I'll just sit back and watch." *As you do it all wrong*, was implied.

Sammy flushed a beet red. "Listen here—"

"You can't refuse to let him be here," I told him. "He was invited. He would have been here for the engagement party tonight in any case."

Sammy muttered something, but there wasn't much he could say to that, so he didn't try. Instead, he kept his eyes on me as Tom wandered over to shake Francis's hand and bend over Constance's and wish them both well on their engagement. While that was going on, *sotto voce*, in the background,

Sammy addressed me. "I have a few questions for you, Miss Darling."

"Of course," I said politely.

"You were supposed to share a room with Mister Christopher Astley."

I nodded.

"The two of you occupy a flat together in London."

"That's correct."

"But last night, he ended up sharing with his cousin instead." He flicked a glance at Crispin, who looked amused.

"His other cousin," I confirmed. "Yes."

"Pardon me?"

"I'm also Christopher's cousin. On the distaff side."

Sammy chewed this over for a moment before he decided that it didn't matter and moved on. "You spent the night alone."

"I did."

"Did it upset you that your cousin chose to share with his other cousin instead of you?"

"Of course not," I said. "It's not like we share a room under normal circumstances. Christopher has his own bedchamber and I have mine, just as we did during the twelve years we lived here at Beckwith Place. We were only sharing in the first place because the house is full and some of us had to double up. If Lady Laetitia hadn't been here—" I gave her a look, "I assume I would have been in Constance's room. As it was, it made more sense to put me with Christopher than with Francis or Crispin, although I don't suppose either of them would have minded sharing, either."

Someone emitted a choking noise in response to this. I expected it to be St George, but when I glanced over, it was Francis who was choking, not on horror but on mirth, as Crispin eyed him irritably.

"No, Pipsqueak," he told me, voice uneven with the

laughter he was desperately trying to suppress, "neither of us would have minded sharing."

I sniffed and ignored him. "Obviously, when Francis ended up downstairs in the library with Constance, Crispin and Christopher shared the second floor room and I took the empty one. We don't go out of our way to be shocking."

It was the Countess's turn to sniff. She and Laetitia exchanged a look before they both ostentatiously refused to look at me.

"So you spent the night alone," Sammy said.

I nodded. "I did."

"And no one can vouch for your whereabouts."

"Aside from the fact that I went to bed on the second floor, and woke up on the second floor, and nobody saw me in-between, I suppose not. No."

Sammy nodded.

"Out of curiosity," I added, "why do you think I might have wanted Abigail Dole dead? That's what you're leading up to, isn't it? That I somehow figured out that she had left the infirmary and made her way here from the village, and instead of letting her in and showing her that her baby was well taken care of, I whacked her over the head with the ubiquitous blunt instrument and left her on the croquet lawn?"

Sammy opened his mouth and then closed it again. I guess he didn't want to out-and-out say it, but yes, that's what he thought.

"I had no reason to want her dead," I pointed out. "I certainly didn't get her with child. Nobody would expect me to do anything about it. And she didn't stand in the way of me marrying anyone."

I had meant it to refer to Laetitia, of course, who had slept in a room of her own and who had every incentive not to want St George to step up and marry Abigail. But instead, Sammy gave Constance a narrow-eyed look. She had little Bess on her lap, and with Francis next to her they looked quite like the happy little family.

I sighed. "Not Constance. She was in the library with Francis."

"But he was in no condition to hear her leave," Sammy said triumphantly. "That's what everyone says, isn't it? He was too drunk to go anywhere. Too drunk to do anything but sleep it off on the sofa in the library."

He waited, but none of us could really, in all honestly, disagree with that.

"Well," Sammy said triumphantly, "if he was too drunk to do any of that, he was too drunk to notice his fiancée leaving, too!"

Well... yes. He probably would have been.

That hadn't been what I'd been trying to draw Sammy's attention to, though. I'd done everything except point directly at Laetitia, and apparently I should have done so, because he hadn't caught on to what—or who—I meant.

"Constance would never—" Francis growled, and Tom put a hand on his arm.

"Have you found the murder weapon?" he asked.

"The croquet mallet—" Crispin began, and then stopped when Tom flicked a glance his way.

Sammy looked sour. "The croquet mallet went to the village with the body."

"But the croquet mallet wasn't the murder weapon. You've spoken with the doctor since he did his on-site examination of the body, haven't you?"

"We're looking," Sammy said shortly.

Crispin lifted a hand, like a dutiful pupil in class. "Wait a second. If the mallet wasn't the murder weapon, what was?"

Sammy fixed him with a fulminating stare that would have

been more effective had St George been easier to cow. "We don't know. When we find it, you'll be the first to know."

"Oh, will I?"

I cut in, before Crispin could dig himself a deeper hole. "You didn't find anything in the carriage house?" That must have been what whoever was in there had been rooting around for, after all. The actual murder weapon.

Sammy eyed me sourly. "No. At the moment we're checking the residence."

That explained why the light had been on in the cellar stairwell when Tom and I passed by. It also explained the rather heavy footsteps I had noticed passing back and forth above my head.

Lady Euphemia clutched her not-prepossessing bosom. Like her daughter, she was built tall and willowy. "What do you mean, you're checking the residence? You're going through our rooms?"

"Routine," Sammy grunted, while Tom nodded apologetically.

"I'm afraid that's true, Lady Euphemia. The premises are always searched for the murder weapon and anything else that might pertain to the crime."

"Well, I have nothing to hide," I said. "Anyone's welcome to search my room."

It was hard to say who was most put out by that statement, Laetitia and her mother, or Sammy.

I smiled brightly at the Countess. "By the way, my aunt instructed me to tell you that breakfast is almost ready. She said you were starving. It shouldn't be long now."

That's not what Aunt Roz had said, of course, not in those words, but Lady Euphemia gave me the kind of fishy stare that ought to have dropped me into a heap on the carpet.

When it didn't, she turned away with a sniff. I grinned, and caught an answering twitch of Crispin's mouth across the room. "Where's Kit?" he asked. "Not back from the village yet?"

Sammy brightened. "Done a bunk, has he?"

I rolled my eyes. "He drove Doctor White to the mortuary, since you and your colleagues are getting around on bicycles. I'm sure he'll be back shortly."

"Was Wilkins not available?" Uncle Harold wanted to know, in a sort of distant voice, as if an Astley should not have had to drive the doctor anywhere when there was a chauffeur around to do it.

Or perhaps it was distant because it was me, and he doesn't like to address me. When he has to, he often pretends that I'm not here, like he's talking to the air instead.

"I haven't seen him lately," I said. "He was here this morning. Constable Entwistle spoke to him—" I glanced at Sammy, who nodded confirmation, "but the motorcar was gone by the time Tom arrived."

"Probably assumed his services wouldn't be needed today and retired to the village pub," the Earl of Marsden grunted.

"No doubt," I answered, as pleasantly as I could manage. "He's not wrong, after all. None of us are going anywhere anytime soon. Are we?"

Tom and Sammy both shook their heads, and then Sammy shot Tom a disgruntled sort of look and Tom hid a smile. Before he cleared his throat and told us all, "No. No one will be allowed to leave until the police are satisfied that they have all the information necessary to solve the crime."

Uncle Harold heaved a sigh. Lady Euphemia sniffed.

I was still leaning in the doorway between the foyer and the sitting room, one shoulder against the jamb, and now I became aware of noises behind me. First there was the sound of the front door opening, and Christopher's voice. "Hullo, Pippa. What's going on?"

At the same time, there was the clatter of crockery from behind the door at the landing to the cellar steps. Christopher crossed the foyer to open that door instead. Meanwhile, a set of ponderous footsteps began to descend from above, the regulation boots of a uniformed constable.

"Hello, Mother," Christopher said from behind me. "Let me take that."

His steps approached, and then his voice said, "Excuse me, Pippa."

I stepped out of the way. Christopher breezed past with a large tray full of cups and saucers and a steaming teapot. Hughes followed, carrying an assortment of teatime delicacies. Small, crustless sandwiches and biscuits and the like. Without Cook, I guess we wouldn't be getting a hot breakfast today. Elevenses it was, a little early.

"Hello, Christopher," Aunt Roz beamed as she brought up the rear.

Meanwhile, the constable—the same one who had been squatting on the grass outside—reached the bottom of the staircase and stopped in front of me. "Miss."

I glanced down at the object in his hand. "What have you got there?"

There was a wooden handle, as far as I could see, and on one end, something wrapped around it, or screwed onto the top of it. A bolt or something like that.

"Trench club," the young policeman said, in a vaguely apologetic way.

"I'm sorry, but I'm not familiar with the concept. Come again?"

He opened his mouth to tell me, but by then, Tom had reached us, with Sammy right on his heels. "Trench club, you said?"

The young man nodded, brandishing it. He'd had the foresight to keep his gloves on, I was happy to see. After all, this trench club, whatever that was, must be important if he had carried it down to show it off.

"I'm sorry," I said again, looking from one to the other of them, "what is it?"

By now Francis had also reached us, and was looking at the club with revulsion. "That," he told me, with a nod to it, "is the handle of an entrenching tool. Standard issue during the war. They came in two parts: this handle," he flicked his finger at it, "and then a metal part that was a spade on one side and a pick axe on the other, with a hole in the middle. We'd use it to dig trenches and latrines and graves, and sometimes to break heads."

So a weapon. "I don't see a spade."

Francis shook his head. "That's gone. What you're looking at is just the handle. Someone's fitted it with hobnails to use as a melee weapon."

I eyed the rounded head of the stick with its small metal protrusions (and dried blood) and tried to imagine it making contact with Abigail's head. "That's barbaric."

"I've seen worse," Francis said grimly.

Tom nodded. "We all have."

"A man in my outfit at Ypres had one with spikes running through it," the constable holding it said. "Not something you'd want to meet on a dark night."

Definitely not. Not at Ypres or in the garden of Beckwith Place, either. "So that's the murder weapon?"

"So it seems," Tom qualified. "Where did you find it?"

The constable glanced at Sammy, who told him, grumpily, "This is a DS from Scotland Yard, name of Gardiner."

The constable arched his brows, but told Tom, willingly enough, "It was under the mattress in one of the bedrooms on the second floor."

"My brother's and cousin's room?" Francis shook his head. "Neither of them were old enough to have been in France."

Sammy eyed him. "You sure this isn't a souvenir of yours from the war, Astley?"

Francis's jaw clenched. "I'm positive, Entwistle. I still have the Webley. It's in the gun cabinet in the study. But that's all I brought home. If I never see one of these again, it won't be too soon."

Sammy smirked. "Gone soft?"

"I killed my share of men in the war," Francis said. "I've no desire to do it in peacetime."

His voice turned rough. "For God's sake, she was a tiny little thing. Just a slip of a girl, with a new baby to care for. What kind of man picks up a trench club and bashes in the head of someone like that?"

"Someone with nothing to lose and everything to gain," Sammy said.

CHAPTER TWENTY

A QUICK ROUND of questioning elicited the information that no one present had seen the weapon before, and only a few people knew what it was. Among them, the Earl of Marsden.

"Oh, yes." Maurice nodded knowingly. "That'd do it."

"It wasn't in the young gentlemen's room," the other constable finally got around to saying. "It was in the other bedroom, where the young lady slept."

Everyone turned to look at me, and I could feel myself turn pale. "That can't be. I would never—!"

"Blood spatter?" Sammy inquired, and his colleague shook his head.

"None so far."

If I was reading the shorthand correctly, whoever had wielded the weapon—me in this scenario—was likely to have gotten some of Abigail's blood on him or her, and so far, none of our rooms had yielded any bloodstained clothing.

"May I be excused?" I asked tightly. "I'm not hungry."

The display of food was actually turning my stomach. Sammy opened his mouth, took one look at my face—it was probably green—and closed it again. Aunt Roz nodded. "Off you go, Pippa. Do you need anything?"

"Just to get away from that thing," I said, already on my way towards the outside. "Some fresh air. Excuse me."

I stumbled through the front door, shut it behind me, and dropped onto the step, where I closed my eyes and fought air into my lungs in slow inhalations as I struggled to keep the nausea at bay. Images of the head of the trench club colliding with the back of Abigail's head, of blood spatter and the noise of eggs cracking under the pressure of a spoon, filled my head, and I swallowed hard against the feeling of bile rising in my throat.

It didn't come as a surprise to hear the door open again just a few seconds later. I should have known that someone would come after me. If not Christopher, to check on how I felt, then Sammy, to make sure I wasn't trying to make my escape. I must look quite guilty at this point, with the murder weapon hidden in my room.

But it turned out to be neither of them. It was Francis. And when I thought about it, I guess it made sense. Tom was inside, sticking close to the investigation, and so Christopher had stayed inside to stick close to Tom. Crispin probably couldn't leave Laetitia even if he had wanted to, and there was no reason to think he'd prefer my company to hers or that he'd be concerned about how I felt. Constance was holding the baby, and had Aunt Roz for backup. But Francis had been just as fazed, if not more so, by the trench club as I had been, and it wasn't surprising that he might want some fresh air, as well.

"Cigarette?" He held an open case under my nose.

I shook my head. "Thank you, but no. I really do want fresh air."

"I find that smoking settles my nerves," Francis said. He chose a cigarette and then closed the case and dropped it back in his pocket. "I'll probably have nightmares about trench raids tonight."

His hand was trembling when he pulled out a lighter and lit the fag before sucking in a deep lungful of smoke.

"I wouldn't blame you," I said. "I might, too, and I never took part in them."

"Be glad you didn't. Nasty business." He blew the mouthful of smoke out.

"I'm sure of it." I hesitated a moment, and then I told him something I'd never told anyone else, not even Christopher. "Sometimes I wonder what happened to my father. I know he died—he was on the casualty list, my mother told me that much before the influenza took her—but I don't know the details."

Of course, he had been on the other side, in the German trenches. But if it hadn't been in a battle, then it might have been in a trench raid, with a whack on the head by someone wielding the kind of weapon that had killed Abigail.

"Better if you don't think too much about it," Francis advised.

I nodded. "I don't often. It isn't pleasant. And sometimes I feel like that was someone else's life. That I've always been here with you and Christopher and Aunt Roz and Uncle Herbert."

Francis took a seat next to me on the step. He didn't look at me, just sat by my side and stared at the bushes on the other side of the lane while he smoked his cigarette.

"But then something like this happens," I added, "and I remember that my father died in the war, and that it wasn't very long ago at all—less than half my life, really, and I haven't lived that long—and then I start to feel a little strange about it all."

"Sometimes I think about that, too," Francis admitted. "Sometimes I worry that I killed him."

I slanted him a look, and he met my eyes for a second before he added, "I probably didn't. So many people died, on both sides. So many people were involved. It would be a very big coincidence if it was me. But sometimes I worry."

We sat in silence a moment before I leaned into him so I could put my head on his shoulder. "Sometimes I'm afraid that my father was the one who killed Robbie. We'd never know it if he did. And I know he'd never have wanted to. He didn't want to be there. But it's possible that he's the one who did it."

Francis didn't say anything.

"Even if you did," I told him, "even if you were the one who killed my father, I forgive you. I'd never not forgive you, Francis. You and Christopher are my brothers in every way that matters. There's nothing I wouldn't forgive. Even this."

He didn't answer, and I added, "You did what you had to do. So did he. Neither of you had a choice. You were there, and you had to make the best of it. You had to survive. And now it's over and you did. You came home."

"And he didn't."

I shook my head. "No, he didn't." Whether the 'he' he was talking about was my father or Robbie, or perhaps both. "But he —neither of them would have wanted you to spend the rest of your life miserable over what you had to do. You were drafted, Francis. You didn't choose to go to war. And since you came back, the only person you've hurt has been yourself. It's all right to be happy now. You deserve Constance, and marriage, and all the happiness in the world. If anyone's earned it, you have."

He nodded. "I didn't kill her, you know."

"Abigail? Of course you didn't. I never thought you had."

"Sammy thinks I did."

"Sammy wants to think you did," I corrected. "You have an

alibi, so you couldn't have. Of anyone in the house, you're the one least likely to have done it."

"Sammy would say I'm the most likely."

"Sammy doesn't know what he's talking about," I said. "Constance was with you all night, and you were too drunk to move from the sofa. I saw you, don't forget. Several of us did. I know you couldn't have done it. You're still hung over now."

"It's not my baby." He shot me a look. "She looks just like me—"

"Not just you. Christopher and Crispin, too."

He nodded. "But I swear, Pippa, she isn't mine. I had a few bad years right after the war—you missed the worst of them, you and Kit, being away at Oxford—but by last spring, I wasn't doing badly. I still did a lot of things I shouldn't have done, drinking and doping and the like, but I wasn't walking around in the kind of stupor where I'd black out and not know what had happened. If I'd taken this girl to bed last year, I would remember."

"I believe you," I said. "Just out of curiosity, have you ever been to the Hammersmith Palais?"

He looked at me with an almost comical look of disbelief on his face, mixed with a healthy dose of amusement. It was nice to see, after the conversation we'd had. "A dance hall? No, Pippa. Whenever I'd go up to London, that wasn't the kind of place we'd visit. We'd have darker haunts than that."

Like the opium dens in Limehouse and someone's flat where they could enjoy getting doped up on cocaine without worrying about being caught, I assumed.

"We found a note in her bag that indicated that she had met whoever he was at the Hammersmith Palais. Constance didn't mention it?"

"We haven't really had a chance to talk," Francis said. "I was thoroughly foxed last night, and this morning you woke us up with the news that the girl was dead. We haven't had the opportunity for a private chat since then."

And yesterday afternoon, he was already gone by the time we'd found the tote with the list in it. "Well, perhaps you ought to tell her."

"It wouldn't matter anyway," Francis said. "I'm marrying Constance. Even if the baby had been mine, they couldn't have forced me to marry her."

No, they couldn't have. "I still think you ought to tell her. Find a few minutes for a private conversation. She might be worried about it."

He didn't move. The cigarette was long gone, and must have done the trick in calming his nerves, because he didn't reach for another one. But he didn't get up, either. "What about you, Pippa? Are you worried?"

"I'm not sure what you think I'd be worried about," I said. "I know you didn't do it. I know Christopher didn't. And Crispin was with him, so I know he couldn't have. Aunt Roz and Uncle Herbert had no reason to want Abigail Dole dead. Not that I think either of them would be capable of that kind of thing. And Constance is surely too small to deliver such a blow. Everyone I care about is in the clear, it seems."

Francis nodded. "And yourself?"

I shot him a look. "Why would I kill her? I'm sorry to have to put it so bluntly, but she and her child were nothing to me. If one of you were responsible, I would have wanted you to step up and take responsibility, but it certainly wasn't important enough for me to kill anyone over."

He hummed. "Do you suppose Sammy sees it that way?"

"I can't imagine that he'd see it otherwise," I said. "You're engaged to Constance, Christopher's queer, and St George... well, if I wanted St George I wouldn't just have to kill Abigail,

I'd have to kill Laetitia, too. And probably a dozen other women who are ready to step up as soon as Laetitia's out of the way."

"But the murder weapon—"

"I have no idea how that got into my room," I said. "It wasn't last night, after I whacked her over the head with it, I can tell you that much."

Francis shook his head.

"I haven't been up to my room in hours, so anyone could have put it there."

"But between that and the fact that you slept alone, you're not worried that Sammy's going to think you're a viable suspect?"

"I'm not." I was fairly certain that Sammy had no plans to try to pin the murder on me. He was probably trying to prove that Francis owned the trench club and had hid it in my room sometime between dawn and now. "Just out of curiosity, have you been alone at any time this morning?"

Francis shook his head. "I went upstairs with Kit, and came downstairs with Kit, and I've been with the rest of you since. Kit would have noticed if I'd had a trench club hidden down my trouser leg when we climbed the stairs."

Of course he would have. "There's no way Sammy can say that you were the one who put it in my room, then. You couldn't have done while I was sleeping—I would have woken up if you'd started lifting my mattress—and you couldn't have done it since."

Francis looked relieved.

"Although," I added, "I would feel better if I had some idea of who might actually be guilty. It's one thing to know that I'm not, and that you're not, and that Christopher isn't."

Francis nodded.

"But someone killed her. And not just that, but someone's

the father of that baby. And if we don't figure out who, all of you are going to go through life being suspected of it."

He shook his head. "I don't know how to help you, Pippa. I just know it wasn't me."

I nodded. The answer, of course, was obvious: it had been one of Uncle Herbert's illegitimate children. But I had promised my uncle I wouldn't talk about that.

"You wouldn't happen to know who Sammy's mother is, would you?" I asked instead. Maybe I could get at this from a different angle.

Francis looked at me with his brows elevated. "Of course I do. I've lived in this village my entire life. You should know that, too."

"Well, who is she?"

"Amelia Entwistle. The butcher's wife."

Butcher? Sammy probably wouldn't baulk at a bit of business with a trench club, then.

Although Amelia sounded nothing like Maisie. Amelias are usually called Amy or Ammie or, in a pinch, Melia or Lia. Not Maisie.

"What about the other constable? The one who found the truncheon?"

"Phil Hemings," Francis said. "Nice lad. Took some shrapnel in France and was sent home early, so he missed the rest of the war, the lucky devil."

"Do you know his family, too?"

"Of course." He still eyed me strangely. "His father drives a lorry and his mum's a housewife."

"Names?"

"Vicky—Victoria, I suppose—and Philip Senior. Is there a reason you're asking me these questions, Pipsqueak?"

"There is," I said, "but I can't tell you."

He nodded and pushed to his feet. "I'd better get back

inside. Don't want to give Sammy too much of an opportunity to bully Constance."

No, it was probably better if he didn't. "I'll be right there," I said. "Just... give me a minute more to think something through."

"Take all the time you want. We know where to find you."

He closed the door behind him. I turned my eyes back to the bushes, but without really seeing them.

Both Sammy and Phil Hemings had been in the war. Either of them might reasonably have brought home a trench club as a souvenir.

Neither of them was old enough to be Maisie's son. Sammy was Robbie's age, two years younger than Francis, and in order to have been in France during the war, Phil Hemings had to be either the same age or older. He did not look like he was older than Francis, however, and the latter had called him a lad, which indicated he was probably the same age as Sammy and Robbie.

Either of them could arguably be Uncle Herbert's younger child, the one born during his marriage. Although they had both lived near Beckwith Place for as long as I could recall, and so had their families. You would have thought, if Uncle Herbert had seduced one of their mothers, that there would have been some sort of talk about it at some point. It's difficult to keep secrets in a village, and until today, I had never heard a single, solitary whisper about my uncle's infidelity.

Other than the fact that Sammy and Phil Hemings were both here at Beckwith Place this morning—which had a logical explanation; it wasn't as if either of them had inserted themselves into a situation they didn't belong in—was there any actual evidence to suggest that either of them was involved in this case beyond investigating it?

There wasn't, I decided. Much as I wanted someone else to

be guilty, I was back to the family and friends—I use the word loosely—gathered at Beckwith Place.

Francis, Christopher, and Crispin had had no opportunity, at least not unless someone was lying. The same, I assumed, was true for Aunt Roz and Uncle Herbert and the couple Marsden.

Take all of them out of the equation, then.

Geoffrey had had opportunity, but probably no motive. He had missed the draft by a year or two, so I couldn't imagine where he might have gotten his hands on a trench club.

Then again, Maurice knew what they were, so there was a possibility one had been at Marsden Manor. But even if Geoffrey had had one at home, there would have been no reason for him to bring it to Constance's engagement party. He didn't have a beef with Francis, or with anyone else in the family as far as I knew. He also had no motive for wanting Abigail out of the way, and no way to know that she'd even turn up here this weekend.

Laetitia had had motive, if she believed that Crispin was responsible for little Bess and that he would be forced to marry Abigail. She'd also had opportunity, but again, probably no access to the murder weapon. And from her reaction to it earlier, she probably wouldn't have chosen to use it in any case.

Unless that had been a reaction to actually having used it, of course, and the memory of what it had done to the back of Abigail's head.

Would she have put the truncheon in my room to implicate me if she were the one who had used it?

Of all the people here, I thought she actually might have done. She doesn't like me much, and I suppose I was partly to blame for that, after the way I had greeted St George when we arrived. And then, of course, there was the fact that I had spent the time since I got here diligently trying to talk him out of marrying Laetitia.

None of that had happened until after we were both here, though, and I didn't think she'd come here with a plan to kill me. And she would have had to, to have brought the trench club with her. But of everyone, she'd had both motive and opportunity, as well as a reason to try to frame me with the murder weapon. She stayed on the list.

She had not been upstairs at the time when I had seen the shadow against the window in my room, however. Not according to Christopher. And if that had been when the trench club had been hidden under my mattress, then Laetitia hadn't done it.

Constance had had opportunity to kill Abigail, since Francis had surely been too drunk to notice her moving about last night. She'd been close to the back door, which would have made going outside easy. There had been no one else in the back of the house to see her come and go. And if Abigail had knocked on the back or side door—which she might have done when she arrived in the middle of the night—Constance was the one most likely to have heard her. All the rest of us had been upstairs, with the exception of Francis.

She'd had motive, if she had believed that Abigail might take Francis away from her.

I wasn't sure she would have had the strength to crack someone's skull, but given sufficient motivation, it was possible. I also had no idea where she would have got her hands on the trench club, but that was true for all of us.

And she had been upstairs when it had been put in my room. But try as I might, I couldn't imagine Constance framing me for murder. Why would she? We were friends.

I had had opportunity, of course. I'd slept alone. I'd had no motive—I had felt bad for Abigail, and had wanted to know who her baby's father was, but I hadn't felt threatened by her. Her situation certainly hadn't been worth committing murder over.

Who else?

There was Uncle Harold. He'd slept alone. He'd had motive, if he thought Abigail was after Crispin. He wasn't above knocking his only son around when he felt like it, so I knew he had at least some capacity for violence. I had no idea where he might have got his hands on a trench club, but he could have found one had he wanted to. You can acquire anything when you have enough money.

Would he have framed me for murder, though?

I wouldn't like to think so, certainly. I was part of the Sutherland family, practically a daughter to Aunt Roz and Uncle Herbert, and if he did that and was discovered to have done it, he would completely destroy his relationship with his brother, his sister-in-law, and both his nephews. His son might not like it much, either, not that Crispin's opinions seemed to hold a whole lot of weight with His Grace.

And if Uncle Harold had committed murder and was trying to avoid being arrested for it, family relations might take a back seat to the gallows, anyway.

Cook was surely out of the picture. She belonged here at Beckwith Place and would have had no reason to know that Abigail and Bess even existed.

Hughes? She would have heard about Abigail during that weekend at Sutherland Hall, when the rest of us had first heard the story about the girl with the baby who had visited Sutherland House. I couldn't think of any reason why Hughes would have killed her, though. And anyway, she hadn't been here last night. Like Cook and Wilkins, she had lodged in the village—

"Pippa," Christopher's voice said from behind me, and I

jumped. I'd been so caught up in my thoughts that I hadn't even noticed the door opening again.

"Is everything all right? Are you feeling better?" He looked concerned. "You've been out here a long time."

"I'm fine." I jumped to my feet. "Do you require me?"

"Sammy does. He wants to go over some of your answers again."

"Where?"

"He has taken over Father's study," Christopher said. "Tom's with him."

"Perhaps he has realized that he needs help." I crossed the threshold and waited for him to close the front door behind me. "Or at least that he'd be better off accepting it, when it's available. Hopefully that means this will get figured out sooner rather than later."

He nodded, and I added, "Anything else I should know?"

Christopher shook his head and fell in behind me. "I think he suspects you, Pippa."

"He would." I pulled the door to the back of the house open and stepped onto the cellar landing. Behind me, Christopher followed.

When both doors were closed, the one in front of me and the one behind Christopher, I added, "He knows I had both motive and opportunity, and the real murder weapon was found in my room. Why wouldn't he suspect me?"

"Because you didn't do it?" Christopher suggested.

I smiled. "Of course I didn't do it. Tom knows that. Between us, we'll be able to set Sammy straight."

"See that you do," Christopher said, leaning a shoulder against the wall. "I'll tell you straight out, Pippa, I'm worried. I know it isn't my baby, and I don't believe it's Crispin's or Francis's, either. But if not ours, then whose?"

I shook my head, since I couldn't tell him what I knew that he didn't.

He added, "I have no idea what's going on. I don't see any of us committing murder, but I also don't see how it could have been anyone else."

"It'll be all right," I told him. "I have an idea."

"Will you tell me?"

"Not now. I'd better not keep Sammy waiting. Let's not give him the idea that I'm reluctant to talk to him."

Christopher nodded. "Come find me when you're done."

I promised I would, and he gave my hand a final squeeze for luck. Then I pushed open the door into the back of the house and stopped in front of my uncle's study and applied my knuckles to the wood.

CHAPTER TWENTY-ONE

"COME IN, MISS DARLING."

I took a deep breath before I pushed open the door with a smile. "You were asking for me?"

Uncle Herbert's study is a lovely, masculine little room with dark wainscoting and heavy wood furniture, that smells of leather and smoke. Sammy had positioned himself in my uncle's chair behind the desk, I saw to my displeasure, and was lounging there like he owned it. Tom, meanwhile, was sitting in one of the chairs in front of the desk, the one usually occupied by Christopher when he and I had been called on the carpet in front of Uncle Herbert as children. I headed for my own usual chair before Sammy could even gesture to it.

"Yes," he said drolly, "have a seat."

"I assumed you weren't going to make me stand." I sat and folded my hands demurely in my lap before I added, "Not even my uncle did that."

Not usually anyway. Not unless we'd committed some particularly heinous crime, like the time I had locked St George in the cellar and left him there. It had been in retaliation for a spider down the back or something like that, no doubt. That time, I got my dressing-down on my feet, while Crispin sat in the chair. His face had been blotchy and his eyes red, and I had felt quite good about the whole thing, even in the face of his tears.

At least until Uncle Herbert informed me of my punishment, which had been to spend the next day in my room instead of accompanying the others on a trip to Salisbury. I quite liked Salisbury, it usually had things like ice cream and tea cakes, and now I'd be stuck at Beckwith Place instead, all by myself. Crispin had smirked then, and I had stuck my tongue out at him, and then...

Tom cleared his throat, and I came back to myself with a flush. "Apologies."

Sammy smirked. "Something you'd like to share?"

"Just a memory of being in here with my uncle and Lord St George, getting dressed down for locking him in the cellar for the best part of an afternoon. We were eleven."

Sammy looked nonplussed, but Tom chuckled. "There never was much love lost between the two of you, was there?"

"He used to take me into the garden maze at Sutherland Hall and leave me there. I was just getting some of my own back."

He nodded, and I added, "But no. We got on the wrong side of each other almost immediately. He was such a horribly mean little boy."

"Mean enough to commit murder?" Sammy wanted to know.

I gave him the sort of look I frequently bestow upon St George, as if he were something that had crawled out from beneath a flat rock. "No. Or not this murder, at any rate."

"If I were to tell you that I have proof that Lord St George killed the girl—"

My stomach did a sort of swoop, but I shook my head. "I wouldn't believe you."

Tom arched a brow. Sammy said, "Why?"

"First of all, he spent the night with Christopher. Christopher would have woken up if Crispin tried to leave the room. He's a light sleeper."

"Perhaps he woke up and is lying about it."

"Christopher's not a liar," I said. "And Crispin had no motive."

"If the baby was his..."

"It wasn't. And aside from that, he wouldn't hit a young woman over the head with a truncheon. He might have abandoned me in the garden maze when we were eleven, but he never hit me."

"The trench club..." Sammy began.

"Was found in my room. That's what Constable Hemings said."

"There were fingerprints on the handle—"

"Not Crispin's. And not mine. Besides, I don't believe you. Nobody would have been stupid enough to leave a weapon with their fingerprints on it. Not someone who was thinking clearly enough to substitute the croquet mallet in the first place. Certainly not Crispin. He's too smart for that."

Tom smirked. Sammy sighed. "If not Lord St George, then who?"

"I told you," I said, or perhaps I hadn't. I had been over all this so many times in my head by now that I had gotten confused. "I don't know who did it. But it wasn't Christopher, Crispin, or Francis. They all have alibis."

"You spent the night alone."

I nodded. "But I had no reason to kill her. I love them—or I love Francis and Christopher, at least; I can take or leave St George. But I wouldn't commit murder to get them out of taking responsibility for siring a child out of wedlock. Besides, Abigail met St George at Sutherland House in March. If she was still looking for her baby's father in July, that means Crispin isn't it. And if Crispin isn't it, then Christopher isn't it. And if Christopher isn't it—"

"Mister Astley..." Sammy began, and I shook my head.

"It's not Francis. I know you don't like him, but just like I have to admit that St George isn't guilty, it's time for you to admit that Francis isn't, either. He has an alibi."

Sammy looked sour. "His fiancée would lie for him even if he were guilty."

"He's not, so that's moot. And it's not just that he was with Constance. He was so drunk last night that Wilkins had to help him across the grass. We put him in the library because he couldn't make it up the stairs. He wouldn't have been sober enough to kill anyone even several hours later. He certainly wouldn't have had the presence of mind to switch the murder weapon for the mallet."

Nor would he have tried to frame me with it. Francis loved me.

Sammy accepted defeat. Not graciously, but he accepted it. "Moving on," he said.

I nodded. "Good idea. Were there really fingerprints on the trench club?"

"No," Sammy grumbled. "It was wiped clean. Same as the mallet."

"I don't quite understand why someone would bother to substitute the mallet for the trench club, and then leave the trench club in my room. If you were going to leave the actual murder weapon, why substitute the mallet in the first place?"

"Opportunity," Tom said before Sammy could open his mouth.

I tilted my head. "Opportunity?"

"The trench club was a weapon of opportunity. Something handy. But also something that might be traced back to whoever used it, so he or she fetched the mallet and tried to make that look like the murder weapon."

I nodded. I followed so far. That's what we'd always believed anyway. Or at least what we had believed since Doctor White had told us the mallet was not the murder weapon.

"Then something happened, some reason or opportunity presented itself that made it seem like a good idea to hide the club in your room."

"Hughes," I said.

"Excuse me?"

"Nothing." Had Hughes realized that I had overheard her conversation with—or blackmail of—Uncle Herbert, and decided to frame me for murder?

But that would mean that Hughes had killed Abigail, and that made no sense whatsoever.

"Never mind," I said. "Carry on."

Tom's lips curved, as if he knew exactly the progression of thoughts that had made their way through my head. He didn't say anything about it, however. "Your room was mostly empty all morning, so it might have been simple opportunity. It might be that someone knew you'd slept alone and had no alibi, so you'd make a handy scapegoat. Or it might be personal. Someone wanted you, specifically, to look guilty."

"I did see someone in my room earlier," I said. "It was while a few of the Marsdens were still making their way downstairs. We'd sat in the kitchen—Christopher, Francis, and I, and Crispin, along with Aunt Roz and Uncle Harold—and when the others went to the front of the house, I went back out on the terrasse. And someone was upstairs in my room. I saw a shadow against the window."

"Someone might remember who was where at what time," Tom said to Sammy, and the latter looked unhappy about taking the suggestion, but nodded.

"I already asked Christopher. I think he told me that only Geoffrey and Constance were not in the sitting room. Of the guests, I mean."

The two coppers exchanged a glance. "Lord Geoffrey Marsden?" Sammy said.

"Too young to serve," Tom answered. "Although his father did know what the trench club was."

"He doesn't like me," I supplied. "Geoffrey, I mean. He tried to push me into a corner of the Chesterfield at the Dower House two months ago, and St George had to rescue me. I've been avoiding him since yesterday, which I can't imagine that he appreciates."

There was a moment's pause while they both chewed on that. Tom had already known about the incident at the Dower House, of course. It had come up during the murder case in Dorset. But it was news to Sammy.

"And also Miss Constance Peckham," he said now, and I felt myself stiffen. "I don't know where she might have gotten her hands on a trench club. Astley—"

"Francis," I said.

Sammy shot me a look. "Yes, Mr. Francis Astley said that he hadn't brought one back from the Continent, so it wouldn't have been here. Unless he lied, of course."

"I lived in this house with Francis from 1914 until a few months ago," I said, "and I've never seen it before."

"Her motorcar?" Tom suggested. "Didn't you say that Geoffrey Marsden motored up from Dorset in it, Pippa?"

I nodded. "Gilbert Peckham was too young to have been in the war too, though."

"But they had a chauffeur, didn't they? I think I met him when Lady Peckham died?"

He probably had. I hadn't paid much attention to the chauffeur—didn't think I'd heard him speak once. He had arrived at Sutherland Hall with Lady Peckham, Constance and her brother Gilbert, and the late Johanna de Vos, and I hadn't seen him again until several days later, when he arrived back at the Dower House with Lady P's luggage. I didn't even know his name.

And he certainly wasn't at Beckwith Place now. The only chauffeur here was Wilkins. "Are you thinking that the club could have been in the Crossley? That the chauffeur kept it around as a weapon, should he get held up by a highwayman on a lonely road at midnight? And when Lady P died and he was out of a job, he left it behind?"

"Something like that," Tom said. "People do keep weapons in their motorcars."

I'm sure they did. And if a man had gone through the war with a trench club at his side, it might make sense to him to keep it behind the seat of his car in case of trouble.

Although if he had gone through the war with a trench club at his side, would he have left it behind in someone else's car after losing his job?

"Are you thinking that Geoffrey went to the village in Constance's Crossley after everyone was in bed last night," I asked, "and he picked up Abigail on her way here, and killed her? Why would he do that?"

"Not Lord Geoffrey," Tom said.

"Who, then?" Not Constance. Constance wouldn't have tried to frame me for murder. We were friends. And she was marrying my cousin.

They exchanged a look.

"Not Constance," I said. "She wouldn't have left Francis for long enough to drive to the village. And she wouldn't be strong enough to crack anyone's skull. And even if little Bess was Francis's—and she isn't—they couldn't force him to marry Abigail. Constance had no reason to kill anyone."

"Calm yourself, Pippa," Tom said. "We aren't talking about Constance."

"You're not?" Somehow that didn't feel good, either. I wasn't Hercule Poirot, by any means, but surely I should be able to figure this out. "Who are you talking about, then?"

"We," Tom said, "are talking about someone who participated in the war, who had access to this house and to a motorcar, and who might have kept a trench club behind the seat in case it came in handy..."

"Not Francis!" The Astleys had the Bentley, but there was no trench club in it. There never had been. I had spent enough time in that car to know.

Sammy looked sour. "No," Tom said. "Not Francis."

I sat back on my chair. "Then I don't know who we're talking about."

Tom nodded and turned to Sammy. "What I'm about to tell you can't go beyond this room."

"I can't promise that..." Sammy began, but Tom wasn't listening to him. Instead, he turned back to me.

"Be a dear and go fetch your uncle, Pippa."

I got to my feet, a bit reluctantly. "Which uncle do you want? Herbert or Harold?"

"Better make it both," Tom said, "actually."

"Really?" If this was about Uncle Herbert's illegitimate child, or children, was that something Uncle Harold needed to hear?

He might already know, of course. Duke Henry might have shared it with him, as his successor to the title. Or Uncle Herbert might have done the same, brother to brother. But if not, did Tom really want to let that particular cat out of the bag?

I tried to convey all those thoughts with the power of my mind, without opening my mouth, and—

"On second thought," Tom acquiesced, "perhaps just Lord Herbert for now."

I nodded and headed for the door. Only to be brought up short by his voice behind me.

"And see if you can make Lord St George follow you out of the room, Pippa."

"Excuse me?" I stopped in the doorway and turned around.

Tom smirked. "I need Lord St George for a moment. Try to make it look natural."

I eyed him down my nose. It was made easier—made possible—by the fact that he was sitting and I was standing. "I'm not sure what you're implying, but I suppose simply asking him to accompany me is out of the question?"

"You can go ahead and ask. Just make it look like you want him personally and not for me."

I sniffed. "That'll be difficult to feign, but I'll do my best."

"Do your best, Pippa." He waved me off. "Close the door behind you."

I did, and then eyed it resentfully. Clearly part of the purpose of this errand was to get me out of the way while he brought Sammy up to date on things I wasn't supposed to hear. I contemplated staying where I was and putting my ear to the door instead of fetching Uncle Herbert from the sitting room, but if I did, and didn't produce him and Crispin in a timely manner, Tom would likely guess what I had done, and I didn't particularly want to end up on the wrong side of Tom Gardiner. So I stuck my tongue out at the door, but buzzed off past the cellar steps and into the foyer.

"Uncle Herbert? You're wanted in the study."

In my absence, most of the tea tray had been demolished, and everyone looked a bit more genial. Constance and Francis were cuddled up together in one of the oversized armchairs, while Euphemia Marsden had lost most of the pinched look. She was watching her daughter use her wiles on Crispin with a benevolent expression on her face. Little Bess had fallen asleep, and was tucked into a corner of the Chesterfield next to Aunt Roz, her pink rosebud lips parted and her tiny chest rising and falling under her embroidered blanket. Her wispy fair hair stuck straight up from her small head.

"St George," I added, dragging my eyes from the baby and over to where he was sitting, perched on the arm of Laetitia's chair. "May I have a moment of your time?"

He blinked. I'm not usually so polite when I want his attention, I suppose. Laetitia's eyes narrowed and Uncle Herbert shot me a quick glance on his way past.

"Good luck," I told him, and he nodded and headed for the door to the back of the house. Crispin, meanwhile, clearly needed more time to decide whether he wanted to oblige me or not. So much for Tom's inference that he'd follow me if I just crooked my finger at him. All he did was eye me with calculation from across the room, as if trying to figure out what my angle might be.

"You know what, St George?" I said, annoyed. "Forget I asked. It's obviously an imposition."

Laetitia's lips curved up, pleased.

"I'll just ask someone else for help. And the next time I need assistance—"

By the time I was halfway through the sentence, Crispin

was up from the chair and on his way across the floor. "Stop being manipulative, Darling, and tell me what you want."

He grabbed my elbow as he moved past, and tugged me along into the foyer.

"You, St George," I told him sweetly, just before we disappeared through the door into the back. Hopefully my voice was loud enough that Laetitia heard it. "I should have thought that was obvious."

Then the door shut behind us, and he dropped my arm like it had burned him, and pushed the next door open in front of us. "A likely story, Darling. What do you really want?"

"You, as I said. But I'm just the messenger. Tom needs you for something. He just didn't want to make it obvious."

I gestured to the now-closed door to the study. Crispin looked at it, and looked at me, and then gave the door a brisk knock. He turned the knob and walked inside without waiting for an invitation. When I tried to follow, he shut the door in my face. I rocked back on my heels, my mouth open in outrage.

It took a second to battle back the instinct to pull the door open again and start ranting at him. Instead, once I had, I leaned in and put my ear to the crack.

"There you are," Tom's voice said, sounding smug. "I thought she'd get you to follow her."

"Yes, thanks a lot, Gardiner." Crispin's voice was as annoyed as I felt. "Very funny. What can I do for you?"

"We need a very small favor," Tom said. His voice was fading, I assume as Crispin walked closer to him and he didn't have to speak so loudly. "If you could go next door—"

And that was all I heard. I made a face, but kept my ear to the door for another few seconds, until I heard footsteps approaching on the opposite side. By the time Crispin came back out, I was standing on the other side of the hallway looking innocent.

Or perhaps not. He looked me up and down, and snorted.

"What?" I said.

"Nothing, I'm sure."

He turned down the hall towards the back of the house.

I trotted after him. "Where are we going?"

"*I'm* going to the library. I don't know where you're going."

I was going wherever he was going, but I couldn't say that without opening myself up to some sort of sarcastic remark. So instead I said, "Where's Christopher? He wasn't in the sitting room when I fetched you, was he?"

"He didn't come back after going to tell you that Sammy wanted to talk to you." He pushed open the door to the library, and walked in.

I followed, looking around. The room was deserted, but the blankets from last night were still on the sofa, thrown off and forgotten when we'd burst in to tell Constance and Francis about Abigail's death. I headed toward them and began folding.

"I have an idea where he might be, though," Crispin added. "I'll help you look for him once I've made this telephone call."

"Are you sure you wouldn't rather go back to Laetitia?"

He gave me a look but didn't respond, just picked up the ear piece of the telephone. I put one folded blanket down on the sofa and picked up the other and shook it.

"Do you need me to leave?" I'd listen at the door if he did, of course, but it seemed polite to inquire.

He shook his head. "It's nothing. Just a call to the village to ask Wilkins to come back up."

"Sammy talked to Wilkins this morning," I said, while I watched Crispin deal with the exchange.

"And now I suppose Gardiner wants to talk to him." He turned his attention to the receiver, with a noticeable increase in charm. "Hello? Is this the Beckwith Arms? This is Crispin Astley, calling from Beckwith Place..."

There was some noise from the other end, and then a smile from Crispin. It warmed his voice when he said, "Yes, that's correct. My father and I are visiting from Sutherland..." He chuckled. "Is that so? Yes, of course I do..."

I rolled my eyes and put the second blanket down. Some woman at the pub remembered him from some other time he'd been here, and wanted to know if he remembered her, no doubt.

He caught it, and smirked at me, but without losing the thread of the conversation. "Yes, for Francis's birthday next week. That's right... Yes, with all the visitors we have a full house at Beckwith this weekend. Our chauffeur is lodging with you, which is why... Yes, that would be simply spiffing, if you would be so kind."

There was a pause and then all the charm dropped off and his voice turned businesslike. "Wilkins. Thank God. It's St George."

There was a faint quacking on the other end of the line.

"Not that I know of, Wilkins. Would you mind bringing the motorcar in this direction? Along with a bottle of the most expensive gin the Arms can provide? I can't stomach my uncle's sorry excuse for a gin and tonic anymore..."

The phone quacked again, and then Crispin answered, "Yes, thank you, Wilkins... Yes, we'll be here. Nobody's going anywhere, it seems... No, I don't believe they're any closer to figuring anything out. Why would they? Village idiots, the lot of them..."

He leaned a shoulder against the wall and examined his nails. "Yes, Wilkins, I'll be here. I'll meet you outside the carriage house. And Wilkins... don't let my father know, eh?"

The quacking continued for a moment and then went silent. Crispin hung up the receiver and arched a brow at me.

"Masterfully done," I said. "Tom wanted gin?"

He shook his head. "Tom wanted Wilkins. I wanted to give Wilkins an excuse that didn't include the police."

"So you don't want the gin?"

"There's nothing wrong with Uncle Herbert's liquor cabinet," Crispin said and headed for the door. "Come along, Darling. Let's go make our report."

CHAPTER TWENTY-TWO

WE MADE OUR REPORT, which essentially meant that Crispin knocked on the door to the study, stuck his head through, and said, "He's coming. I told him to bring me a bottle of the most expensive gin the Arms can lay their hands on so he wouldn't suspect anything."

"I don't know what you think he might suspect, Lord St George," Tom said blandly, "but thank you for the help."

"I told him I'd meet him when he gets here. So I suppose I should keep myself nearby, to intercept."

"Of course you did." Tom's voice was resigned. I pressed my lips together so I wouldn't snort. "Then yes, please. If you wouldn't mind intercepting."

I couldn't see Crispin's face, but I could hear the smirk. "Delighted to be of assistance, Detective Sergeant."

He pulled the door shut and the smirk turned into a grin. I grinned back. "Well done, St George."

"Thank you, Darling. Now..." He glanced around, "you were looking for Kit?"

"I wondered where he was," I admitted. "You said you thought you knew."

He nodded. "Follow me."

He strode off down the hallway. I gave the study door a last, longing look before scurrying after, and caught up just as he pushed open the back door onto the terrasse.

"Out here?" I looked around. "I don't see him."

"Watch and learn, Darling."

He headed across the flagstones and down the stairs with me trailing two steps behind. But once on the grass, instead of turning towards the crime scene and the driveway, he took a left, skirting the terrasse in the other direction.

Back here, below the scullery window, is the vegetable garden, and on the grass, a table and chairs under the overhanging branches of a large, old English Oak. Beyond that again is an arbor, and then there's a part of the house where a lot of ivy grows around the window of Uncle Herbert's study.

Crispin turned to me and put his finger to his mouth. I peered past him and saw Christopher sitting on the ground below the window, his back against the worn brick and his knees up. His eyes were closed—the better to concentrate on what was being said inside, no doubt—but he must have sensed our approach across the grass, because he jerked his head in our direction. It seemed to take a second—perhaps he hadn't expected to see us together, or hadn't expected to be found by anyone at all—and then his eyes widened.

He started to move—his face when he looked at Crispin was horrified, and I guess it's never really a pleasant experience when you realize that someone you've listened to knows you've eavesdropped, although it wasn't as if Crispin had said anything important during his scant few seconds inside the study—but the latter waved him back down, silently. Christopher settled back into his spot on the ground and turned to me. His expression was apologetic. He must have eaves-dropped on my conversation with Tom and Sammy, too, I assumed. Or the part of it he had caught after walking out here.

It didn't really matter to me—I hadn't said anything impor-tant either, and I would have shared every detail I remembered with him later anyway if he wanted to know—so I just smiled and took the hand he extended, and sat down next to him. Crispin dropped down on the other side of me, silently, and we all started to pay attention to what was going on inside.

"—only time it happened," Tom said, and I felt Christo-pher's hand jerk in shock.

"Apparently not," Uncle Herbert answered bitterly.

"When did you first learn—?"

"This morning, believe it or not." He made a sound that might have been a very ugly laugh. "Hughes told me."

"Hughes?" Sammy echoed, and Tom provided the explana-tion: from Marsden Manor to Sutherland Hall to Beckwith Place. After it was concluded, Sammy asked, "How would the maid know?"

"Apparently the other maid told her," Uncle Herbert said. "I'm more interested in how *you* know."

It was Tom who answered, so the question must have been directed at him. (Really, it is so much more difficult to follow a conversation when you can't see the people involved in it.)

"I know all sorts of things about all sorts of people," Tom said blandly. "I had access to Simon Grimsby's blackmail notes at Sutherland Hall, remember?"

"Of course." Uncle Herbert sounded sour. "And you decided not to say anything about it at the time because...?"

"It wasn't my place to say anything. It didn't pertain to the investigation, and besides, how was I to know that you didn't already know? You knew about the other matter."

"The other matter was entirely different," Uncle Herbert said coldly, and this time it was Sammy who made the noise.

He apologized immediately, and I imagined that both Tom and Uncle Herbert must have given him identical death glares. When I stole a glance at Crispin, a corner of his mouth twitched in response, so he must have thought the same thing. Christopher's hand was still in mine, limp now, and I gave it a comforting squeeze. He slanted a look my way, and I smiled back, as reassuringly as I could. It took a second, but then he managed a smile in return. Crispin glanced over, noticed the byplay, watched for a second, and looked away again.

Inside the room, the conversation went on.

"Tell me about Maisie Moran," Tom said.

"What's to tell?" Uncle Herbert sounded resigned. "She was a parlor maid at Sutherland House. A few years older than me. Beautiful girl, one of the Black Irish. Bright blue eyes and black hair. I was just down from University. I imagine I thought I seduced her, but it was probably the other way around..."

From the corner of my eye, I could see Crispin's mouth curve in what looked like sympathy, or perhaps rueful memory of his own experience. Laetitia Marsden wasn't Black Irish, not to my knowledge, but she had bright blue eyes and black hair, and she had definitely once seduced him.

"I didn't know there was a child," Uncle Herbert added. "I didn't know my father knew about the affair, either. It was never mentioned, until one day I got up to Town and she wasn't there. I can't recall what he said when I asked—just that she was gone, I think; moved on to a different situation—but from the way he said it, I could tell it was because of what had happened between us. But by then I had met Roslyn, so I didn't think much about it after that, what with the courting and the wedding and then a couple of years later, Francis..."

He trailed off, and for a moment there was only silence.

Then— "I never heard from her after that. My father never brought her up again. I didn't, either. If I had known..."

"You would have done something different?"

There was a beat, just a second of silence before Uncle Herbert said, "No. I wouldn't have done anything different. I didn't want to marry Maisie. I had fallen in love with Roslyn by then. I wouldn't want to change anything about my life. But if I had known that there was a child, I would have made sure it was taken care of. She probably thought I'd abandoned her to cope on her own."

"I imagine your father made the situation clear," Tom said. "He paid her quite a lot of money to go away and never darken the doorstep of Sutherland House—or Hall—again. She wasn't thrust into poverty or made to live in the gutter."

Uncle Herbert didn't respond to that, but I thought I could feel a lessening of tension in the air, as if a weight had been taken off his shoulders.

"She married," Tom added, "and used the money to buy a public house. Over time, she and her husband had two more children. From all I can gather, she's had a good life. Your son—"

"Don't call him that."

There was a moment's pause before Tom's voice came back, still calm. "He went to war, along with his younger half-brother. After the war, he approached your grandfather for a job. I don't know whether there was any coercion involved, or whether that was a promise that had been made originally. That when the child came of age, he'd have a position waiting for him at Sutherland."

Incredibly cruel and blind of old Duke Henry, if so. To make the child who should have been the firstborn son of the house work for them as a servant instead.

Unfortunately, that didn't mean it couldn't have happened

that way. Henry hadn't been known for his charity or generosity of spirit.

"Grimsby?" Christopher mouthed, incredulously, and I made a face. It made sense, I supposed. The old Duke had been strangely lenient with his valet, when he hadn't been known for forbearance with anyone else, not even his own family members. He had basically let Grimsby run wild: had let him take over the use of the motorcar (and Wilkins) and roam all over England digging up secrets about the other family members with no oversight whatsoever. They had been in London every other week, it seemed, following Christopher around. Grimsby's notes had had page upon page of minutia about Christopher's rather uninteresting doings: taking tea at the Savoy and shopping at Fortnum and Mason. I had been followed, too, and of course Grimsby had had a fine time gossiping with the servants at Sutherland House about all of St George's shenanigans.

He had been alive until late April this year, so he could have met and seduced Abigail the April before. He hadn't struck me as someone who would appeal to a young girl in a romantic way—I had found him a rather reptilian sort, with his flat, black eyes and slicked-back black hair—but there's no accounting for taste, I suppose.

And then my train of thought was derailed when, on the other side of me, Crispin scrambled upright with a silent curse and took off running. At first I couldn't imagine why, but then my ears picked up the sound of the motorcar turning into the driveway on the other side of the house, and I understood. Wilkins must be arriving, and Crispin had said he'd be there to meet him.

Tom would want to talk to the chauffeur about what Grimsby had been up to while in London last year, I supposed.

Wilkins would be the only one who had any information about that.

Christopher arched his brows at me, and I shook my head. "Nothing to worry about. Just Wilkins with the motorcar." And a bottle of gin for St George.

He nodded and settled back down.

Inside the study, the conversation went on. "I think," Tom said thoughtfully, "that this accounts for everything. He is unquestionably the grandson of the Duke of Sutherland, as much as Francis and Kit and Lord St George are. He had access to your father's Crossley, which is a black motorcar, as Abigail Dole noted on her list. With your father's goodwill, he could easily have been in London and at the Hammersmith Palais in April of last year. We may be able to confirm that if we ask the staff at the Hall or at Sutherland House. He spent time in the trenches, so could have brought back a trench club at the end of the war..."

All that was true. However, Abigail's list had had the words 'fair hair' and 'blue eyes' on it, and those didn't fit Simon Grimsby at all.

Besides, Grimsby was dead. I had seen the body, in the heart of the garden maze at Sutherland Hall in April. There was no question that Simon Grimsby was dead.

So how could he be here, committing murder?

And then there was a brisk knock on the study door and the sound of Crispin's cheerful voice—"DS Gardiner? Here's Wilkins to see you,"—and suddenly it all rearranged itself in my head with a clatter.

For a second or two, the mental noise blocked everything else out. Then Tom's voice cut through, pleasantly. "Mr. Wilkins. Come in. Have a seat."

There was a pause. I imagined Wilkins standing in the doorway, chauffeur cap in hand, with his sandy hair exposed and his cool, blue eyes—not Astley blue, more the washed-out color of the summer sky—flicking back and forth between Tom, Uncle Herbert, and Sammy.

Sensing the trap and unsure whether he could talk his way out of it. Knowing he had Crispin at his back, so retreat was impossible.

Then—

"Thank you, Lord St George," Tom added, pleasantly, "you may go."

There was another moment of silence, then a burst of noise. The sound of flesh on flesh, a grunt, a thud—the door hitting the wall?—and a rattle of footsteps.

"After him!" Tom's voice said, and then there was the scraping of chair legs and quick breaths and more footsteps pounding. They faded into the distance, and there were a few more, farther-away thuds: perhaps the boot room door opening and shutting a few times.

Christopher and I looked at one another, wide-eyed. I was just about to suggest that we get up and go around the house to see what was going on when Uncle Herbert spoke up.

"All right, my boy? Did he hurt you?"

"Not enough to matter," Crispin said. "Uncle Herbert..."

"Yes, Crispin?"

But Crispin must have changed his mind, because I don't think what he had originally planned to say was, "Perhaps we should go and see what's happening?"

"If you'll forgive me," Uncle Herbert said, rather formally, "I think I would rather stay here and not watch."

That was certainly understandable. Christopher and I exchanged another look, and without a word, got up and headed towards the back of the house. Uncle Herbert might prefer not to watch his newly discovered son be arrested for murder, but I had no such qualms.

It was strange, naturally. I was shocked and appalled that Duke Henry hadn't seen fit to tell Uncle Herbert that he had a son he didn't know about, especially when that son came to work at Sutherland.

But right now, there was the fact that Wilkins must have killed Abigail, because if not, why would he have run? He must have recognized Tom from back in April, and must have assumed that if Tom was there, and was asking for him, it was because Scotland Yard knew what was up.

And so he had run, instead of waiting to be asked the questions that would clear it up.

The only reason why someone would do that, it seemed to me, was if he was guilty.

By this point in my cogitations, we had turned the corner of the house onto the croquet lawn, and were trotting alongside the terrasse at a jog. And that's when the sound of a gunshot sliced through the silence and made both of our steps falter.

From the other side of the trees several voices rose into cries, and then settled back down into murmurs again.

By the time Christopher and I had fought our way through the bushes, the situation became clear. Tom and Sammy, along with Phil Hemings and the other constable, the one whose name I didn't know, were grouped around the Duke's Crossley. The motorcar's door was open, and beyond them, I could see a pair of legs in gray uniform trousers and tall, shiny boots sticking out, at an angle that indicated that their owner was limp.

Crispin had made his way over from the study, and was standing in the boot room door, his face pale and his eyes enormous, with both arms folded across his torso. Uncle Herbert was nowhere to be seen, so he must have done what he'd intimated he'd do, and stayed behind in the study.

I took Christopher by the elbow and tugged him in

Crispin's direction instead of towards the coppers, who were deep in conversation. From the way none of them did anything about Wilkins, I assumed he was no longer a threat, nor capable of being arrested. I didn't quite know how to feel about that, to be honest, so I made myself not think about it.

"Are you all right?" I asked Crispin instead. "Did he hurt you?" Hopefully it wasn't his head again.

"Not enough to mention. Elbowed me in the stomach on his way past. It took me a moment to catch my breath, but I don't think he broke any of my ribs."

He wasn't looking at me, but at Christopher. "You all right, Kit?"

Christopher nodded, although he didn't look it. He kept glancing at the Crossley, and then away again, and then back, as if he couldn't stop himself. "What happened?"

"I was a little slow off the mark," Crispin said dryly. "Entwistle and Gardiner both ran by me. By the time I made it through the door, he was already at the car. He opened the door and threw himself inside, across the passenger seat. A few seconds later, there was a shot. He never tried to hurt anyone else, only himself. Gardiner had got there by then, and was trying to haul him out, but it was too late. He went limp."

After a second he added, "I'll make a guess and say he kept a loaded pistol under his seat along with the trench club, and he'd rather do this than go to prison."

It was a blunt assessment, but probably accurate. And not to be callous, but it would solve rather a lot of problems. For the Astley family, anyway. Wilkins's relationship to Uncle Herbert might not need to come out, nor his relationship to Abigail.

Publicly, I mean. We'd all know, I assumed. At least the family, which at this point included Constance. But perhaps we could keep it from the Marsdens, at least. It was none of their affair, after all.

I put my arm around Christopher's waist to give what comfort I could. I'm not sure he noticed, but it was all I could do, so I did it. Perhaps when Tom could remove himself from the other constables and come over, it would help. But until then, it was up to me, so I did what I could.

"He must have picked her up in the village last night," I said softly, "and offered to drive her up here. He had no reason to be here last night otherwise. And instead of helping her find Bess, I guess he decided to get rid of her once and for all, somewhere where there were a lot of other Astleys who could be blamed."

"She might have said something to him," Christopher said distantly. "Perhaps she made some sort of threat."

He glanced at the car and the pair of legs protruding from it again, before he added, "I guess we'll never know."

Not unless we could piece it together ourselves, no. We probably wouldn't.

For a moment, I wished fervently that Tom had forced Wilkins to speak in the study, that he had maneuvered the chauffeur into a chair so perhaps we could have gotten a few answers before it was too late.

But it was what it was, and we had to be satisfied with what we already knew.

And it wasn't as if we didn't have most, if not all, of the answers. Or like we couldn't extrapolate the rest. The man had killed himself rather than be questioned: he must be guilty. Tom had filled in the backstory in broad strokes for Uncle Herbert while we'd listened, and Uncle Herbert had done the same with the earlier story for Tom. I don't know what Wilkins could have told us, apart from how the murder had come about, or the reason for it, that we didn't already know. Abigail might have threatened to have him sacked, or she might have insisted that he marry her when he didn't want to, or he might have had another girl he wanted instead and this one was in the way...

I shook it off and turned to Christopher. There was no sense in us standing out here staring at a tragedy we could do nothing about. Not when there was something helpful we could do inside.

"Let's go check on your father. He can probably use a visit from one of his sons right now."

Christopher glanced at Tom, still in conversation with Sammy and the other constables, and then at Crispin. A moment passed, then—

"Topping idea," Crispin said. "Let's all go."

He stepped backwards, out of the doorway, and I nudged Christopher into the boot room ahead of me. I closed the door behind us, and when I turned back, I heard Crispin say, softly, "I'm sorry I didn't tell you."

Christopher gave a harsh bark of laughter, one with not even a trace of humor in it. It might have been a sob, and not laughter at all; I don't know. "I don't blame *you*, Crispin. You found out... when? Two months ago?"

Crispin shrugged, and Christopher added, "I imagine it must have been a shock to you, too. And it isn't *your* responsibility to keep me up to date on Father's shenanigans. Even this. Besides..."

He hesitated. "If you had told me back then, or even between then and now, I might have resented you. And now I don't. And I'm glad I don't. So it's better this way."

Crispin didn't respond, but as they set off down the hallway towards Uncle Herbert's study, he nudged Christopher's shoulder with his own and got an answering nudge back. If all wasn't perfectly well with the Astleys at the moment, at least it looked as if they'd get through this tumult in time and be all right for it.

EPILOGUE

TOM LEFT with little Bess in the late afternoon. Ian Finchley had come back from Whitechapel with the names and location of the Dole family, information which he had passed to Tom via telephone, and Sammy was only too happy to relinquish the responsibility both for the baby and the death notification.

He had his hands full with the new crime scene, the one in and around Uncle Harold's Crossley. The official responsibility for going to Southampton and telling Maisie Wilkins that her son was dead would be his, although by the time Tom left, Uncle Herbert and Francis had already set off in the Bentley on that errand. Maisie shouldn't hear about her son's death from the constables if he had the opportunity to tell her himself, Uncle Herbert said, and Aunt Roz agreed with him, so off they went. She would have gone herself, I think, had she not had a house full of guests she had to attend to.

She wanted to keep Elizabeth. She did, however, realize that we had no claim to the baby, or if we did, it would be much better for everyone if we pretended we didn't. So Bess was off to the Doles, with the promise of a substantial monetary settlement from the Astley family, ostensibly because the Duke of Sutherland's chauffeur had seduced and then murdered their daughter.

That was really all they needed to know, and it was all we were prepared to share with them. If Abigail had told them that the baby's father had told her he was an Astley, it could easily be explained away by his employment, and there was no need for them to know any more of the sordid details.

Aunt Roz impressed upon Tom, anxiously, that he must tell her if there was any reason at all to think that little Bess wouldn't be safe or happy in the Doles' care, because if so, to hell with the conventions and what people thought: she would bring the baby up herself rather than leave her somewhere unsafe, and the whole world could think—and say—whatever it wanted about it.

"Promise me, Thomas! If you get any inkling, even just a feeling, that something isn't right, you will take her out of there, and bring her back here. I won't be responsible for anything bad happening to that precious baby!"

Tom assured her that he would not leave Bess with people who wouldn't take care of her, and then he set off in the Tender with Hughes beside him, allegedly so she could help with the baby, but really because she couldn't wait to get away from us all, and we—mostly Uncle Herbert—couldn't wait to be rid of her.

He impressed upon her the need to get in touch with us with a forwarding address once she was settled—and used the missing Lydia Morrison as an excuse—but I heard it, and I'm certain Hughes did as well, as an assurance that the cheque for a thousand pounds would be forthcoming.

Her blackmail had lost rather a lot of its sting with these last few events, of course, although I suppose giving her the hush money still made sense. Uncle Herbert had it to spare since Uncle Harold was coughing up the settlement for the Doles. I guess perhaps the new Duke felt somewhat guilty over his late father's actions and wanted to contribute something.

"I'd still like to know how that trench club ended up in my bedchamber," I commented, after the Tender had vanished down the lane behind the Bentley with Uncle Herbert and Francis. "It makes no sense that Wilkins would have put it there. He had the opportunity, I suppose, but why would he frame me, out of everyone here? I had nothing to do with any of this, and he couldn't possibly have known that I didn't have an alibi. He wasn't here last night when we went to bed. And there was no reason why he'd single me out. There was no bad blood between us."

There was a beat, then—

"Probably thought he was framing Astley," Geoffrey grunted. "Someone who had been in the war and could have brought home a club of his own. Someone who could have been the baby's father."

I blinked. That was a very sensible suggestion, and I was rather surprised that Geoffrey, of all people, had come up with it. Up until now, I had been convinced of his utter uselessness. But it made sense, at least as far as Wilkins's hypothetical motivation went. Frame Francis, not just because he had been in the war and knew how to use a trench club, but because Francis was the firstborn legitimate son, the one who had taken Wilkins's place.

"Shouldn't he have put it in the room on the other side of the landing, then? That's where Francis was supposed to sleep. Or the library, where he actually slept? Or even the room Uncle Harold was in, which is Francis's usual room when the house isn't full of guests?"

There was a moment's silence. Then the Duke cleared his throat.

"I don't imagine you'll ever discover the reasoning behind it, Miss Darling," he said smoothly. "The man's dead, and can't tell us."

I smiled politely, even as I resisted the urge to roll my eyes. Talk about pointing out the obvious. "Of course."

He eyed me down the length of his nose. "Surely there can be no question that he did it? Who else would have had access to the weapon?"

He clearly meant it as a rhetorical question, although I could think of one other person who might have had access to it. Harold, Duke of Sutherland, might have found the trench club in his own room after Wilkins put it there with the idea of framing Francis.

That would mean that my courtesy-uncle-by-marriage had deliberately tried to frame me for murder. And while I had always suspected that he and Aunt Charlotte didn't like me much, that seemed rather like a serious accusation.

Unless he, too, had tried to frame Francis. He wouldn't have wanted to put it in the other upstairs room, after all, where Crispin had been asleep. Nor would he want to wander all over the house with it, I assume. Nor admit that he had it at all.

And he was right, anyway. Maybe Wilkins had done it. We'd never really know.

While I cogitated, His Grace turned to Crispin. "I'll have to travel back to Sutherland with you, St George, since the Crossley—and Wilkins—is unavailable."

"I suppose we'll need a new motorcar after this," Crispin said brightly. "Can I talk you into one of the New Phantoms? Overhead-valve straight-six engine and four gears? Ninety miles an hour at top speed?"

Uncle Harold looked somewhere between revulsed and fascinated despite himself.

"Looking for more and better ways to kill yourself, St

George?" I wanted to know, which was really quite a stupid turn of phrase under the circumstances. At least half the room flinched.

Crispin, who has no finer feelings to speak of, merely gave me a supercilious look. "Not at all, Darling. I'm a changed man. From now on, it's the straight and narrow road for me."

"If you say so," I said dubiously.

Laetitia tinkled a little laugh. "Oh, Crispin," she cooed, fluttering her eyelashes, "you're so droll."

I saw no reason to refrain this time, so I rolled my eyes with abandon. Crispin smiled, and Uncle Harold said jovially, "Why don't you come back to Sutherland Hall with us for the rest of the weekend, Effie? Maury? With Francis gone, the engagement party is surely off—"

Surely, and not just because Francis had motored to Southampton.

"—and Roslyn undoubtedly has other things to think about than keeping us entertained."

Like the fact that her husband's son, whom she hadn't known about until today, had killed her grandchild's mother and then himself on the grounds of her childhood home.

"Of course, Harold," Aunt Roz said peacefully. I'm sure she was as eager to get rid of them as they were to leave.

Euphemia said herself willing to share the amenities of Sutherland Hall for the next few days, and so the following thirty minutes were spent in a mad dash as everyone gathered up their belongings and beat a hasty retreat out the door to the remaining motorcars. Laetitia got in beside Crispin as if she belonged there, and left Uncle Harold to choose between squeezing into the back seat, or going with the Earl and Countess. He chose the latter, and ended up in the back of the Daimler with Geoffrey. I guess they all trusted that Laetitia and Crispin could do without a chaperone for the trip, or if not that,

that a chaperone was unwanted, because they'd all like to see them married and would do whatever seemed necessary to affect that outcome.

"Be careful," I said as we stood outside seeing them off. "No sudden moves, St George."

"Don't worry, Darling." He flicked me a glance. "I'll drive as carefully as if I had a dozen bottles of port in the boot."

For once I wasn't worried about his driving—if he wanted to put Laetitia in the hospital on the way to Sutherland Hall, he had my permission—but of course I couldn't say that with her sitting right there. Especially when she told me, with utter condescension, "How kind of you to concern yourself, Miss Darling. But I'll take care of him."

She put a possessive hand on his arm. I eyed it for a moment, but since she'd have to move it anyway as soon as he started driving, I didn't bother to say anything sarcastic. I could have, so I gave myself full marks for restraint. Although I did take a step back from the vehicle to avoid further temptation. "Safe travels."

Crispin nodded and let out the clutch. The Hispano-Suiza rolled off down the driveway followed by the Daimler.

"Aren't you afraid they'll be engaged by tomorrow night?" Constance wanted to know. She came up to stand next to me as we watched the cars turn the corner into the lane, one after the other, leaving only the Peckhams' Crossley parked in front of the carriage house.

I glanced down at her. "I wouldn't say that I'm afraid. And anyway, it's none of my affair, is it?"

"Isn't it?"

"All I can do is warn him," I said. "If he chooses to propose to her, there's nothing I can do to stop him. I wasn't invited along. And he knows what I think, because I've told him, and if he refuses to listen to me, then that's his problem. He needn't bother to come crying to me about his unhappiness later."

Constance tucked her hand through my arm. "I can't tell you how glad I am to be rid of them. I guess they mean well—at least Uncle Maury does, I think, and I suppose Aunt Effie too, when she isn't busy trying to arrange an advantageous marriage for Laetitia—but I really could have done without them this weekend."

I could have, as well. Especially Laetitia. "This wasn't how I wanted your engagement party to go."

She sniggered and shook her head. "No. But it doesn't matter. All I want is to marry Francis, and now we can get married with nothing whatsoever hanging over us."

I nodded, even as I reflected that there were still plenty of things hanging over us. There was Uncle Herbert's second love-child, and Laetitia Marsden, and I would still like to know how that trench club ended up in my room, if it came to that.

But Constance didn't know about Uncle Herbert's extra-marital shenanigans, and she had better things to think about than Laetitia's and Crispin's romance, so I merely squeezed her arm and smiled warmly as I turned her towards the boot room to follow Christopher and Aunt Roz back into the house. "Let's go inside and plan the most wonderful wedding ever."

"That sounds wonderful, girls," Aunt Roslyn said brightly over her shoulder, and tucked her arm through Constance's as we entered the boot room. I relinquished Constance to her future mother-in-law and took the arm Christopher extended to me. "Everything all right with you?"

"Never better," my best friend told me, and although it might not be strictly true, it was close enough for jazz as we closed the boot room door behind us and entered a quiet Beck-with Place.

Dear Reader,

Here we are again, with another installment of the Pippa Darling mysteries.

First, the ubiquitous warning about the language. Pippa is British (and half German), and I'm Norwegian, but I have spent most of my adult life in the US. I wrote more than 40 novels in American English before I started this series. As a result, what I'm giving you is a mish-mash of both. There are nappies—in this book in particular, lots of nappies—and lifts and flats and trousers and pants (which are underwear) and knickers (which are women's underwear), while knickerbockers are those trousers that end at the knee, and plus-fours are the knickerbockers that extend four inches below. There are also flannels, which are trousers, and bags, which are flannel trousers with extra room in the legs. Flannels can also be wash-cloths, and of course flannel is a term for nonsense.

On the other hand, the cars have tires, not tyres, although I know that tyres is the British spelling. I also leave the u out of glamor and clamor and humor and the like. So, again, a mish-mash. You can tell me that I've done it wrong, but I'm pretty sure I already know.

The Hammersmith Palais de Danse was a real place, and was owned by William Mitchell, the same gentleman who owned Rectors nightclub, which featured in *Murder in a Mayfair Flat*. William Mitchell existed, although nobody knows what happened to him after the mid-1920s. Rectors was ordered closed in 1924 for violations of the liquor license, but the Hammersmith Palais was still open for dancing during the spring of 1925, when Abigail Dole must have gone there, probably with a friend, and met the grandson of the Duke of Sutherland.

The Maternity Hospital in Stepney, where Abigail gave birth to little Bess, was a real place, and so were the Blackwall Buildings on Thomas Street in Whitechapel, where Tom told Pippa that Abigail lived. They were built in 1890 by the Great Eastern Railway, and although the Whitechapel area itself wasn't great, the Blackwall Buildings were a nice, safe, gated community for someone like Abigail to reside with her baby. While I didn't go into detail in the book, I imagine she probably had a girlfriend she shared her flat with, the same way Pippa shares hers with Christopher. If Abigail hadn't had support from someone, I imagine she would have run home to the elder Doles when little Bess came along.

WWI trench clubs are, of course, a real thing. You can Google them if you like visuals, but they were standard issue at least for the British Empire soldiers. As Francis describes, they consisted of a wooden handle with a metal attachment that had a pickaxe on one side and a spade on the other. There are some nasty examples online, including ones with hobnails and ones with spikes. I decided to spare Pippa's feelings—and my own— and use a hobnailed one for this murder, rather than having to describe the effects of the ones with spikes.

So doth conscience—or at least squeamishness—make cowards of us all, as Shakespeare would say.

There are no real people in this book, and while Wiltshire

and Salisbury do of course exist, Beckwith Place and Sutherland Hall do not.

ABOUT THE AUTHOR

New York Times and *USA Today* bestselling author Jenna Bennett (Jennie Bentley) has written more than fifty books, most of them in the genres of mystery and suspense.

For more information, please visit her website,
www.jennabennett.com

To purchase Jenna's books, please visit
Jenna Bennett Books
www.jennabennett.myshopify.com